FROM THE CITY OF DREAMS,
A BOX FULL OF NIGHTMARES . . .

They were coming up the stairs.

He didn't know what they were, what they looked like, how they moved. He didn't *want* to know. They made noises that his mind rejected as unreal, though his heart and mind knew better. They skittered and slithered and fluttered and muttered and howled like brain-damaged hyenas from Hell.

One of them made the walls shake as it approached.

I will not move, he urged himself with a silent, sickly whining voice.

I will not scream . . .

Bantam Books by John Skipp and Craig Spector:

THE LIGHT AT THE END
THE CLEANUP
THE SCREAM

.........DEAD LINES.........

A NOVEL OF HORROR

.........JOHN SKIPP.........

.........CRAIG SPECTOR..

BANTAM BOOKS

TORONTO · NEW YORK · LONDON · SYDNEY · AUCKLAND

DEAD LINES
A Bantam Book / January 1989

Grateful acknowledgment is made for permission to reprint the
following lyrics: "This Must Be The Place" copyright © 1986
Index Music, Bleu Disque Music Co. Inc. Administered by WB
Music Corp. All rights reserved. Used by permission. "Take Me
To The River" by Al Green & Mabon Hodges, copyright ©
1974, 1978 Irving Music Inc. & Al Green Music, Inc. (BMI) All
rights reserved. International copyright secured. "Solitude Standing," "Language," and "Woodenhorse," music and lyrics by
Suzanne Vega. Copyright © 1987 by AGF Music Ltd./Waifer-
songs Ltd. All rights reserved. Used by permission.

ISBN 0-553-27633-6

Published simultaneously in the United States and Canada

Bantam Books are published by Bantam Books, a division of
Bantam Doubleday Dell Publishing Group, Inc. Its trademark,
consisting of the words "Bantam Books" and the portrayal of a
rooster, is Registered in U.S. Patent and Trademark Office and
in other countries. Marca Registrada. Bantam Books, 666 Fifth
Avenue, New York, New York 10103.

For Mikel Jean
and
For Lori
... with love.

ACKNOWLEDGMENTS

Once again, we'd like to waste valuable wood pulp extending warmest thanks and appreciation to our families and friends for their love, support, and sheer endurance, with special thanks for:

Adele Leone and Richard Monaco; Lou Aronica, Pat LoBrutto, Janna Silverstein, Laura Nixon, Susan Sherman and all the other fine folks at Bantam; Marianne and Melanie, Lori, Linda, Beth and Tappan, JK, Joe and Greg, the *Fango* gang, Matt and Alli, only sister Kim (for the title assistance), Dave Schow (for the triple-digit phone bills), Everett Burrell and Tom Savini (for the icky pictures), Mr. Page 511 and Mr. Wraparound (just for being themselves), Chris and Mango (for animal antics), Phil Nutman, Jesse Horsting, Bob Sabat, Beth Gwinn, Leslie and Adam, that Amazing Invisible Krafty Polekat, the guys 'n' gals at the Edgar Street Bookland Video, and all Steves everywhere.

Portions of this book have previously appeared in *Twilight Zone, Night Cry, Borderland, The Architecture of Fear,* and *The Year's Best Fantasy*. We'd like to thank everyone involved. Even Stubby.

SERIOUS AUTHOR NOTES

Now that John Skipp and Craig Spector have achieved Serious Author status, they want the world to know that they have changed. Grown up. Matured. Gotten . . . well, *serious*.

For example, you'll notice the absence of a funny author cartoon, as provided in the past by Leslie Sternbergh. Not this time. They've outgrown that. Also missing are the whimsical so-called "facts" so prominent in their previous bios, such as, "Skipp enjoys body surfing, so long as the bodies are fresh," or "Spector's 'Caramel/Drano Puff Balls' are a perennial holiday favorite." *Au contraire.* As Serious Authors, they have a standard to bear, a great responsibility to themselves and to us all.

And, yes, they know this all too well. Today's John Skipp and Craig Spector are caring, concerned, socially committed. They're vibrant, magnetic. They just say "No." They have little tweed patches on the elbows of their leather jackets. They are every mother's dream.

John Skipp. Craig Spector.

Think about it.

They say that New York is the city that never sleeps, and in certain respects that's true.

On the other hand, one might also say that New York is a city that never awakens from its long, strange dream of power. They call it the city of dreams, after all; never citing, or minding, the contradiction.

But you know how they are.

If you ask me, there are other truths: less often said, but closer to the point. Of all of them, I'd settle on this:

New York is the city that eats its young, with high-rise teeth and pavement tongue.

I came.

I saw.

I was digested.

John Paul Rowan
July 15th

1
JACK IN THE BOX

Jack wanted only two things out of life, as he watched the sun throw long shadows across the floor leading up to the ladder. He wanted another drink.

And he wanted the rope to be nice and tight.

Actually, he'd have opted for a good deal more than that, but Life was a bitch. Life had whittled him down until there didn't seem to be much that Jack felt up to grabbing at, nothing that wasn't chock-full to the rafters with pain and pointlessness and rancid, gray despair. No lifelines. No callbacks. No eleventh-hour reprieves.

No, he'd decided, those two would suffice.

First things first: a drink. Something strong. He was fairly sure Glen had left a bottle of peppered Finlandia around somewhere. Probably stashed in the freezer, along with the exotic concentrates and the Stouffer's frozen entrées and the other reasonably nonperishable goodies that would remain preserved, like a woolly mammoth in a Pleistocene ice floe, until Glen returned from his latest bicoastal expedition.

Glen was like that, Jack knew; he kept his shit wired tight. He'd strike off for la-la land, for weeks unto months on end, secure in the knowledge that no matter how far he strayed in pursuit of his next double-platinum album shoot or magazine cover or MTV video-verité technofest, his funky, stylish loft slash studio would be waiting: the fridge all full, the bills all paid, the CD and the TV and the black-leather passion pit all snug and warm and willing. He was as different from Jack as the sun and the moon. As success and failure.

3

As life and death.

Yep, Jack knew, Glen would probably have the Finlandia tucked into the far left corner of the icebox, right next to the frozen lime juice and the turkey tetrazzini. He checked. Bingo. The liquid inside was slimy green and viscous: itty bits of deadly jalapeño had been stewing within since roughly last October. Fire and Ice, they called it, and Glen always kept some ready for those moments of ritual self-destruction that swept down from time to time.

Jack pried the bottle out of the freezer's glacial expanse with no small amount of effort, ice clinging in frozen fingers from its base and sides. A few of the heavier shards fell chattering to the floor, where he crunched them under bared feet. He felt it as he felt everything else in his existence: too intense, like rock salt on raw flesh. And like everything else, he took it in.

But all that was about to change.

Jack plunked back down on the sofa and stared at the phone, which was slim and black and had lots of buttons. It was a fiber-optic marvel, capable of performing any number of great and important high-tech tasks: it could record messages, wash the dishes, feet the cat, or juggle upwards of a dozen people at once, like the Amazing Wallendas or something. Yep, it could do anything.

Except maybe ring when he needed it to. Like now, for instance.

Oh, well. Fuggit. He didn't expect he'd be hearing from her again. That was all ancient history now. He held the bottle up to the light. It glowed, amber-green. This was his favorite time of day, no doubt: when the sun's rays were longest, and everything they touched seemed to burn like polished brass. As if lit from within. As if aflame. He couldn't have picked a better time, he decided. The light transformed the bottle into a magical vessel; the liquid inside, the purest ambrosia.

He looked up at the ladder to his right, which stood poised and ready to bear his weight. It was glowing, too. Anticipation? Perhaps. Whatever. It would wait for him.

Just a little bit longer.

Immediately before him was the coffee table, which

held the clutter that had come to symbolize his life. The
telephone that refused to ring. The ashtray, filled as
ever to overflowing. The blank white sheets of bonded
paper. His trusty Smith-Corona. The cardboard cathedral—
his dead-tree legacy—was already sealed and hidden
away. The only words he had left to say, he would say
now.

Or forever hold his peace.

The typewriter hummed, a crisp white sheet of Strathmore
Bond unsullied in its grasp. Hell of a time for writer's
block. "Oh well. Here's to you, Pop." He gestured grandly,
toasting the fading sky. "Must be in the goddam DNA."

He took a long pull straight out of the bottle, felt his
sinuses drain in self-defense as first his gullet caught fire,
then his stomach, then on, and on, clear down into his
emptied bowels.

"Feh!" He winced. "Oh shit, that burns . . ." Every inch
of the vodka's wake was ablaze as it churned its way home
to his bladder, burning like Sherman marching to the sea.
The cloud in his brain was an opaque, instantaneous buzz
that burgeoned in the center of his forehead, soft and hot
and dimly throbbing. It was good. He leaned forward,
fingers hovering above the keys, and typed:

TODAY
IS THE LAST DAY
OF THE REST
OF MY LIFE

"Nah," he muttered, yanking the page. "Too facile." He
crumpled it up, fed another sheet in. This was gonna be a
bitch. He had to get it right the first time, because the
opportunity for a rewrite looked pretty slim. "How 'bout,
'Dear Glen. Thanks for letting me crash here. Sorry 'bout
the mess.'"

He squinted up at the rope.

It was top quality, scored down on the west side of
Canal Street, which was always a good place for hardware
bargains: fifty yards for a buck ninety-nine, more than
enough good stout nylon cord. He'd considered going
natural, but nylon was stronger. It would hold more

weight, and longer. The last thing he wanted was a botched attempt, to end up in a fractured heap on the floor. Where was the style in that?

Jack had come to rely on style. Not the ephemeral, transient trash that fed the fashion machines and media mavens. Piss on that. No, he was talking true style here: the unmistakable voice, the unreplicatable signature. The mark that he would leave on the world.

As muses go, style had staying power. It had driven him long after the hope of Love or Honor or Understanding had knuckled feebly under to the mean streets and cold sheets of his life. It honed itself within him until it was sharp as a blade of Madagascar steel, and twice as hard; until he could thrust it, Arthurian-like, straight into the stone his own heart had become.

And it would not accept failure.

It would not accept defeat.

It prodded him: to do it right, to forgo food and then enema up 'til his belly and bowels were yawningly empty, the better to be certain he'd leave no embarrassingly telltale chocolate trail down the back of his pants at that inevitable loss of control. No style in that. You'd better believe it.

No goddam style at all.

Beside him on the sofa sat a fat book, profusely illustrated and imposingly titled. Part of Glen's vast reference library, sick fucker that he was. The cover was antiseptically white and unappealing, the words set in a plain red type, evidence that the publishers felt no need to hype an audience; that those who sought the contents knew exactly what they were looking for. A ripped-open envelope served as a bookmark, sandwiched between the pages after sex crimes and airline disasters but before gunshot wounds and automobile accidents.

Forensic Pathology:
The Medicolegal Implications of Death
Volume III

Catchy title, Jack thought. He took another hit off the bottle and flipped the book open to the marked chapter.

Page after well-thumbed page of text rolled by, in clinically obsessive case-by-case detail, interspersed with postmortem portraits of the only souls in the book who actively auditioned for their part.

Jack couldn't help but hold them in contempt. They all looked so weak and sad: a cavalcade of the lost, each of whom was saved from complete oblivion—not on the basis of their great works or good hearts or fine family name, but on pure and simple accident of technique. Whether gun or pill, razor or rope, each had done something—some tiny variation on the theme—that set them apart and made them, if not special, then at least noteworthy.

But did they have style?

Ah, that was the question.

Jack was not inclined to think so. His new peers, as reflected by *Forensic Pathology*, were a sorry, threadbare lot: largely illiterate, incapable of articulating what drove them to the brink beyond the barest, hastily scrawled sentiment—i am sory please forgive me god will hate me o god im so sory.

Jack had no such illusions, about gods or forgiveness, and no one left to apologize to. Fuck God. And piss on forgiveness. God had not lifted so much as His finger to help these people in this their hour of need. Jack knew better than to even ask.

And as for what had driven him to this, the answer was simple as simple could be: When he had stared into the abyss too long, he found it staring back.

And Jack blinked.

Suddenly, inspiration struck. Oh, wonder of wonders: his muse had stuck around 'til the bitter end. He leaned over and typed furiously for a moment, then sat back and sadly smiled. A masterpiece of understatement.

Perfecto.

Which meant that the time had come.

It's time, he thought, and the moment jarred. No more excuses, and nothing left to do. He looked at the bottle, thought about taking a farewell swig. There was no point. He left it go.

Then he turned off the typewriter, got to his feet, walked over to the ladder, and started to climb.

His legs shook on the way up, which surprised him. He actually lost his balance a bit near the top, and scuttled to regain his footing. An adrenaline rush flooded his senses, making his heart pound in his ears. The irony of it all was not lost on him—that he could be so prepared to die, and yet flinch at the prospect of falling. Wouldn't want to break a leg or anything, might spoil the suicide. A little gallows humor, hyuk hyuk hyuk.

The view from the top was very high; it occurred to him that most people in his place would opt to tippy-toe off the perch like a swimmer inching into a freezing pool, or kick over the ladder and let gravity do their dirty work, or just piss their pants and crawl back down and wait for old age to claim them.

Not Jack. No fucking way.

Only a swan dive would do.

He reached the last step, calves trembling, and reached for the rope, for tenuous balance. Fear and anticipation did a Keith Moon solo on his heart, going *bubbada-bubbada-bubbada-bubbada* in mad, terminal polyrhythms. He noted, appalled by the perversity of it, that he hadn't felt this alive in ages.

The rope felt waxen and slick in his hands. He placed it carefully—carefully—around his neck. It occurred to him that it would probably rip off one of his ears if he lost his balance and fell before it was properly seated. That did not pose a pretty picture. No style in that. Oh, jesus god . . .

A sense of perspective was sinking in. He was standing on a ladder, with a rope around his neck. Is this trip really necessary? lisped across his consciousness in Daffy Duck's voice. When he laughed, there were tears in his eyes.

Yes, he was definitely getting scared. No, he amended, scared didn't quite cover it. Petrified, maybe. Or abject terror. He looked at the bottle of Finlandia below, had second thoughts about that final swig

(don't be a wimp, just do it)

as he pulled the cord over his head, tightening it at the base of his skull. He closed his eyes, could see himself swinging, and

(do it)

his hands reached out to heaven, as if the Big Guy's

booming voice might rescue him just in the nick of time, and

(DO IT)

suddenly he was flying.

For an instant, it was almost like he'd pictured it: time stretching like an old rubber band as he hurtled toward the floor, the wind whipping past, feeling that nine-alarm adrenaline surge that screamed holyshitireallyfuckingdidit . . .

. . . then came the unforgiving snap, as the rope played crack-the-whip with his spinal column, shearing the vertebrae at the juncture of head and neck with an audible pop . . .

. . . and then there was nothing but white heat and pain, incredible pain, incomprehensible pain, rendering him oblivious to the whirligig motion, oblivious to his body's swing back into the ladder, the ladder's collision with Glen's big-screen TV, the shower of sparks and glass that littered the carpet beneath his spinning legs, his legs which wouldn't stop kicking . . .

. . . because there was no room in the whitesizzle paincrackle infinite Now for thoughts of the body, for thought at all, the body was on its own, nerveless fingers clutching at the rope-bound throat, tendons and muscles wrenching loose in rudderless abandon, bladder voiding to darken the lap of his pants, lungs rupturing under the trapped air pressure, eardrums popping, sealing out the city sounds and sealing in the roar of blood in his brain as his larynx collapsed like a moist cardboard tube, tongue blocking what little scream was left in his throat as his teeth bit it clean through, tip careening to the floor, blood and spittle foaming at his lips . . .

. . . and still he continued to twitch and spin, twitch and spin, feet doing a spastic midair tap dance three feet above a floor they would never feel again, every cell in Jack's brain screaming NO!NO!NO!NO!NO! as they winked out like embers off a burning building . . .

. . . and still he wasn't dead, unconscious yes but not dead not gone still trapped in a tortured bag of swinging meat . . .

. . . until gradually the spasms tapered off, and his limbs grew livid with trapped and blackening blood . . .

... and finally death came, a suffocating nothingness that rose from all sides up to smother him as his body gave in, gave in to the simple physics of the situation, pain mercifully abating as his nervous system shut down and locked up for the endless night.

There were no words to convey the surprise, no personality left to be shocked. His awareness had imploded, random bits of memory scattering like the refracted light in a shattered watch crystal. Death froze his discorporated soul in mid-scream like a bug in black amber, sealing it into the atomic structure of the walls, the floor, and the ceiling of the room which had become his tomb.

The rope held admirably, winding and counterwinding itself under the strain of its burden. Then inertia set in, and the swinging stopped.

Eventually, the sun went down, and darkness settled into the quiet apartment. Outside, cars honked, and life went on.

A week later, they found him.

So much for style.

.................AUGUST

2
BAYAMO BLOODBATH

It all started with the *Pollo con Fuego*.

Okay, Meryl thought. Picture this:

She sits at her table, overlooking the balcony, the Bayamo Restaurant menu in her hands. The menu, like the table and the rest of the room, is immense and largely blue. Bayamo is special in that it claims to be "the home of Chino-Latino cuisine." She doesn't know what this means. She doesn't care. She would rather be anywhere else in the world, and there is nothing on this menu that she wants.

"Do you know what you want?" her father inquires.

Yes, she thinks. I want to explode. I would not feel too badly if you did, too. At the very least, I want to believe that you will not suggest a dish for me. I have no such faith, however. Damned and doomed.

Her father sits across from her at the table. He's the picture of elegance, as always. He scrutinizes her from the peak of his imperial nose; through his bifocals, those regal eagle eyes are huge. He is imposing, as always, dressed even on an off day in an expensive summer wool suit, an intricate weave of midnight blue, russet, and gold. He wears no tie, and the top two collar buttons of his ivory shirt are open; a few sprigs of graying hair curl at the hollow of his throat, which is tan and taut as the rest of him, from the vast hairless desert on the top of his head to the cushy-clad soles of his feet. No gold chains; that would be tacky. In fact, no jewelry at all; even the blanched band of skin on his left-hand ring finger is all but tanned away. Life goes on, in the world of Charles M. Daly. Yes, time marches on. Tittee-rump. Tittee-rump.

He's so pleased, she thinks. Pleased to buy his little girl a nice lunch. Pleased to come to the rescue, with a helping hand and a word to the wise. Pleased to have the upper hand. Again and again. Forever. Amen.

She stares at the menu, which is big and multilingual. It makes a great shield; the better to hide behind, thereby buying a few more microseconds of time before having to make a decision. Any decision. It's a ruse, she knows; and a pointless one; and if Charles M. Daly detests anything more than anything else, it's a pointless ruse. Very soon now, he will grow impatient and start offering pleasant suggestions: choice items from the menu that—though he's never had Chino-Latino cuisine; though he is far far away from his Boston Back Bay home; though he has never even set foot in this restaurant in his entire life—will be right up her alley and yummy to boot.

And when that happens, Meryl Elizabeth Daly will finally go berserk. She can see the *Post* headlines already: KILLER COED SLAYS DAD, OTHERS, IN BAYAMO BLOODBATH. Sez "I didn't want the chicken." *X-Clusive Photos, pg. 9.*

On the table, her salad fork wickedly gleams. She can feel it coming, even before he opens his mouth.

"Why don't you go for a nice chicken dish?" he says.

She feels herself snap then: an audible crunch. Even Charles M. Daly cocks a tremulous ear. Very quickly, the pieces clickslam into place. She meets his big eyes for a moment, then proceeds to read out loud.

"The chicken," she says.

"Yes?"

"The chicken," she reasserts. "It all looks so good."

Her father nods warily.

"Mmmmm . . . Pollo Barbacoa."

"Meryl," he says.

"Or Curri de Pollo Chino."

"Meryl."

"Lookie here! Pechugas de Pollo Barbacoa con Queso Flameado! *Mmmm-mmm. My favorite!*"

"Meryl, that's enough." He doesn't shout. He never shouts, or rants, or raves, or loses his grip in any way. He delivers her name like a blowdart dipped in curare, hushed and numbing and deadly accurate. It pushes buttons in *her that she's spent her whole life trying to deny. Between that voice and those eyes, there is no room for hesitation.*

For one second, meeting those eyes, she falters.

Long enough.

"I didn't come all the way down here to play childish games," he says. "And I really think it's time you stopped fighting me tooth-and-nail on this."

Meryl stares at the ceiling. Blue Corinthian columns and track lighting everywhere.

"You drop out of Hempshire College and an excellent program at the end of your junior year, and disappear to Mexico. Fine."

Meryl stares at the wall. Big gaudy mural, happy carefree natives in their quaint native garb.

"You come back destitute and determined," he gestures, "to experience all this." His hand dismisses the city en masse. "That's okay, too."

Meryl stares at the menu. More ways to cook chicken.

Pollo con Fuego.

Chicken on Fire.

"I will endure all of this because I am your father, because I love you, and because I have no choice. I will even underwrite this, use my connections to help you secure acceptable housing, all because I don't wish to see my only child adrift in a sea of winos, junkies, and losers as she completes her quest."

She thinks about the dreaded fire-chicken: so hot it had been known to fry men's tongues right out of their heads. A plan takes form, suddenly. She knows what she must do.

There is a couple being served, some three tables away on the narrow swath of balcony near the windows. A plate of Pollo con Fuego hovers perilously before them.

"But there are some things that I simply will not have," *her father continues. His voice fades out. She no longer listens.*

She looks at her gleaming salad fork.

It only takes a second to heft it up and sling it headlong at the neck of the waitress. It moors its tines to the flesh and bone beneath the waitress's long blonde hair. The waitress pitches forward, the flaming chicken soaring off to strike its intended devourer in the face, the woman patron's hair erupting in bicentennial sparks that promptly plume into flame.

The customer screams. Her male friend dittos, falling back and cracking his head against the table behind him. He slumps to the floor. The waitress collapses astride him. The flaming chicken woman catapults to her feet. Blindly, she flails her way toward the stairs. She slams into the venerable Charles M. Daly, who spontaneously bursts into sparkling combustion.

Meryl is the proud owner of one white virgin marshmallow. She impales it on her butter knife and holds it up to her dear old dad. Alack and alas, he is moving too quickly: like a comet, he streaks to the balcony's edge and over, then plummets to impale himself on the pointy beer taps below.

And as flaming death spreads to engulf the home of Chino-Latino cuisine, Meryl picks up her trusty violin . . .

"Okay," her father said. "So you don't want chicken. It looks like they have some good shrimp dishes . . ."

"Dad." She squeezed the word out from between clenched teeth; all the joy from her fictive conflagration wheezed out with it like the air from a ruptured whoopie cushion. All five-foot-three of her was tight as a rail, clenched white flesh dressed in basic black. Her thin-lipped, bookish features betrayed a fine blush of angry red.

"So you don't want to think about food. Okay, fine." His hand carved an arc of dismissal in the air. "Have some soup and an appetizer. Have a salad. Just have drinks. Whatever you want. You're all grown up now."

"Oh, really." A halfhearted butterknife slice at the jugular. She blew at the blue-black bangs that dangled down over her brown-black eyes.

"But you're not going to get out of this roommate thing that easily. Not while I have any say in the matter."

And so, ah-hah. The crushing black heart of the matter had been lobbed back to her at last. She sank under its weight, still rigid.

"You see how the interviews are going," she said. "They're a bunch of geeks."

"So you're surprised? Where did you solicit them?

Some ads on bulletin boards and the back pages of the *Village Voice?*"

Meryl sighed. She'd set herself up, and now it was coming.

"The fact is," Charles continued, "that I have some very highly recommended referrals coming over this afternoon, and I have no doubt that someone suitable will turn up." Meryl made a sour face; Charles continued, undaunted. "Do you know what the client who secured this apartment told me? There are three thousand legitimate bidders for every decent available apartment in Manhattan. By that he means people who have the means to pay the rent, and would be more than happy to."

"But I don't want a roommate! Don't you see? Jesus!"

"Don't swear. I know you want to do it all by yourself. You're stubborn to a fault; you always have been. But it should be evident by now that you can't..."

...do it all by yourself. God, how she hated those words! Had there ever been a phrase more calculated to suck the spirit from your veins? She'd tried to go it alone, to find a studio that cost less than eight hundred dollars a month, as the pressure mounted and the dog days of August baked the city to a crisp. Maybe she shouldn't have cut so deep into her personal resources, running off to Mexico like she did. Maybe by the time she got back, all the deals were already scarfed up. Maybe this just wasn't her lucky day. Or month. Or year. She didn't know.

All she knew was that she needed to be here in the city now, more than anything.

And she couldn't do it alone.

"You don't have the money," her father continued, rubbing it in. "Do you have any idea how much I'm spending on that apartment? Three thousand dollars a month, and the only reason we got it at all is because the building's owner is a client. I'm willing to underwrite the expense, since you insist upon coming here."

Of course you are, Meryl thought. It's the only way you can retain control. It was a Charles Daly power play of the first order. She stared hard into the menu, and hated him for it.

"Rent, utilities, books . . . fine. I expect as much, as an investment in your future. But I will not finance your bad habits, and I will not supply you with spending money. That you can derive from charging your roommate for rent."

Meryl glowered.

"Why are you doing this to me?" she muttered.

"I'm teaching you a valuable lesson," Charles replied. "Money is power. It's something that you direly need to learn."

There was a pause of uncomfortable duration as father and daughter dug in.

"So maybe I'll find a cheaper apartment."

"There simply isn't a decent apartment for less . . ."

"Well, maybe I want an indecent apartment! Maybe I don't think I warrant a penthouse suite!"

"Listen, young lady." His patience was thin. "I know how you like to pretend that you're one of the poetically long-suffering masses. But in the final analysis, you are still a Daly. You were born into a certain strata of privilege. You have never been without it. You will never be without it. You are in a position my father would have killed for at your age—"

"Maybe he should have," she muttered.

"I beg your pardon?"

"Nothing."

"The discussion is settled, then."

"My ass," she growled.

"Maybe you should grow up."

"Maybe you should butt out!" she yelled. The conversation stopped dead; they had arrived at the moment of The Unpleasant Scene. And if there was anything Charles Daly detested more than anything else, it was an unpleasant scene. The conversation had nowhere to go but down, a belly landing on all-too-familiar terrain. They had been there so many times before.

And at that moment of impasse, their waitress arrived at last.

"Hi," the girl said. She was the same one that Meryl had fictionally forked earlier. Meryl avoided eye contact, feeling weirdly guilty for a moment. "Can I get y'all something to drink?"

Meryl peeked up over the edge of the menu; her father's face was instantly transformed. The merry widower, smiling his best successful-attorney-from-New-England smile, cobalt eyes crinkling warmly, peppercorn-colored mustache tweaking wryly upward as he said, "Just a Perrier, dear, with lime. I have a plane to catch." He smiled some more and nodded sagely; the waitress smiled and nodded back. "And my daughter will have..."

"A Devil's Tail," Meryl cut in, glancing up. Rum, vodka, apricot brandy, and wine: four great tastes that taste great together. It was the deadliest drink on the menu, with a limit of one per customer. "Actually, make that two. Two Tails, dear," she said, archly imitating her father's tone. "I ain't goin' nowhere."

The waitress glanced back toward Charles, seeming to glean in an instant the web of tension stretched thin as razor ribbon between father and daughter.

And then she did something remarkable, which was to wink and smile, not at the great Charles M. Daly, but back at merely mortal Meryl.

"I'll tell ya, darlin'," the waitress said, leaning close. "They don't put a one-drink limit on them things for nothin'. One Devil's Tail is a whole lot of fun; two of 'em and I might just want to bring a bucket. But it's your party."

Meryl laughed, a hard bark of surprise aimed less at the statement than the underlying reality. She didn't defer to him! her mind crowed, exulted. She didn't defer! It was a first, in her mythology. She checked to see how her father was taking it; he seemed somewhat taken aback, as though he had missed some secret joke.

"So what do you say we start with one, and see how you feel after that?" the waitress continued. She had a charming voice, with just a little south'rn twang peeking out. She also had a mean wink, offset in her otherwise Miss American features by a semicircular indentation of scar tissue that followed the hollow of her left eye. A conspiratorial gleam flashed between them.

"That's fine. Thanks..." Meryl snuck a glance at the name tag on the waitress' ample bosom. "...Katie?"

"Katie. Yup." The waitress winked again, then turned back to address them both. "You all think about what you want to eat; just about everything's pretty good. I'll be back in a minute." Then, before Dad could say a word, she turned and whisked away.

Meryl watched him watch her leave, noting that Katie-girl had what is known in the parlance as a killer bod: not a discernible ounce of flab, and a rear view that was to die for. In some ways, it was painful: she was sweet-faced and blonde and built and was probably a varsity cheerleader in college and an aerobics instructor by night and all the things Meryl never was and never would be. Further, she knew that he would have already logged those and a dozen other details, filing them away for future reference. She watched him track the waitress down the winding stairs that led to the bar, then ducked behind the menu again—

"As I was saying, we have four more appointments this afternoon..."

—while a plan took form in her mind.

3
THE LOFT

Katie Conner waited for the doors of the service elevator to fully open before stepping inside. A grizzled old black man was sitting by the controls, like a figure in a slightly decrepit Norman Rockwell print.

"You checkin' out Nine?" he asked.

"Ninth floor. Yep. For a friend." She stepped inside and smiled at him. Her pulse was pounding.

"It's a beautiful place," he said, clanging the doors shut behind it. "Wish ah could afford it." He threw the lever.

Katie felt her stomach lurch as the iron box started its upward slide. She could scarcely believe she was doing this. Not so much because of any problem leaving the restaurant while on break—she did that all the time, to hook over to Tower Records or Shakespeare & Co. and score something for the evening's diversion. And not even because the invitation itself was so bolt-from-the-blue weird: the father-daughter power-tripping so thick in the air it was like serving food in a field generator, then the girl piping in with an offer that was so obviously an end run around Daddy Bigbucks that it wasn't even funny.

No, it wasn't any of the above. It was the simple fact that she'd agreed. Agreeing was a little like acknowledging there was a problem in her life. Agreeing was a lot like admitting the very thin condition of the ice she skated on.

So maybe agreeing wasn't the greatest idea.

But if that was true, then why was she so damned excited . . . ?

104–106 Broadway was a fairly old building; nowhere was that fact more evident than in the service elevator. Its caged-in walls and nonexistent ceiling gave an open-air view of the elevator shaft itself. She could see the ancient cables and greased mechanisms that were hefting her upwards. She'd seen such things before.

What she hadn't seen were the interior walls of the shaft, covered as they were with posters from all over the world. With every floor, the motif changed: Two to Three was China, Three to Four was India, Four to Five the Caribbean. Travel posters alternated with works of native art, all neatly spaced and heavily stressing their native esthetic charm.

"Wow," Katie said, staring at the ascendant imagery. "Who did this?"

The black man smiled with pride, like he'd been biding his time for a long while, just waiting for somebody to come along and notice. "Let me put it to you this way. Ah spend round 'bout sixty hours a week in this thing, jus' goin' up and down. By itself, that ain't no way to see the world."

Katie turned to look at him. "So you did this."

"Little bit at a time. Got a niece, she works for American Express Travel Service. She sneaks 'em to me."

At the sixth floor, it ended; a flat expanse of dirty gray walls and doors concluded its trek to the vanishing point.

"Looks like you got a ways to go yet. Still," she told him, "I have to say: this is the finest elevator shaft I've ever seen."

"Well, shoot." He laughed. "You do what you can, so long as you're here."

"The best of us do, anyway," she said, then caught herself subconsciously before she could go on. Colin's voice was in her head, sardonic as ever, saying it's nice to be nice to the nice, isn't it, dear? She hated his snotty inbred British cynicism, but she had to admit, there came a point where she tended to lay it on a bit too thick.

The elevator man seemed to sense it, had the grace to ride the last two floors in silence. "Good luck to your friend, sunshine," he said at last, braking them at the ninth floor doorway. "I got a good feeling about you."

"'Preciate it." She beamed. "I hope you're right."

He threw open the door.

"Thanks again . . ." she began, stepped out onto the floor, and then stopped in mid-thought, staring.

At the loft.

It wasn't the largest she'd ever been in; she'd seen, and slept in, a few that would put this to shame, both in fixtures and cubic footage. But that didn't diminish the fact that it was huge; and no one, but no one, had ever actually offered her a shot at anything comparable that didn't involve a whole lot of bending over.

The central room was sixty feet long by thirty feet wide, with wide-plank hardwood floors and smaller renditions of the same Corinthian columns that graced Bayamo's cavernous expanse. In the far corner, a kitchenette—evidently somewhat of an afterthought—nestled near what appeared to be a short set of stairs leading up to the bathroom. Lots of plain white shelves on a plain white wall, all in need of a good cleaning and a fresh coat of paint. There were quite a few boxes and garbage bags sitting around, a few empty St. Pauli's and Classic Coke bottles, a half-eaten sandwich adrift in its wrapper. Otherwise, the east end of the loft was functionally nondescript, and demanded little more than her passing attention.

Unlike the other side, which consumed her entirely.

The wall was ablaze with light. The sun's westward descent tracked straight across the main room's three huge windows, and it put on a helluva floor show: brilliant golden fire, shining through to warm the exposed brick walls, the rich wood of the floors, and Katie's heart. She felt a sudden rush of peaked anticipation; Bob Fosse couldn't have timed it better. This place got sunlight, alright. God, did it ever. It would be great for her plants. It would be great for just plain basking in.

She'd taken another five steps in the room, transfixed, when a voice came from behind.

"You came. Great." The girl bounced off the bathroom steps and made for her, hand outstretched. It was the one from downstairs, alrightee: Meryl something-or-other. "Yesyesyes. I desperately need your help," she whispered, shaking Katie's hand.

"Excuse me?"

"You're excused. But I still need your help."

Katie was somewhat stymied. She'd never seen anyone drink two Devil's Tails and retain basic motor control, much less be lucid. "I'm afraid I don't quite follow you . . ."

"Shhhhh, they're coming." Meryl-girl gestured to the front room, and Katie saw the telltale vapor trail in her movements. She held it well, but she was lit, no two ways around it. "Listen, be a pal, huh? Just say you'll take it."

"What?" Katie wondered what the hell she was talking about. She heard voices, coming from what looked like the bedroom.

"I give you the tour and offer you the slot," Meryl-girl said. "*You* say you'll take it. Simple." She slurred her sibilants, just a bit. Katie was about to press for more information when the voices rounded the corner.

And Daddy Bigbucks reentered the picture, beaming as a squeaky voice squealed ". . . ooooooh, this is just wonderful!"

He was busy showing the apartment to a girl that filled a definitive type-slot in the city, particularly that section of the Village dominated by New York University: perfect hair in a perfect little ponytail, perfectly clear skin, perfectly straight teeth shining out from behind perfectly tight little lips. Body by Nautilus. Brain by Hostess. The kind that would marry well and age badly, fighting off the march of time by stretching every character line down at the Park East clinic until her cheeks were tight enough to bounce a quarter off of. She saw a lot of them in the restaurant, sucking back five-dollar margaritas all night long and talking about their last trip to the Caribbean or their next trip to the south of France. She could see that Dad approved. She was not surprised.

She could also see, for what it was worth, that Meryl had about as much in common with this princess as a Ming vase had with a Skippy jar. One good look at Meryl and Katie knew that Daddy was about a million miles off the mark. His little girl was a different one indeed.

Not just strange; strange had become a way of life for Katie. Strange was normal. Strange was boring.

It was just that Meryl was different in a way Katie had a

hard time putting a finger on, something that had nothing
to do with her hair or her clothes or her attitude. Maybe it
was her mouth, the way the corners turned down in that
peculiar kind of inverse smile that looks almost like a
frown and makes the smiler appear privy to some very
private punch line. Maybe it was her voice, which was a
throaty, melodious rasp that she could scarcely believe
coming from someone so young. It sounded, slurs and all,
like the voice of an old soul.

It sounded like a voice Katie wouldn't mind getting to
know.

Enough so that she hung around for the next sixty
seconds, which counted among the strangest in her life. It
reminded her of a John Cage performance, lining up two
different marching bands playing two different scores on
opposite ends of a football field and marching them toward
each other. Because Meryl-girl grabbed her by the arm
and started touring around the place, in full view of Dad
and the princess.

"This, of course, is the living room, and over here is the
kitchen," she said, with the kind of enthusiasm normally
reserved for a Catskills condo timesharing salesman. "It
gets lots of light, as you can see. Used to be a studio of
some sort. Great for plants. You like plants?"

"I, uh—"

"Great. Now if you step over here," she whipped Katie
around like a passenger on the Coney Island Tilt-A-Whirl
and pointed her at a doorway. "This you're gonna love."

Meryl turned and leveled a pointed stare at Dad and
the princess. "This," she said, not slurring at all, "is your
room."

Fifteen minutes later, Katie was sliding back down the
greased shaft. The elevator operator, whose name was
Lee, smiled as she got on but otherwise kept to himself;
the mark of a true New Yorker. Be nice, or butt out.
Whichever way the wind blows.

As it was, Katie's head was spinning, trying to figure out
exactly what just went down. Was Meryl-girl really offering her a place? Or was it an elaborate ruse? For that
matter, was she really even looking?

The facts and figures were a blur. She'd given her name and number, and of course they knew where she worked. They promised to contact her within the week.

Meryl seemed really biased in her favor, much to the twinkie's dismay; come to think of it, Daddy didn't seem too terribly upset, either. She wasn't really surprised by the turnaround, the way he kept feeling her up with his eyes. But he'd be in Boston. She could handle Daddy just fine. Yes, the smaller bedroom would be fine. Size was relative; small here was downright gargantuan compared to her current accommodations. There were already bookshelves in the room. Four hundred a month? Are you kidding? And a big closet. And exposed brick walls. She could handle anything. Phone in Meryl's name? No problem. At last, a sanctuary.

Somewhere to call home.

Free of Colin.

Free of anyone . . .

Just before they hit the ground floor, Lee glanced over at her. "So what's the good word? Think your friend'll like it?"

"I'll have to ask her." Katie smiled. "But I think she just might."

4
COLIN'S WORLD

It was a loverly evening for a knob-job. Colin felt, Heisenberg's Uncertainty Principle notwithstanding, that he could assert as much with very little danger of contradiction whatsoever.

True, he'd had a bit of trouble getting his willie to stiffen: the downside of the cocaine. Fortunately, the drug had quite the opposite effect on the lovely little bird whose lips were now so lugubriously a-twitter at his loins. For girls like her, just the thought of that lily-white powder was a social lubricant *nonpareil*. When he cut the lines, her knees were already en route to the carpet; such a delightful display of causality in motion could scarcely be imagined.

And so he had lain back on the bed, bearing his wand to her, abandoning himself to her pharmaceutically inspired ministrations. It seemed to him a quite benign way of wiling away the dreary hours remaining before his intended's anticipated return. Certainly better than wanking off, which always struck him as a dreadful waste of perfectly good semen not to mention bath tissue.

Colin Bates was a bit of a scoundrel, as he would be the first to admit. He would also point out, if pressed, that he failed to see much point in being any other way. It had been, after all, his great misfortune to spend forty-three years, seven months, five days, eighteen hours, and twenty-seven minutes on a planet entirely too stupid for words. That came out to fifteen thousand, nine hundred and twenty-three days, plus the one thousand and twenty minutes ticked off thus far on today's spectacular yawning stretch. All in all, a grand total of twenty-two million, nine hundred and thirty thousand, two hundred and twenty-seven minutes had been witnessed by Colin Bates thus far, most of them spent wondering why this wearisome accident had bothered to take place.

So long as he was here on Spaceshit Earth, he had resigned himself to the task of remaining amused. As such, he had virtually no patience with that which failed to amuse him. And seeing as how it was an incredibly stupid planet, its social behavior governed largely by rules evolved over the centuries by apes who insisted upon the conceit of calling themselves a "higher" species—as if that meant anything at all—genuine amusement was painfully hard to come by. A handful of truly great works, generated all too rarely by a far smaller handful of truly great minds; beyond that, the seemingly endless drool that comprised the plebeian human stew.

While he waited for another infinitesimally rarefied spark of brilliance to brazenly ignite in the undifferentiated goo, Colin had to console himself with what scant pleasures the earthly plane afforded. Mind-altering chemicals, for one: in quantity, whenever possible. As he was often wont to express, reality was for people who couldn't handle drugs.

Of late, cocaine was his controlled substance of choice; the insular numbness it provoked was in line with his preferred worldview. But he was also fond of the occasional psychedelic, the doorways of extraordinary perception to be found there. And tobacco was a mainstay time-waster, in a life filled with far too much time for the wasting.

Sex was another of his favorite pastimes: as varied as possible, as often as possible. Though he not infrequently found it a dawdle, as predictable primate rituals go it was certainly one of the best. He liked the way it made the tick-tocking seconds run together into molten continuums, Daliesque clocks of jism and flesh. He liked the simple, pleasurable self-absorbtion that his stimulated member demanded.

The moment at hand was a case in point. Whatever little else of note could be said about his companion of the moment, she certainly was an ardent little cocksucker.

Her tongue had a way of darting thither and yon, rather the way he fancied a hummingbird might if enclosed in a mason jar. It seemed to be everywhere at once, lighting with feathery enthusiasm all about the length of his shaft. Of particular appeal was the amount of attention she expended on behalf of his cushy german helmet.

This was not to suggest that she was in any way remiss with regard to the up-and-down pumping motion so important in such matters. To this task, she brought both hands to bear, and skilled little workers they were. In addition, she made quaint little mewling sounds which, he had to admit, added greatly to the overall excitement.

Colin raised himself up on his elbows, in order to better observe the proceedings. Her name, if he was not mistaken, was Abbie. Not that it made the slightest wisp of a difference. The names and faces of his many coke-whores had a tendency to run together, so interchangeable were they.

At any rate, Abbie—or whatever her name was—was a jolly bit of fun to watch. Her cheeks bulged delightfully as she harbored his vessel. She was blessed with ample buttocks and breasts that wibbled and wobbled as she worked. Her dark and rather severe bangs fell over her eyes, which was to their mutual advantage, as he doubted that she would really want to know what the look on his face revealed with regard to his true feelings about her.

It was in this state of recombinant contempt, amusement, and excitation that Colin found himself when he heard Katie's key penetrate the front door lock.

"Oh, bloody hell!" he blurted, jolting rather abruptly into a seated position. This came as quite a surprise to Abbie-or-whatever as well; she let out an undignified glorping sound as the tip of his cock hit the back of her throat.

At the far end of the flat, the front door swung open. Colin's nerve-endings, stimulated as they were, registered the *skreee* of the functioning hinges much as they might a hearty bite of tinfoil. It piqued the beginnings of his very foul temper, brought his bad back molars together in a grinding clench.

He hated the mathematical imprecision of the compromised position, the fact that his meticulously orchestrated agenda could be so easily thrown out of whack. He specifically hated the inevitable cataclysm that he knew was now coming, as surely as her footsteps closed the distance in the hall.

Most of all, in the moment, he hated Katie: for her chronic inability to hold to schedule; for the batty-eyed innocence with which it was done; for the way she would wilt as the damage unfolded.

In short, for being herself.

"Colin?" her voice piped up: Scarlet fucking O'Hara in Eighties regalia. The coke-whore hastily withdrew his digit from her dainty palate and looked up at him, panic aswarm in her eyes.

"Colin, honey, are you in?"

"Just a moment, dearest," he answered back. First things first: the honey, then the boot heel. "Have a seat. I'll be out in a jiffy."

Abby (or Tabby, or whatever she was) was upright in a flash, hastening to straighten her many many straps and buttons. Colin made the token gesture of pulling up his trousers; it was, he knew, far too late to manufacture the pretense of innocence, but it seemed the very least he could do. If he had to get caught in the act, he'd bloody well do it with dignity, not *flagrant delicto*, in foolish and full red-membered repose.

The bedroom door squeaked open, and Katie-love was there: twinkling eyes and red lips smiling, no doubt in preparation for some quaint and cozy expression of how very much he meant to her. The gesture, whatever it was meant to be, transmuted with alarming speed into something far less flattering. He looked at her, but her eyes were no longer for him; they were locked, instead, with unblinking fixation, upon his little prick-attendant.

"You're early," he said.

Her attention snapped back toward him, then; he could see the flint where her anger would spark within the shock-dilated eyes. That moment had not yet arrived, however; if he seized it first, and kept her reeling, the battle could yet be his.

"Whatever," he continued, fastening his trousers in an absent gesture of utter calculation. "Katie-love, this is Abby... that is Abby, right? And this is Katie, the love of my life."

"Hi," Abby muttered, still struggling with her raiment. Katie simply stood there, blinking, as if she'd just sustained a sharp blow to the head. It was difficult for Colin to conceal his amusement; the reek of absurdity was a tangible presence in the air.

"At any rate, Abby just popped by for a quick quartergram. She's got to scurry on now. Mustn't you, dear?"

"Uh, yeah!" She certainly was fleet of foot and wit. "Uh, thanks, Colin. Nice meetin' ya. Umm..." And with that, she propelled herself out of the room at a pace just short of supersonic.

Which left him alone with his long-suffering sweet, who had not yet managed to capture her breath. She resembled nothing more than a singularly lifelike statue, one of those animatronic amusements that were rumored to populate Walt Disney World. He contemplated her static beauty for a moment, felt a twinge of remorse that he promptly scuttled, and then went on with the charade.

"Nice girl," he said. "A bit aggressive... what brings you home so early? I thought you were stopping by..."

"Bastard," she said. The voice sounded hollow, and not at all pleasant. Tears began to sparkle in the corners of her eyes. "You bastard. How could you?"

She looked at him then. Yes, the spark had ignited. Her look was intended to render him gelatinous. He simply shrugged, disinclined to oblige.

"How could I what?"

"You bastard!" she shouted, and wheeled from the doorway. Her footsteps thundered fiercely down the length of the hall. Moments later, his ears were greeted with the *skreee* and slam of the front door, signaling her departure.

"Ah, well," he informed the room. "The fire when it comes."

But in truth, he felt not nearly so casual as that. A fire was already burning within, old as his years and mad as the planet he so thoroughly despised. He had no patience, no patience whatsoever, with that which failed to amuse him.

And he was not amused.

It had been better in the beginning, those three short years that seemed so much like eternity ago. She had been captured by his knowledge and his charm (not to mention his Brit accent, with the mysterious and foolproof aphrodisiac effect it had on American women); he, in turn, had been taken by her beauty, her sumptuous athletic build, her naivete, and her willingness to listen with rapt attention to any and every word he cared to say. Their coming-together had been the closest thing to a magical occurrence in all of Colin's forty-three years. For six entire months—a personal record by which he was mightily impressed—he had scarcely entertained even the thought of another woman.

But for a man of his boundless intelligence and appetites, even six months in Paradise began to grow tiresome. For one, she started referring to them in terms that were the province of that most revolting of archaic social units: the couple. Colin found the simplistic inflexibility of the binary primate utterly revolting. In addition, he noticed that her interest in reaping the benefits of his bottomless wisdom had not only plateaued, but was actually flagging. She was beginning to call him on things, to challenge his insights, to assert her fledgling intellect in a way that he found most irritating.

And so Colin withdrew, bit by bit, from the Garden: with occasional *soirées* of the utmost discretion, with increasing antagonism to her increasing arrogance. Before long, he realized that it had all been an illusion; not only was the magic gone, it had never even existed.

They broke up, then, in a nasty sort of way, but a strange and powerful dynamic survived the explosion: a perverse shifting magnetism, alternately attracting and repelling, bringing them together and tearing them apart at its leisure, almost always without warning, and certainly for no reason unless it was to drive them both utterly insane in the end. She would take her leave and saunter off for a week or a month or six, trying vainly to absorb herself in the pathetic ministrations of a lesser love, an occurrence Colin inevitably regarded with a bemused contempt that was directly proportionate to the intensity of her attempted escape. The last go-around particularly so: it had dangled the promise of true love before her moist and greedy eyes, and Colin couldn't have been more pleased. He knew it was destined to sputter and die, just as he knew she'd come limping back when all was said and done. And, lo! Miracles of miracles, it did, and so did she.

And so it was that they were together again, for bitter and for worse, in sickness and in stealth. Did he love her? No. Was she part of him? Yes. Would it ever end?

God, he could only hope . . .

The front door creaked back open exactly forty-two minutes later: forty-two minutes duly logged on his life's grim grand total. He had spent them gearing up, oiling his strategy; honing the razor, in a manner of speaking.

Now she was back, amid much opening and closing of cupboards and drawers. She always stalked the kitchen when angered or upset. He had no doubt that she would hammer on the evening's disclosure: it was, after all, the first time in their history that she'd literally caught him with his knickers down.

Well, he was ready: in casual recline across his comfy chair, fresh cigarette alight and at his lips, stereo redolent with the lilting strains of Mozart's *Ein musikalischer Spass* (the aptly named "A Musical Joke") in F major. Let her do her worst. He would nip this little beauty in the bud, *tout de suite*.

Presently, Katie appeared in the living, stoically featured and hooded of eye, just as he'd expected. He smiled benignly, biding his time, reading the liner notes that the Smithsonian had so graciously provided, a perfect smoke ring blossoming in the air before him, She would, of course, be waiting for him to initiate this dreary discourse. And that, of course, would be the first of her many mistakes.

The moment stretched. She stood by the door, evidently endeavoring to bore holes into him with her righteously smoldering gaze. He waited. The moment stretched. She cleared her throat. He blew another smoke ring.

Twenty-two million, nine hundred and thirty thousand, two hundred and seventy-one minutes into his life, she finally began to speak.

"Why?" she said. A compelling introduction.

"Why what?" he answered gently.

"Why do you do these things to me?"

"Ah." He smiled. "Oh, why indeed? Don't you think a more appropriate question might be, why do I do these things to myself?"

Katie said nothing. Words failed her; it would appear that her emotional apparatus had gone on the fritz once again. Colin, however, was no longer content with silence. It was time for the dissection to begin.

"I mean," he continued, "how many times have we traipsed down this road together, you and I? One might think that by now you'd have figured out what to expect from me. I'm not altogether unpredictable, you know. My habits are quite nearly as tediously repetitive as anyone else's."

Her eyes fought the flood, brave little soldiers that they were. But alas! Her lower lip had already begun to tremble. Naturally. Jesus wept, while Pavlov yawned.

"Say, yours, for example. You know as well as I do that you'll begin to make little weeping noises at any moment. For my part, the temptation is to ask, is it live or is it Memorex?

"In fact, perhaps we'd be well advised to videotape this entire sordid melodrama now, as it unfailingly unfolds. Then the next time we're tempted to play it out, we can just sit back and watch it on the telly instead."

On cue, the tears spilled forth. Any second now, the whining would commence. Colin blew a pair of concentric smoke rings, one after another, the second neatly penetrating the first.

"I just don't understand how you can be so cold!" she blurted. "Like you don't care about my feelings at all!"

Abruptly, Colin's hands came together, like a thunderclap in the small apartment. It jerked her eyes up to commune with his as he launched himself from his seat.

"My God!" he cried. "It's a revelation! The Good Lord Himself must have lighted on your head! The fact is, I don't care about your feelings! The fact is that they bore me to tears! Would you like to know why? Righty-right! Here we go!"

He was advancing toward her now; she retained her customary runny-eyed cowering stance against the wall. She was taller than he, and quite possibly stronger; but in the battle of wits and wills, she had never stood a chance. His weariness was exceeded only by the thrillrush of poisonous anger and bile that always accompanied this stage of the game.

"It's because they're not even your feelings!" he roared. "They're the same old crock of pious platitudes and simpering pea-brained middle-class slope-browed sentimentalisms you inherited from your mother, and she from hers, and she from hers, all the way back to the pitiful dawn of time! If you ever had an actual feeling of your own, I'd be honored to witness it, but I won't hold my breath!"

She turned to flee the room then, but he would not allow it. The thrill of the hunt was giving way to the chill of the kill; he was on her in an instant, apprehending her arm and yanking it back, eliciting a tortured yelp as he affixed her once again to the wall.

"I mean," he breathed, melifluous now, "what are you upset about, really?" He was directly in her face now; when she tried to pull away, he grabbed her by the cheeks and forced her head back 'round. "No, really. What is it? What has upset you so?"

She let out a dreadful high-pitched sound: a trapped-animal sound, far more expressive than words. It was rare indeed that he pushed her this far; the "relationship" could only take so much, all perverse shifting magnetism aside. But, God, it was a sound worth waiting for. One could spend their whole lives searching out something that pure.

"Come on," he cooed. "Give us a clue. Surely it can't be just about my little peccadillos. Surely it's not just because I fed that trollop my prick."

"Leave me alone!" She squirmed. He held her fast.

"Because the last time I checked, love—and you may

want to take note of this—my prick still belonged to me. I am still the sole proprietor of my most private parts, even to the extent that I might wish to bare them to the world!"

"Get your hands off of me, damn you!" She could barely speak the words, so boisterous were her sobs.

"But I don't think that's the *sum en toto* of what's bothering you, my dear. I think it runs a wee bit deeper than that." His fingers dug into her cheeks until she made that sound again. "I think the problem is that you want so desperately to change me, to get me to conform to your stupid God-fearing chickenshit morality. And the fact that I won't do that makes you feel like a failure.

"Well, let me tell you something, sweetheart. I feel like a failure, too. Way back, when I used to love you . . . yes, you heard me correctly. When. I. Used. To. Love. You . . ."

He rapped her head smartly against the wall, in tandem with the words.

". . . I thought perhaps that I could help you awaken from your stupid conditioned robotic trance. But evidently I was wrong. You don't want to be awakened. You want to spend your life as a fucking drudge; the better to fit in, I suppose, with the rest of the fucking drudges!

"Well, to hell with you! I'm bloody well fed up! So you can pack up the lot of your pitiful possessions, and your vomitous creeching sentimentality, and you can get them the fuck right out of my li . . ."

It was at that precise moment that her knee met his groin.

The effect was instantaneous and incandescent, with no room for more than a microsecond of incredulous alarm. Colin felt his wind take flight, and the fireworks began: great spiraling pinwheels and blossoming blooms of crackling Technicolor pain, overwhelming his inner vision with their majesty as he sagged to his knees on the floor.

Katie pulled away from him then, and his upper torso connected with the wall. She was still sobbing violently, and she moved with a graceless shambling gait, but this was not of the tiniest concern to him at the moment. She had put every bit of her considerable strength into the act, and his testicles felt quite thoroughly pulped. He cupped them gingerly in his hands; the gesture succeeded only in unleashing another grand salvo of brilliant agony. His lungs sucked on nothingness, stoking the display. He could do nothing but wait for the anguished entertainment to abate.

Dimly, behind him, he heard the sound of her finger tracing circles on the telephone dial. A moment later, she began to speak, with a voice rather desperately struggling for control. He could make out only bits and pieces of what she said, through Mozart's absurdly comic dissonant pomp and the air raid sirens blaring in his ears; still, snippets of phrases made their way to his attention. "Meryl, I'm sorry . . . Katie, the girl who . . . were you serious . . . bit of trouble . . . can I come? . . . tomorrow . . . thank you . . . look for another . . . promise. . . . thanks . . . how can I . . . thank you!" The click of the phone.

By that time, the pain had receded to the point where he could, though barely, turn in her direction. His own wheezing hacks were coming under control as well: the beginnings of normal breath. He watched her turn to stare at him; and though she was no longer crying, she did not have the eyes of a victor. There was uncertainty there, and sadness, and fear. He could see her attempting to cling to her anger; but the more she clutched at it, the more it turned into something else.

Colin understood, understood perfectly. Curiously enough, his own anger was gone. Perhaps it had gone the way of his wind, replaced by the nausea he choked on instead. He felt quite certain that it would be back.

But for now, what he felt was a twisted amusement, provided by the understanding that, in this game, there were no winners. If he had lost, then so had she. Another great triumph for the meaningless void. Another medal on the chest of Absurdity, his only true friend.

"Congratulations," he croaked. It was the best that he could manage. "You severed the Gordian knot. Alexander would be proud."

"I'm moving out of here tomorrow morning," she informed him. There were no more tears, but her voice still hitched. "I'll pack up tonight. You can sleep in your chair."

"Whatever you say. You've the pants in the family."

"And I swear to God: if you touch me again, I'll kill you."

"Of course, of course." He chuckled, or at least made the effort. "I think you may have succeeded in your ultimate aim. I may never be able to fuck again."

For one split second, she almost smiled. Then her face went hard, and she turned away. Fine, Colin thought. Let her stew in her old Christian guilt.

This conversation may have ended.

But the magnetism remains . . .

....
.........**SEPTEMBER**

5
SLAVE OF NEW YORK

It was late Saturday morning by the time she got her stuff down to the street, apprehended and bribed the requisite cabbie, loaded up, and headed off toward her new abode. No simple task, in any respect. But it had to be done.

And it certainly wasn't the first time.

The hardest part wasn't the leaving itself. As always, once she'd made up her mind, the process took over completely. In the resulting flurry of motion, there was no time for doubt or regret. At least not yet. That was the good news.

And Colin, to his credit, was astoundingly thoughtful this time around. He took off, and didn't come back. It spared them both the need to replay any more ugly tapes from the past. No attempts to charm or browbeat her into submission; no killing silence; no tense charades; no emotional reneging; no sarcasm; no sulking; no insults; no nothing.

It was far and away the wisest choice. She had to give him that.

So, no, leaving was easy. It barely even agonized her. The hard part was in recognizing how very little it actually changed. Tama Janowitz was right, dammit.

Katie was still a slave of New York.

For in a city that offered unlimited employment but could not happily house its millions, finding a roof over your head to call your own was the single stickiest survival chore on the roster: harder than mugging-and/or-rape avoidance, harder even than catching a cab in the rain or finding a cop when you really really needed one. To be a slave of New York was to live in the shadow of someone else's name on the lease, never knowing when the caprices of Fate or your property master would dash you out from under that roof and onto the cold cold streets.

Katie had been in New York for a little over three years. She'd spent a good bit of that time bolting from one asylum to another. It was a pattern she'd already established back home in Selma, but Manhattan had upped the voltage substantially.

The worst thing about moving was that it flashed you back, and back was not a place you necessarily wanted to go. Bad enough that you'd already been there. Sitting in the back of the cab, those few possessions she refused to part with piled up all around her, Katie felt like an urban boat-person on some kind of bizarre emotional exodus.

The cab hit a pothole and sent the blunt, battered edge of her cheval up to rap her on the chin. She bit her tongue and cursed under her breath. Not even God knew why Katie hung onto it. Certainly not for its beauty: it was an ancient, scarred oval frame of oak ringing a mirror that only a forgiving disposition could consider as being rustic. The silver had cracked and blistered and flaked away in innumerable places around its periphery, leaving a pitted varicose latticework that curled around the reflective surface of the heavy glass. Only the center was clear, and staring into it was a vaguely disconcerting effect, like seeing the fabric of reality itself unraveling all around you.

Once upon a time that had been appealingly romantic, way back when they'd first found it, abandoned in the weekly flea market that was trash night in the Village. Once upon a time it had been worth lugging the twelve blocks home, simply because it was funky and free and she and her lover had found it together as they strolled down Ann Street, and that had consecrated it, made it unique among the cast-off furnishings of the world and thus a thing to be kept, and cherished.

That was a long time ago.

Why she still held onto it, she wasn't sure. She'd shown up on Colin's doorstep with it six months ago, lumped in with her clothes and bags and boxes like a big wooden albatross, a clunky memento of the last good thing in her life before it had gone sour. Why she'd dragged it with her into this very compromised position, however, was clear enough: she didn't want the sole remaining symbol of what they'd had to fall into Colin's cynical clutches...

The cab hit another bump, and Katie's thoughts jarred back into the real world, the world of forced marches and slavery.

The world of Colin.

He was notable for several reasons. Topping the list was the fact that he was a repeat customer: Katie had shared space with Colin on three, count 'em, three separate and distinct occasions. She couldn't fathom it to save her life. The first time started good, got bad, and ended worse. The second skipped the first stage, and the last went more or less directly to hell from the git-go. Each time she swore she'd never see him again; each time, it hurt a little more. This time being the worst of all.

She swore it would be the last.

Five dollars later, the cab slid up to the curb. Here we go again, Katie sighed. Guess it's where the heart is, after all.

Home.

The ordeal proved to be quick and relatively painless. Meryl didn't ask many questions, and for this Katie was very glad. She'd answered the door sporting freshly spotted bib overalls, a paint roller, and little else. "I'm busy," she said; then, "C'mon in."

Katie smiled and lugged her stuff through the door. Meryl turned around and went back to work. Katie breathed a sigh of relief. It was hard enough to deal with the very personal decision of jettisoning her rightful claim to what few material possessions had found their way into Colin's lair during their three rounds together—her stereo, her TV, her plants—without having to explain why she'd showed up with next to nothing. No one who hadn't actually been around to witness their diseased relationship could really sense the taint that its terminal last gasps left on the things they'd shared. And certainly very few knew what a colossal prick Colin could be when he didn't want to give something up.

To hell with him. They were things, they could be replaced. She wasn't about to go back and fight for stuff that would only serve to remind her of him. It was as if his scent was forever upon anything he touched. To hell with it.

Besides, Meryl seemed to have the necessities covered. Looked like a lot of the boxes she'd seen turned out to be stuff coming in. In fact, it looked like Meryl had been pretty damned busy. The place was transformed from the last time Katie had seen it. There were plants now, hanging in the windows and sitting on the sills. They weren't hers, but it helped. In the middle of the living room was a big floppy couch and some chairs, plus a color TV and a black steel shelf that housed a stereo system that put hers to shame. The Talking Heads were playing at mondo volume; David Byrne's tremulous voice rode over the band:

> "Home—is where I wanna be,
> pick me up and turn me round
> I feel numb—burn with a weak heart
> (So I) guess I must be having fun . . ."

"Whatcha up to?" Katie asked, gesturing to the back wall, which was half-coated in an explosion of bright pastel colors. A half-dozen cans of acrylic paint lay open on a canvas drop cloth.

"My father wanted to hire painters," Meryl replied. She dipped her roller in a tray. "But I said fuck 'em. I want to do this my way."

She rolled a neat stroke of violet onto the wall, pushing the color right up to the corner, where it abutted a swath of mandarin orange. Other colors—greens, yellows, purples, blues—graced other parts of the shelves, the pantry, the whole back wall. It was as though no surface could match any adjoining surface, an unwritten rule in the World According to Meryl.

And strangely enough, it worked. Meryl had great color sense; though there was no logic to speak of beyond that one golden rule, it appeared unified, complete. It made the whole end of the room come to life, a jumbled kaleidoscope of vibrant kinetic planes.

Meryl reached up on tiptoe with her roller, the stretch exposing a paint-speckled glimpse of her right breast. She worked with an almost obsessive intensity, covering the walls in quick, deft strokes. Katie watched for a moment, admiring her control. Meryl didn't talk much.

"Can I do anything?" Katie asked. She was antsy from wanting to form some social bonding with this complete stranger. The music boomed its bouncy, naive melody:

> "the less we say about it the better
> make it up as we go along
> feet on the ground
> head in the sky
> it's OK I know nothing's wrong..."

"Huh? Oh, sorry," Meryl said. "I space out sometimes. There's a ladder around here somewhere that I sure could use."

"Coming right up," Katie burbled. On turning away she felt foolish, like she was trying too hard. She should just chill out, not try to buddy-buddy it up so badly. Meryl wasn't aloof so much as neutral. Some people don't warm instantly. She reminded herself not to push it.

The ladder was in the back of her room, where a lot of the excess boxes had also been shoved. She tried not to view this as anything but an accident of convenience. She pushed her way through the cardboard obstacle course, thinking it's okay, it don't mean a thing, don't be so damned paranoid.

The ladder was leaning against the wall, inert. By the time she reached it she had rallied, conjuring up scenarios of handy helpfulness that would make them feel more like a team, make this place feel like a home and not some well-appointed way station.

She grabbed the ladder and felt a sharp stab, an almost static shock of pain.

"Ow! Shit..." she hissed, and pulled her hand back.

Blood flecked back and spotted her shirt. "What the hell?" She held her hand up.

She was bleeding from a small but nasty slice across the center of her left palm. "Oh, great," she bitched. "What next? Tetanus? Rabies?" It didn't look like a nail wound. A mean splinter, maybe. A rabid termite. She examined the wood for the offending protrusion.

A curved, thin shard of glass was embedded in the wood, one edge cleaving through the grain like the fin of a shark. *What the hell is that doing there?*

She left the ladder where it lay and went out to the bathroom.

"Jesus, what happened?" Meryl asked when she saw the blood, which was etching thin, trickling grooves across the pale skin of Katie's wrist. "Are you okay?"

Katie held it out for inspection. "I think so. Goddamned sliver of glass on the ladder."

"Yeah, I found a bunch more sweeping under the radiator in the living room." There was no hint of apology in her voice; the lack of it irked Katie just a little. "Was it real thin?"

"Uh-huh."

"Looks like somebody blew up a video monitor or something."

"Why would anyone do that?"

"Who knows? I heard this used to be a studio. Maybe it was a performance piece." Meryl looked at the floor. "You'd better get cleaned up. You're dripping."

Katie looked down; droplets of blood were plopping down to spatter the floor, the drop cloth, the tray of violet pastel. "Oh, shit, I'm sorry," Katie moaned.

"There's some iodine and peroxide in the medicine chest," Meryl said, as she turned and made for Katie's room. "I'll get the ladder."

Katie watched her go, wondering if she could ever feel close to such a person. Then she walked up the stairs to the bathroom, closed the door, ministered to her wound, and then sat on the toilet and cried, very quietly, for the next five minutes.

The music drifted through the door, its obscenely cheerful beat bopping along:

"I'm just an animal looking for a home
share the same space for a minute or two
and you love me till my heart stops
love me till I'm dead..."

When she came back out, the song was over. The tape flipped automatically; another tune took its place. Meryl was up on the ladder, painting to beat the band. Katie went back into her room. Blood and pastels covered the wall.

And Katie unpacked her bags.

6
CARDBOARD CATHEDRAL

At ten o'clock that evening, Meryl discovered the cardboard cathedral.

She had been working tirelessly since the early morning hours, but that energy was all but petered-out now. By the time she actually wandered into her bedroom, she was running on fumes and sheer stubbornness; and when she saw the pile of boxes and crates and garment bags, she threw up her arms and moaned to the heavens, "Uh-uh. No way, Jose. *Hasta mañana.*"

Still, she couldn't get past the fact that, though her body was fatigued to the point of collapse, her mind was wide awake and a-rarin' to go. Surely there had to be something to do that didn't involve loading, unloading, lifting, setting down, painting, cleaning, or rearranging clutter.

"Okay," she said to the bedroom, but mostly to herself. "What options does that leave me with?" Because she was not a delusional schizophrenic—at least not yet—she answered the question within the solitude of her own mind.

Food? Nah. She'd nibbled a bit through the course of the day, but she was really too amped for a sit-down meal. Drink? Well, she was already doing that: a pint of Seagram's had spent most of the day making its leisurely way into her system, buffered by the tonic of the same name. Drinking, at this point, wasn't an event; it was an ongoing process.

TV? No way. Even with the cable turned on, her mind was too restless to sit still for that dreck. Read a book? Ha! That was a good one. Unless it was telling the story of her life, she doubted very seriously that it could capture her attention. Maybe write? That was a double har-har. Until she got this place straightened out, no way could she concentrate on tiny matters like the soul.

That left taking a walk, which she was too tired to even consider, or talking to Katie, which was doubly likewise. Whatever had happened to her surprise instant room-mate, Meryl didn't especially want to know right now. It gave every appearance of being depressing as hell. Not exactly what the doctor ordered.

"How about just standing here, talking to yourself?" she inquired. "Might be fun. But I doubt it. Nah." With all of her options gone, it seemed the only thing left was to disperse into gas.

And that was when she took a good look at the wooden contraption that was holding the loft bed aloft.

"Hmmm," she said, appraising the structure, weighing the value of keeping it up against the pain of tearing it down. On the downside, it ate most of the room: a sprawling confluence of drywall and two-by-fours, held together by bolts as thick as a big man's thumb and apparently anchored right through the wall and into the steel skeleton of the building itself. Whoever put this thing up wasn't fucking around, and that was a fact.

That figured heavily on the upside, as did the fact that it was well designed. The sleeping area was high and wide, with a sturdy railing guarding the two open sides and enough headroom that she could move freely without stooping, and could thus afford the ultimate luxury of privacy in her room without having to shut the door.

Meryl hopped down off the ladder and peeked inside the structure, which she'd only given cursory examination prior to her father's departure. Yeah, this was okay. Plenty of storage underneath. This was great. She wandered around the side. There was a door there, a rubber-lipped, hollow-core job held shut by a brass-plated doorknob. She twisted the knob and gave it a yank. The rubber lip hissed across the floor.

The door opened.

Inside was a room no bigger than a walk-in closet. A wide shelf ran waist-high around the interior. It was cluttered with shallow, crusty plastic pans and cast-off detritus. A faintly pugent chemical taint hung in the air. A tiny utility sink sat tucked into one corner, its single rusty faucet going drip . . . drip . . . drip. A light fixture hung on one wall, a dull red sixty-watt bulb poking darkly from the socket. Its purpose was unmistakably, wonderfully apparent.

It was a darkroom.

"Oh, this is perfect," she whispered to herself. "This is too much." Dreams of shooting the city danced in her head. This place was, she realized, a score and a half. Maybe Dad wasn't so out to lunch after all; at least sometimes. She was struck by a fleeting impulse toward gratitude. It passed.

But she was still in a terrific mood, thrilled by the discovery that vaporization wasn't her only option after all. What she had, instead, was the chance to do some Big City spelunking. What mysteries might she uncover, here in the Tomb of Forgotten Images? Discarded shots for toothpaste ads, perhaps? Nudie pictures of would-be models or aspiring stars of stage and screen?

Only one way to find out.

It took a moment to find the light switch. Once found, it did not help matters one whole hell of a lot. The red light brought some things into focus, but only served to deepen the bulk of the remaining shadow. She shrugged, wished idly for a flashlight, and then started to snoop around by hand.

Her excitement turned fairly rapidly into yawning disappointment. Whoever the previous tenant had been, he or she had taken all of the good stuff. The most promising item was the plastic trash can, which was back in the corner behind the sink. Still, it appeared to be about half-full; the eternal optimist in her, waxing prophetic-like.

"Welly-well," she murmured, "what do we have here?"

It was yet another in the long list of personality traits that her father found utterly incomprehensible. She could hear the mental admonishment echoing—what!?!! A Daly picking through garbage!!?!!—down the corridors of her mind.

Fuck it. Meryl refused to feel shame. She was by no means a pack rat; hell, she eschewed most of the opulent abundance her family had heaped on her by the shovelful, living a Spartan existence by comparison. It was just that there was something mysterious and wonderful lurking in the cast-off and forgotten relics of other people's lives. She found secrets there. Sometimes, she found magic.

Kinda like the artist she met on Broadway one day, who had collected little bits of junk, little textures and patterns and shapes, and made the most amazing jewelry out of it: earrings and necklaces and bracelets and pendants. All unique. All from seeing something beautiful in things everyone else had simply ignored. It was a gift.

She peered into the can. Looked clean enough, mostly throwaways of prints and stuff. Her rule was, if it didn't ooze, it was worth a cruise. She pulled a few out. The first two were deservedly forgettable: wrong paper, bad exposures, poorly cropped. Garbage.

The third one, though, was kinda cool. It was a big print, very obviously shot in the apartment, in front of those big arched windows. It was a portrait of someone, and judging from the light and the long shadows it was taken either very early or very late in the day. He was in three-quarter profile, one leg up on the ledge, half-sitting on the windowsill. She couldn't see his features clearly— partly the shadows, partly the fact that whoever had taken it had set the shutter speed too long, or maybe the film wasn't fast enough, or maybe they were just going for an artsy effect. She had no way of knowing for sure. They'd obviously used a tripod, because the apartment itself was super clear. But the light looked like it was crawling across the floor, and the guy in the portrait . . .

He was a blur: one arm waving like a hummingbird, dark hair swept back to reveal the shadow-pits where his eyes belonged. The rest of his face was indistinct; a bit of mouth in motion, the hint of a nose line. But those eyes . . . there was something about the way those two smudges of silver nitrate stared out at the world beyond the curling borders of the photo paper that intrigued her. Something intimate, something compelling and tragic and boundlessly mysterious.

Meryl liked it. There was no way in hell she'd ever

know who this guy was. It was like having a portrait of a ghost.

"Yep," she decided. "It's a keeper." She'd bop down to Basics in the morning and pick up a box frame; she could hang it on the same wall it had been shot against. There was a nice bit of poetry in that. Yep, she was really starting to like this place.

Finding the keeper had derailed her junk hunt somewhat; she suddenly became fixed with the idea of finding something heavy to flatten it out with.

And that was when she spotted the cardboard cathedral.

It was, in fact, merely a cardboard box, pretty scrupulously sealed up with silver duct tape and jammed into a niche that the trash had concealed. Indeed, if it weren't for the red glint off the silver, she wouldn't have spotted it at all. It appeared as though someone had shoved it there and forgotten all about it. On closer inspection, she could see why. It was pretty forgettable-looking.

But it also looked like it would do the trick, flattening-wise, and it sure wasn't going anywhere. Alright, she thought. Now we're cookin'. She grabbed a paper towel, moistened it in the sink, and swabbed the back of the print. She laid it face-down on the counter on another paper towel. Then she reached under the counter, hooked her fingers through the side flap of the box, and gave it a yank. It was a heavy sucker, roughly the size of a file cabinet drawer. So much the better. Something was written in big black letters on one side, but she couldn't read it in the absence of legitimate light. Probably THIS SIDE UP or HANDLE WITH CARE, or some other message of earth-shaking import.

It wasn't until she'd actually maneuvered the damn thing onto the picture—carefully, carefully, not wanting to crack or bend or tear her prize—that she saw how close her flippancy had actually come.

The side of the box said DO NOT OPEN 'TIL DOOMSDAY.

"Huh," she said. Now there was something you didn't see every day. It definitely got her curiosity going. Perhaps the rest of the goodies in the garbage can could wait.

She thought about the heft of the thing, the way its weight had shifted. Not books, or any single large object:

no solid clunk or thud within. Her guess was paper. A lot of paper. More photographs? Maybe. Or maybe magazines.

But why had the thing been left behind? And why the cryptic witticism, if witticism it was?

Right, she thought. This is deadly serious. I've just stumbled onto Pandora's Cardboard Box.

And she knew what that meant.

The first thing she had to do was get her X-Acto knife. It was out in the main room somewhere. One simply did not open the Doomsday Box without the Ceremonial X-Acto Dagger. To do otherwise was heresy.

Meryl darted out of the darkroom, trusting that the box wouldn't crawl back into the corner while she was gone. Her own belongings, which held no mysteries, warranted nary a second glance. She had a big ol' smile on her face as she raced into the main room and began her holy quest.

Katie was sitting on the couch, watching something or other on the tube: a commercial, at the moment. Infidel, Meryl thought. No sacred rituals for you. The lowly couch potatoes of the world would tremble when Princess Daly, High Priestess of Broadway, unleashed the terrible secrets of the darkroom.

"Hi," Katie said. She still looked pretty gloomy. "I guess you're still unpackin', huh?"

"Guess so. Have you seen the X-Acto knife?"

"Is this it?" Reaching for the Day-Glo-orange unit that was, sure enough, on the coffee table.

"Yeah. Thanks." She leaned over the back of the couch, and Katie handed it over. What followed was a somewhat awkward moment of silence in which Meryl realized several things: (a) that Katie was feeling very lonely and out of place here; (b) that Meryl wasn't doing a thing to help; and (c) that she wasn't very likely to in the immediate future. It gave her a little pang of guilt that she didn't know quite what to do with. For a moment, she contemplated inviting her guest to investigate the mysterious box with her.

Then the tiny voice of self-interest piped up, saying, uh-uh, that puppy is yours, thrill to the disappointment yourself and then come play with her if you're still feeling guilty. It seemed like a good plan.

"Umm...what are you watching?" she asked, a token gesture of concern.

Katie brightened a little. *"The Haunting,"* she said. "It's this great old haunted house picture..."

"Wow. Yeah, I love that movie." Meryl smiled. "Especially the scene where the two women are in bed..."

"...and one of 'em thinks they're holding hands..."

"...but it's really the ghost. Yeah, great scene."

"Well, if you want, I could scoot over a little..."

"Uhh...not right yet." Meryl stalled; she'd almost forgotten her quest. "I really have a few more things I gotta do..."

"Okay..." Playing down her disappointment with admirable style.

"...but let me finish up, and maybe I can get back in time to watch whatsername wrap her car around that tree, or the gate, or whatever the hell she does."

"Gotcha," Katie said, as the commercial block ended. "You better skedaddle 'fore the movie starts, and you get caught up."

"Yeah. See ya."

"Later!"

Well, that was painless, Meryl thought as she made a rapid beeline back to the darkroom. The fact was that Katie was a very nice lady; maybe when the smoke cleared and the dust was swept away, they could settle into the kind of buddy-buddy thang that her roommate seemed to so desperately want. It was always good to have a friend; at least that was the rumor. Meryl didn't have one whole hell of a lot of them, but she'd heard that they were swell.

Meanwhile, back to the task. She had her magic blade in hand, and in two shakes she was back in the darkroom. The box was still just sitting there.

"It's Doomsday," she said.

And sliced it open.

For a moment, it looked like a case of much ado about nothing. She had been correct in guessing paper, and lots of it; beyond that lay the heartbreak. No photographs. Not even any magazines. Just dozens and dozens of manila folders, holding reams and reams of what appeared to be plain old typing paper.

Great, she mused. No wonder it said DO NOT OPEN 'TIL DOOMSDAY. A little boredom would probably be just the ticket when the world blows up. Take your mind off your troubles.

The folders were all hand-labeled. Just for the hell of it, she decided to inspect them. At this point, she expected to see nothing but TAXES and RECEIPTS, maybe GRANDMA'S FAVORITE RECIPES. The folder in front was a skinny little item. She pulled it out and held it to the light.

The label said NIGHTMARE, NYC.

"Huh," she repeated. Another surprise. She opened it up and read the opening page:

NIGHTMARE, NEW YORK CITY
Tales From the Last Days
Of the City of Dreams
by
John Paul Rowan

"Wow," she said, scrutinizing the page. Nice paper. Good thick bond. The typing and alignment were clean and dark and flawless, though she imagined it would be pretty hard to fuck up eighteen words on five lines of type.

She turned the page, saw a table of contents. There was a lot of scribbling on this one, names of stories or whatever crossed out and interchanged, little arrows, etc. She scanned it quickly, then flipped to the next. It started out with INTRODUCTION: WAITING FOR THE GIANT TO AWAKEN, then went on with a full page of type.

Intrigued now, Meryl began to read:

I have lain awake in the City of Dreams and listened to its breathing. Long after the others have gone to sleep, staggered home from their jobs or their nights of debauchery; long after the streets have been reduced to canyons bearing only the echoes of the day's cacophonous rat-race patter; long after all but the last of the lost have closed their eyes and shut out the world beyond their skin, I have lain awake.

And listened to its breathing.

The city stands: a million trillion tons of cold, unblinking concrete and glass and steel. Eight million people, day by day, scuttle across its flesh and hurtle through its bowels. Like parasites, like crumbs of food, like microscopic organisms, they eke out their existences within the body of a host too enormous for their comprehension.

It tolerates their presence.

It has reasons of its own.

The city is alive. Countless billions of dollars and lives, over centuries, have more than seen to that. Over two hundred years of human hopes and dreams that fed and fouled, nurtured and polluted the sleeping giant. Now it has dreams of its own. I can only begin to guess at their nature. I may never know for certain.

But as I lay there, my own tiny lungs bellowing within the confines of my own four walls, I know it is the city's breath I hear. It rushes in and pulses out; steaming on the rain-slick summer streets, spinning ice-devils down the frozen boulevards. The city's breath: equal parts carbons monoxide and dioxide, oxygen, dust, rust, blood, and sweat. The city's breath: carrying with it the passion and pain, the labor and love, the life and death that have given it sustenance and form. I taste of these things as I lay in my bed.

Listening to the sleeping giant breathe.

And waiting for the day it will awaken.

"Jesus," Meryl exclaimed, closing the folder. "Who is this guy?" She checked the front page once again. John Paul Rowan. It didn't ring a bell.

All sorts of questions were rising up now, vying for her attention. Was this the original manuscript for some famous book she'd never heard of? Was this the original manuscript for some great lost work that she'd just discovered? Was this a box full of useless drivel that was better off stuck in that corner forever?

And why had it been left behind?

DO NOT OPEN 'TIL DOOMSDAY.

Curiouser and curiouser.

Whatever the case, Meryl knew one thing for certain: this was pretty darned interesting. She could feel the mystery sweat begin to prickle at her pits. The impulse to drag the box out to the middle of her room and do a full-scale excavation was almost irresistible.

Then she thought of the picture underneath, and that opened up a whole 'nother batch of questions. Was John Paul Rowan the keeper? Had this been his studio? What else was he into? Were there any other pictures where you could actually see his face? Where the hell was he now? And did he know that this box was still here, or what?

Too many questions, and not enough answers . . . at least not until she got down to the digging. She couldn't really drag the box if she wanted to get that picture flat: a result she hankered for more than ever. "Well, damn," she muttered. "My kingdom for a simple solution."

The best thing, for now, was to grab a handful of the front-running folders and toddle off into the light with them. This she did. There was a chair in her room that she cleared off in seconds; the box that had been sitting there made a dandy footrest.

"Okay," she said. "Let the nightmares begin."

As she opened the first of the stories . . .

THE LONG RIDE
by
John Paul Rowan

The man in the backseat is a haughty little fart who smells of Brut excess. He keeps holding his watch up to check it in the passing streetlight, as if the future of humanity itself hinged on his punctuality tonight; but Harry knows that the guy is no big deal. Neither hot nor cold, this lukewarm man will be spat out into the New York City night...hocked like a phlegm-wad from the back of Harry's cab...and it won't make any difference at all.

But you couldn't tell that to this guy, overdressed at the center of his own universe. He wipes an executive amount of sweat from his forehead and checks his watch again. "How far away *is* this place?" he whines, desperation latching hold of his face.

Without a glance to either side, Harry answers, "This is 57th Street. You wanna go ta Penn Station, right?" The guy digs around in his brain for a second, mumbles a high-pitched affirmation. "Okay, that's on like 33rd Street. So you figure it. We got twenty-some-odd blocks to go, right? We'll be there in a coupla minutes..."

"Can't you go any *faster*? Jeezis!" He squeals like a pig with a corncob up its ass, and for some odd reason it makes Harry think about the country. *Ain't seen nothin' but dogs, pigeons, rats and cocka-roaches for years,* he muses, *an' I probably never will again.*

Then he shrugs. So he and Betty never got their house in the boonies. So what? One of life's little regrets: too little, and too late, to worry about.

Harry drives a cab, and he probably always will. Right now, a fragrant little man in a big hurry is playing backseat driver. Harry pulls himself back and decides to have a little fun.

"Sure," Harry says. "Sure, I can go faster." Before them, the light is as yellow as they come. Harry leans on the horn and steps down hard on the gas. The cab shoots forward. The light turns red.

"Look out!" the man screams, as a garbage truck and a station wagon surge out from 56th Street and straight for them. On the passenger side, no less, Harry notes, resisting the urge to laugh. Instead, he just floors it and veers slightly to the left, making it close enough to set the guy back in his seat a little without ruffling anyone else's hair in the least.

Harry's cab screams like a bullet down Seventh Avenue. When a red light at 48th finally forces them to a grinding halt, the little man doesn't say another word.

"Almost there," Harry deadpans.

Not another word.

Harry's cab spits the guy out in front of Penn Station and sits there, purring, at the curb. Harry pops the sweaty ten-spot in a clean white envelope, pockets it, and chuckles, patting the dashboard lovingly. They are two old friends, sharing a treasured and time-honored joke. *I love ya, old crate,* he thinks as the engine purrs back at him, and is amused by his own sappy sentiment.

Betty'd have to laugh, seein' me like this, he thinks. The smile saddens. *If only . . .*

Then a rap on the passenger side brings him out of it. A long-haired kid is playing his knuckles across the window and peering in. "Anybody *home?*" the kid mouths, his voice lost in the *hummmm* of the city.

Harry motions the kid inside, then watches as two young cuties pile in behind. *Hoo boy! A blonde and a brunette! Lucky bastard,* he thinks ruefully. *No more chicks for Harry, by gum.* Then he pictures Betty, on the day that they were married, and he shrugs again.

No regrets.

The three of them are in now, with the door closed behind them, and they are wrassling with their backpacks for space. The cab is filled with their laughter and commotion. "Wait a minute," says Blondie, in the middle of everything. She's up to her elbow in a jumbo handbag, digging for something.

"Where to?" Harry asks, though in no particular hurry.

"Yeah!" says the kid, with a trumped-up southern accent. "Where in Sam Hill *are* we goin', Bessie May?"

"I said *wait* a minute," she responds curtly, then adds, "Don't call me that. It sounds like a cow." The girl keeps looking. A minute drags past.

"Umm . . . I think it's on Saint Monkey's Face, or something," says the kid, feigning helpfulness.

"Oh, shut up, Tom!" yells the brunette. Blondie rolls her eyes. Tom cowers. They all start laughing.

These are good ones. I can feel it. Good kids. Harry thanks God that he can still feel. It makes the long ride go down easier.

Blondie, meanwhile, finds a scrap of paper. She unfolds it, and her face lights up. "All right!" she exclaims. Everyone turns. "We're going to . . . uh . . . 124 St. Marks Place. Is that right?"

"Right," says Harry, switching on the meter and then sliding out into the street. "Here we go."

"New York *City*!" yells the brunette, rolling down her window and howling like a coyote. This seems to strike her friends as a good idea, and within seconds they have practically raised the roof right off the cab. Harry shakes his head, laughing as he taps their maniac glee. Then Brownie leans back inside and says, "Hey, Mr. Cab Driver! I thought you guys were supposed to drive like . . . like *crazy*!"

"You want a *ride*?" Harry yells back at her, mischief in every line on his face. His passengers let out one loud unisoned "*Yahhoooo!*" and . . .

. . . Harry takes a banshee left on 28th, zips over to Broadway and gives them a full-frontal shot of the Flatiron Building, its breathtaking cutaway design. "Oldest skyscraper in New York," he informs them as they gasp with awe. Tom mutters something about "a wedge of cheese from heaven," and they laugh some more, while Harry weaves in and out of traffic like a thread in some master's loom, pulling off stunt after stunt with a cool half-smile.

Makes me feel like a kid again, Harry owns up silently. *Makes me feel really. . . alive again.* The admission floods him with images both tragic and sublime, leaves him swimming in the bittersweet. They pull up behind an impatient cluster of traffic, held at bay by the baleful red lights, and Harry finds that his cargo has also slipped into a thoughtful silence.

Blondie breaks it up by looking suddenly at Harry and saying, "I don't want to be a party pooper or anything, but . . . you aren't giving us the *scenic* tour, are you?" Her voice betrays discomfort with the need to ask. "I mean . . ."

"I know what you mean," Harry cuts in, understandingly. "You don't wanna get snookered by a New York cabbie, am I right?" She nods reluctantly.

"Well, hey," Harry adds cheerfully, reaching across to flick off the meter. Three sets of eyebrows raise in disbelief. "Does that take care of it?"

The kids don't know what to say, but they sure are smiling when the light turns green and the cab kicks back into gear. Tom does a thumbs-up motion and points at Harry, while the ladies nod vigorous agreement, but not a word is spoken. Harry decides to break the ice again.

"Where're ya from?" he asks. A time-honored line.

"We come from deepest space," Tom monotones.

"Ahhh!" Harry replies. "Coneheads, eh?"

This brings startled laughter from the rear. "You watch *Saturday Night Live*?" Brownie wants to know.

"Hey! This is th' Big Apple, kiddo: home of *Saturday Night Live* an' all things cultural!" The back echoes for a moment with *yeahs* and *wows*. "Yep, this is one hell of a little town, if you never been here before. You'll love it."

"First time," says the blonde, "and I think I already do."

"It's scary, though," says the brunette suddenly. There is an anticipative pause. "I mean, we're from a really small town in Pennsylvania . . . Stewartstown. You ever hear of it?" Harry hasn't.

"Anyway," she continues, "we come up to New York City, and . . . woe my God!" She sighs heavily, then adds, "I mean, don't you ever get *scared* living here all the time?"

Harry thinks about it. *Not anymore* occurs to him instantly, but that's not what he wants to say. Before he can answer, Blondie interjects.

"If you're not afraid, you'll be all right, Kathy. It's the *fear* that attracts negative energies. If you don't . . ."

"It's always *energies* with you two," the first one complains. "I don't know what to think about all this *energies* shit." She practically spits out the word.

"No, seriously," says Tom, and it's the first serious thing he's said. "It's like a dog, Kathy. A dog can *smell* when you're afraid. You don't have to carry a sign that sez I'M SCARED OF YOU for a dog to know what's on your mind. They just *know* it."

"I hate dogs," Kathy mutters.

"See?" Tom insists. "It's because they can see right through you . . ."

"But *really*!" Kathy interrupts, turning the conversation back to Harry, who's been listening the whole time. "When we got off the train and came upstairs, there was some guy in the lobby with one of those huge radios, an' . . ."

"*Kathy!*" The blonde in the middle sounds genuinely distressed.

"It's okay," Harry says slowly, quietly. He knows what she's going to ask. "Go ahead."

Kathy looks furtively at her companions, who are shaking their heads at her in disapproval. She sends back a telepathic message to the tune of *well, he said to go ahead;* then she clears her throat and continues.

"Well, the radio said that . . . that something like eighteen cab drivers have been killed so far this year already, and . . ." The silence is leaden. ". . . and I just wondered: doesn't that scare you at all? I mean really, seriously." When nobody speaks, she adds, "I'd be scared, that's for sure."

The atmosphere in the cab has been dampened, as if Kathy had just thrown a big shovelful of graveyard dirt over the lot of them. Harry has so many things that he could say right now, so many things drilling holes in his brain and screaming to get out, that he wishes he could just scream and let them out, spray them around the upholstery like bits of shattered skull. But these kids are fresh in town, and nothing horrible is gonna happen to them, and he doesn't want to haunt their dreams with his nightmares.

So he weighs it all very carefully in his mind before speaking, and he tries to make it as meaningful as possible. He says, "It's a dangerous job. No doubt about it. There are a lotta crazies runnin' around here, and some of 'em would just as soon kill ya as look atcha."

They are hanging on his words now, Kathy's gaffe entirely forgotten.

"But," he adds, and this is the difficult part, "as far as my experience goes, dyin' is no big deal. I mean, it's bad," and they all laugh nervously, "but it's worst for the people that're left behind. You know?" They know. "It's like, I lost some of my *favorite people* ta fuckin' creeps and crazies..." and then he stops, knowing that he's going too far.

They wouldn't believe it if I told 'em, he reminds himself. He takes a deep breath to calm down. It works. He looks in the rearview mirror. They're waiting.

"...but, ya see, I'm a cab driver. I been drivin' this cab for twelve years now, an' I think I'll probably be drivin' it forever. It's as simple as that. You know the risks. You take your chances. And you hope ta hell..." pausing, great difficulty in his voice, "that nothin' ever happens to ya. That's what life is all about, I think." And he leaves it at that.

"Yeah," says Kathy, after a respectable pause. "I guess there's really nowhere safe anymore, is there?"

Tom's voice, as he stares out the window at the City of Hollow Mountains, is strangely soft and faraway. "Nowhere," he almost whispers.

Nowhere. The word echoes in Harry's mind. *Nowhere.* He sees himself on the long ride, endlessly drifting through the endless night...

...and then, mercifully, somebody changes the subject.

By the time they get to St. Marks Place, they've rapped about everything from Reagan to rubber love dolls, and Harry wishes that this part would never end. But the street is alive with blue-haired punks and neon and smoke and intensity, and Kathy's boyfriend is waiting in his wild East Village apartment, and Harry knows the end of a road when he sees one.

The fare comes out to a whopping $1.30. A quick pooling of resources, and four smackers are plopped into Harry's hand. He pshaws a little, but it's to no avail. "That was better than a roller coaster, man," Tom informs him. "Have one hell of a good night."

"*You* have a good night," Harry replies. "An' welcome to the city, kids."

There are a couple of moments of awkward, well-meaning cheerfulness, and then the kids slide out of the cab. The other two start to wander off, stunned by their new surroundings; but Blondie stops at Harry's window and crouches before it, giving him a look that makes his old heart flutter. "Take care of yourself, Harry," she says finally.

"You don't have to worry about me," he answers, warm and slightly embarrassed. A tiny smile plays across his lips. She gives one back. It says *but we will, anyway.* Then she turns (her friends are waiting now), and they disappear into the East Village shadows.

"Have the time of your lives," Harry whispers, watching them sadly. He doesn't envy them their life, their vitality. He's already had his turn, and . . .

Forget it. He issues the silent command. *Just forget it.*

Harry pulls the white envelope out of his pocket, counts the bills. *$126.00 so far,* he notes, rounding it off with the four new bucks. He looks at his watch. It says 10:45. The night is young, so far from over.

"You're good ones, God bless ya," he calls after the kids, long gone. Then he pats his pal the dashboard and wheels into the street again. Just the two of them, machine and driver, on the long long ride.

Harry picks up one of the bad ones around three that morning. A freaky-looking guy, all dressed in black, with mascara and an earring and a terrible nervous twitch that gives him instantly away. Harry picks him up anyway. *You don't have to worry about me.*

"Where're ya goin'," Harry asks as the guy clambers into the backseat.

"Uh, 110th Street, man." He talks fast, this one. Probably hopped-up on speed or something. "110th and, uh, Columbus."

The guy slumps back in his seat, looking nervously from side to side. Harry doesn't like him a bit, quickly dubs him Weirdo. The alarm is ringing in the back of Harry's head. It's a sound that he knows too well.

It's too late to worry about that shit, Harry tells himself, but it doesn't do any good. He thinks about what the kid said, about the dog, and he wonders if one's fear really *does* bring the bad things down.

There is a night that Harry will never forget, and he knows that he was scared when it happened, and he wonders . . . driving fast though there is no joy in it this time, just wanting this weird bastard out of his car.

Weirdo lights a cigarette, drops the match to the floor with a shaking hand. He cracks the window and watches the smoke drift out like a ghostly skeletal claw, and Harry thinks *hot damn, boy. You picked yerself a winner.*

Harry tries to strike up a conversation. It doesn't work. He tries to ignore the chill that's creeping up his spine, the deathly cold certainty, the knowledge and the responsibility it entails. That doesn't work either.

So he drives.

And he drives.

And he drives, coming nearer to the point where he knows that it all must come down. He watches the signs flash past on his left . . . 59th, 69th, 79th, and onward, while Central Park sprawls out like a great dark monster on his right, a beast of unfathomable size and appetite, seeming to go on forever.

Like the long ride, forever and ever . . .

I wonder if he'll try to dump me in there, Harry muses. *Dump me in the bushes, drive my cab for a coupla blocks and then dump it, too, takin' off with the money I work my ass off for, the money that Betty needs so bad . . .*

"Pull over," says the voice from the back.

You can't HAVE it, Harry screams in his head, and it's so much like a déjà vu that it makes his head swim. He pulls himself together with tremendous effort and says, "I thought you said . . ."

"I said *pull it over*, man. *Now*." And Harry feels the familiar coldness press against his neck. The nightmare coldness. Of the barrel. Of a gun.

Very slowly, Harry eases off on the gas. The cab complains, as if it wants to resist but is powerless to do so. Harry mouths something inaudible; the cab mellows out...

...and then *surges forward*, Harry slamming down hard and flooring it. Weirdo flies backward like a wild pitch, hits the backseat, and curses wildly. "What the hell are you *doin*?" he shouts, shaking like a leaf and pointing the gun at Harry's head with both hands.

"You gonna shoot me when we're movin' this fast, big man? You gonna take control of this baby from the backseat? Huh?" The words are loud and wild and crazy. His eyes are like saucers with bright red trim. "We're goin' to 110th fuckin' Street, an' then we'll *see* about this!"

Weirdo doesn't know what to do. Harry is pushing seventy and running red lights like they weren't even there; cars and trucks and buses are honking and swerving to avoid him; brakes are screeching; the engine is roaring. "You bastard!" Weirdo yelps at one close call. Harry bites his lip and keeps on driving. He can see the gun, swaying back and forth like a cobra, very clearly in the rearview mirror.

Harry howls around the corner at 110th, a hard left followed by a harder right, jostling Weirdo around as much as possible. He slams the brakes down with all his might, fishtailing and flinging the guy forward in the process. Weirdo smashes against the front seat with tremendous force, knocking the air out of him and making him groan.

But he does not drop the gun. No. The gun, he hangs on to.

He drops back into his seat, practically crying now, and aims at Harry again. He can no longer control the shuddering. That's a good sign.

"You know what this is all *about*, then, right? You know what's goin' on!" His voice is a high-pitched squeal that reminds Harry of the little guy with the Brut O.D. "I want all your goddamn money, man! An' I want it *now*!"

Harry turns around slowly. He is thinking about his wife. He is thinking about those kids. He is thinking about all the genuinely good people he has known, and he is thinking *the world would be better off without this son of a bitch, this miserable creeping scum. If only I had . . .*

But there is no time to think of that. It's too late for that now. So he turns, very slowly, and says, "You can't have it."

"I ain't kiddin'!" shrieks Weirdo. "I'll kill you!"

"You're not gonna kill me, you little shit." The words are ferocious. Harry's eyes have taken on a strange light. "Little bastards like you think you run the world. You make it bad for everybody. Your best bet would be to give me that gun, while you still can."

"What're you talkin' about? You're crazy!" Weirdo's teeth are chattering, but his aim is there. Harry can feel the black hole boring into his head.

If a déjà vu is a flash from another life, then this is a déjà vu. Harry has been here before, and he will be here again. Harry is a cab driver.

Again and again and again . . .

Harry's eyes. A strange light.

So very calm.

So very calm, as he reaches forward with one hand and says, very firmly, "Give me the gun."

And Weirdo pulls the trigger with a tortured little cry, and Harry's brains explode out of the back of his head to run like fat misshapen slugs down either side of the shattered windshield. Harry jerks like a clipped marionette and slumps against the steering wheel, smearing his old pal the dashboard with gore.

But the light in his eyes, it doesn't go out. Weirdo has a few seconds to register the sight.

Then everything changes.

And the man in the backseat starts to *scream* . . .

Betty Stone awakens with the rising sun. She groans a little, haunted by a bad dream from somewhere deep in the night. She struggles with it for a moment, but it refuses to come clear. Something about Harry, no doubt. She always dreams about Harry.

She is alone in the double bed, of course. No surprises for Betty Stone. She takes her time getting up, wraps her old housecoat around her aging frame, hits the bathroom, and then makes her way to the kitchen.

She gets the coffee perking, then starts on the couple of stray dishes lying around. *It's always been like this,* she muses, still slightly bleary. *Seems like it's always been like this.*

Seems like forever.

Betty Stone drinks a cup of coffee, watches *Good Morning, America,* then flips to some nature documentary. Time passes, an hour at a time. Then she goes and checks the mail.

Several bills. There are always, always bills. Every bit as certain as death and taxes, they roll in every month. Thank God she's still able to pay 'em.

A letter from her sister in Vermont. Thank God for Loretta. She's been writing regularly now, ever since . . . ever since . . .

And, of course, the white envelope is there. The white envelope full of money. The clean white envelope that has been in the mailbox every day since . . .

. . . since Harry was murdered, shot through the head in his lousy taxicab, that horrible goddamned dream-shattering night . . .

How long has it been? she thinks to herself, trying to place the date, count down the lonely days. *How long?* she asks herself.

Three months, the answer comes to her. *Three months now. And every day the money keeps coming. And I don't know where it's coming from. And I don't know who to thank . . .*

Betty stands at the mailbox for a long long time.

There is a woman at the corner of 34th and Fifth Avenue, in front of the Empire State Building. She'd had one of the best days of her life, taking in the infamous Big Apple's million and one attractions. Freshly returned from the summit where King Kong himself once stood, she breathes deep of the gritty air and considers her options. Where to go, what to do?

She still hasn't made up her mind when the cab comes cruising down Fifth in her direction. *Well, I've got to go somewhere,* she ventures wildly, and then waves for the cabbie's attention.

The cab slides gently to a stop in front of her. She beams winningly at the driver and hops in the back, stepping over a mangled New York *Post* with its pages flipped open to the following story:

GRISLY MURDER IN CENTRAL PARK

Horrified strollers today discovered the mutilated body of a young man near the 110th Street corner of Central Park West, in what police call one of the grisliest murders of the century.

"It was horrible," said officer Glen Roark, who first investigated the crime. "It's as if every bone in his body were broken..."

"Beautiful day, isn't it?" says the lady in the back.

She's a good one, Harry thinks, noddingly agreeing. *I can feel it.* Harry thanks God that he can still feel.

It makes the long ride go down easier.

"Well, damn."

Meryl took a minute to let it sink in, feeling the peculiar, tingling rush that always came when a story hit a nerve. The room came back into focus; she could hear the movie playing on the tube, feel the delicate threads of expectation emanating from Katie's camp. She thought about going in there.

But she didn't. She just didn't want to lose the buzz. It was as though—for a few minutes, anyway—the entire world had disappeared, gently deferring to the pages she held in her hands. Time, space, all things both Meryl and not-Meryl, became transparent in the face of the words.

And then even they disappeared, as the story came to life in her hands and her heart. It sparked a torch of bittersweet melancholy that she harbored always within her breast. It was a familiar, albeit complex emotion. It didn't happen often, or often enough. Too few people even had a clue of where to look.

But John Paul Rowan, the mystery man, knew right where to find it.

In the living room, the movie played on. The couch called in vain. Meryl sat alone in her chair, wondering what other tricks the mysterious Mr. Rowan had up his sleeve.

Then she opened the next folder in line, and proceeded to find out . . .

GO TO SLEEP
by
John Paul Rowan

4:27 in the morning. Streets, naked and shimmering under a twilit patina of frost. Against the gray wall, the goat man is sleeping. Rick is watching, weighing. And nobody else is there.

Rick can't stop looking at the goat man's feet. Something nasty has spawned down there ... some black, bloating, hideous decay gone well beyond all hope of repair. They're the kind of feet that some well-meaning doctor would like to amputate, in fact, because whatever slow death has taken hold down there will eat its way into his bowels. The massive body will blacken and shrivel, and the eyes will bug out, and one last inarticulate goatlike bray will rasp out against the night in agony ...

And, of course, nobody will be there, Rick muses, scanning the length of 34th Street for some sign of life. Over Herald Square, two sheets of old newspaper do a ghostly mating dance in the wind; the fate of one derelict couldn't interest them less. And the statues are there, as always. Eternally vigilant, with their spears and armor. Eternally looking the other way.

There are pigeons, too, in more or less the same boat as the goat man. Sick. Homeless. Slowly dying. Rick watched them hobble around for a minute, flapping their wings abortively and pecking at the dirt for sustenance. *Just be glad you don't drink,* he advises them silently. Then he drags on his cigarette and looks back at the goat man's naked, horrible feet.

The goat man sleeps, huddled against the gray wall at the mouth of the subway stairs. It would have been warmer for him down there, but apparently he just couldn't

make it. An empty bottle of something pokes its mouth
out from under his jacket; a thin pool of whatever is
freezing on the sidewalk before him. He snores, a sound
resplendent with burbling phlegm. Rick sighs wearily and
then crouches down in front of him.

That leaves me, am I right? A rhetorical question. The
goat man doesn't answer. *Just you and me, buddy,* Rick
confirms with a nod of his head. The goat man snores,
oblivious.

His hands are shaking a little; he'd like to believe that
it's just the cold. The cigarette almost slips from between
his fingers as he brings it up for one last drag. It tastes like
shit. He snubs the butt into a crack in the sidewalk, sticks
it in his back pocket when he's sure it's dead, returns to
the task at hand.

In winters past, the night would find Rick locked in a
parlor liberal's paralysis, debating the morality, letting
right and wrong slug it out while the dangerous seconds
ticked past. But the years had hardened him, filled him
with chilly resolve. Right or wrong, he will do it. Now.
Before anyone comes, or the goat man wakes.

Like all the times before.

Quickly, Rick rubs his freezing hands together, wipes a
thin trail of mucus onto the sleeve of his winter jacket.
Then he reaches over... slowly, slowly... to rest his hands
on the matted gray Afro of the goat man's head.

He listens first, as he always has, for any sign of hope. He's
not surprised to find nothing there: nothing worth saving. Just
the muttering voices. Rick had known, from the first time
he'd seen him bellowing on a street corner, bellowing at
nobody, that the goat man was simply taking too long to die.

Pictures of the twitching dog come creeping back into
Rick's mind. He pushes them away, grimacing. The goat
man jerks a little in his sleep, as though he, too, had seen
them. Then he stops.

Rick closes his eyes, summoning the power. He focuses,
sending it out through his fingertips. And he whispers
three words into the goat man's being.

"Go to sleep," he whispers, gently. "Go to sleep."

It only takes a moment. Rick pulls his hands away,
straightens, and turns. In the back of his mind, he hears

the car barreling down Broadway in his direction. He walks up Sixth Avenue, not looking back. The statues stand watch, seeing nothing.

The shitty taste is still in his mouth; but Rick has resigned himself to that much, at least.

It will be hours before anyone notices that the goat man's tortured breathing has stopped.

■

In his dream, he sees the twitching dog again, whining in its pool of mud and gore. He feels the wild thumping of its tiny heart, the wet rattle of its lungs, as surely as he feels the rain that spatters on his head. Behind him, Daddy is digging around in the trunk for something. Ricky, age seven, follows the skidmarks on the highway to the side of the road where their car is stopped. Daddy pulls out something long and shiny.

And for the millionth time, he watches his father's grim approach. The cold, set features. The tire iron. For the millionth time, he sees the shadow loom enormous, Daddy towering like God over dog and boy. He hears the voice like thunder, telling him to stand aside. He feels himself obey.

And he watches the cold steel come down in a shimmering arc, whistling through the wind and the rain. He watches the fur-covered skull split in two, the redmeat streams of horror launching off in every direction. The scream spirals up and up, crazily, as it has a million times before; and in the last moment before he turns away, opening wide to part with his fried clams and HoJo Cola, he notes that his father's hand is coated to the wrist in glistening darkness.

"It's alright," he hears his father say. "I couldn't just leave him like that, Ricky, you know it? He was suffering." The massive hands reach down, grabbing him by the shoulders, and the sickly-sweet smell of death assails him from his right, soaking into his T-shirt and haunting him forever. "I had to put him out of his misery," Daddy says from far away, and he feels himself starting to drift . . .

■

It was shortly after his ninth birthday that Richard Hale discovered his power. Their tomcat, Tom, had ripped a sparrow to shit and left it bleeding in the backyard. He had shushed Tom away and picked the poor thing up, sensing instantly that death was sliding in like a dagger. The dog's death was still vivid, even after a year and a half; and when he heard Daddy's booming laughter from the living room, a tiny voice that he recognized as his own said *not this time. Not like that.*

He had put the bird to sleep, effortlessly, with that simple incantation. It had staggered him so much that he threw the sparrow into the woods behind his house, hardly breathing, and gone off by himself for an hour. Daddy'd paddled his ass something fierce when he got home, but he wouldn't say a word about what happened.

He never told anyone.

Through junior and senior high school, he was one of the quiet guys that nobody knew. He got in with the partying crowd, to be sure; but he was the guy zoning out by the stereo, while others played guitar and cracked jokes, punched each other out, or pawed each other in the corners. He was the one who, when conversations turned to Ouija boards and UFOs, reincarnation and dope-spawned cozmic concepts, looked away with a face that spoke silently of pain.

Graduation found him heading for New York University, where he would study medicine. Summer in the Village was an amazing experience, frightening and exhilarating all at once: he'd had no idea that humanity could rise so high or sink so low. He was staggered by the proximity to famous people, famous places, and the thousands more who aspired to that glittering stratum.

And then there were the bums.

Shuffling, shambling, dragging the wreckage of their lives behind them in grocery bags, staring vacant-eyed at invisible things while their voices told the same stories, over and over and over. Even in the sunlight, in comfortable weather, they sent chills down his spine. There were so many of them. Their presence was something that refused to leave him alone. Sometimes his fingertips would tingle just a bit. He tried not to think about it.

He got a job as an orderly at NYU Medical Center. Classes began, and he threw himself into them. He made friends. He went to parties. He sampled the fruits of romance and rejection. And in weaving his way between the brilliance and the ruin, Rick felt something coming together inside of him. Not quite there yet. But coming. And soon.

He never told anyone.

And he never used the power.

But when the broken bodies of accident victims and the criminally assaulted were wheeled past him in the hospital corridors, he would find himself praying for an opportunity to act. And when the news would come of somebody dying quietly in their sleep, he would experience a strange kind of jubilation: a thrill in the knowledge that cruel fate had been cheated of its option for imposing and sustaining misery.

Then his first New York City winter had come; and with it, the discovery of his purpose.

■

Like a dream. Like a dream. Turning the corner, a little tipsy, staggering slightly in the cold night wind . . . and almost tripping over the old woman on the sidewalk. Stopping, frozen, and staring at her: the flesh like chalk under a pale blue light, thin as tissue paper, barely covering her bones; the thin, tattered jacket, barely covering her flesh. And feeling the tingle spread across his fingertips.

It took forty-five minutes to get up the nerve, and almost two weeks to get over.

But it only took a moment to do.

She was the first.

There were more, then. There were always more. Rick found that it became easier as he went along. The pain and guilt faded, giving way to a sense of . . . what? Call it duty. Call it purpose. Call it chilly resolve. It was something that he could do. The only thing, when you got right down to it.

And nobody else was there. Nor did it appear that there ever would be.

So he took them out, one after the other. He cut them loose from their misery, his misery, the whole miserable world's pain. He said goodbye to the forgotten grandmothers, the abandoned children, the former friends and

*lovers. He hushed the tortured voices of memory: their
only remaining dreams. He tucked them in with a touch
and a whisper, sent them gently off into that good night.*

*How many? Not less than forty, he was quite sure
. . . although, in truth, he'd lost count somewhere in the
middle of January. It was hard to say. There were so many
of them.*

And there were always, always more.

■

"Gimme some coffee." They are in the waiting room at
Penn Station, waiting for the Boston express to take his
friend Joe home for the weekend, when the bum's rasping
voice first accosts them. Joe brushes him off like a seasoned
New Yorker; but Rick stops, staring into that face.

"Gimme some coffee," the bum says again, and his
eyes are so blank that Rick shudders involuntarily. Filth
covers him like a second skin, and the grotesque parody
of a clever smile creases both layers on its way to Rick's
sight. He has the face of a mongoloid, without the excuse
of having been born one. He is a shambling, vomitous
wreck.

Rick pauses for a moment, tightening inside, before
draining half of his coffee and handing it over without a
word. He can feel Joe bristling with anger behind him, but
he doesn't care. *Let him drink,* the small voice inside
admonishes. *The last supper.*

The bum doesn't thank him. He takes a swig and spits it
quickly onto the floor. Then, as if nothing at all had
happened, he looks back up at Rick and says, "Gimme a
cigarette."

"Wait a minute, pal," Joe says, coming up beside his
friend. "He gave you some coffee, and you spit it all over
the fucking floor. Get a cigarette offa somebody else,
alright?"

"Joe!" Rick is as surprised by his own outburst as he is
by Joe's words.

"Gimme a cigarette," the bum repeats, now adamant.

"Fuck you! Get your *own* cigarettes, goddammit!" Joe's
nostrils are flaring, his face turning red. Rick grabs him by
the arm and starts to drag him away, but not before Joe

can add, "You're the scum of the earth!" at the top of his lungs.

The bum starts laughing then: a dry, utterly humorless sound. The laugh of a man who has turned his back on everything, who no longer cares at all. It cuts through the air like hot shrapnel, forcing startled heads to turn. One of them belongs to a woman seated directly behind the bum. He turns to her and speaks, as though the laughter had never happened. He tells her to give him a cigarette.

"What's the matter with you?" Rick demands, pushing Joe into a seat beside him, down the aisle from the bum.

"It just gives me the shits, man," Joe mumbles, fists clenched in his lap. "I mean, we bust our balls for every penny we get, and we're paying out the ass for our lousy degrees, and here this joker just sticks his greasy paw out and says *gimme gimme gimme,* and we're supposed to hand the world to him on a silver platter so he can piss all over it. Makes me sick, that's all." He shakes his head furiously. "Makes me sick to my goddam stomach."

"You could have a little more compassion," Rick says, but the words sound suddenly hollow.

"Shit. You give it to him, he spits it out. He has no shame. He doesn't care. Man, he forfeited his right to my respect when that coffee hit the floor. I'd sooner respect a dog turd. I mean, *look* at him!"

Rick looks. The bum has a cigarette now, probably culled from the poor woman behind him. He has taken maybe three or four drags off of it. Now he tosses it to the floor and stomps it with his bare foot.

His bare foot...

Five pairs of socks are strewn around the floor, along with what passes for a pair of shoes. The bum's pants are ripped up to the knees, and his legs are red and swollen. For the first time, Rick notices half a buttered bagel on the bum's lap; with horror, he sees that several pieces are also on the floor, buttered side down.

The bum takes a bite and chews it slowly. Then he rips a chunk, equal in size, from the bagel and tosses it. When it hits the dirt, Rick feels it like a slug to the stomach.

"See what I mean?" Joe says, and Rick is unable to

argue with him. "This guy is the lowest of the low. I can't believe that nobody's gotten around to *killing* him yet."

Rick's whole body shakes at the comment. He cannot bring himself to meet Joe's gaze.

"I mean, doesn't that make you want to punch that guy's *lights* out? Doesn't it make you wanna just grab him and shake him and say, 'Hey, asshole! Wise the fuck up!'"

"No." Rick states it with conviction. "No, I wouldn't say that."

But when the hardass cop comes strutting over and tells the bum to get out . . . when the bum stoops to pick up his filthy socks and shoes, leaving the area strewn with spilled coffee and bits of bagel . . . when the bum disappears, laughing his soulless, inhuman mockery of laughter, Rick looks at him and silently says *you're next, baby. You're next.*

■

That night . . . this night . . . the dream comes swiftly. He is kneeling over the dog, and his father is coming: a deadly leviathan, gaining unholy mass with every step, the tire iron glimmering cold as a thousand New York winters, obscenely huge in the grip of his clean right hand. As the shadow falls over them, Ricky hears a voice that he recognizes as his own say not this time. Not like that.

Daddy tells him to stand aside, but the voice is strangely impotent: the thunder, the authority, is gone. Rick hesitates only a moment, pulled by the past and its endless repetitions. Then he moves. Shielding the dog's body with his own, reaching down to take its head in his hands.

To end its suffering, bloodlessly.

To put it to sleep.

Now, he whispers, and closes his eyes.

That's when the dog whirls suddenly, lunging with its sharp-fanged death's-head grin, and rips his hand off at the wrist.

■

4:27 in the morning, again. Manhattan, asleep under a thin, shabby blanket of snow. Behind the glass doors, three of them are sleeping in the entrance to Grand

Central's subway station. Rick watches and weighs, leaving round blobs of mist on the glass with his breath. And nobody else is there.

The dream will not leave him alone. It claws at the back of his head like a rat behind a wall, trying to break through. He tries to ignore it.

But he can't.

But here I am, aren't I? Smiling sadly. *Doing it anyway. I must be crazy.* Rick takes another drag off his cigarette, a creature of two minds, watching over the broken men. Under the heavy winter coat he is sweating; and the violent shaking of his hands has very little to do with the cold.

Rick lets the cigarette slip from between his fingers unfinished; he grinds it into the snow with his boot. No time for amenities. If he's going to act, it has got to be now: before anyone comes, or his fear overwhelms him, or the bums in the foyer awaken.

God, I'm scared, he thinks. *I must be outta my goddam mind.* Then he opens the door, almost independent of thought, and steps quietly inside.

Softly, slowly, Rick moves toward the far wall, where the men lay sprawled out in filthy, tattered heaps. The air is thick with spilled liquor and piss, ripening in the heat from the tunnels below. It turns his stomach, and he almost stops. But not quite.

For as he draws nearer, and the foyer widens to meet the top of the stairs, Rick realizes that the man in the center is the very one he'd been looking for. The realization jolts him, while the rat behind the wall in the back of his head claws away with renewed vigor.

Shut up, he tells himself, fighting for inner control. The entranceway seems suddenly brighter, the bums starker in relief against the bareness of the wall. He lingers, trembling, while his eyes take in every detail of the three figures before him.

The one on the left is small, slight, almost completely hairless. His skin is incredibly smooth and thin. There is an embryonic quality about him; curled up on the floor with his beak nose and bulging eyes, he reminds Rick of a chicken fetus floating inside an egg.

The one on the right is much larger, with thick graying

hair and a massive beard surrounding his strong, finely chiseled features. Years of drinking have eroded his face, like a statue left standing through a thousand acid rains; but there is still something commanding about him, an air of regality lost.

And then there is the man in the center: the bagel-strewer, the spitter of coffee, with his blank eyes and horrible laughter. Sleep has not softened the apelike features or brought to light any hidden attributes that might have redeemed him. He is still ugly as a slug; and the wet trail behind him suggests an aptness to the comparison that makes Rick shudder.

He catches himself in the midst of a deep, miserable sigh and realizes that he has been standing there for the last three minutes or more. *Come on,* he urges himself. *Get it over with or get the hell out of here. One or the other, man. Now.*

But there is no question as to which it will be. After only a moment's hesitation, he advances once again toward them.

The man on the left is closest. Rick goes to him first. His naked scalp is baby-soft and clammy as Rick touches him with fingertips that feel drained of all circulation.

And listens. Like all the times before.

It only takes a moment.

Then Rick is on his feet again, moving like a man in a dream toward the center figure. Kneeling there with his hands outstretched. Touching. Hearing. Saying the words. And rising again, amazed by how little he feels, how simple and quick and *nothing* it was in the end.

Now there is only the man on the right: the fallen king, slumped against the wall like a monarch dozing on his throne. Rick stares at him for a moment, hesitating. *What is it?* he asks himself, but his mind offers up no useful explanations.

Only the continuous scraping of the rat.

Shut up, he angrily commands. *Come on. This is stupid.* But there is a tentativeness in his step that he has never known before as he moves to the head of the subway stairs and kneels before the broken man . . .

. . . *who reaches up suddenly with one gnarled graying talon and grabs Rick firmly by the wrist.*

Rick screams.

"You're the one, ain'tcha?" The voice is sibilant, horrible. The rheumy eyes are a baleful red. They are judge's
eyes. They latch onto Rick's and hold them helplessly, as a
hideous grin crackles across his lips and begins to bleed.

"I been waitin' for you," the man says, leaning forward
until his face is mere inches from Rick's. "I knew you'd
come. Sooner or later. I knew."

Rick screams again. Crazily, instinctively, he pulls himself backwards and to his feet. The bum comes up with
him, smoothly, as though they were two dancers in a
neatly choreographed routine, one hand holding firmly
onto Rick's wrist, the other reaching down to grab a bottle
of Mad Dog 20/20 by the throat.

"Who appointed you *God*, mister? That's what I wanna
know. Who the hell do you think you are, decidin' when it's
time for *me* to die?" The words are loaded with so much
violence that Rick feels them rather than hears them.
Nothing makes sense, suddenly. Nothing is clear.

A part of Rick wants to offer some kind of explanation:
about the power, the dog, the whole mad succession of
events leading up to this moment. It's a ridiculous thought,
he knows, yet it persists, the parlor liberal inside him
making one last pointless stand. His body, infinitely more
sensible, tries once again to pull away, without success.

The wine bottle comes up in a strobing slow motion, a
dance of light across its surface. Rick watches it, frozen.
Something prickles at the boundaries of his conscious
mind from somewhere beyond; he struggles, for a moment, to identify it . . .

. . . *and then it strikes him with horrible, infinite clarity.
It is sound: a billowing, echoing cacophony of sound,
overwhelming in its density and texture and tone. It is the
sound of inarticulate, goatlike braying; it is the sound of
mocking, inhuman laughter; it is the sound of falling
plaster, of a rat's triumphant chittering song.*

*It is the sound of a dog's dying howl. Gnashing teeth.
Breaking bone.*

*It is the sound of a heart, wildly pounding. And pounding.
And pounding . . .*

It is the last thing Rick will ever hear.

Then the bottle comes around in its deadly shimmering arc and smashes into the side of his head. Pieces of glass splinter off and imbed themselves in his soft face and temple. The world goes black and mercifully silent, yet he remains on his feet, staggering.

Rick has no idea that the bum lets go of his wrist. He doesn't feel himself falling backwards, carried by his own weight and the force of the blow. He is not aware that his feet leave the ground. And as he rolls down the stairs, the loud crack of his neck breaking is not anything that he can hear.

■

They are standing in the doorway, a tight throng of five. The shortest woman, curiously in command, reads from her clipboard. The others nod, poking at *their* clipboards with ballpoint pens, occasionally scribbling.

"This is Richard Hale," she reads aloud, and then proceeds to enumerate the damages. The list is long and quite specific. She also details the measures taken in emergency, his current critical status, and the nature of Richard Hale's life-support system. It takes about two minutes.

The nurse watches them leave. She is standing at the foot of Rick's bed, monitoring the flow of liquid that seeps into him from the IVs. Or so it would seem.

Actually, she is staring at the broken man and waiting for the footsteps to recede. Slowly, then, she moves around the edge of the bed and gently sits down beside him, with something like love in her eyes.

She puts her hands to his bandaged head and listens. Like all the times before.

She is not surprised by what she hears.

"Go to sleep," she whispers.

"Go to sleep."

Meryl turned the last page of the story, let her vision unfocus on the vast manila plain that followed. Again, there was the odd shimmering glitch as she segued back from the world of words to the self in the body in the chair in the room in the world in which she lived.

And again, traces of the story came back with her, lingering wisps of imagery. She could taste the cold, the sour taint of subway urine, the antiseptic commingling of hospital scents. Most of all, she could taste the sorrow at the heart of the mystery man's work.

"Damn," she began, and then a yawn took over. It was a doozie, neatly obliterating all thought as it rumbled between her ears. For the first time, she realized how completely spent she actually was.

Meryl shut the folder and set it down, dragged the back of one hand across her blearing eyes. She didn't know whether it was the hour, the long day catching up with her at last, or maybe the story's mantra tapping a direct line to her subconscious.

Whatever the case, exhaustion had come, and come with a vengeance: sinking her weight into the chair, tugging at her eyelids, whispering *you are getting sleepy* in a hypnotist's melodious drone. She looked at the loft bed, the stairs leading up to it, and the thought was purest anathema. "No way," she mumbled, and then another yawn hit, more powerful than the first, nearly propelling consciousness away as she exhaled it.

She drifted. The last thing she remembered was, strangely enough, a smell: faint enough to be her imagination, distinctive enough to catch her vanishing attention.

An overripe and rotten smell.

Then she, and it, were gone.

7
AWAKENING

In the dream, she was falling.

It was a rare but familiar sensation. A childhood sensation. It took her back. She could feel the bed, all soft and warm. She could feel it begin to rock and sway. Like a boat on the ocean, adrift on the waters, the bottomless waters of the liquid abyss, and she pulled the covers up tight around her neck.

Slowly, slowly, she felt herself drifting off, sinking down, the bed spinning, spiraling down and down into those endless black depths...

In the dream, there were voices.

Shadowy voices, murmuring, flitting across her REMscape like bats in a belfry, darting this way and that, too quick to pick up on. She felt herself snatching at them instinctively and to no avail, catching only inflections, cadence, random bits of emotion. Excited babble. Snatches of laughter...

In the dream, he was with her.

They lay entwined on the falling bed, arms and legs curled together like hot vines, fingers crawling tendrillike across the planes of their skin. She couldn't see his face, buried as it was in the crook of her neck. But she could hear him, voraciously nuzzling, digging in. She could smell his sweat on her skin. She could feel the hunger, the warmth of his body...

In the dream, then, the terror came.

And suddenly he was clutching at her, clawing like a drowning man, the connection between them broken as the madness took its place. She felt the panic and despair arc off of his body like sparks from an electrical generator.

It burned into her skin, heat without comfort, pain without comprehension as her own panic grew. He engulfed her with the rush of his smothering fear, and she could feel him painfully surrounding her, could smell his warm and welcome scent go cold and foul in her nostrils, could feel his flesh rippling with the motion of things that burrowed beneath the surface, could hear the buzzing and the scream trapped inside his lungs welling up in her own throat as together they fell and clutched and kicked and spun and swung and...

Katie awoke with a start, batting at the shadows around her head, batting at the sounds of fear. The sudden darkness of the real-life room overwhelmed her, fanned the spark of the chill in her bones. She reached for the covers and found none there. She had dreamed the covers.

She had dreamed the bed.

The sounds of fear were coming from the TV set. Katie stared at it, an unpopped kernel of nervous laughter wedged between her teeth. It was one of those Mexican vampire movies; she remembered it, helplessly, from when she was a kid. *Nostradamus* or something. *The Evil of Nostradamus*.

She blinked her eyes. She was still on the couch. No big surprise there. Evidently Meryl had not come back, and she had slipped off into slumber. Further absence of big surprise. It seemed to be that kind of night.

But the memory of the terror remained.

On the TV, a dopey-looking hunchback with a Moe Howard hairpiece was chasing a screaming señorita through some dusky old catacombs. Aside from that, the room was dark. The streetlight below and the moonlight above came together into something just barely visible through the big loft windows behind her. She rose up slightly and turned toward them, checking out the night skyline.

Behind her, the TV changed channels.

She whipped back around, and the channel changed again. Her breath caught in her throat.

There was nobody there.

The channel changed again. And again. And again. She got flickers of visions: the Home Shopping Channel, the late Lorne Greene and a can of Alpo, the revolting prettyboy rock band, Europe. Something hard dug deep into one cheek of her ass. She jolted back in her seat.

The TV died.

No time for thought. The terror, resurging in the chaos. Instinctively, she reached under her ass-cheek as the room went utterly black. The hard thing was there. She wrapped her hand around it, and recognition flooded in. Remote control, it said. You fool, you fell asleep on the remote control . . .

In the sudden silence of the apartment, something moved.

It was the last straw. Her nerves, already frazzled, went painfully incandescent as she froze at the end of the couch, thinking the light, I've got to turn on the light, if I turn on the light I'll see that I'm alone and it's okay . . .

. . . except that there was another voice in her head that wanted to know about what if it wasn't okay, what if there was somebody in here, moving in the darkness, watching her . . .

Clearly, then: the sound of footsteps, lightly treading her way. In panic, she flew from the couch, barking her shin on the coffee table, letting out a yelp as she stumbled and nearly fell through the glass. There was the *skreeee* of whining hinges as, behind her, the door to Meryl's bedroom flew open.

And then Meryl was standing there, staring at her.

"Oh, shit!" Katie blurted. She felt horribly embarrassed, despite the fact that she had practically jumped out of her skin. "I'm so sorry! I just . . . I don't know, I just . . ."

"What's going on?" Meryl's voice was pinched, and higher than usual; for the first time, Katie realized that Meryl seemed frightened, too. "Is everything okay?"

"I . . . yeah, I think so." She felt like an idiot, standing there shivering in the dark. "Um, where's the light in here? I'm all disoriented . . ."

"I'll get it," Meryl said, moving forward. There was a tinge of irritation in her voice, reinforcing Katie's sense of stupidity. "It's around here somewhere . . ."

She began to grope around at the wall to Katie's right. There was a lot of wall. Katie joined in the quest. "I hope

I didn't wake you up," she offered lamely. "I had a kinda bad dream, and then . . . okay! Here it is."

She clicked on the switch; the room flooded with light. She was surprised to see Meryl dart her gaze around the room, mostly because Katie was doing the exact same thing. Checking for interlopers. She didn't see any.

"Looks like we're alone," she said, and then Meryl shot her a very strange look: as if she were trying to see into her head. It shut Katie up, and amped her discomfort. "What?" she said finally.

And then Meryl looked away.

It was nothing, of course. What else could it be? It was stupid to think it was anything but. The last time she'd checked, her pertinent stats had not shown up in *Ripley's Believe It Or Not*.

So what if she'd also just had a bad dream? So what if it had also awakened her with a keen sense that someone or something was watching? Forget the fact that she never had nightmares. Forget the fact that, nine times out of ten, if she felt like she was being watched, it was only because it was true.

Forget all that. It meant nothing or less: just another piece of stupid, random synchronicity.

Forget the cold that still rolled down her spine.

"Are you okay?" Katie asked her then.

"Um . . . yes. I'm fine."

"You sure?"

"Uh-huh."

"I didn't wake you up, did I?"

"Oh, no. Not at all."

"You weren't still up workin', were ya?"

"No." Agitated as she was, these questions were starting to get under her skin. "Why do you ask?"

"Aw, hell. I'm sorry." It was Katie's turn to avert her eyes. "I didn't mean to give you the third degree or nothin'. It was just the way you looked at me . . ."

That quickly, Meryl felt the mantle of embarrassed stupidity shift from Katie's shoulders to her own. She really hadn't meant to stare like that: it was rude, and she knew it; she'd been told often enough. It was just a little thing she did when things took a turn for the peculiar.

Except that nothing that peculiar had happened. Right?

"So what happened?" she asked, glossing over her pointless trepidation. "You say you had a bad dream?"

"Oh, yeah..."

"You want to talk about it?"

"Uh... naw. Not really."

"Okay." Meryl let the moment hang, took the moment to ask herself why she was asking. Was she really that interested in what this woman dreamed?

Or was it her own dream, now mercifully fading, that she wanted to talk about?

"To be honest," Katie said at last, "I don't even really remember it all that well. It was pretty damned unpleasant, though. That much I know. Ugly sexual shit..." She stuck her tongue out and grimaced; on a picture-perfect face like hers, it was kind of amusing, kind of fascinating. "Not that I don't like sex."

"Okay." Meryl smirked, simultaneously got a flash of a bed, slowly spinning. She shrugged it off. The smirk was still on her face, for some reason. Too much nervous, meaningless energy. She knew just how to dispense with it.

"I don't know about you," she continued, "but I'm a little wired out. Would you care for a drink?"

Katie smiled. "You don't know the half of it. What've you got?"

"A little bit of gin, and a fifth of tequila."

"We'll be sicker'n dogs in the morning, you know."

"Do you have to work?"

Grinning slyly. "Nope."

"So, fine. Let's do it."

"You know," and Katie was shy as she said it, "I was kinda hopin' we'd get a chance to talk a little tonight. I feel so strange, bargin' in on you..."

"Don't worry about it..."

"But I really do..."

"You don't know how massive a favor you did me, getting my dear old dad off of my ass."

"I sorta sensed the tension."

Meryl's turn to smile. "You got that right."

"And I don't mean to get all gushy or anything, but I kinda liked you right away."

Meryl couldn't believe it but she was blushing; she could feel the evidence on her cheeks. Nor did she believe the words that now issued from her lips. But there they were. "I kinda liked you, too."

"So whaddaya say we boogie down?"

"'Boogie down'?"

Katie shrugged. "Figure of speech."

Meryl smiled. "I'll get the drinks."

She headed on down to the kitchenette corner, smiling and strangely excited. I think I might have made myself a friend, she thought to herself. Imagine that.

Then the feeling came back. Just a tickle. Just a second. Just enough to call the hairs on her neck to attention.

That I'm-being-watched feeling.

And then it was gone.

In the dream, they were sitting on the couch. Two young women: one light, the other dark. The details were fuzzy, but they appeared to be drinking. And talking. The conversation was clear.

"Yeah, Colin's one regular son of a whore." The blonde. She was speaking. "But I'll tell ya—and I hate to admit it—but when I was layin' here on the couch, I really missed him."

"That's dumb." The small dark one. "From what you're saying, he's a complete fucking bastard."

"I know. I can't stand it. I hate myself for it. He's a complete fuckin' bastard, and he even admits it, which I don't know if that makes it worse or not. I mean, he's real self-aware, which translates into completely intolerable, because he's got this genius IQ that makes him certain—even when he suspects he might be wrong—that everyone else has got to be at least twice as wrong as he is."

They laughed. They seemed to pour another round. The clinking of glass was unmistakable.

"Are you sure that he's really that intelligent? Are you sure that he doesn't just have a good rap?"

"Listen, honey. I've seen 'em come and go. I'm a

brain-fucker, to be truthful. I have to admit it. If they look half-decent and their discourse is elevated, I latch hold of their ass like a fly on shit. I mean, I'm not all that smart, myself..."

"Yes, you are. You're very bright."

"No, I'm not."

"Yes, you are."

"No, I'm not! Don't argue with me!" They laughed again. "But I'll tell ya, I know within five minutes whether they're full of it or not. And believe me: Colin can sit there and explain Einstein to me; and even though most of it goes right over my head, I know that he knows what he's talkin' about. You get to the point where you can tell the difference between conviction and bravado. You know what I'm sayin'? When a guy's just sayin' things to impress you, that's one thing; but when you know that he's just sittin' there, impressin' the hell out of himself, then that's another thing entirely."

"I don't know... I've met a lot of guys who are really impressed with themselves, but they still don't know what the fuck they're talking about."

"That's true. Touché." The blonde drank. "Augh! That's smooth."

"And I still don't see what that's got to do with wanting to sleep with him."

"Okay. The way it is, is... *BRRRAWP!*" A belch. They laughed very hard. "'Scuse me. That was gruesome."

"S'okay." Still laughing. A sweet and raucous sound.

"I'm sorry. Okay. The way it is is that, bottom line, I need the mental stimulation... although, from the looks of it, that's not gonna be a problem here." Pause. More clinking of glass. "But the other thing is just a simple warm body. It's stupid, I know, but I hate sleeping solo. It's probably my least favorite thing to do. I guess I just want to know that somebody is there, and I'd do just about anything to guarantee it."

The small dark one took her shot now, made the requisite *acking* noise.

"You okay?"

"Oh, yeah. You're just making me think." Pause. "It's funny, but I really don't feel that way at all. I like sleeping by myself. I like being by myself. Every time I get involved with someone, he winds up dominating the thing. It makes me crazy, 'cause it makes no sense. You know? Most of the time, they're not even as strong as I am. But they still get it over on me, and I can't figure it out."

"Who breaks it up, then? You or him?"

"Me, mostly. Unless he beats me to it."

"That's weird, 'cause I'm exactly the opposite. I'll hang in there forever. I don't know why. Maybe it's just my upbringing. All I know is, it has to get pretty goddam bad before I'll leave. It hardly ever happens."

"It happened this time."

"Yeah, it did. Good for me . . ."

In the blackness, a sudden sweet sadness erupted. Self-awareness was dim, but it seemed to be mounting. Fragments of memory. Inklings of identity.

A scene from a movie . . . could that be possible? . . . flickering briefly across the mind's screen. Something about a fly who dreamed he was a man. But the dream was over. And the fly was awake . . .

Something else, then: an idea set to paper. Too vague, too vague. Not even a tongue to sit on the tip of. Awareness of frustration, and sadness, and loss.

But, most of all, the black.

The empty.

The cold.

Watching the women.

And wanting to be with them.

While the Pull beckoned softly from behind.

NOT WITH A WHIMPER
by
John Paul Rowan

This is the way the world ends
Not with a bang but a whimper.
                    T.S. Eliot, "The Hollow Men"

Last night Jack Fitzpatrick committed suicide by attacking the President of The United States with a fully charged cream pie. Lemon meringue, in full honor of the occasion—history redrawn in an explosion of frothy yellow goo. He did not pull back, as I might have come to expect—as he had so many times before. He didn't even pull back *after* the fact: retracting the move, chalking it up to youthful folly and wiping it forever from the face of Time.

No, this time Jack stayed to the bitter end. Through the nine-millimeter staccato death-dance that accompanied the Secret Servicemens' gunfire, and beyond. He jerked off the platform like a marionette with its cables cut, toppling backwards through the bunting and into the Hereafter. The media swarmed instantly around his ruined form, a jumble of lenses and shutters providing state-of-the-art coverage far superior to that afforded to the Hinkleys and the Oswalds and the Sirhan Sirhans of their time. Millions of Americans watched in slack-jawed silence as Jack Fitzpatrick's radiant nightmare visage stared into their living rooms and straight through the veil, grinning through the blood.

And when I turned, half-hoping to find him miraculously beside me, popping the tab on another brew as he played back yet another videotape of Something That Never Really Happened, laughing and toasting humanity for the wonderfully gullible bunch of patsies we were and still remain . . . he was simply not there.

Nor has he appeared, in the ticking hours since. No, this time Jack Fitzpatrick—my friend, the Man Who Could Do Anything—remained in his awkward spread eagle by the podium steps, lifeblood seeping from the innumerable smoking holes that the President's men had expertly opened in him. He died—no, he *let* himself die, right there; his body, blown to bits. His mouth, still smiling.

A lot of people have been wondering about that smile. And I guess it's time to tell someone about it.

Jack and I were buddies of long standing. We worked together, a few years back. At the time, we were both poor young struggling nobodies: I was caught up in the desperate struggle to get published, often to the point of forsaking the selfsame compassion that spurred me to write in the first place. And Jack . . . well, Jack was strange.

He was a gentle soul, kamikazie-cream pies notwithstanding. He genuinely gave a damn: about people, about the world, about the details you or I or most of the other scuffling hordes nosing the grindstone to get-us-this-day-our-daily-bread never even stop to think about. Maybe he cared *too* much, I don't know. Despite our friendship, Jack was a loner. There was always this impenetrable wall of self-sufficiency that he never let slip. Jack Fitzpatrick took care of himself . . . even if it ultimately came to mean wiping that self clear off the face of the earth: erasing all traces, wrapping all loose ends, and letting anyone involved go on with their lives, unencumbered by the tiniest scintilla of knowledge regarding a Mr. Jacob B. Fitzpatrick—regardless of how intimately he had known them in any concurrent reality.

Sounds weird? Sure it does. It can't be helped. I am proud to be the bearer of this lunacy, just as I am proud to have been his friend throughout, knowing as I now do that he could have wiped himself out of *my* existence at the drop of a hat. He didn't, though, and I love him for it.

So you may well understand if I am necessarily biased in this account. If you want the bum raps, read it in the funny papers. File under the Freedom of Information Act, if you're really that ambitious; find out what miserable inaccuracies they will inevitably concoct. That'll be illuminative. The government is adept at disappearing that which they cannot readily explain, and the press loves nothing better than to take things out of context, only to bring them back in a more preferable form. They do it all the time. They're good at it.

But not nearly as good as Jack. Believe me.

■

I think it first dawned on him when he was about twenty-seven. Now, that might seem a long time to wait to find one's gift, one's destiny; but in the scheme of things, it's nothing. Certainly in *Jack's* scheme of things, it was nothing. Preliminary estimates are that he logged in a good ten thousand years before the bullets splattered and snubbed him out, all at the ripe old age of twenty-nine.

It began, as I recall, with a girl named Jamie Morganstern, whom Jack intended to date and hopefully fuck the bejesus out of. She was a receptionist for Whitley, Greene, and Pimkin, a posh Madison Avenue consultation firm and one of our largest clients. She was also dazzling in the extreme: chestnut hair, emerald green eyes, lips to die for, and a body whose upper and lower hemispheres seemed to be perpetually competing for perfection. I mean, this girl could stop traffic if she was wrapped in burlap, and her customary office attire tended toward curve-hugging silk blouses and skirts that filled me with dreams of dying and being reincarnated as her seat cushion.

Jack was slightly more ambitious. Nothing new there: he always did aim a little higher than me, and both of us were notably more driven than the vast bulk of our coworkers. We were messengers by day, crazed cyclists for an outfit called *Speed Demons, Inc.* In most peoples' eyes, we were nothing but proles: shit-toters and delivery boys, the feebs and dweebs that made sure that flak men got their flak distributed and lawyers got their lawsuits filed by five o'clock, when all bells ring in Midtown and the young turks break for the Tex-Mex fern bars.

And in most cases, they were right. I only ever met two types during my stint on the streets: those on their way up, and those on their way down. Most fell firmly into the latter category, destined to shuffle along with their bags of broken dreams until old age finally coughed up its pay-load of fixed income and Little Friskies. The fear of failure was an oftimes palpable thing. But those in the minority kept up the good fight, certain in the desperate determination of our dreams (and I guess we were right. I went on, anyway, to become a published writer. Oh sure, I'm not ready for *Lifestyles of the Rich and Famous* yet. But I eat. I work. And I'll tell you something else: in every jaunt Jack took into future possibility, I was a *rich* published writer . . .)

But we were talking about Jamie Morganstern, who was gorgeous beyond belief. Jack hungered for her with a fervor that would have made Jason tremble, hands inches from the Golden Fleece, with inferiority of purpose. Seismographic disturbances were reported if he so much as thought of her. It was a pointless obsession, I thought, because it was common knowledge that Midtown receptionists occupied a pinnacle so far above lowly messengers that they would have to stoop clear through the stratosphere just to recognize our faces above the clipboards we daily held out for their immaculately illegible signatures.

This was clear to me and the rest of the civilized world. But it didn't mean squat to Jack Fitzpatrick, who was so rakish and recklessly canny that Jamie Morganstern didn't report him the first time he propositioned her. Nor did she discourage him on the second attempt. Nor on the third.

I remember him well, barreling the wrong way down 47th Street and skidding onto Third Avenue, where I was freshly emerged from what may be the only skyscraper in the free world that features a life-sized, clinically accurate bronze nude permamounted in its revolving door. When he saw me he careened across the oncoming traffic and dismounted at a dead run. "Ohmigod, ohmigod, I can't fucking be-lieve it! I done died and gone to Hebben!"

I had a sick feeling inside. Only one thing could get a rise like that out of Jack Fitzpatrick, and I wasn't entirely sure that I wanted my intuition verified. "So, chuckles." I tried to be nonchalant. "What's the deal?"

"She said *YES*!!" he blurted. "She said YES! To*night*! *Din*ner! *Dan*cing! *Fore*play!" He was jumping up and down and shaking me by now, all blonde-haired blue-eyed handsomeness disassembled. "Man, this is a goddess I'm going out with! This is fucking Venus herself!"

"What, no arms or head?"

He ignored me. "Oh, god, I can't believe it! I'm gonna die!" He twirled and feigned a heart attack, falling back into what he trusted would be my waiting arms.

Maybe I should have let him fall, but I didn't. I had seen guys lose their cookies over affairs with the opposite camp before, but nothing like this. This was storm troopers taking over the Vatican. This was intense. I still figured there must be some kind of catch he wasn't hip to, and I felt morally compelled to blunt the edge of his fervor. So I said to him, by way of artful deflation, "Look, Jack. Something's wrong here. The chick has AIDS or herpes or something. That's all she wrote, man. You'll jump into the sack with her, and you'll end up toting around these little fungoids for the rest of your days. So what the hell are you so worked up about, anyway? So *what* if she's beautiful! A legacy of genital leprosy is worth all this precoital leaping about?"

I was only teasing, trying to keep him from being too smug in the face of the fact that though we'd both always lusted for her, he'd been the one who ultimately scored. Nothing new there. We always lusted for the same women. He always got them. I always teased him.

But I wasn't always right . . .

Jack and Jamie went out and had a spectacular dinner together, scarfing steak and seafood at Dobson's, engaging in the kind of high-octane conversation that always got a little weird when he tried too hard. But it worked: he finally charmed her back to her apartment with a grace and economy of motion that you never see in the *How To Pick Up Gurls! Gurls! Gurls!* ads. They made the kind of love that conjures up the theme music to *National Geographic* specials; all tongues and teeth and sweet soul-fire. To hear Jack tell it, mountains were reshaping themselves on the other side of the planet.

And then, in the sweet, sweet afterglow, when all was perfection, she started to cry. He asked what was wrong, and she told him, and my future as the Amazing Kreskin was assured: she was so sorry, but she couldn't help herself, it had been so long since she'd dared even risk it, but she just couldn't hold back anymore, and she really liked him, and it *wasn't* under control at all, and she was so sorry. . . .

. . . and Jack had felt the bottom drop out of the pit of his stomach, and he lost it, thinking oh shit, oh shit, I wish this had never even happened *and a blinding pressure like an embolism imploding bloomed in his head . . .*

. . . and suddenly they were back at Dobson's, finishing their coffee, and he was saying, "and that's why we just can't go to bed together, Jamie." She gazed at him with a strange mixture of shock, confusion, sorrow, and relief. And, all in a flash, he realized what had happened.

Of course, he walked her home, and they wound up not going to bed with each other. Jack always spoke wistfully of it. "Getting herpes was a lot more fun than *not* getting herpes," he said. "In the short run, anyway." He grinned thoughtfully and added, "But at least I got to do it, didn't I?"

Now, I know what you're thinking. I know, because when he finished telling *me* I started checking his bike helmet for bumper dents. Brain damage would have explained everything, to my ultimate satisfaction. But he was clean, and the fact that he was so adamant left me no conclusion but that my best friend had come completely unhinged. She shot him down, and he was driven bonkers by his own rabid libido. He smiled the smile of the perfectly just. I began to worry.

It was quite some time before we spoke of it again. And that comes much later. After the change.

After the proof.

■

In the first few months of his strange new life, and going strictly by the purely linear time-sense the rest of us are bound to, Jack Fitzpatrick spent the bulk of his newfound extra time screwing around. By all estimates, he slept with well over a thousand different women. And I do mean different; *every conceivable combination and configuration of comely female flesh that a loving Creator had seen fit to bless humanity with ultimately yielded to the carnal colonialism of Jack Fitzpatrick. From tall, leggy blondes with faces of sculpted alabaster and breasts like ripe mangoes to tiny, dark-haired, smoky-eyed girls whose deeply banked fires might go unnoticed by all but the most perceptive gaze. All races, all ages. All types of women knew his touch. And all without ever remembering exactly what had left them smiling so sublimely.*

He also saw every film that rolled through Times Square, every play on Broadway, every performance at Lincoln Center, and read every book, every periodical, and every newspaper in Barnes & Nobel, B. Dalton, Forbidden Planet, and the entire New York Public Library system. He ate in every restaurant in every borough, and tipped generously. He saw the World Series, took every course offered by the Discovery Center and the Learning Annex, and sat through all three Madison Square Garden shows of David Bowie's next world tour, a total of nine times.

He also learned very quickly not to talk about it with anyone: not with anyone but me, anyway. That was not so good for me, but very wise for him. Opting to not enlighten the general populace spared him the likelihood of an involuntary holiday at Bellevue, ass-end hanging out of a paper smock.

But most of all, it allowed him to get his earthly rocks off. He had more fun in those first few months than most people have in their whole family tree. He sowed more wild oats than the Harvest Queen herself. It was great therapy; he just worked off the need for vicarious thrills and pointless liaisons. I estimate he must have picked up a good seven years in stolen moments—a nonstop two thousand, five hundred fifty-five day party weekend—all in the space of six months, all without aging one crinkle.

■

By now you are either dying to know how he did this or you're busy speed-dialing the bozophone. In the too-few hours since Jack's death I've been searching for, among other things, clues as to *how* he could do whatever it is that he did. I wish I could tell you I've been successful. As near as I can tell, he called his talent—his gift, if you will—a sort of mental "squeeze." Some lamebrained group of researchers two years from now are going to explain this as an acronym for *Synchronistic Quantum Universal Energy Enveloping Zeitgeist-Entropy* and receive a huge grant to investigate its military applications. Jerkoffs. As near as I can tell Jack called it a "squeeze" 'cause that's how it *felt* while it was happening. Maybe he squeezed his pineal gland, you tell me.

Regardless, his technique, such as I've been able to tell, was ridiculously simple:

1. Roll with the flow of linear time for as long as required to do what is desired,

2. "Squeeze" back in time to the moment *before* said event occurs, and

3. Do something else.

Simple, huh? Sure. And all you need to do to play the flute is (1) blow into the big hole, and (2) move your fingers up and down on all the little ones. But that was Jack's style. Anyway, using these three "simple" steps, Jack Fitzpatrick claimed that he could, for example, watch fifteen movies on Times Square in a single two-hour stretch, for a single six bucks, and go home ten minutes before the first movie ended with the same six dollars still in his pocket.

Or he could walk through the same Times Square, having already seduced every woman he saw in little more than the time it took to see them. He could do whatever he wanted to whomever he wanted, no matter how indulgent or depraved; in the end, no one was the wiser. A marginal fraction of "real" time passed in the "real" world, something on the order of a year to the minute; he could be in and out of a girl's bed and back on the street in the time it took for her to shoot him down. They never knew what hit them. Only Jack knew.

The only place it showed was in his eyes.

■

As the new year loomed on the horizon, the world's collective prospects looked gloomier than ever. It sometimes appeared as though the forty years of bad hype courtesy of George Orwell had not missed the mark by much. We didn't quite have Big Brother yet, but the lag-time had allowed the climactic thrust of the Reagan administration to foment into a secret war in Central America, the Meese commission bashing sex, the PMRC bashing rock 'n' roll, and a tee-vee holy moe offering to run for President if God-fearing patriots everywhere would fork over a cool three hundred million toward the cause. Everyone on the other side of the fence seemed to have just a real sour feeling about the future of the species.

It wasn't until right around the Republican Convention that the full extent of his potential became clear. Jack had always been the kind of guy who could have been anything; the simple truth of that was a blessing, and a curse. He showed promise as a gifted painter, writer, photographer, musician, architect and auto mechanic. He had a firm grasp on three languages, a head for figures, a way with words, and a keen sense of what constitutes a good deal. He learned quickly and retained knowledge like a microchip. He could have risen meteorically to the top of any of a dozen fields; indeed, there didn't seem to be anything beyond the scope of his grasp.

But he couldn't seem to *focus* it on any one thing long enough to see it through. He had dropped out of NYU in his third year, a fact which had slaughtered his parents even more than the knowledge that he had changed majors so many times that they'd simply lost count. Then he bopped through everything from mysticism to metallurgy to heavy metal to motorcycle maintenance; still, nothing ever seemed to stick. Finally he left New York altogether, taking his quest out into the world at large. He hitched through Europe and hiked through Central America, smoked hash in Amsterdam and got blasted on *basura* in Bolivia.

Eventually he came back, and landed the job where we first met. That was two and a half years ago. Time took its stately, measured course. And there he still was, like me: working as a messenger, making not much more than two hundred dollars a week. Before taxes.

So, one damp February eve found Ronbo on the tube, lying through his wisened puss about the State of the Union. Jack and I sat in the back of the Blarney Stone pub on Madison, downing cheap drafts and blowing off steam after another cold day on the streets. The conversation has come back to haunt me in the last few hours:

"Scott?" he said. Scott Wachter is my name, by the way. You'll be hearing a lot of it in the future. Make sure you get the spelling right: W-A-C-H-T-E-R. "Scott?" he repeated, leveling an extremely pointed gaze in my direction. "If you could think of one thing the world needs more than anything else, what would it be?"

"Hamsters," I muttered, mocking his *el serioso* stance. "The world just needs more of the little furry fucks. Three for every boy..."

"I'm serious—"

"...and five for every girl," I continued, undaunted. "Six for fearless leader." I gazed at the flickering screen behind the bar. "He can stuff them in his cheek pouches." On the tube, the President smiled his homey, inward grin, revealing ample storage facilities.

"You're a jerk," he bitched, blowing smoke in my face. He was trying so hard to be topical.

Weary, I drained my mug and let the rag die. "We solved all the world's problems *yesterday*, remember? Everything's fine now."

"Scott," he said, his features wound tight. I looked up; his eyes, far wiser than they had any right to be, flitted over my features like a bar-code scanner. "If you could do *anything*..."

There was no escape. I sighed, gave it a microsecond of serious thought, shook my head, and replied, "The world needs a major overhaul, my friend."

"No shit." There was an uncomfortable urgency in his tone. "But how would you kick it off? What approach? Politician? Scientist? Corporate Turk?"

"Butcher, baker, candlestick maker..."

"Asshole," he spat. Jack was deep in his cups. My feet hurt. I sat, thoughtfully pouring the last of the pitcher into our mugs. Then I took a hefty swig off mine and wiped my mustache, which I'm sure all great philosophers are wont to do at such times, and delivered my verdict:

"No one man is *ever* going to be able to do it, because no one *thing* is ever going to do it."

Jack stopped in mid-swig. His eyes opened wide and he stared into the middle distance as if he'd just taken a faceful of seltzer. And when he turned that gaze back to me, it was filled with a realization that puzzled me then, and awes me now. Because Jack Fitzpatrick suddenly saw

it all very very clearly. **Q:** *If you could do absolutely
anything, but no one thing is ever going to do the trick,
what would you do?*
　A: *I'd do it all.*

■

Jack Fitzpatrick lived over one thousand full and pro-
ductive lives over the next eleven months. They all shared
the same childhood, the same adolescence. Their common jumping-off point was twenty-seven-year-old Jack
Fitzpatrick, a young nobody who still toted flak and
subpoenas for a living by day... and who each night
engaged in what may possibly be the most radical transformation in human history.
　He started with the sciences. One by one he tackled
them all, devoting one entire lifetime to each individual
discipline. He took Buckminster Fuller's concept of the
Deliberate Generalist to its penultimate extreme by becoming an expert at everything.
　Not that all this information just leaped into his head,
mind you: mild-mannered messenger one moment, Wile
E. Coyote, genius, the next. He worked his collective
duplicitous butt off. Twenty-seven is a little late to be
starting in some fields of endeavor, like med school, for
instance. But he had support: parents who were again
and again overjoyed to see their wayward boy finally get
his life on track, and with several lives' practice he got
very good at filling out student loan forms. The challenge of being the perpetual latecomer only helped fuel
his fire.
　And, like ol' Bucky Fuller, Jack endorsed the principle
that anyone of average intelligence, given enough time,
could get a basic understanding of the perfect technology
that underlies Universe. Jack had a good bit more than
average intelligence.
　And, quite literally, all the time in the world.

■

His first life he spent as an astronomer. It seemed as
good a place as any to start. ["Best to know where you is
before you try to get someplace you ain't," from *The Wit
and Wisdom of Jack Fitzpatrick,* copyright 1999, Bantam
Books.] He lived well into his seventies, and did some

distinguished work—nothing flashy, didn't redesign the cosmos or anything, but it helped to lay the groundwork for his next life as a master of Quantum physics. And his next after that, as a biochemist. And his next four, as a neurosurgeon, psychiatrist, physician, and homeopathic healer.

By the sixth or seventh he was starting to pick up Nobel prizes. On a very regular basis.

■

He made two overwhelming discoveries in April: one of them marvelous, the other absolutely terrifying. I'm leaping ahead in my narrative to tell you this, and I apologize for the disruption; but it was at this precise point, when Jack told the story to me, that *he* was forced to make the same digression:

"What do you want first," he asked me, "the good news or the bad news?"

"The good news," I muttered, hoping that he might say *April Fools!* and smack me in the face with a pie. I was getting a wee bit concerned about my erstwhile best friend. Lord knows, I must have looked like a man receiving a ball peen suppository, because Jack busted up laughing.

"Okay, okay," he said, "the good news is that I found out that I can bring back artifacts from the future. I'm not sure why, but anything I create—anything by my hand or bearing my likeness—can squeeze back with me." He grinned beatifically.

"Uh-huh." This was a twist in his otherwise ridiculous fantasy. To date, I'd seen no evidence. "So, what, are you gonna show pictures of your grandchildren?"

"They're at home," he said, deadly earnest. "All one hundred ninety-seven of 'em. Three volumes worth. Don't you want to hear the bad news?"

"They were all ugly." I sniggered. "A hundred and ninety-seven little mutants."

"Not funny. I was a geneticist twice and lived through three meltdowns, bucko. Saw a lot of that shit. But that wasn't the worst of it."

"Oh, no?" My sarcasm was a thin veneer disguising how miserably uncomfortable I was, watching Jack do his

I-are-a-mental-case schtick. "And what, pray tell, *is* the worst of it?"

"The worst of it"—he lit a cigarette with steady hands—"is that right around fifty years up the road, the world always ends."

"Uh-huh . . ." I began, and my voice kind of fizzled in my throat. Maybe it was the chill certainty in his eyes, sorrow wrapping his words like an orphan's threadbare blanket. Maybe it was simply succumbing to this relentless departure from reality as I understood it. Any way you slice it, the walls of my skepticism started caving in like a sand castle against the onslaught of high tide. I stared at him. He smiled and nodded.

"Happens every time," he said.

■

And it was true. Every single time, somewhere between the years 2032 and 2037, the human race wound up biting the big one. The methods varied, as well as the dates—Jack found that intriguing, even a little hopeful—but in the end, it always came to the one grim realization: we always went kablooie.

The human race was doomed.

■

By Labor Day, Jack Fitzpatrick was the most scientifically learned man in history. From there he went full-tilt into politics and law. Playing by the rules, knowing when to bend them and when to break them, he graduated top of NYU and Harvard Law Schools no less than eight times. Alternately Working Within The System and molding it to his purpose, he inevitably rose to high-ranking office. He was a chief presidential advisor six times; he was U.S. Ambassadors to the Soviet Union, China, and Nicaragua; he was governors of the states of New York, New Hampshire, and Massachusetts; he was a justice on the Supreme Court. He did many great and laudable things; he championed the rights of oppressed millions everywhere. He was bold and wise and absolutely incorruptible.

It didn't change a thing. The world continued to blow up.

In desperation, he became a crusader. He wrote scathing attacks on the Powers That Be conducting Business As

Usual. He organized rallies and marches, tapping into his vastly expanded experience to build strong organizations around his lofty ideals. He actually started making headway: his moving and shaking began being heard clear around the world. In fact, he got so very good at being a mover and a shaker that a new and highly unpleasant pattern emerged:

Jack Fitzpatrick began getting assassinated. On a regular basis.

It was an extremely frustrating period in his lives. Every time he'd get a strategy rolling to the point of success, some bastard would blow him off the podium or wire a bomb into his car's ignition or arrange for his chartered plane to crash mysteriously. It wasn't the dying, per se, that bothered him—he'd raced down that black velvet tube so many times that detouring back to the present was no big deal anymore. What bothered him is that he never got to find out what happened. Did his cause succeed? Did his organization endure? Did the world eat it? He had no way of knowing.

So, the next time around Jack tried another tack. He met a man named Carey Hatcher, who had a good heart, a noble bearing, and oodles of charisma; he was a born showman, an excellent speaker, and a knock-down-dragout debater who put smarmy simpletons like Ronbo to shame. In fact, the sole thing that Carey Hatcher lacked was the vision that marks a true leader.

Enter Jack: he met Carey in '91, they became friends, and then partners. Jack became the invisible man behind Carey's beautifully hewn image: together, they went on a human rights campaign that shook everyone from the White House to the Kremlin to the Boys In the Band. They came to symbolize the power of the people: they fought apartheid in South Africa; they quelled the brutal race riots of Boston in '96; they so successfully exposed and embarrassed the Administration on the eve of the covert Honduras invasion that far-reaching policies were put on the floor of Congress that the War Powers Act be updated and enforced.

By 2011, the popular referendum had Congressman Hatcher aceing the Populist party nomination in the upcoming election, and Jack Fitzpatrick was content in the knowledge that he had never built an organization more sound, more trim, more exquisitely run.

Carey Hatcher received the Nobel Prize posthumously in the year 2012, after his car was forced off of I-81 near Harrisburg, PA, and tumbled down a thirty-five-foot embankment. In the resulting scramble for power Jack watched his entire dream turn to shit. He was the Man Who Could Do Anything, but he couldn't bring back the dead, and he couldn't stop the vultures. Or the worms.

■

For the next thirty years, he made five other successive attempts. All of them ended in death and corruption. In 2036, we kicked the bucket, once again.

■

By Halloween, Jack Fitzpatrick was the bitterest man in human history. His dreams had been shattered, again and again and again. Something in him went cold and hard; his humanitarian stance gave way to a sharp-edged and cynical rage. He was tired of getting murdered, tired of putting faith in people who constantly let him down and tired of knuckling under to the murderous impulses of insensate boobs. His mind took a decidedly militant twist, turned cunning in the worst ways.

He spent his next forty-three lives in the service of Death.

■

The first twenty or so went pretty quickly. Wielding Death, he found, was something for which he did not have a natural aptitude. But he got the hang of it, with practice: he bought weapons, went to a clandestine guerrilla training camp in the Everglades, answered ads in Soldier of Fortune *magazine. He became a mercenary, eventually; and from there he went on to participate in some pretty vicious Third-World revolutions, stage some reasonably devastating coups and countercoups, and ultimately came to preside over some rather bloodcurdling reigns of terror. Finally, he tapped into Der Führer within us all, and went on to become bona fide Ruler of the World.*

By that time, of course, he found he'd become so bitter

*and hateful that he destroyed the world himself, in the
year 2029, a full three years before anyone else.*

■

In his despair, his thoughts turned to suicide. It only
lasted a weekend, but he expended a total of ninety-eight
lives from his seemingly inexhaustible reserve. He walked
in front of buses, slit his wrists, O.D.'d on smack, leaped
off the Brooklyn and Verrazano bridges and the Empire
State Building; he swallowed both barrels of a Smith &
Wesson over-and-under twelve-gauge pump, guzzled an
economy sized Janitor In A Drum, hanged, flayed, filleted,
and immolated himself, and even fed himself to the lions
at the Staten Island Zoo. Ninety-eight ways he fired himself into the nothingness of that long black tube; still, he
could not allow himself to go all the way through to the
other side. Suicide, for Jack Fitzpatrick, was just not an
option.

It was only logical that he should turn, from there, to
religion.

■

He studied them meticulously. He became adept in
every major denominational faith, all of the occult sciences, and several well-known lost arts. He accepted
Jesus Christ as his own personal savior. He became a
whirling dervish. A *brujo*. A bishop. A warlock. He danced,
chanted, prayed, swayed, shaved his head, and yodeled
like a pilgrim in a Muslim minaret. He hung out with the
Sufis, learned how to manipulate their life-sized puppets:
it reminded him, in a joyful way, of politics. He sacrificed
goats to Ba'al; he became a macrobiotic vegetarian. He
trance-channeled with Shirley MacLaine. He chanted *Nam-e
Hyo Ho Ren-ge Kyo* 'til the cows came home; he fasted,
witnessed, handled serpents, spoke in tongues, took Erhardt
Seminar Training, and laid in sensory deprivation tanks
until his skin puckered white.

When he was ready, sometime around Thanksgiving, he
went ahead and took one lifetime to become the Spiritual
Leader of the World.

They crucified him.

He rose from the shadow, some three days later: just in
time to see the mushroom clouds bloom.

And, having risen, knew just what he should do.
◾

By Christmas Eve, Jack Fitzpatrick was the wisest man in the history of the earth. It was only fitting that then he made his wisest move.
He became a child again.
◾

Let me explain something. I spent the lion's share of this whole time getting more and more estranged from my friend Jack Fitzpatrick, who was putting on a virtuoso performance as the World's Most Intense Schizophrenic. It was a hard time for me, because I really cared about Jack, and I hated watching him switch personalities like a couch potato changes channels. But I had problems of my own: it was not the greatest of years for me emotionally, despite the fact that I had sold my first novel and was finally able to retire from the messenger biz; I was considerably more secure than I'd ever been, but I was still lonely and womanless and still subconsciously sitting on the edge of Armageddon, thinking *what if it's all for naught?* Newfound success will do that to you. And if I'd had any inkling of what Jack knew—that we had another fifty years, give or take a few—I would have puttied my face shut. But I didn't.

And when he told me, of course, I didn't believe him.

Until early early Christmas morning—4:30 A.M., to be precise—when he proved it to me.

"I've got a surprise for you," he said. It was 4:15 A.M., and we were trashed; the previous five hours had been spent at my apartment on West 37th Street, drinking Watney's Red Barrel and arguing passionately about what he called the truth and I called absolute fucking insanity.

"Oboy," I moaned, staring out the window of the Checker Cab that bore us down Broadway toward his 13th Street studio. The snow was new and dainty-white, whipping by the window in thick swirls above, muffling the cab's tires below. My mind contrasted this pristine vision with lunatic imaginings of his "surprise": an urban update, perhaps, of Ed Gein's Wisconsin charnel house, complete with a Frigidaire full of viscera and his mother's face soaking in the sink. *What's he gonna show me: a*

pound of homemade meat loaf and a dried-skin lampshade?
I felt ill.

"No," he said quietly, as if he'd heard my thought. He
smiled—a deep, bittersweet smile—and reached into the
canvas biker's bag in his lap. He pulled out a rather
hastily wrapped package. When he handed it to me, my
touch confirmed what my eyes suspected: it was a large
hardcover book.

I held it motionless for a moment, as the cab took a
muted left onto 14th Street and headed toward Second
Avenue. "Don't open it quite yet," he said, still smiling
that strange smile.

No problem there. Something about the weight of that
book, the way it lay in my hands, filled me with a sense of
awe and dread. I think the meat loaf would have been
easier to deal with.

We pulled up to his place at 4:27. I handed the cabbie
ten bucks for a four-fifty fare, and we walked in white
silence to the door of Jack's building. He turned at the
entrance and said, "You can open it now."

"Let's get it out of the snow," I replied. "First thing I
want to do is fuck up the cover, right?" He smiled and
nodded; we stepped through the front door and paused in
the foyer.

I opened the package while he fumbled with his key.
Peeling away the bright green and red paper, the first thing
that hit me was the title: *RENEGADE SAINT—The Secret
Lives Of Jacob B. Fitzpatrick.* The second thing I saw was
a holographic photoplate of a face. It was a decade-plus-
change older, easily. Careworn, matured, victorious—but
no doubt about it: it was a face I recognized. It was Jack.

I flipped instinctively to the back. There was another
plate there, and another face, similarly aged and weathered.
It was the author's face.

It was my face.

My mind reeled. I scanned the brief blurbs beneath the
picture. According to the blurb, it was my tenth book.
According to the blurb, it was already a best-seller.

According to the blurb, so were the other nine.

I looked at Jack, tears in my eyes and a knot in my
throat. Jack looked back, that impossible peace and wis-

dom in his eyes. "It's a good book, man," he said, and nodded. "You've been very good to me, over the centuries. You're the best friend I have. That's why I have to show you this, now."

He opened the door. I followed into the darkened entrance hall, glancing once again at the impossible book, the worlds within worlds layered within his face, the publishing date: 2004, Year of Our Lord. Jack flicked on the light at the end of the hall, turned with a flourish, and showed me a thousand futures.

It was staggering. A thousand future histories, meticulously logged and gift wrapped for posterity. My eyes rolled like minnows in a mudslide as I scanned the sprawling mass of information packing his studio apartment; twelve by twenty-five feet of living space, plus kitchenette and bath. Every square inch of which was crammed with tier upon tier, shelf upon shelf of books, periodicals, videocassettes, laserdiscs, photo albums, notebooks, and manuscripts. There was some stereo equipment that Japan hasn't even dreamed of yet. A twenty-seven-inch color TV that was about as thick as the Weehauken yellow pages. A lot of framed certificates.

But the centerpiece was, by far, the computer: a formidable-looking IBM equipped with the largest-capacity hard disks I'd ever born personal witness to, humming contentedly beside a four-foot-tall rack of floppy disks.

In short, proof.

I stood, starkly and suddenly sober in the face of Jack Fitzpatrick's incontravertible evidence. Like I said: I was a working writer at that point, squeezing an average of 3,500 words a day out of my little Macintosh word processor. I could double that pace for the rest of my life and not produce one one-thousandth of what laid before me.

"That's all she wrote, pal," he said softly. "It's all here: a thousand possible futures, all cross-referenced and catalogued. It's all mine," he added. "And yours."

I stared at him blankly. "Whu . . . what do you mean, *mine*?"

Again, that secret smile.

"You'll see . . ."

* * *

Last night, Jack Fitzpatrick committed suicide by attacking the President with a fully charged cream pie. It contained no hidden explosives, no poisonous chemicals, no flesh-devouring corrosives. Knowing Jack, it probably didn't even have any preservatives. The President-elect had just accepted the reins of power, and was busy spoon-feeding the faithful the same dangerous mixture of pious platitudes and get-tough posturing that had carried the election. Everyone sounded hot and ready to march on down to Central America and kick some commie butt. The media was out in full regalia, transmuting the event from reality to electron-fodder for the benefit of the folks back home. Jack appeared virtually from out of nowhere, and *splat!* the new President flailed back into the Vice-President, who in turn bumped the First Lady and the Secretary of State into the Second Lady and the Chief Justice, who pitched three members of the Cabinet sprawling and knocked the ex-First Lady clear off the podium and down into the band shell, where her spindly anorexic legs stuck out of the cacophonous tangle of Marine Corps band members like a blue-veined victory symbol. The former President managed to grab hold of the draperies before being bowled over by the Head of the Joint Chiefs of Staff, who landed whoofing and wheezing squarely atop him, and the pull of their joint impetus managed to bring the lion's share of bunting crashing down on the entire fiasco like the finale of a Spike Jones road show. Jack was clear of the melee and leaping from the stage when . . . POW!

I'm sure you've seen the pictures.

I was working when it happened. The last three weeks had brought us closer than we'd ever been, largely because he was busy showing me through his archives, sharing memories I haven't even *had* yet. Then, about a week ago, he suddenly dropped out of sight. I was worried, but what could I do? The future's great stuff, but I still had the present to deal with, and books don't write themselves. I left about two dozen increasingly uneasy messages on his machine, and otherwise left it at that.

Until last night.

I sat at my desk, completely unable to work on chapter

seven of a novel which is already five months behind
schedule, shell-shocked in the dawning light of realization. The TV was blasting, hashing and rehashing the
details of the attack. In my lap sat the box that came by
messenger yesterday morning. Its contents: a photograph,
a cryptic note, and a key. The photograph was something
he hadn't yet shown me, a shot of myself and some very
beautiful girl, waving from a boat in some subtropical
locale. The inscription on the back says, "*Honeymoon is
great. Don't wish you were here at all ha-ha.*" The date
is two years hence. The handwriting is mine. The girl is
gorgeous, the spitting image of that long-ago bronze beauty. I may just die.

The note said simply:

GET ON DATANET. RUN FITZ: 12788; PP87; ENTER.

For those of you as yet uninitiated to the halls of the
silicon gods, Datanet is one of the many national elec-
tronic mail storage and retrieval services. I dialed it up,
logged on, typed in the code, and waited.

The screen went blank.

When it blinked back on it asked me a very specific
question, to which it wanted a very specific answer. A
password

Q: *If you could do anything, but no one thing is ever
going to do it, what would you do?*

I racked my brain, searching for the answer. I searched
all night, no doubt while a platoon of police, Secret
Service, and federal investigators were simultaneously kicking
down the door of Jack's apartment. I finally found the
answer around 4:30 this morning. Right there, staring me
in the face, on page 87 of *RENEGADE SAINT*—the chapter titled "Conundrum." Sly bastard.

Bleary-eyed, I logged on Datanet. Typed in the code.
And when those little green letters lit the screen, gave the
reply:

A: *I'd do it all.*

The screen blanked momentarily. When it lit up again,
it was Jack. I cried as I read it. It said:

Scott—

You made it, which means I did it. I decided to go all the way this time. I think that's what might be holding us back: until I go on to the next step, and blow this whole thing wide open, we'll keep going kaboomskie.

Am I some kind of kosmic keystone? Or is this just a little kick in the pants from God? I don't know. Forty-five hundred years of cumulative experience later, and I'm still not qualified to say. I only know it's time to move on.

And that's where you come in: when you punched in the code, it signaled Datanet to send precoded letters to every major wire service, newspaper, and periodical in the country. TV stations, too. The delivery times are all staggered, as well, so they can compete with each other for primacy. All-sides-against-the-middle time. I won't be easily explained away.

The key is to a safety deposit box at your bank. In it are papers appointing you legal executor of my estate, and a diskette containing the locations of other safety deposit boxes across the city. In them are directions to storage facilities containing duplicates of every work in my apartment. There's also some stock in companies that are soon going to make you a very rich man. It's all yours, buddy. Use it as you will.

It's funny; after everything is said and done, I still think one of the best times I ever had was that first night with Jamie Morganstern. Remember her? I even went back and married her, once. Love conquers all, I guess. Life is so strange: we can never find enough time, and yet we spend so much of it all caught up in the bullshit. Politics and war, in particular; science and religion can get pretty loopy *in extremus,* but the first two are by far the worst. Sometimes I think that laughing those two particular practices right off the face of the earth might must be Humanity's highest possible achievement.

      Oh, well. Gotta go, pal. Good luck.

      You'll need it. And thanks.

      ....Jack

Was he right? Is the world going to fry in fifty years? How should *I* know? Not much reason to expect that it won't, of course; but then, Jack never did *this* before. He may have changed everything with that one final act. And who knows? He may even be right about Humanity's highest possible achievement. You've got to admit, after all . . .

. . . the President looked awfully damned silly picking pie off of his face.

I'VE BEEN WAITING ALL MY LIFE TO MEET YOU

I wander the streets of this fucking city for the umpteenth millionth time; and though I know it to be pointless and worse, I do it. I do it I do it I do it out of habit, out of hatred for the patterns that have emerged to torment and enslave me: moist and meaningless shadow-things, liaisons with waste and nothingness in an endless cold cold night . . .

Let's face it, kiddo. The thrill is gone. The thrill of the chase, of poking my nose at scented tails and letting my tongue go wagga-wagga . . . it's gone. Too many nights going *yeah* and *really,* bumpity-bump *did you cum?* and *I'll see ya later.* Too many nights senselessly pumping sperm into women who didn't want it to grow and probably didn't deserve its growth anyway, would treat it to more of human stupidity's boundless milk in the hopes of spawning a *lawyer* or some other luckless creepy-crawler. No, man. It's too goddam easy to climb in bed with the wrong person and let the fluids fly, your promise to tomorrow just a yucky inconvenience that there's some pill to take care of.

No, man. Fuck it. *Beyond* the habit and the hate and

the slavery, *beyond* the hitherto-sacred-cow-enshrined sexplay; *beyond* all that, there is something that is screaming to be *found*!

And. I will. Find. It.

Oh, what's this? A can. Hey doggies. I'll kick it. THWUNK clitta clitta clitta and nothing. Who am I kidding? This whole deal is a kick-the-can across infinity, and I'm infinitely weary. I'm going home.

No, I'm not. There's nothing there. Nothing I haven't sucked all the life from, anyway. Not even my art, clamoring (not as hard as I clamor) to be finished, waiting for me in the huge and empty darkness of my room. Not even my fabulous, breathtakingly beautiful art, which is displayed on all the right walls and between all the right covers, all over this great slobbering nation of ours and beyond! Oh yeah, it's waiting for me; but not like I'm waiting for *you*, honey. Not like I'm aching for you.

So where the hell are ya, anyway? I'm out on a main drag now, the cars are racing by with typical brainless fervor, this scene is obviously *happenin'*, man, *happenin'*, so . . . where the hell are ya? Huh? Please?

I don't know. There are so many people out here, doing their dingy public dances, stacking veneers like layers of paint on an old old structure. Well hey, people! I got news for y'all! Sucker doesn't need a new paint-job; it needs to be torn the fuck DOWN, babies! It needs DEMOLISHED! It needs . . .

One may well wonder, I suppose, how this foaming maniac hopes to find any kind of woman at all in this state of mind . . . much less *the one*. (Oh, how that phrase rings in my ears. And what sweet promises it holds.) But it's not true. Already the woman-eyes are locking on me like rivets, doing the slow turn as I do the slow burn past them. They sense my hunger. They don't know what it *is*, mind you; wouldn't know how to sate it, even if they did. But they feel it.

How could they not? It is the brightred red of lust and lifeblood, the penetrating yellow of keenest wisdom, the permeating green of calm and reconciliation, the soul-sucking blackness of utter despair and whitewhite light of utter clarity. It is a rainbow and more of energy, pouring out of me, eating and replenishing me so I can continue on my goddam brainless quest. Quest of the Ultimate. Ultimate that I just gotta have.

I cringe inwardly now, thinking. Thinking: *people, don't think that I think that I'm better than you. Don't think that I'm thinking, "I'm looking for someone much better than you'll ever be. Sorry, babe... nice tits, but no go." Because I'm as little and creeping and pathetic as any of you, out here blowing my brains out for something I'll never have. Just like you. And none of us will ever find it. Not a ...*

OOPS! What's this? "Oh, I'm sorry, hon. Bumped right into ya," I say without even thinking about it. I catch myself with a consoling hand on her shoulder, and wish that I would think once in a while before I do shit.

Because I recognize the light in her eyes; know that she won't be articulate enough to come up with anything witty and table-turning; know also that there's nothing in this world she'd rather do right now. She has felt the energy: it has touched her there, there, and (oh yes!) *there*. I can see her thoughts, like two Championship Wrestlers having at it, one edging toward the ropes for a bit of tag-teamwork. It's so sad, and so innocent, and I wish like crazy that it wasn't happening.

PROCTOR'S FIRST LAW OF SEXUAL DYNAMICS: don't touch unless you really mean it. One little touch is all it takes. Once done, you either gotta follow through or do the Wormlike Wriggle. Both are more trouble than they're worth. Honest.

It's the Wormlike Wriggle for *me*, doll. The indicator lights in her irises tell me that she's coming up with something. Just as her lips part to let me have it, I withdraw my hand and kick in the deflector shields, saying, "Uh... sorry again," with averted eyes and a doleful brush past her. Utterly uncharming, I'd think... but no.

"It's alright!" she assures me hurriedly, pitter-pattering up from behind. It's all I can do to keep from smacking my forehead with a flat palm, invoking the clownface gods. I don't stop walking. I cut a swath through the social intercourse of two happily chirruping couples, leaving them as a roadblock for Ms. Cutesiepie Hotpants. It slows her only a little.

"Hey!" she calls, sidestepping the parrots and doing (I just know) the silly little hands-up running bit. It is cruel and thoughtless to let her chase me halfway across town for nothing. Sighing ponderously, I decide to kick in . . .

PROCTOR'S COROLLARY TO HIS OWN FIRST LAW: the Wormlike Wriggle can sometimes be disguised as the Sabertoothed Snickass. This is to be done only in cases where corrective surgery is absolutely necessary.

"Hey," she says, laying her hand on my shoulder. I stop, and steel myself. I start to turn, and she's met me halfway.

Having faced me, she is again at a loss for words. I take a moment to appraise her. She's a nice girl, it's obvious. She's cute, she's ample, she's warm all over and eager to please. A couple of years ago, we coulda had *some fun hey!* I quite thoroughly hate myself for what I'm about to do.

"I . . ." she starts to say, shy smile creeping crossways, happy taffy-pullers at either end of her ripe red lips. I'm about to spazz them out when some fool bumps into me from behind, pushing me flush against her. It feels good. *Damn* you, God or whatever you are! for making us all so vulnerable.

The stunned silence lasts too long. She inflates it to triple its actual worth. My eyes burn like hot pus behind the eyelids, and I feel an unwanted tear gathering substance there. My hands come up to her shoulders and push me gently away. Maybe, just maybe, I can play this one straight.

"Darlin'," I say with just the right blend of tough 'n' tenderness, "you're a very sweet lady, and cute to boot, but I really gotta get going." Then I give her the patented winkansmile, and turn to walk away.

Winkansmile. Frankenstein. Here's the evil Dr. Winkansmile, building monsters from the pieces of dead and moldering dreams! Where are the goddam torch-bearing villagers to put me out of my misery? Do I have to come back for yet another dreary sequel?

Yup. I hooked her like a small fish: no matter how many

times I throw her back, she just got to have that worm. "No, wait a minute!" she cries, stopping me. "Umm . . . couldn't we, like, get together lat . . ."

"See, I've got this little problem," I butt in quickly, working my best understated Bruce Dern imitation. "I've got to disassemble my piggy banks. By my estimation, I'm up to roughly two hundred and fifty thousand pennies. That's a lot, don't you think?"

She nods, confused. We're almost halfway there.

"Well, tomorrow, I'm going up to the top of the Empire State Building during rush hour and flinging them all right over the side."

Her stare is blank. It's working, God help me.

"You've heard about how, if you toss a penny off the Empire State Building, they can go straight through a person? Faster than a speeding bullet?" I giggle in an unhinged manner. Go git 'er, Sabertooth!

"Well, I figure, it's going to cost me, sure, but I'll probably go down as the single most fiscally extravagant mass-murderer in American history, not to mention the biggest." I allow myself to shift into full-tilt hysteria now. "Fuck Charles Whitman! Fuck Henry Lee Lucas! Nambee-pambee, penny-ante, piggly-wigglee diddlee-shitty . . ."

I turn away then, making tracks, still singsong ranting far beyond her audible range, my last impression of her face embossed across my inner eye. I don't wait to see the taffy-pullers yank her face downward, don't wait to see the hurt and confusion. Can't *bear* to see it. I walk off hurriedly, contemplating the underside of speeding cars as a final resting place . . .

Yeah, I can see it now. THE JOSHUA PROCTOR STO-RY: closing reel. Our hero finally realizes what a loath-some, heartless monster he has become. Like all those who flip God the bird by pursuing the unreasonable, like all those who aspire to Godhood themselves, his heart's been corrupted and his demons unleashed. The bitter irony of it, the sorrow and revulsion, brings the tears and laughter bubbling up in one last mad paradoxical burst.

The city blurs, goes soft and runny. Close-up of his face, hideously transforming: yellow slit-eyes above the long-toothed snout, spilling watery slime down his cheek's matted fur. He wipes his eyes with two monstrous claws, howling now, and tried to refocus.

A thousand lights pierce the soft gray smudge, homing in on him like spotlights from heaven. They are calling him home. A repentant human voice echoes inside his mind, saying LORD JESUS, FORGIVE ME (who wrote this script?), while the outer beast flails and bellows its rage. No more commercials now, kiddies; this is the dumb old climax you've been waiting for.

Full-body shot of the thing, rearing back as the multi-fold lights start to bathe and envelop it. Lashing out at nothing, now glowing from within, oblivious to the screams of the gathering crowd, it howls and is blind and in frenzy.

A stupid cop runs up and clubs it from behind. Whirl. Slash. So fast that the body stands, teetering slightly, while the face wetly exits stage left. This time, the creature hears the screams all around it. With one last shriek of anguish, it takes five stumbling steps backward. Into the street.

The first car has got to be doing forty when it hits the monster and sends it spiraling crazily, like a poorly tossed football, into the opposing lane. The wide receiver is a ten-ton semi. There is no time to brake. Or scream.

Ground-level close-up of all those wheels.

Omigod.

They're so terribly fast . . .

And the head of the thing that was Joshua Proctor explodes in a shower of luminous gore. No longer the painter of bleeding flowers, of crystals and beasties with knowing smiles, this thing that death-kicks upward, catches on the chassis and drags like a broken muffler. No more the embellisher of human core visions and painter of blushes on warm feminine flesh, now painting the streets with garish smears of meat and radiance. The legs snap off just above the ankles. This journey is ended. As if to lend this emphasis, the truck swerves suddenly to squeeze viscera from either open end of the flopping carcass and mash it flat under rubber rollers.

No matter that he's left his indelible mark on the world, pressed pavement-tight and ever-glowing. The quest is finished, and he has failed.

And, of course, she is there. We recognize her instantly,

although we've never seen her before; standing alone in the crowd, with the bright tears coarsing down her cheeks. Bright tears, mirroring the stupid brilliance of his remains, reflecting his soul as she turns, defeated now as well, and staggers half-dead into the empty city night . . .

Shit.

Okay, so I'll stay on this side of the street, dammit. I know how the fucking Fates like to deal with quitters. And I *hate* pathos, believe it or not. Damned if *I'm* gonna be the object of it in my own friggin' movie.

It's just that it's so hard, man. It really is so very very mercilessly hard to just keep going like this that I just can't believe it's happening sometimes . . .

But I've stood here long enough. There are enough people around here to choke a sperm whale, and I know you're out there somewhere. Ol' Josh hasn't wasted himself yet, darlin'! And he's been waiting all his life to meet you.

So don't make him wait too much longer, okay?

I don't know how much longer he can take it.

Mmmmm, this is good mocha java. I savor it between lungfuls of streamlined tobacco, eyeballing the girl at the very next table, and I think about compensations (of which there are many). The joint I wound up sharing with those high-school kids detached me somewhat. Things look a little less bleak now. Hey! It's time to rethink again. Think about . . .

Compensations. Perhaps it would be a good idea to (long as I'm sittin' here) count the old blessings for a change! I pull out a fine-point marker and the trusty pocket sketch pad, and I briefly jot down the following:

YOU OUGHTA BE ASHAMED, BUNKY! LOOK WHAT YOU GOT!

Because I'm an artist (also because I'm stoned, and not a little crazy for starters), I take the time to put this in a word balloon and issue it from the mouth of my best friend Linda, all white-robed and smiling angelically with a nifty little halo over her head. This takes a bit more time than I'd originally intended, of course, but I'm absorbed while it's happening.

Now I look at the clock on the dark burnished wall and say "Shit!" out loud, omnidirectionally. No big deal, but I'd only planned to stop in for a quick cup. Oh, well . . . maybe the Great White Goddess will drop by for some cappuccino. I could certainly dig another cup o' dis! My eyes cast around for the waiter, come up instead with the dark burnished girl at the next table. She is looking at me. I engage her glance. She pulls it away. I smile at the air, then look back to my sketch pad.

Linda's more sensible than I am, really. That's why we couldn't hold it together as lovers. I look at her face, play some scenes in my mind, and then remember what I wanted to be writing. Okay! Smooth movin', Josh! Let's see . . .

    1. You're selling.
    2. You've got a little more than enough money.

Okay, we got that covered. I will eat tomorrow. What else?

    3. My work is good.

Yeah, man. After all those years of doubt, of quivering fragile inquiries as to the quality of my material, I can finally sit back feeling good. I've learned to reproduce what I see, precisely. And I've learned to see so *much* . . .

    4. I love my work.
    5. My consciousness seems to be expanding
    nicely.

Yeah, great. But I seem to have changed perspectives here. When I started out, Linda was talking. Now *I'm* talking. I create CHAOS from the swirling subconscious! Ha . . .

It's because I was thinking about Linda again; and, truthfully, all of the really great women I've managed to come across (or cum in) over these last several years. WHY WASN'T I SATISFIED? I ask myself for the umpteen-millionth time . . .

"Can I get you another cup?" asks the waiter, appearing magically to my left. I jolt upright and turn, surprised, to look at him. He laughs and says, "Hey, I didn't mean to terrify you . . ."

"It's alright," I say, hurtling back to my body. "Yeah, I'll take another one." He is checking out my list and smiling, wry. He nods twice when I finish speaking and then splits, tossing one backward glance before disappearing from view.

Why wasn't I satisfied? I ask myself more calmly. Better prepared to answer reasonably in this less-feverish state of mind, I pause to consider.

Earlier on in life, I decided that no one woman could possibly do it all; further, that no one woman could be reasonably expected to even try. Leading, of course, to the subsequent decision that I'd have to work out some arrangement with a bunch of 'em, tailoring each one-on-one relationship to its unique matrix of matching parts. You know: I'd ski with the ones who were into skiing; I'd eat Chinese with the ones who were into Chinese, Italian with the pasta-lovers; I'd share cozmic revelations with the more spiritually inclined, drink toasts with the tibblers, take trips with the acid-heads, eat meat with the carnivores and tofu with the Aquarians. I'd share my wit with similar senses of humor, my art with similar tastes in culture, and my bed with similar . . . appetites. The best of all possible worlds, right? One big marriage to all womankind, most assuredly made in heaven.

But it didn't work out that way. Not at all. I even got a chance to try, something that most people never get; I spent two years trying to ride Enlightened Polygamy, only to find it was a wild horse that refused to be tamed. And you know why?

Sex. Pure and simple. Immediately, the wet funk of genital interaction slopped itself all over everything that happened. Alchemical transformation took place. Previously innocuous and unrelated events took on new meaning somehow, always sinister and usually false. Ski trips were no longer ski trips, for example: they were excuses for shtupping Suzanne in front of a big fireplace (only once, in fact . . . months after the accusation). Not being able to see someone for three weeks meant that I no longer wanted to see them at all, but that's alright (sob sniffle), they'd survive. It was utterly insane, an experiment gone mad: half the time belly-up and ready for mauling. I could . . .

Ah, but the waiter has returned with a big steaming

goodie. I say "Thanks" as he sets it down before me, and dig in my pocket for change.

"No problem. I make my living by taking orders." It's such an offhand comment that it makes me laugh. He said it because he knows I can handle it; already, he's back to studying my work-in-progress, looking as though he'd never spoken. I like this guy.

"You haven't gotten very much further on this. Are you running out of blessings, or what?" he adds casually, that same smile on his face.

"Naw. I just cruised my biocircuitry for a minute. Spacin' out. You know." He nods while I give up on the concept of change and pull out my wallet.

"This is really good stuff here," he says, pointing to Linda in particular. "You are an artist by trade?" I nod affirmation; he acknowledges it with another one of his own. "Great," he cheerfully concludes.

"Here, man. Keep the change," I say, handing him a five. He goes wow and really lights up. I flash him the patented winkansmile and hold out my fist, thumbs up. He thanks me very much and sorta dances away. I watch him, while my mind slides over to the subject of friendship; and from there, back into the past...

I lost lot of friends with that two-year foray into The Unknown. A lot of bitterness, a lot of hurt, and a lot of confusion. It forced me to a new set of conclusions, perhaps wilder and more dangerous than the last. And it set me on this quest.

Quest of the Perfect Love...

I take a tentative sip of my java. It's perfect. I tingle. A cigarette comes to my lips and ignites (purely mechanical act); my thoughts tumble inward.

Perfect Love. It wasn't Linda, much as I love her. She was the closest I've come, but the differences were glaring, irreconcilable: we kept totally different hours, and she was far gentler than I. My outrage still frightens her more than I like.

Trish. She was wilder, more than kept up with me in the all-nighter department, and was a barrel of laughs besides. But when she asked me to tie her up, I hung it up instead.

(Felt like a prude that time, yes indeedee; but the idea's just too fucking alien to me. I'm sorry.)

Then Patty let me know what bondage was really all about, and I'm sure that I'd have been better off with Trish. Because nothing is worse . . . a hand grenade up the ass couldn't be worse . . . than the million tiny hooks that the love-loonies wield. That Patty used on me in our hideous year-anna-half together. They're the kind that you don't feel 'til they're in; and they don't hurt until the first time that you try to pull away.

Ah, the love-loonies. Those miserable scumsuckers. You don't know how deeply I hate what they do. They know that the hooks go in all the soft places, the weak spots that only a lover can know. They seek out the puffy underdeveloped portions of your personality and then sshhHHHTOOK! The hook sinks in so easily, and holds so snugly . . .

. . . and it won't let go without ripping a nice big steaming chunk out of you. It won't let go just because you're getting sore. No, boy. It won't let go just because you're crying out and the blood is starting to trickle from all those ugly little cracks. You're gonna bleed, baby! Bleed, before those bastards will let go of you. You're gonna bleed from every lousy hole that's capable of it, baby; gonna take every ounce of will you've got to endure the fucking pain, to take it beyond any point of reason, to keep pullin' and keep pullin' while the million tiny hooks just bide their time, happily hangin' on, groovin' to the high-tension hum of invisible wires that absolutely will not snap, waiting for you to end the symphony with a final supreme effort, with an enormous flurry of sucking staccato notes as the hooks finally yank free, studding you with a million wet puckering wounds that will never fully heal.

Yeah, man. And to top it all off, there's the fact that they really do love you, insofar as they understand the phenomenon (precious little, I can tell you); they put in the hooks because that's what they know, that's all they know about love, damn them: the fear, the clutching, and the redmeat punishing-of-imperfections that underlie their fatuous, wide-eyed blissy-wiss.

At any rate: because they love you and because they're

human and because you are less than perfect yourself, you love them as well. Though I crawled away from Patty like a savaged dog, like a leper, like an Afghani villager with nothing but Soviet shrapnel in his belly . . . though she and her kind have so thoroughly defiled the name of love that I cringe every time a voice intones it . . . though I hate the wretched motherfuckers and everything they so blindly stand for with a passion that leaves me wondering why I never got around to killing . . . I still love 'em.

I guess that makes me a real nice guy, huh? Or a bottomless fool. Either way, Patty: if I learned one thing from your guided tour of the goddam pits, it was that you're never too smart to get hooked. You're always capable of that killing stupidity. I was watching out for vampires. I really was. But I was tired, and I let down my guard for a second, thinking I was cool. And you got me.

Never again, man. I'm never letting it down again, man. Not until I know for sure. It's too damn easy to crawl in bed with the wrong woman and let those fluids fly.

Back again, I chug half the cup and kick up a smoke-screen. My eyes return to the list I was making, and my hand moves to set down these new illuminations:

      6. I got away from Patty (love all bloodied, but intact)

      7. I will not give up.

Laughter turns my head. It's naughty-girl stuff (one of my favorite kinds), resonantly issued from the table next door. The dark girl's been joined now by two other women; she's still the most striking of the lot.

I watch her face as she laughs. I marvel at the exquisiteness of her features, the strength in the lines that life has carved across them. Her eyes catch the sparkle of a shaded lamp briefly, and I decide in that instant to draw her.

I light a new cigarette on the last sparks of the old and then put Grampa Filter to rest (a modern metaphor for reincarnation), while my other hand flips the page and proceeds to draw. Meanwhile, the criteria of my quest goes chikka-chikka through the ol' data banks.

Looks? **chikka-chikka-chik.** Yeah, I definitely like good looks, as my marker so reverently testifies. But I'm not real picky. No particular dimension or hues, no particular hairstyles or dress codes on my checklist. I'll never find her in a computer printout of nose lengths and nipple circumferences. That beauty behind the skin, able to shine through even the lumpiest countenance, is what I seek.

Mental attributes? **chikka-chikka-chik.** Yeah, I definitely like mental attributes (chuckling, as I sketch in the character lines on her face). Wit, keenness of insight, a logic not so constricted as to exclude the towering absurdity; a dexterity with symbols, a grasp on their meaning, a taste for the eternal. (All of these things appearing in the girl's likeness. Am I just embellishing them, or are they really there?)

Kindness. Gentleness. Inner strength. A sense of wonder, of harmony with the rest of creation. Honesty. Courage. Do I see those, too? **chikka-chikka-chik.** My hands begin to sweat. I put down the marker for a moment, mind behind the damp forehead reeling, and wipe myself off. Nicotine. Java. The girl at the next table. A hot groin, setting my juices to a boil.

I am terribly close to something: something important. That sense of proximity hangs in the air, thick as dope smoke at a Grateful Dead concert. Thought impulses flash through my head faster than I can decode them, going **chikka-chikka-chikka** What? **a-chikka-chikka** ASK HER **ikka-chikka** OMI **ikka-chikka** GOD, I **chikka-chikka** THINK **a-chikka-chik** SHE MIGHT **a-chik** SHE MIGHT **a-chik** I SHOULD **a-chikka-chikka-chikka** WHAT IF IT'S . . .

I snap back into the room, and instantly freak. She's getting ready to pay her bill; the waiter approaches her now. Hey, man! I thought you were my friend! Break your leg on the way over or something! *Detain her!* Just a . . . oh, shit. I pick up the marker and furiously darken in the portrait's hair. The wild lines give her an adventurous air. We hurtle down dreamslopes together, dodging trees and laughing at Fate. **chikka-chikka-chikka.** My mind floats to . . .

Interests. Wild movies, wild music, wild books and art and theater and dance. Philosophy. Metaphysics. Wholism and synthesis and the global transformation movement in general. The environment. Law, and the absence of justice. The future. The past. And most of all, the ever-present: site of all-there-is. (I wonder . . . does she share these concerns?)

Then she has paid, and is rising to leave. A testicle-sized lump rises in my throat, unbidden; I half-rise out of my seat in alarm. The rest of the goddam details will be there for your head to fill in, darlin'. It is time for me to . . .

. . . very rapidly . . .

. . . sign my name (and address and phone number) to the back, just as she and her friends move their shapely ways toward me. It is a classic moment of split-second timing, definitely one to fossilize and file for the genera-tions a-comin': the last penstroke, just in time for the first footstep to resound in the floorboards at my feet. Flipping the page over and looking up just in time to catch her eyes and hold them for a second. Just in time for me to open the floodgates of patented Joshua Proctor charm and say, "Hey . . . !"

Just in time to watch those precious features twist into a mixture of annoyance and contempt. Just in time to let my picture-bearing hand petrify in midair as that soft and surely God-sent woman/child nails me with those eyes and says, "Aw, just *fuck off*, would'ja?"

Just in time to see her rope one arm around one of her woman-friends, who gives me the kind of look usually reserved for lumps of shit on living room floors.

Just in time to watch her stalk past, leaving a blast of crypt-warm air in her wake, and go out the door.

The picture hangs useless and stupid in my hand. I give it one last quick appraisal. It sucks. I tear it into little pieces and immediately wish I hadn't (it wasn't *that* bad). "I guess that wasn't her," I say to myself, preparing to stick the shreds of vision into my pocket.

The door opens again.

I turn, slowly, to look.

And *you* walk in.

I am seeing you; and though there is no thought involved . . . no thought, no thought at all . . . I know that you are seeing me. The universe (save us) has locked in stasis: beer frozen halfway between tap and mug, incomplete words dangling in midair. This moment exists for us alone.

For you and I.

We each take a first, tentative step toward each other (me not even fully out of my chair) and then stop: stupidly, mortally afraid. Though no more doubt could possibly remain, it's a whole lifetime of doubt and fear that sends a rational mind into a desperate flurry of brattling rationalization: *what if it isn't her, you know how close you came a minute ago to fucking up again, what if it is her and you are no longer worthy . . . ?*

I am caught in the sensory distortion of that logical maelstrom, paralyzed by that which passes for reason. Reeling in fear of my heart's ultimate betrayal, because my heart keeps screaming *it's TRUE, dammit! It's TRUE!* My eyes snap shut, focus with insane clarity on the brilliant subatomic dance, and I think *omigod, this is too intense to be just another dead-end street. This has got to be, it's got to be . . .*

And my eyes snap open. And they lock on yours. And I see the same conflict that must show in my eyes; see them mirror my shock at recognition; smile, as we simultaneously reach the same conclusion.

It's true.

My God, it's *true!*

IT'S TRUE! I let out a howl of lunatic joy and leap into the air, knocking my chair over and not caring the tiniest damn bit. You are here, you are here, I can't fucking *believe* it! I watch as the chair goes ka-boom behind me, turn to see you suddenly giggling.

As if on cue, the world grinds back into action. It's like opening time at Robot World: everyone jerks to life in ultra-slow-motion, while the Great Soundtrack rumbles ponderously into our ears from all directions and steadily accelerates. I spot one old geek who's had his finger in his nose this whole time, withdrawing the dirty digit and examining it verrrrrrrry slowwwwwwwwly; that's the end of the line, boy. I lose it entirely.

Suddenly I am running in mock slow motion, arms outstretched, toward you. You get it instantly, break into matching hysteria. But this ain't Hollywood, and you can't quite bring yourself to sink that low. Besides, you're helpless. I, too, only manage another three or four steps before I'm forced to stagger the rest of the way, clutching my belly and blinded by tears. I stagger, chest flooded with joy, and then we are in each other's arms.

We are in each other's arms, laughing and hugging, while the universe stabilizes. Everything is back to normal, except... you are here. I squeeze you as tight as I can, indescribably happy, wanting to kiss but afraid that we'd bit off our tongues. We gasp for breath, pressed-tight chests pounding.

I love you, I think/feel in one massive burst of internal fireworks, but no words will come. I manage a quick, noisy kiss to the side of your head instead. Suddenly you bury your face in my shoulder, desperation appearing in your embrace; and it is only a moment before I realize that you are no longer laughing, though you shudder more ferociously than before.

Instantly, one of my hands is up to stroke your hair. Wordlessly consoling, my mind fishes for the right words nonetheless. I drop my line into the vast unreason; I cast about in the confusion wrought by your abrupt turnaround. I look for something that will help, put things in perspective. I hear my mind whisper *why are you crying?* and it seems like as good a place as any to start.

But before I can articulate my thought, you bring your lips to my ear; and in a quivering voice both husky and tender, you very quietly exclaim, "I thought I'd never find you..." and then break into loud, irrepressible sobbing.

"I know," I murmur, pouring every bit of empathy I have into you, painfully aware of every little scar that the long cold years have lain on me and knowing that each of them has found its counterpart in you. My mind races through the past, flashes on a billion distinct moments of loneliness, futility, and despair; I reexperience the anguish in tidal waves of feeling that wash us overunderthru.

And my mind cuts loose from my body somehow to run down the corridors of *your* mind. To see the billion split-second agonies of your parallel quest. To see the forms that your pain and joy have taken.

I see them all. They're all there.

And, omigod, how *good* it feels to have someone to share it with! Someone who understands *completely*!

It is only a moment before I realize that I am crying, too.

The ride home is one unspeakably beautiful kiss. It is something from beyond my wildest dreams; it is exactly the way I always knew it would be. Two mouths that were made to engage at the lips, a pair of telepathic tongues. Two souls that have been starving for the taste of each other, now able to feast in boundless abundance. The cabbie may be heading to my place by way of Australia; we'll never know. This is a covenant, written in spit and swirling motion. This is most holy communion. This is . . . *more important*.

Similarly, the walk through the front door and up the steps fades from memory almost before it happens. Almost as if it doesn't happen; as though ghosts have slipped in from the void to inform us subliminally of the occurrence.

Then we are at the door, laughing again, while I fumble with the keys to my apartment. I think (not remembering, even now) that I never *do* find the right one, but we kinda just float through the door anyway. I *think* that's what happens, but I'm not exactly sure.

What the fuck. I don't care. We are inside now; inside. That's all that really matters. We are free now to fully explore each other, without further delay; unencumbered by any physical reality that isn't thoroughly conducive to our . . . explorations. We pause to hold each other with our eyes in the hallway, then take hands and slide dreamily inward. Deeper. All the way in to where I live.

We wander, then, through the trappings of my life, scattered like flotsam on the shore of my sprawling loft apartment. Here, a series of canvases near to completion. Here and there, the components of my massive stereo system. Here, a pile of crumpled sheets and clothing, slopped randomly on a sofa that sits in the spaciousness like an island. We wander like spirits through the huge and emptiness, through the only occasionally brilliant clutter spewed about it.

We wander, comparing notes on this and that: movies

we both love; foods; philosophies. It's hardly necessary; a relic from that other life, the life that ended about an hour ago. A mere formality, fun on top but a trifle scary below the surface. We do it anyway, not knowing what else to do, until we reach the bed.

"Seat?" I ask, gesturing with my free hand. You give me a look that says *of course, you fool,* and we sit. Snuggle. Pause, then, to survey the vastness.

I am overwhelmed, suddenly, by exactly how empty my life has been up to now. How *miniscule* my accomplishments: what measly Bic lighters in an infinite dark *sea* they've been, flicking on punily to illuminate so *little*! So *little*! I clench up suddenly, jerking you toward me without meaning to. You have me by the shoulders in an instant, while I grip my face and cower away from the horror of it.

"What is it?" you ask me, all concern and certainly knowing; entertaining only that fraction of doubt that keeps one from jumping to conclusions (another relic). I pull myself together inwardly, try to put a label on it myself. I fish for the words. They come up from the depths like Godzilla and I am dragged by their force.

"It's just so sad," I say with effort, "to look at what I've been. It's like I've been a scrap of a human, picking through the graveyard of my own bones, trying to find the rest of me and rejoicing over every discarded shin I find." No, that won't do it. I try again. "Like I've caved in on the inside, and everything's just rubble all over the place." No. "Like . . ." and then you shush me, and I am silent.

"It's like one-half of you has been missing for all these years," you say, and the blinders start to slip from my eyes. I blink at you; you are glowing like heaven. I almost cry out, but you are not finished.

"Listen," you say. "Nobody can fill up this empty shell for you. You are not this empty shell. We'll move out, we'll set up the place where we were meant to live. Okay?"

I nod.

"Do you understand what's going on?" you ask. I struggle for a second, while white light burns the last vestiges away.

"We are one being," you say. *"We are really, truly, but one being."*

And the room suddenly goes shimmery-white. Timeless.
Motionless.

And we are on the bed, and I am undressing you
And you are undressing me
And after I am done, then you undress me
And I undress you
And I am you are running flesh over flesh inna hot
pulsing HOO boy your my arms legs wrapped around in
me you I'm in o
                            ■

I've been waiting.
All my life.
To meet.
Me.

....
....
..................**OCTOBER**

8
SECRETS

So much to recount, since last we spoke. The good, the bad, the perverse, the sublime, the tragic, the fantastic, and the merely absurd. From boring busywork to spooky manifestations, from friendly fun to forbidden longings, these last thirty-odd days have had it all. To lodge it firmly in historical context, to whit, toot sweet, and dot dot dot:

Having successfully navigated a full month in the City of Dreams without crapping out of college, falling in love with a loser, getting ravished by hooligans, or crawling home to Daddy, our heroine pauses to savor sweet victory. The scene: Cafe Degli Artisti. The time: the present (no time quite like it). Her mission: to get it all down on paper, then craftily scheme ahead.

First, the boring part.

Looking back on it, the first week of school was a tactical nightmare, but our heroine has expected no less. She has braved the crowds of scuttling paper-pushers with grace and aplomb, coming away with: (a) a laminated I.D. card emblazoned with a photo so unflattering that it lacks only a tendril of drool dangling from her lower lip to make the insult complete; and (b) a roster of classes as diverse as they are unchallenging. All smoke and fury, signifying nothing; just the way she wants it.

She does not move toward any officially sanctioned goal; no piece of paper or cushy job-slot propels her

dreams. Far from it. No, our heroine's path is a
subtle, meandering thing, full of mystery and in-
trigue. She steps from moment to moment as she
would cross a rocky mountain stream, scarcely knowing where her next step will take her until she gets
there.

All of which is lost on the mighty educational
juggernaut, she knows, as well as on the Beast of Back
Bay, who has long since returned to his lair, where he
growls often but writes regular checks. No matter.
Our heroine uses the routines to keep the Beast at
bay. Schedules are established, noses are placed to
grindstones, and the juggernaut chugs forth. Our
heroine knows the institutional ropes like any good
rat knows the corridors of its maze; very quickly she
can run them by rote.

Which leaves her free to explore the City, and the
myriad miracles to be found therein. Not the least of
which is the book, into which she loses herself at
every opportunity.

And the Keeper. Who is nowhere to be found at
all . . .

Meryl paused over her journal and stared into the cup
of cappuccino, as if to divine some secret in the cinnamon
and steamed milk. The coffee shop was darkly warm and
inviting, decorated in sooty wood and glass and brick. It
smelled of coffee and chocolate, of sugar and spice and
clove cigarettes. It was a big favorite of brooding writers,
poets, and *intelligentsia*, an ideal place to wile away the
hours lost in thought or pointlessly pointed discourse.
Meryl had fallen in love with it instantly.

She wondered if J. P. had done the same.

But if he was the man in the photograph, she hadn't
seen him, and didn't now. And if he wasn't, then how the
hell would she know? She clearly couldn't go up to every
stranger who looked like he might have a brain and say
excuse me, but your name wouldn't happen to be . . . ? It
was too goddam ridiculous.

Outside, Greenwich Avenue bustled, drawn entirely in
shades of gray. Fall had fallen early this year; the tempera-

ture was cool, and the clouds hung like a shroud in what sky you could see if you looked straight up between the buildings. It was perfect weather in which to contemplate mysteries.

Or better yet, to jot them down...

With regards to J. P., my mystery man; i've been digging around everywhere, from Waldenbooks to B. Dalton to The Mysterious Book Shop and Forbidden Planet, not to mention the college and public libraries, and nobody's ever heard of *Nightmare, New York City* or anything else he might have written. Not only that, but his name's not listed anywhere in the five-borough area. i suppose i could check out Hoboken and such, but somehow i don't think New Jersey holds the key to the answers i seek. It's getting to the point where i'm almost tempted to call the Beast and beg for the name of his real estate connection. But not quite. That would tend to take the fun out of it.

And what fun it is. Dearest Diarrhea, i tell you true: i think i should like to buy that gentleman a drink. He has so completely colored my perceptions of the City... so completely brought to life its hidden corners and shadowed depths... that i often find myself seeing it as if through his eyes. As if he were not only beside me, but inside me (pant pant, more on that later), informing my perspectives with his own experiences both real and fabricated, breaking down the line between and making them mine.

And it extends beyond the internal (as if that weren't enough). His book is a walking tour of the City. i visit the sites of his various stories, and they're just as i had pictured them... no. More precisely: just as he said they would be.

i walk through the City and every step of the way, i'm haunted by a prescience, a *déjà vu*–like sense of familiarity. It's an intimate recognition, core-deep and vivid, rendering the sights and smells and tactile sensations as much a part of my personal history as the life i've actually led. i feel as though i'm inside his

people: living their lives, dying their deaths. i feel as
though i'm inside his place.

i lay awake at night, sometimes, and can hear the
City breathing.

His stories have made an urban empath out of me.
And his stories are bringing me closer, with every
turn of the page, to a world that exists beyond the
paper in my hands. Bringing me closer to him.

Which brings me to the dreams, and the truly
strangest aspect of this phase of my life. To call them
beguiling and bewildering is a sizeable understatement. *Hot*, i think, is a more accurate description.
And perplexing as all get-out.

Because, though i've spent the bulk of this past
year in self-imposed celibacy—with nary a complaint,
i might add—the last two dozen nights or so have
been spent in fairly animate sexual abandon. Which is
to say that i've been fucking my brains out. In my
dreams. With the mystery man.

Now, i know what Daddy's shrinks would say; and
in certain respects, they would probably be right.
Twelve months of libidinous inactivity would tend to
indicate a motherlode of repressed sexuality, simmering
down there beneath the surface, and under a considerable amount of pressure. Enough to turn coal into
honey, so to speak.

Except . . .

Except for the way that the dreams have unfolded.
In the beginning, they were frankly pretty terrifying.
Erotic at the outset, and then flip-flopping suddenly
into panic, with an underlying motif of corruption (by
which i mean physical decomposition). Yucky stuff,
which never failed to wake me up feeling unpleasantly
wired and ready for a nerve-balming drink (or three).
It went on like that for about a couple of weeks, until
i didn't even want to sleep anymore; i'd just stay up,
working on stuff, until i literally collapsed from
exhaustion.

But then the pattern shifted, as if the dream had
gotten crafty. i would no longer find myself appearing
in the bed, already in motion and ripe for horrific

disappointment. Instead, a gradual process of seduction began, maddening in its precision and ultimate inexorable success. i tell you true: if anyone on the physical plane ever wooed me this way, i'd throw it all away, every dream of doing it all solely on my own terms. Shoot, i'd throw myself away, in true zen fashion, giving in to the river and letting it take me away, if anyone were to ever treat me this way in real life. Which is, in itself, a terrifying revelation at best.

i know what you're thinking, dearest Diarrhea. A classic case of neurotic transference. i find the stories. i become obsessed. i begin to fantasize, fitting the face from the picture to the man the box reveals. The corruption motif is my fear of involvement, my fear of men period, my undeniable distrust. Maybe even throw Daddy in there: as a symbol of masculinity and corruption hand-in-hand, he certainly can't be beat.

Then my mind strives to make the thing palatable, and so concocts the ultimate seduction sequence, geared completely to my needs. Before long, i'm whining to have the damn thing come true. Reading the words down on paper, it's almost enough to convince me you're right. It's so fucking obvious, in fact, that i should probably tear these pages right out of your body and forget i even mentioned it.

Except . . .

Except that there's more going on here than your simplistic Freudian bullshit. There is more in Heaven and Earth, Horatio, than is dreamt of in your philosophy. Because Katie's dreams are running an interesting (to say the least) parallel to my own.

Which means that it's probably time to tell you about her.

She's my roommate, as you ought to know. What's more, and even more surprising, is that she's my friend. i like Katie so much that it's kind of unnerving; i've never had a close friend like her (like this is news? i've never had a close friend, period,) and i certainly wasn't in the market for one. But Katie's different—certainly different from most people i know, and about as far from yours truly as two people can get and still be classified as the same species. She's really beautiful in that disgustingly blonde and built and tan way, and she's so damned sweet that it's kinda hard to not like her, which is the last kind of statement i though i'd ever make about a person.

You know how i feel about sweetness in general. It makes me want to puke. i had enough saccharine sweetness in my father's idea of heaven to send me all the way to Alpha Centauri, running solely on puke propulsion. Too many preppies from make-nice-money families, always on their best behavior. In public, anyway. The funny thing about phony smiles is that you always notice the teeth first. Go figure.

But Katie comes from a different world (white trash from Selma, Alabama, to hear her tell it), and i'm surprised she's managed to survive. She's extremely sincere: a commodity so impractical that no one has bothered to build an exchange around it. There's no percentage in it. It begs to get screwed. People see sincerity, and they get out their cutlery. ("Mmmmmm-mmm! This looks good enough to eat!") No wonder she keeps winding up in horrible relationships with predatory fuckers.

But, i digress. Back to the evidence.

At the same point that my dreams began, Katie began her own somnambulant voyage. Only hers has not gotten better. It has stabilized at the erotically unpleasant. It started out—and this is important— exactly like mine in every respect. The grunting turned to grasping, turned to rotting. i about shit when i realized that it was the same pattern; but i didn't say anything to her about it. i mean, sharing dreams is not exactly normal behavior, you know?

And then, right about when mine grew seductive, hers turned perverse and nasty. She won't tell me, past a certain point, what happens. But i can tell: a pattern remains.

i don't know what to talk about next: the need for the retaining of intimate secrets, or the parallax view of our dreamstates taken together. It's like trying to describe the split in a family tree using no graphs and only in complete sentences. You need to go both ways at once, but you can only go one way at a time. The limits of language and form. Oh, well.

Let's talk about secrets. i know i've got mine. For example, i have still not told Katie about the book, or about finding the Keeper. Or about my side of the dreams, for that matter. Crisscrossed, they comprise my cross to bear. You know what the shrinks all said: i don't share my feelings, i hold things back, i repress all my pent-up rage and hostility and guilt and all those other great psychoanalytical buzzwords. Guess i must have picked that up from Mom and Dad— remember how good they were at sharing. Dad viewed intimacy as a threat, like letting the other side see your briefs. And Mom—well, you know what Mom did.

i suspect that Katie's holding things back. She is not very good at it. Hell, the girl gushes on and on about intimate shit that i really have no interest in knowing . . . well, maybe not no interest. Fact is, i'm intrigued . . , but also embarrassed by her bared-throat approach. She's so vulnerable. She makes me want to tell her things that before i would tell only to you, things I would barely admit to myself.

Then, in the midst of all this forthright sweetness and light, she goes cloudy on me. The girl is definitely holding out. Some deep, awful secret. She gets right up to the lip of it sometimes, like any minute it's going to come blurting out like one of those *Alien* face-huggers, all claws and slime. Then she chokes. *Silencio*. So what am i supposed to say? So how 'bout those Mets? It's not a pretty sight.

Anyway . . . the other thing? Oh, yeah: the parallax view. That's a much harder factor to peg. In fact, i doubt that it would hold up in court. But both she and i know that the connection is there. She takes it personal, like she's being punished for something. That might explain her, but what about me? There are so many unknowns.

Which, of course, comprise the essence of the mystery. Which, of course, comprises the essence of the fun. As is most often the case, the mystery is doubtless more gratifying than the answer at the end. But i will wait for the answer.

i will finish the book.

And see what is waiting for me on the far side of revelation.

MEATMARKET

A rustling on sheets. The sliding of flesh over flesh, softly merging. Wetness, spreading slowly from the center of the bed. All motion. All flow.

Above, always above, the clock is ticking. Ticking of seconds that turn into hours. Slicing time into measured increments with a sound that cuts like a scalpel's blade. Cutting staccato gashes across the near-perfect stillness of the room.

They try to ignore the ticking. To be lost in the motion. And the flow.

■

When Doreen left him, Tom Savich was in some serious pain. His chest ached. His balls ached. His spine felt as though it had been yanked out, bone by knobby bone, then sewn back in the wrong way. His guts felt mangled and savaged from the inside. His eyes burned. His lips chapped and bled.

In his brain . . . in all the soft places where he stored his memories of her, his estimates of her worth, his plans of a future together . . . there were black, puckered holes. They bled so tangibly, so profusely, that he found himself wondering when *all* thought would be drowned and buried by the copious flow.

Once again: he was in some serious pain.

It was painfully obvious. Anyone could tell that he'd just been hit, and hard. They stayed away in droves: the women, particularly. Tom found that he really could not blame them a bit. He knew how unappetizing he looked.

So he toughed it out. He waited for the wounds to scab over and heal. He gave himself the time and the solitude he needed to recover, to get his bearings, to go out and love again.

It took about a month.

And then his friend Jerry called up to ask if he felt like hitting Dio's after work on Friday. Maybe pick up a couple of sweet little pieces.

"What can you lose?" Jerry asked.

"Everything," he replied. "My heart. My mind."

"Name of the game," Jerry said.

■

Moving, now. The ticking, forgotten. Nothing but the waves of passion and immersion. Rushing over them, now, with mounting fury.

As they move.

■

Tom Savich thought about it. He gave it some intense consideration. The idea simultaneously attracted and repelled, which was pretty much what he had come to expect, considering how much emotional baggage he was carrying around with Dio's name written all over it.

Because Dio's was *the* pickup spot in the garment district, the stretch of Manhattan that gave Fashion Avenue its name. It was the place where hawkers of overpriced clothing went after hours to find their partners for the night. It was the place where business and pleasure, predator and prey came together in an atmosphere of dim light, alcohol, and smoky haze to consummate their endless affairs.

It was the place where Tom first met Doreen, in fact. And Kirsten. And Molly. And the one before that. And the one before *that*. Ad infinitum. It was the place where he had always gone when the need became too great, because it was designed to meet such needs, and it had never failed him.

The question is, he told himself, *do I really need it that badly?* It was not a question that could be answered rationally. It could only be measured in terms of scar tissue and hunger. How much of one, to appease the other? And was it really worth it?

In the end, Jerry persuaded him. It wasn't that hard. Tom Savich had gone a month without. He had pulled himself back together, admirably, from a nasty piece of circumstance. The hunt must go on. If he wanted it, all he had to do was go out and get it.

And as it turned out, he really did want it very badly. More than that: he *needed* it.

■

Inside, now. Dark. Deep. Firm parts over firm parts touching soft soft parts, probing deeper. Pushing, pulling. Into each other.

While the clock. Is ticking. Ticking.

Overhead.

■

Inside Dio's, insanity reigned. By 6:30, there was no more room to stand. Warm bodies vying not only for attention, but for a square foot of floor space to call their own. Large color screens curled over the corners, flashing jump-cut images of perfectly undulating flesh. The big neon clock over the entrance swept round and round, reminding all players of the need for speed. From the balcony, Dio's looked like an army ant farm: a swarm of expensive suits and low-cut blouses, limbs and backs and faceless heads, swaying with the beat, crawling all over each other.

"It's a jungle down there," Tom said. "I'd forgotten what a jungle this is." His eyes flickered between the videos above and the spectacle below and the sweeping, glowing hands; his drink sat, unattended, on the table before him. He might as well have been talking to himself.

"You're just wired, Tommy." Jerry, too, was staring over the rail; but he grinned, white teeth showing under the flat gleam of his eyes. "You just need to loosen up some. Get your thumb out of your ass. This is supposed to be fun, remember?"

"Yeah, right." Down below, somebody had finally scored with the gorgeous blonde by the cash register. A dozen men turned despondently to look for other prey. Tom Savich felt suddenly very tired. Of it all. He sighed deeply. The clock swept round. The bodies writhed. The music throbbed on.

"Listen. Killer." Jerry's tone was derisive, a wee bit impatient. "I'm not going to babysit you, man. If you're bound and determined to have a miserable time, there's no sign up saying you have to stick around. I just thought you had yourself patched up better than that." Tom looked over sharply, stung. "I just thought you were ready to get over that shit."

"It's just..." Tom knee-jerked, suddenly on the defensive. He found that he couldn't look at his friend for a moment; there was something in Jerry's expression... something ugly and feral... that made him distinctly uncomfortable. "It's just that this place is such a meat rack, man. I..."

"Oh. And you're *above* that sort of thing, I take it." Jerry laughed. Tom felt stupid. Jerry continued. "Come on, Savich. Cut me a break. The Virgin Mary has never been your patron saint. I've been in this bar with you more times than..."

"It's just been a long time," Tom countered. "And I don't see anything that really gets me going. And I just can't seem to feel it."

"Well," and now Jerry sat beaming like a Buddha, convinced that he'd finally broken through. "You might want to start by finishing your goddam drink," he said, indicating the untouched glass on the table. "A few more of those, *I'm* gonna start lookin' good to you!"

And it was true: at least halfway. Though Tom made it clear that Jerry would always be an ugly sucker, he did find that Dio's became far more appetizing about two drinks down the road. He began to loosen up. He began to have fun. He began to ignore the dull pangs that went off, deep within.

And that was, of course, when he spotted her.

■

Building up. Sharp breaths. Sharp movement. In. Out. In. Out. Consuming.
The wet spot, slowly growing in the center of the bed.

■

Her name was Linda. She said that she worked for Murjani, International. "I wanted to be a model," she continued, "but they told me I was too short. So now, instead of modeling clothes on the cover of *Vogue*, I hustle 'em in the showroom."

"That's a damn shame," he told her. "I mean it." And he did. *She must have been tremendous as a kid,* he thought. *When she was fresh. Wish I could've been there.*

That would have been some fifteen years ago. Linda wasn't a kid anymore. Very faintly, he could see the scars that the years had left on her. She'd borne them well. She was still a looker. And there was something tough about her. . . a worldly wisdom, a sense of having learned to survive . . . that he found very appealing. With Linda, he knew, there'd be no need for bullshit and fancy dances. She wouldn't stand for it. It made him happy.

He wanted it to be with her.

Perhaps they'd find it.

In each other.

█

Moaning, now. Breath coming in firebursts. Backs arching. Eyes flashing. Teeth glistening. Loins pounding.

As the climax builds.

And the moment draws near.

And the clock slices holes in the night.

█

They spoke for a while, of a number of things. Her eyes were large and dark and penetrating. Her face had a slight flush, blood tiptoeing gingerly to the surface. When she smiled, her lips were red and full. They made themselves clear.

She wanted it as badly as he did.

After that, there was nothing left to say.

█

Hoarse cries in the darkness. The animals, revealed. Flesh sliding over flesh over tensed muscles, writhing.

As he nibbles at her throat.

And she digs into his back.

And the rhythm drags them forward, like the pounding of their blood. Like the ticktock scalpel slashing at the warm body of Time.

While the wet spot grows. And grows. And grows.

█

They went to his apartment on Riverside Drive by taxi, nuzzling each other and the hip-flask that she carried in her bag. The pain was gone now . . . the hunger firmly in its place . . . and all seemed propelled by a drunken exhilaration, pounding through him like a thousand primitive drums.

And then they were in the apartment, where they quickly dispensed with formalities, as well as their clothing. He was startled, but not surprised, by the red gash that ran the length of her soft underbelly, dwarfing the scores of other old wounds that pockmarked her flesh.

Tom Savich glanced down at his own scars for a moment: some as recent as Doreen, some dating back to his very first piece in high school, all those many years before. Some of them gleamed whitely, like bleached bones, like that fabled picket fence; others blushed red, embarrassing memories that he didn't want to think about. Not now. Not now...

And then he was looking at her again, as she moved toward him. Memory drowned in the sight of her body; the sagging breasts, the tightening nipples, the hips that undulated in a dance as old as the first woman, converging with the first man, on the day of the birth of human hunger.

And as they descended on the bed together, he only knew that it was alright. That the past was irrelevant, as irrelevant as the future, in the face of the moment itself.

It was only natural.

■

Now.

The first scream. Ten thick grooves, carving lengthwise down fleshy expanse. Jaws, clamping down. A hot spray. Muffled howl.

Taste of meat, raw and steaming. An audible tearing away. Head, whipping from side to side while its mouth bellows agony. Twists with rage. And attacks.

In the moment.

In the flow.

While the clock ticks off seconds that slice like razors into the soft parts that no claw could reach, no tooth impale, no casual glance reveal.

And the dark wet tendrils stream outward from the center of the bed...

■

Linda was gone when he awoke. It was better that way. It was hard enough to face his own wounds, in private. He didn't want to see what he had done.

She had left very few traces of herself behind. A bit of blood, on the bathroom floor. She was meticulous. He was glad. It meant that she still had her presence of mind; she would be okay; she would make it.

Of course, there was still the bed. There would always be the bed.

Later, after breakfast, he would definitely have to burn the sheets.

And put on clean ones.

For the next time.

9

DRESS FOR EXCESS

Somehow, the last thing Meryl expected to see was Katie's behind poking out the backside of a black leather teddy. It was late in the afternoon, classes had been a veritable meat grinder of boredom, and the bag of groceries she'd scored down Broadway was offering to free her arm from the constraints of her shoulder-socket at a moment's notice. Katie's behind was the last thing on her mind.

But there it was, in all its glory, wriggling backwards through the door of her room, just as Meryl finished prying her key out of the front door dead bolt and squeezing past the police lock. The Talking Heads were on again, pumping out of the stereo at maximum intensity. Meryl let the door *ker-chunk* shut behind her.

"Oops," Katie blurted, wheeling around on a pair of three-inch patent leather pumps. She positioned herself in the doorway of her room so as to block the view. "Oh, hi. You're home."

"Yes, I am," Meryl replied, feeling rather sheepishly obstinate. "Is this a bad time?"

Given Katie's attire, it was a valid enough question. Meryl almost didn't recognize her. The girl was clad like an S&M hostess from Hell, in shiny black high heels— "fuck-me" shoes, as Meryl called them—torn lace stockings with black lace garters, spiked wristlets and choker and, of course, the infamous teddy itself, which wasn't a teddy at all on closer inspection but rather a bone-strutted bustier and leather tap pants, the latter of which were ripped in a half-dozen places like a preview of coming attractions and were doing their damnedest to compete

149

with the former, which were pushing her perfect titties together and up and out in spectacular fashion.

To top it off, she'd dyed her hair a midnight blue-black and painted her face in a stylized *Kabuki* mask that made her lips ripe and blood-red and her eyes smolder like snow-banked coals. It looked uncomfortably exploitive and kinky as all get-out, and left Meryl feeling a little bit angry, even a little jealous, and mostly just perplexed. "Am I interrupting something?" she asked.

"No, nothing, really." Katie smiled sweetly. Her teeth seemed luminous, peeking out from between those blood-red lips.

"Oh." Meryl replied. "Mind if I ask a dumb question?"

"Go ahead."

"You alone?"

"Yeah, s'just me here."

"What? Oh. What happened to your hair?"

"Hair?"

"Yeah, hair. It's black."

"It's a temporary rinse," Katie offered. "*Zazu.*"

"Oh." Meryl nodded. There was no evading the obvious. "So," she began, "why are you dressed like a bimbo?"

"Oh, this?" It was Katie's turn to blush, even though it didn't register as such through the patina of greasepaint. She shrugged. "I . . . I was just trying on my costume."

"Costume?"

"For the Halloween parade."

"What Halloween parade?"

"You mean, you don't know?" Katie seemed incredulous. "Damn, sugar, are you ever missing out." She gestured toward the window, and Broadway below. "It's only about the second-wildest day of the year in this town."

"What's the first wildest?"

"St. Patrick's Day," Katie replied decisively. "But that's just 'cuz everybody and their uncle becomes an honorary Irishman. Halloween's still the best. I always have a blast."

"You mean you actually go outside like that?" Meryl's turn to be incredulous; she was having some difficulty imagining Katie making it half a block, unmolested.

"Damn straight," Katie asserted. "Gotta see it to believe it."

Meryl shook her head. "Okay," she muttered, mostly to herself. She walked over to the kitchen area and started unpacking her bag of groceries onto the island counter. Katie followed her. There was a pile of Polaroids and an open bottle of brandy there, parked beside a jelly jar glass; two fingers of amber liquid already graced its bottom. Evidently the party had already started.

"It's really something to see," she continued, reaching for the snapshots. "It starts over on the West Side and goes up Christopher Street, then snakes around all through the Village and eventually marches right down Fifth Avenue to Washington Square Park, where they just have this hellacious big party."

"Do they now?"

"Mmmm-hmmm." She smiled, handing the pictures to Meryl. "You ain't never seen nothin' like it. Last year they had four bands set up at different places in the park, all these really wild reggae and Latin and African groups, just poundin' out this beat." Katie leaned against the counter and tipped her head back, exposing the white expanse of her throat. "They got this giant skeleton puppet hanging from the arch, and they move it so it looks like its dancin'. And there's just thousands of people there: all dancin' and jumpin' around, and most everybody's wearing some kind of costume, and photographers are running around in packs . . ." Katie giggled and leveled a vampish glance at Meryl, " . . . I must have gotten my picture taken about five hundred times that night."

"Sounds like fun, all right," Meryl said, flipping through the photos. Lots of pictures of Katie in similarly erotic attire, being ogled and/or groped by characters every bit as odd: ghosts, ghouls, clowns, fools, vamps, masked psuedocelebrities, and other pieces of performance art, up to and including a pair of six-foot garden vegetables.

"Oh, it's fun, alright," Katie enthused.

An elastic moment of silence.

"So, whaddaya say . . . you wanna go?"

Meryl studied her for a moment. "No," she said slowly, "I don't think so."

"Aw, c'mon, it'll be fun."

"I don't think so."

"Sure it will," she insisted. "We can go out and kick out the stops, really knock 'em dead."

"No way."

"C'mon . . ."

"No."

"Aw, shoot. Why not?"

"Listen, Katie. I've done some crazy things in my life, but I'm not dumb enough to go out with you dressed like that."

"But it'll be fine, so long's we stick together. Really, you should've seen it last year. We—"

"You don't get it, do you?"

"Get what?"

"Unbelievable," Meryl said to the ceiling, bunching the grocery bag into a tight little ball. "Jeezus, Katie, look at you!"

Katie was taken aback. "What?"

"You," she began, "can get away with dressing like that. Whereas I, by way of glaring contrast, cannot. So let's say we go out with you looking like Dracula's dominatrix, to the delight of gawkers and onlookers everywhere. Then what am I supposed to be? Renfield's twin sister? Your hunchbacked assistant?"

Meryl's stare flared at Katie, then turned away. She hurled the paper ball at the trash can, and missed. "Shit," she spat.

"You done?"

Meryl nodded. Katie gulped the brandy down and said, "Good. 'Cause I wanna say somethin'.

"First of all, I think you're full of shit," she began. Meryl looked up, startled. "I think you're full of shit because (a) I ain't that pretty, and (b) you ain't that ugly."

Meryl started to say something, but Katie cut her off. "Huh-uh, my turn.

"Meryl, honey, for what it's worth, I think you are one beautiful woman. You got a wonderful face . . . I mean, I'd kill for cheekbones like yours . . . and you got a pretty smile, and positively dreamy eyes." Meryl actually blushed then, and Katie smiled.

"As for makeup, and clothes, and all this shit"—she

figered the lace—"it's nothin' but attitude, darlin'. It's an act, just a role you take on for fun. It's like being in a play. You can be whoever you want, whenever you want. And you ain't supposed to take it so damn serious."

Katie nudged Meryl; Meryl smiled ruefully.

"Hell, girl, I wasn't asking you to go along to make you look bad," Katie added. "I wanted you to come with me so we could both have some fun."

Meryl snickered then, and shook her head. "Kinda hard getting personal identity counseling from somebody who looks like a reject from the *Rocky Horror Picture Show.*"

"Don't knock it 'til you you've tried it," Katie said, pouring another shot of brandy. Meryl drank it. "So . . . you wanna?"

"I don't have a costume," Meryl said.

"Not yet." Katie winked, and took Meryl by the hand.

"This isn't going to work."

"Shut up, and sit still. Now, look up."

A pulling along the lower rim of each eye, first one, then the other yielding to the milky soft tip of the brush.

"Look to the left. Now, the right. Good."

"When can I see?"

"When I'm done. Now, close your eyes and hold still."

Soft darting into the creases of each socket, deepening the shadow. A feathery brushing across fluttering lids.

"Yeah, that's it. Ooooooh, this is great."

"What's great?"

"You'll see."

"Is there any more brandy?"

"A little. Here. Now, hold still."

"Mmmmm."

Music on the stero, pulsing insistently. Talking Heads, "Take Me To The River." David Byrne's voice in the background, crooning . . . "Hold me . . . Squeeze me . . . Love me . . . Tease me . . ."

"Okay, open your eyes. Now, suck your cheeks in, like this."

"You're kidding."

"Trust me."

Feathery brushing, soft, quick strokes across the hollows of her cheeks.

"... 'Til I can't ... 'Til I can't ... 'Til I can't ..."

"Make an *o* with your mouth, like Mr. Bill."

"Ooooooh, nooooo ..." Giggles.

"Wider. Pull your lips over your teeth. Yeah, like that. Excellent."

Creamy gliding sensation over smooth, taut lips.

"Now, smeck your lips together."

Smeck, smeck.

"Lemme see. Look at me. Now, smile. Look evil. Oooooh, yes. Honey, you are done."

A black silk shawl obscured the cheval like a curtain drawn across a stage. Candles sparkled in the twilight glow of the room, shooting pinpoint stars twinkling through the weave of the knit. The mirror awaited, its secrets intact.

Meryl bounced expectantly before it, curiosity mingling with anticipation and terror to heighten the buzz off the brandy. "I don't know about this," she said. "I feel kinda stupid."

"Yeah, well, you look kinda hot," Katie answered from her stance behind the mirror. "Check it out."

She pulled the lace away, and the secret revealed itself.

Meryl let out a clipped squeak that registered in a sonic range she hadn't explored since puberty. A stranger stood before her. "Omigod," she blurted. "Who is that?"

"A whole new person, darlin'," Katie said. "Whoever you want her to be."

Meryl watched as the stranger turned to one side, then the other, checking out the view. She was dressed, from the waist up, in an old square-shouldered man's tuxedo jacket, its sleeves pushed up past the elbow and folded 'til the red silk lining showed. Underneath, she wore a white shirt so sheer that the dark points of her breasts stood clearly etched in shadow as she moved. A string tie with a brooch in the shape of an undulating serpent was clasped at her throat. She turned around and looked over her shoulder.

"Eeeek!" Meryl squealed. "Jeezus, Katie, my ass is hanging out!"

"Yeah," Katie said, eyes twinkling. "Ain't it great?"

She was dressed, from the waist down, entirely in suede and lace. The dense black overlap of lace on lace was all that shielded her: lace tap pants, slit to the thigh, covered patterned lace hose with a weave that looked as if her calves and thighs were spun with the webs of many delicate spiders. At the very bottom she wore a pair of low-heeled, crushed suede ankle boots. A solitary boot chain was strapped across one foot, its petite metal spikes bristling in the candlelight.

Meryl stepped up to the mirror, boot chain clinking, her gaze transfixed on the face of the stranger coming to greet her.

The stranger wore her face, and yet not. The eyes, the nose, the lips, the mouth—all were fundamentally the same, yet all were subtly transformed; as if another person had suddenly taken up residence behind her features. Her skin was perfectly white and smooth, redefined in alabaster and ashen hues. She brought one lace-gloved hand up to touch the smoky hollow of her cheek; the stranger in the mirror did likewise. She smiled; the stranger showed white teeth against taut black lips. Her eyes were shadowy wells that flashed like emeralds. She looked like some hungry and feral spirit.

"Jesus, I feel like someone else entirely," Meryl whispered. "Like . . . like some kind of seductress."

Katie came out from behind the mirror and put her arm around Meryl's shoulder. "You are, honey. You are."

Meryl returned the gesture, smelling Katie's scent on her skin. They stood together before the mirror, taking in the effect. Katie grinned and pulled her close.

"Dracula's dominatrix, and her date." They giggled and swayed back and forth together. "So whaddaya think," she added. "Are we hot, or what?"

Meryl gulped. "I think I need a drink."

Katie gestured to the brandy bottle and laughed. "I think we're out."

"I think that won't do."

"We-e-ell," Katie thought about it, "we could always go downstairs to the restaurant's bar."

"Like this?" Meryl looked at their reflection, titillation and trepidation slam-dancing across her features.

"Sure, why not? Start Halloween a day early." Katie nudged Meryl, and they hugged. "Be worth it, just to see the looks on their faces."

Meryl gazed at their entwined reflection, the mysterious stranger wearing her face and the beautiful creature beside her. "Yeah, it would, wouldn't it?" she replied.

They looked from the reflection to each other, giggling. Their eyes met, and held. The giggling trailed off. Their gaze held. Meryl's buzz spread like a sleeping nerve coming awake, becoming a hot flush across her skin. Then she pulled away, not wanting to break the contact, afraid to maintain it.

"Drink," she said.

Katie nodded. "Yeah."

"Now."

"Yeah." Katie disengaged and walked over to her dresser.

"Katie—" Meryl began, and stopped. Katie turned around and looked at her, eyes sparkling.

"Thanks."

Katie nodded.

"Yeah."

She scooped up her keys, grabbed two twenties, and tucked them, winking, into the crease of her cleavage. Then she leaned over and cupped her hand around the candle. Meryl shivered and took one last look at her reflection just as Katie blew the candle out.

The stranger was smiling.

10
EXTREMITIES

In the walls.

Alive like the earth, the room's six walls. Alive like the air, and the infinite space beyond. Alive like the light. Alive like the darkness. Alive with the energy that bonds them all together.

The room's six walls.

Ceiling and floor, to crown and ground it. Four lateral walls to complete the shape. Crystallized energy, molded in form. Alive in form. Trapped in form.

Trapped inside the walls.

Consciousness, dispersed and random. The ultimate consensus. The room, aware of itself *as* itself: one awareness unfocused, the gestalt of it clear. Awareness, lodged in every floorboard, every inch of plaster, every speck of glass or molded ore.

And then the locus shifted.

The focus became aware of itself as distinct from its surroundings. It pulled together, discovering that most basic, fundamental sentience. i am. Shifting. i am that. Determining. i am that i am. Replicating.

i am that i am.

i am that i am.

The focus tightened around the core. i am that i am i am that i am i am . . .

The focus achieved identity.

The focus was a being.

The being was a soul.

Its awareness pulled tight as a fiber-optic beam, a narrow vessel stretched across a vast swirling oblivion, with a small circle of light at either end. At one end, the door to the world it had so recently departed.

At the other, the doorway to the one that beckoned.

And in the middle, wedged so firmly between, the soul. Hanging on.

Afraid.

It remembered some things: tiny scraps of feeling, of thought, of moments frozen in time. It hoarded them to itself, holding on. It had pitched itself into this place, wanting only to be free of the world it had thrown away, the identity it had shattered into a billion glittering shards. Now it could not let go, could not continue along the path it had chosen. Now, it wanted only to return.

It clawed its way back with strength born of purest will, will born of raw, undistilled terror. Bit by bit, it crawled. Toward form.

Some timeless point later it found a niche, a tenuous purchase in space. Its locus was a point in midair, some twelve feet above the floor: a nondescript stub of rope, knotted tightly around a steam pipe. It clung there: sucking the energy and awareness toward it, feeding the awareness of itself as separate, as distinct.

Concentrating. Fighting for a singular point of view.

i am that i am that i am that . . .

Hovering directly above the couch.

Looking down, then, at the sleeping women. Watching them curl together on the couch, their bodies (energy trapped in form) shifting beneath the blanket, responding unconsciously to the gaze upon them. Reaching out toward their lifeline, fighting the Pull from behind, the terrifying Pull that threatened to suck it back into the blackness, and beyond . . .

The dream came like a thunderhead, rolling across the black plains of sleep.

She felt it before she heard it, heard it before she saw it. The air bore its presence, heavy as the scent of a gathering storm. Every fiber of her being dreaded its coming. There was nowhere to run, no place to hide. Her conscious mind scrambled for shelter, fought to slam the doorway shut

efore the full force of it hit her. Her awareness struggled
p from sleep...

...and in the split-second before the clouds parted, she
w it clearly: the horror dangling above her, the air alive
ith buzzing flies and unbearable stench, the rotting
uman host, flexing extremities purple with settled blood,
eaching blindly out and showering her with a slow pale
rickle of maggot rain...

Katie awoke with a strangled scream welling in her
hroat. She jerked upright, bathed in sweat, feeling the
oom spin madly before her. She looked at the ceiling and
inched.

Above her, only darkness.

She collapsed back into the sofa cushions, feeling Meryl's
leeping form nestled hot beside her. Meryl stirred but
id not awaken. Katie's stomach churned and roiled. The
uzzing in her ears subsided into a dull pinpoint ache in
he center of her forehead. She wanted to get up, go pee,
hrow up, run away. But she didn't. She didn't move.

She just stayed right where she was, staring at the
eiling, until just before dawn. Afraid.

Of the dream. Of the realization. Of the vision with the
orribly familiar face.

Whose dead lips peeled back, black tongue lolling.

And called her by name...

THE SPIRIT OF THINGS

They were screaming downstairs, in Bob Wallach's apartment. He couldn't tell how many people Bob had down there with him. He couldn't even tell how much of it was human screaming. He really didn't want to know.

"Damn it all, I tried to warn him," Wertzel hissed. It didn't help. The floorboards thudded and death-twitched beneath his feet. Books and knickknacks threatened to tumble from their perches. Something snapped and shattered against a wall below: furniture, bone, he couldn't be sure. A window exploded into tinkling shards. The stereo died in mid-song, groaning.

The screaming got louder, crazier. Wertzel swallowed painfully and white-knuckled the handgrip of his .45. Something, decidedly not human, shrieked. The screaming got worse, if that was possible.

A single light bulb burned in the center of the white ceiling. Jake Wertzel sat directly below it on a rickety wooden chair, his back pointed toward the only featureless wall in his third-floor walkup studio apartment. To his right were the windows that faced 37th Street. To his left were the doorways to his closet, his bathroom, the hallway and stairs beyond. Before him lay the kitchenette, the unusable fireplace, his bed.

Every entrance to the room . . . the windows, the doors, the mouth of the fireplace . . . were completely boarded up and blockaded. He hoped that it would be enough.

The walls and the floorboards were ceasing to shudder. The screaming, which had continued to mount, now began to disassemble into its component parts. He could distinguish maybe half a dozen voices, all veering off toward their separate grand finales: this one, a woman's spiraling up toward the ultrasonic as if someone or something were slowly twisting a dial; this one, a man's trumpeting dissonant jazz that closed with a jagged, moist

160

urbling sound; this one, which could have been either
sex, rattling off a string of syllables that ended, very
clearly, with the word *no*. Wertzel knew for a fact that that
was the word, because it hovered in the air for a good ten
seconds before something made a sound like shredding
paper and silenced it.

There was more. Much more. *Wallach must've been
having some kind of a party,* Wertzel thought bitterly.
Maybe he thought there was safety in numbers. A pair of
voices warbled and whooped in screeching, agonized
harmony. *Stupid goddam kid. I tried to warn him . . .*

The screaming stopped, abruptly.

And the feeding sounds began.

Wertzel cupped his hands over his ears, clammy shields
against the horror. A blood-red ocean roared and surged
inside his head. It was better, but it was not enough. He
wanted to hum something, set up a monochromatic drone
that would amplify itself against the confines of his skull,
drown out the cracking and smacking and slurping from
below. He didn't dare. The tiniest sound might be enough
to attract them. Even his breathing was carefully modulat-
ed for silence.

It went on for five minutes that seemed very much like
forever.

Jake Wertzel was a squat, stocky man in his late thirties:
barrel chest, paunch beneath it, massive arms to either
side. Twenty years on the loading docks will do it to you.
His features were pinched and unlovely; his hairline had
receded all the way to the back of his head, crowning him
with a bald plateau that shimmered in the light from the
bare bulb in the ceiling. He looked like a man who had
known much hardship, very little happiness. He looked
exactly like what he was.

He wished to God that he were not so horribly alone.

He remembered the dogs. Fleetingly, absurdly, he wished
that they were still alive, wagging their tails or lapping at
his cheeks or humping his knees with witless abandon.
He had picked them up at the Humane Society three
weeks before, anticipating the holiday rush: a pair of big,
stupid, ungainly mutts that he named Haystacks and Calhoon.
Wertzel had done his human best to remain detached

from them, knowing what fate had in store. But thre
weeks is a long time: more than enough time to grow fon
of them, their brainless devotion. More than enough tim
to make him miss them now.

At 10:45, the absolute latest that he could wait, Wertze
gave the last supper to Haystacks and Calhoon. Th
Purina Dog Chow was laced with enough sedatives t
knock out an army: he wanted to make sure that they fe
no pain. Fifteen minutes later, they were down for th
count.

Wertzel had dragged them out into the hallway, gutte
them, drawn a huge cross on the door with their bloo
and left them on the matt: paws up, tongues lolling.

Then he had gone back into the apartment, locked an
bolted and nailed the door shut, boarded it up with heav
planks he had taken from skids at the loading dock
pushed the chest of drawers in front of it, and moved t
the chair in the middle of the room.

To wait. And hope.

It was now twenty after twelve. The witching hour ha
struck.

And they had come.

"Oh, God," he moaned, and was startled by ho
loudly the words boomed in his ears. His hands jerke
away from the sides of his head, and he realized that th
downstairs had gone almost completely silent. There wa
a faint, airy sound that might have been the hissing of th
pipes. Somehow, he didn't believe it.

Why me? he thought. *Why here? Why now?* Last yea
the worst of it had gone down in Chelsea and the Village
The year before that . . . the first year . . . had laid waste t
much of the Upper East Side. If there was a pattern there
Wertzel couldn't see it; but he'd hoped that the horro
would focus itself uptown again, give him enough time t
save up enough money to maybe get the hell out of Ne
York before the fall.

As if there were anywhere safe to go.

Most of all, he wished that things would revert to th
way they used to be. He wished for the sound of chi
dren's voices, giddy with laughter and hoarse with de

nands. He wished for cheesy plastic masks, eye-holes
sliced in ratty sheets, prosthetic warts and theatrical blood.

He longed for the days when it was easy to pretend that
he whole thing was just a joke.

Gone now, his mind whispered silent. *All gone. All
gone . . .*

They were coming up the stairs.

Wertzel felt his bowels tighten like a hangman's knot.
Ice water drained down his spine and gathered in the pit
of his stomach. His scrotum constricted like a slug under a
magnifying glass, and hot moisture like acid seeped into
his eyes from the unlimited slope of his forehead.

They were coming up the stairs. He didn't know what
they were, what they looked like, how they moved. He
didn't want to know. They made sounds that his ears
rejected as unreal, though his heart and soul knew better.
They skittered and slithered and fluttered and muttered
and howled like brain-damaged hyenas from Hell. One of
them made a noise like a spoons-player in a jug band; it
moved along the stairway wall with incredible speed,
blasted down the hall toward him, clattered across the
length of the door in a split-second, raced halfway up to
the fourth floor, and came all the way back before the
others reached the third floor landing.

One of them made the walls shake as it approached.

I will not move, he urged himself with a silent, sickly
whining voice. *I will not scream. I will not lose control.*
He prayed that the sacrifice would work. Rumor had it
that blood offerings had been known to, on occasion.

Wertzel found himself wishing, suddenly, that he'd sacrificed a child instead: supposedly, they worked the best.
But killing the dogs had been bad enough.

At the time.

They were coming down the hall. They were coming to
his door. The books and knickknacks that had threatened to
tumble now made good of their promise, slamming and
shattering against the floor, filling the room with gunshot
echoes that ricocheted off the walls. The heavy chest of
drawers rocked back and forth on its heels like a Bozo
punching bag. The kitchen cupboard flew open; plates

and saucers and glasses and cups exploded into the sink
like a string of firecrackers.

Wertzel screamed and pissed himself. He couldn't help
it. The crotch of his Lee jeans ballooned with moisture,
and wet sticky tendrils crept down his thighs, while his
mouth flew open and all the terror in his heart flew up, up
and out in a torrential spasm.

*"NO PLEASE GOD NO PLEASE NO OH GOD
PLEASE DON'T KILL ME! I . . . I . . ."*

In the bathroom, behind the boarded-up door, the toilet
flushed.

". . . I . . . I . . ."

A light came on in the sealed closet. There was the
sound of rending fabric.

". . . I . . ."

Something scratched against the window, screeched
and flapped its leathery wings.

"I GAVE YOU A SACRIFICE!" he bellowed. *"I GAVE
YOU A SACRIFICE. PLEASE DON'T KILL ME, OH
GOD PLEASE I'LL DO ANYTHING YOU WANT . . ."*

Silence.

Jake Wertzel fell back in his seat, breath catching in his
throat. The room had stopped shaking. Nothing moved.
Nothing fell.

Silence from the bathroom.

Silence from the closet.

Silence from the windows.

Silence in the hall.

Wertzel held his breath for a good thirty seconds, not
daring to believe.

Silence.

Slowly, then, he let out one long shuddering exhalation.
The muscles in his face twitched; the corners of his mouth
arced tentatively upward in a smile. He let the useless .45
dangle by one finger like an ornament on an artificial tree.

Then he started to cry.

And *God*, did it ever feel good to cry, to let out all the
pent-up emotion, to bask and wallow in the fact that he
was *alive!* he was *alive!* and no sound remained to haunt
him but the manic intermingling of his own tears and
laughter, punctuated by the steady . . .

(Drip. Drip. Drip.)

Of what? He laughed and cried some more. It could have been swollen teardrops, landing at his feet. It could have been the piss, still dribbling down his legs. Lord knew he had dropped enough fluids in the last few minutes to account for any amount of . . .

(Drip. Drip. Drip.)

It was coming from above him.

He opened his eyes.

The room was turning red.

(Drip. Drip. Drip.)

He looked up.

There was a quarter-inch of blood at the bottom of the light bulb in the center of the ceiling, directly above his head. He looked up just in time to watch a tiny blue spark catch off the filament, just before the bulb blew up, showering him with blood and broken glass.

And total darkness.

Wertzel shrieked and hit the floor on his hands and knees. The glass bit through his clothes, his skin, sinking into the meat and lodging there like bee-stingers. He yowled and rolled over. His back erupted with pain.

The toilet flushed.

Light winked on under the closet door.

Something dragged its talons along the window-glass outside.

And the spitfire staccato of the wall-climbing thing burst out from the hole in the wall behind the oven, the hole he had forgotten to patch, the hole that now allowed it entrance. Like a methedrine freak with a pair of spoons, it clattered and streaked toward him so fast that he barely had time to aim the .45 in the direction of the sound and fire.

In the muzzle-flash, he could see the scuttling crabthing turn inside-out and spray all over the kitchenette. Then it was dark again, totally dark. Spots danced in front of his eyes. His ears were filled with the hiss of melting metal as the crabthing's guts ate holes in the oven, the Frigidaire . . .

No.

Not total darkness.

In the fireplace, something was moving. He could see it through the cracks between the boards, red and yellow and orange like flame. But brighter. More solid.

And moving.

A pair of tiny flaming hands pried their way between the boards. The wood crackled and blackened and parted at their touch. A tiny head poked through the opening.

It stared at him.

And suddenly Wertzel knew why there would be no more plastic masks, no tattered sheets with holes for the eyes, no warts and scars and blood from the lab. Suddenly, he knew why they had come.

They had been watching, and waiting, for a long long time. They had watched the Church march arrogantly across the face of the earth, twisting the old pagan holidays to suit it, stripping and homogenizing away all meaning, then positing nonsense in its place.

And though centuries passed like seconds to them, it still dragged on too long. Where the Great Dark Ones had once strode the earth, there now stood Kolchak, the Night Stalker and Caspar, the Friendly Ghost. They had seen the shitty movies. They had read the shitty books. They had seen themselves turned into limp-wristed Bela Lugosis and carrot-headed James Arnesses, heard too many bad actors get the spells all wrong and conjure up demons that couldn't scare the fleas off a pink-nosed bunny.

Worst of all, they had seen All Hallow's Eve transformed into a ritual for posturing, preening babies; had seen their glorious faces mocked and strung up in too many dime store windows. For far too long.

But that was over.

Wertzel understood it all, staring into those coal-black, ageless eyes.

He understood perfectly.

He started to scream.

Then the windows imploded, and the front door flew apart like a matchstick house in a hurricane's hands, and the Old Ones slithered and stalked and soared into Jake Wertzel's third floor walkup apartment in beautiful Godless Midtown Manhattan.

After a while, the screaming stopped.

And the feeding sounds began.

Halloween. It ain't just kid stuff.

Any more.

11
SPEAK OF THE DEVIL

Lee Cave had been at work since seven ayem, as usual: sittin' on his duff in the freight elevator, waiting for something to happen. The day offered up predictable pockets of activity—sweaty homeboys with crates and boxes, props and promo-pieces heading up to Tower Records' storage—but the rest of the time, his job was simply to be there in case something happened.

In the yawning space between, he kept his brain busy: with the endlessly changing cast of characters visible through his hallway-wide window on the world, with the *Daily News* or the *Post*, and the occasional paperback book. This week's entry—he read real slow—was another one of those Ruth Montgomery things that his daughter Bobbi kept handing off to him (enlightening him, she liked to think; barely eighteen years old, born and raised in Jamaica, Queens, and she already knew all the answers to the secrets of the universe).

Strangers Among Us, this one was called, and it was all about spirits from the other side that were poppin' in and takin' over the bodies of people who had pretty much let their own spirits fizzle out. Walk-ins, Ruth Montgomery called them, and supposedly they were friendly spirits (sorta like Casper, he chuckled to himself) that were here to help us usher in the New Age, keep us from blowin' the titties right off of the world.

All kidding aside, he thought that walk-ins were a pretty far-fetched idea, though he could not swear with any certainty that he didn't believe it—some. Lee Cave was born and raised Baptist back in the twenties in Bayou St. John, which was pretty built up now but at the time was a

heavily wooded area in the Lakeside section of New
Orleans. Lots of voodoo, lot of *gris-gris* mojo. Hell, his
own great-gran'mama, a big woman with a face like a raisin
at midnight and the clearest eyes he ever saw, was a real
live *Mambo-Bokour*, a voodoo priestess straight from Africa.
And much as his own mama hated it, Lee grew up with an
ear in either world, hearing all manner of things: how you
could hurt an enemy by putting his name in a dead bird's
mouth and letting the bird dry up, how you could inflict a
slow and painful death on a man by burying his picture
face-down and burning a black candle over it, then waiting
for the image to fade away. About how if you said your
prayers in the dark they went to the devil, and not to
God.

About how ghosts could linger on, hungering for believ-
ers, and how dreams carried messages from the gods...

Lee shuddered. Aw, hell. Piss on Ruth Montgomery.
Gimme the willies. Most of the people he'd met who'd
let their spark go out were still walking around without
one; meanwhile, the world's poor sagging titties looked
closer to blowin' off every time he turned around. And
though he was by nature an optimistic man, most of
what he'd seen from disembodied spirits weren't nothin'
to cheer about.

A buzzer rang. He turned to look.

The ninth floor.

Speak of the devil, he thought.

Not a joke. All at once, it was back in his head: the
sound, the smell, the sight, the stories. It set his own
personal alarm system off; his nerves began to jangle.

"Aw, hell," he muttered.

The buzzer rang again.

Lee Cave was a man who had learned to trust his
feelings. Often enough it had made more sense than
anything else. People lied; his own mind lied; the official
so-called "facts" were lies a good bit more often than not.
But his feelings were cleaner, more straight to the point.

His feeling was that this was not bound to be good.

"Just a matter of time," he muttered. "Damn..."; a
heavy sigh, as he hoisted up out of his seat, slid the doors

shut, set the box in motion. He felt the elevator, rising. And his spirits, sinking.

All the way up, he tried to wipe the pictures from his mind... truth be told, there'd hardly been a day since they found that boy that he hadn't been tryin' to wipe the pictures from his mind. Why today should be any different was a question not even worth askin'.

Still, he couldn't shake the feeling that today, far from wiping the pictures, would ask him to conjure them back up again. And when he saw the girl who had summoned him, he knew it for a fact.

Because it was the l'il blonde from the restaurant—Sunshine, he had called her, and, Lord, had it ever been the truth—only she didn't look quite so sunshiny today. Her hair was black as the ace of spades, for one thing, and when she tried to smile just now, there was no light behind it. What he saw instead were the storm clouds behind a set of sunken eyes, the skin beneath them fretful and taut, their bright blue made hazy by lack of sleep... and something else. She looked haunted. Worse.

She looked ridden.

More booger-bears, creeping back from the shadows: ghosts and dreams and messages from gods. The gods could do so many things: they could give you life, they could tell you to throw it away. They could come to you in your sleep and ride you like the wind. One god might favor a particular person. One god might even kill the favorite of another.

And a ghost might choose to linger, to attract enough power to become a loa, a spirit. And that spirit, gaining power, might wish to become a god itself.

If it could hang around long enough...

Beside him the girl shuddered, an involuntary tremor. He looked at her, and for the barest moment she met his gaze. It was painful to behold. When she looked away, it was almost a relief.

Except that the damage was already done.

Contact had been made.

And the floodgates pried opened...

* * *

The first thing, always, that came to mind—before the smell, before the sight—was the sound of buzzing flies. Surprisingly loud, enthusiastic even. Buzzing. Echoing down the elevator shaft.

He had noticed it on Friday, the seventeenth of July. His hearing wasn't so good, and hadn't been for a while; but when several messengers in a row pointed it out, it singled itself out from the rest of the noise and annoyed him the rest of the day. At six, he went home. End of story.

Until Monday, when the flies were in the elevator shaft.

Not too many, at first, and sluggish as hell; of course, it was only the fourth day in a row that had temperatures up at the top of the nineties. He swatted at them when they lighted, and cursed them when they fell; but he was basically too miserable to give them much thought.

Until Tuesday, when it began to really cut through.

He'd had a little trouble explaining that to the cops, but the answer was as simple as it was pathetic. Fact was, the city garbage strike was in its third week by that point. Leave it to New York sanitation to wait for the dog days. A good, sound strategy—they made their point—but pretty damn unpleasant for the man on the street. From Lee's point of view, it was hard to tell one kind of rot from another.

Except when the stench in the elevator shaft began competing with the stench on Broadway, and winning.

And the buzzing from the top floor was getting louder every day.

It wasn't until Wednesday morning that Rocco the super listened to Lee, and agreed to check it out. He was a lazy so-and-so, and none too clean hisself. But even ol' Rocco made a prune face when he got a whiff of what was going down. And when they took a ride up to investigate, they never made it past the seventh floor.

At 10:15, the police were there. They took one whiff, and that was it. Next thing he knew, he was escorting them up.

And when they opened the door...

* * *

The gods could ride you in your dreams. Lee could well enough believe it; here in the city of dreams, he saw a lot of people who looked ridden.

And sometimes their gods rode them right into the ground...

Sunshine and Lee slid down the shaft. The rumble of the machinery was nothing compared to the roar of the silence between them. It made him think about the flies, the incredible sound they'd made: almost deafening, once the door was open. So loud you could scarcely hear yourself choke. He closed his eyes, and the blackness was alive with their memory: hundreds, maybe thousands, their fat blue-green iridescent bodies so thick in the air you could barely see through to the wall beyond.

Little girl, you don't really wanna know, he thought to himself, biting back on the image. They were coming down by the fourth floor now. The Caribbean. Nice. He wished to hell he was there instead.

He could feel her trembling.

The last few floors seemed to take forever. Too much time to think. Too much time to remember.

The thing on the rope....

The ground floor arrived. He whistled softly, threw open the door, and stood aside.

The girl didn't move.

"We're here," he said softly.

She nodded. Her eyes flickered panic.

"Okay." Heavy sigh. "I been afraid this might happen." She looked at him then. It about broke his heart.

"You wanna tell me about it?"

Her mouth had gone dry, the lips stuck together. It took her a minute to whip up the spit. To speak now would be to cross a line that he was sure she didn't want to cross. Just as sure as the knowledge that she had no choice in the matter. No choice at all.

"I... need to know," she began, "whose apartment it was. Before."

"His name's Glen Fitzpatrick. Photographer fella." Pause. How much? She knew that he knew that she knew that he knew; it was a conspiracy of denial in the face of certainty.

Lee felt awful as he took the next step, saying, "But that ain't what you're askin', is it . . ."

"Oh, God."

He was surprised by the interruption, even more surprised by the confusion and pain in her eyes.

"Oh, God. What happened to him?"

"No, no! He's fine!" Lee blurted, confused. "It was the other boy that hung hisself: a friend of his, some writer fella—"

But she didn't hear; or if she did, it didn't matter. She was running, then, away from him, away from whatever she'd gleaned from his words, the pain of it something she carried with her as she disappeared into the streets.

Leaving him with a very bad feeling indeed: a feeling that things would get a whole lot worse before they could possibly get better . . .

SHELLS

Low tide, and the gentle susurration of baywater waves. Reaching up on the shore, toward the lighter sand some eight feet inland. Falling back in ceaseless cycle, collapsing in the face of the next wave in.

Also reaching, he thought.

Also doomed.

"You're a cheerful guy," Marty dryly informed himself. "It must be your God-given calling in life: to spread happiness and joy wherever you may roam..."

His voice died in mid-rumination. It had plenty of room to die in. The beach was long and chill and all but deserted. It reminded him of the last dozen or so clubs he'd played. His voice had died there, too.

Along with his career, and any hope of its resurrection.

Marty Swansick was philosophical. At this point, it was the only thing left to be. He was forty-five years old. Nearly half of those years had been spent in a grueling, frequently desperate struggle to prove that he really was a hysterically funny guy. His act had been honed to surgical incisiveness by two solid decades of amateur nights, sweaty half-hour stints at places like the Comedy Cellar, the periodic street-corner stand-up routines, and Columbus Circle or Washington Square Park. It was a hard life in search of an impossible dream, but the struggle only served to sharpen his edge. Marty Swansick fought like hell and hustled shamelessly while all around him friends sold out or rolled over for a weekly paycheck and a taste of respectability.

And his folly paid off: a couple of miraculous walk-ons for sitcoms had gotten him a bit part in the ill-fated *Long As It Takes* for CBS. The show bombed, but Lasko (the lovable "flea-bitten super of a Lower East Side slum") had been roundly acclaimed. Lasko led to Letterman led to

Carson led to cable led to a pilot of his own and a slew of bookings in packed houses of increasing distinction.

Suddenly, Marty Swansick had an agent, an upcoming series, and more money than he rightly knew what to do with. Suddenly, the impossible had become the probable had become the likely had become the all-too-easy. And suddenly, over a night that had lasted twenty-seven years, Marty Swansick was a star.

"*Was* a star," he muttered, affirming the past tense. "For one brief, shining moment that lasted all of two years, you were a star, my friend. You had it all." He let out a dry chuckle of joyless amusement.

"And then," he continued, "in the immortal words of Robin Williams: 'I clawed my way to the middle, and then fucked my way down . . .'"

His soliloquy was interrupted by a thunderous boom from across the water. With the sky clouding over as it was, the sound could have passed for real thunder; but Marty knew it was just the boys down at the Aberdeen Proving Grounds, where the combined might of the United States Military got together to test their toys.

Like little kids, he mused, glancing some two hundred yards down the beach at a handful of prepubescents. They were the only other people in sight, and they were busy, busy, busy: oblivious to the chilling clouds and ersatz thunder, hard at work on something big.

It was a sand castle, he guessed. And they labored on it with the same kind of single-minded fervor that he imagined going down at ol' Aberdeen, where the hits just kept a-comin' every couple of minutes.

Someday, he thought, they'll get to test those toys for real. Then ol' Marty Swansick can take his place among the other great comedians of his age: Dangerfield, Cosby, Hope, Reagan, Gorbechev, Falwell . . . too many to list, all topping the charts on the Hit Parade to oblivion.

Such balming bitterness was scant comfort as Marty watched the kids play. He wondered what, if anything, they thought about the constant exposure to the overtures of the Death Machine. *Probably think it's neat; all flash and no pain. They have no idea how genuinely scary it is. They have no idea . . .*

There was a sudden stirring behind him. He turned to see a big old basset hound padding straight for him like a hairy Polish sausage on legs. It came right up, grinning a lopsided doggie grin, snuffling his feet. He stopped and ran his hand along its well-padded back.

"Well, hey, ol' fella!" he burbled, scratching its floppy ears. The dog just panted and lolled its tongue at him. "So how's tricks, huh? How's life as a witless quadruped?" The insult went clear over his fuzzy friend's head. Like most of my hecklers, he observed, continuing to skritch and scratch away.

Another loud ka-boom went off in the interests of world peace and national security. The basset hound pointed its thick head skyward, eyes flickering with confusion. Marty swatted it playfully on the ass and said, "Big storm brewing, buddy. Better get on home, before it's too late."

The dog went galumphing off through the sand, on a collision course with the kids. He guessed they'd be shooing him away in two minutes flat. It was a dog's life.

Ain't it the truth, he thought, feeling the dark clouds gather inside as the surf brushed his feet. A proverbial infinitude of sandy granules lay there, topped by an infinitude of pebbles that sat upon the sand like sprinkles on a sundae. None of which held his interest.

His eyes were focused, instead, on a pretty white shell half-buried at his feet. It was roughly the size of the nail on his pinkie, roughly the color of sun-bleached bone. There was another one beside it. And another. And another. One of them was almost as big as the palm of his hand. But the rest were small. Very small.

There were millions of them, up and down Crystal Beach. They had all been alive once, God only knew how long ago; their deaths had gone unnoticed by all save themselves. And the waves, which pounded them relentlessly into the shore.

So many tiny souls, he thought. *All gone. All gone.*

Just like that.

More sonic booms from Aberdeen. Another chill gust of sea breeze. Marty tucked up the collar of his windbreaker and looked down the beach: two of the kids were playing with the basset by the base of the expanding castle. He chuckled, momentarily charmed by nostalgic pangs, then felt his attention drawn inextricably back. Toward the shells. The sand.

While the changing tide reached its liquid fingers out toward the shore, then slipped back in whispering failure. And the last eight months rolled in like those vanquished waves, drowning him in the details of his fall . . .

He'd been warned. Oh, yes. By old friends. By family. By none other than his agent, Murray the Shark, who drew him aside in an uncharacteristically paternal tone and said, "Marty, you're a very funny guy. Right now you're on top of the world. Watch. Your. Step."

It was a miracle on the order of the loaves and fishes, this concern. It had almost managed to cut through the high-voltage burble that had become the stuff of daily life. Almost.

"I can protect you from the jackals," he'd said, "and I can protect you from the vultures, 'cause that's my job. But I can't. Protect you. From. Yourself."

The words stung with the dead-on accuracy of twenty-twenty hindsight as wave upon lurid wave crashed down . . .

Then there was the drink. The track. The girls girls girls: dozens of them, outclassing him by a country mile, all aching for a piece of the first real money in his miserable life, encouraging him to believe that it would last forever and ever and . . .

Two thousand a month for his Central Park West co-op with the spectacular view. One-hundred-fifty-dollar dinners for two, every night. Broadway shows at one hundred dollars a clip. Nose candy. The occasional nine-hundred-dollar weekend bacchanal at the Plaza Hotel. More nose candy. A trip or two to Europe.

A lot of trips to Plato's Retreat.

And then, when he was too far in to ever escape unscathed, the forty-two grand he'd plunked down on his "summer retreat": a quaint little cottage on Crystal Beach, not far from his ancestral stomping grounds of Cecilton, Maryland. It was a place to escape: far from the hurly-burly, with only the crashing waves and the guns of Aberdeen to remind him of worldly reality . . .

"Ah, but let us not forget," he said aloud, "the way I blew

the pilot. And let us not forget," while the regret and self-pity welled up in his eyes, "the way I came off as an arrogant, sniping blowhard on my third and last *Tonight Show* appearance. And let us not forget," fingering the long-emptied vial in his pocket, "all the many, many dollars I pissed up my nose or down the drain. And let us not forget . . ."

But he wanted to forget. Oh, yes.

Which was why he'd fled the city. To escape, to recoup, to find the edge he'd lost when life got soft. To watch innocent children who had their lives and dreams still before them, playing in the sand.

To say goodbye.

Marty walked, and watched. While the dark clouds gathered.

And the sunlight waned.

The basset hound was gone, which didn't surprise him a bit. The castle was spectacular, which surprised him quite a bit. His eyesight, unlike his timing or his credit, was still pretty close to perfect. He could see a fairly awesome display of moats and turrets and sturdy walls from a hundred and fifty yards away.

One of the kids was calling to him. The rest of them joined in, shouting and gesticulating. He hollered, "I CAN'T HEAR YOU!" and continued toward them, thinking *hope springs eternal, creation lives, sure I've blown it but I hope to God you kids live long enough to make your dreams come true . . .*

The first thing he noticed was the jutting pile of sand. At first he'd mistaken it for a washed-out castle; then he realized that the big white thing poking out of the top was the enormous skull of a fish. Its mere size was disorienting enough: as large as the head of a garden trowel, good eating for any hearty fisherman. He drew nearer, checking it out.

It was a fish, alrightee. No doubt about it. But why had it been buried? And why so close to the water?

As Marty moved abreast of the mound, it occurred to him that the sand beneath the skull was gently stirring. He moved closer still, and the cause became apparent.

There were tiny pools of tiny maggots churning over the base of the skull.

"Yuk," he said, addressing the maggots. "That's disgusting." The feeding continued, unshamed. The little-kid shouting continued, unabated, and it wasn't long before the patter of tiny feet drew near.

"Hey, mister!" his tiny assailant shouted. It was an adorable little boy, maybe six years old: all scruff blonde hair and scrawny tan limbs, huge potbelly poking out of Hang Ten shorts. "You gotta see our castle, mister. It's really neat!"

Marty felt himself momentarily torn between the kinetic bundle of enthusiasm before him and the squirming, sightless death-dance behind. It passed quickly; he knew that this would be his last glimpse of Crystal Beach. The sale of the cottage had been confirmed yesterday. Tomorrow, a Mr. and Mrs. Putnam from Baltimore would take possession, displacing him forever. He would score a modest jump in value which, by the time he settled all his outstanding accounts with the financiers and the snowmen, would leave him just about enough to see through another half a month in the New York City he had come to despise.

None of which mattered doodly-squat to the kid, whose name was Shaun, who really was six and sizzling with energy. "We gotta hurry!" he cried with all the patience of youth. "The tide's gonna change!"

Marty couldn't argue with that. He gazed down into the ebullient blue eyes and felt the crust on his heart soften just a little. "Okay, junior," he said. "Lead on."

Shaun took him by the hand. Aberdeen boomed.

And the mound began to crumble under the tide's first kiss.

■

It was all Marty could do to keep up with the boy's frantic, exuberant pace. They walked on the perimeter of the encroaching surf, heading for the castle. All the while, the kid bubbled and babbled of its glories: how they'd all pitched in, how he'd helped to dig the moat, collect the shells that brightly adorned the walls. All the while, Aberdeen's guns thumped and thudded. As they walked,

Marty felt the bleak existential funk that had been pushed so precariously back, thinking, *they really don't know, they have no idea . . .*

And they were there; the four other kids all standing by, alert and beaming. Two more boys, a pair of girls, not a one of them older than twelve. They all stood unmindful of the chill breeze that blew off the water. They all had the same bright eyes and lupine faces, the same giddy exhilaration at being a part of something really special.

On the other hand, he noted, *they've got every right to be proud.* The castle got better the closer he came. He could see how they'd used trickling water to "age" the walls and turrets, made pillars from driftwood. He flashed on how high the walls were, and how solid; even from fifty yards' distance, it was without a doubt the best he'd ever seen.

All the while, Shaun kept talking: how great his brothers and sisters were, how they did this all the time but this was the best ever! Marty noted that the walls behind the bold front extended easily four feet toward the water. They'd even pulled up weeds and replanted them to look like a manicured arbor of vines. His heart tugged at the sight of such detail. They'd built an ornate walkway, leading from the driftwood drawbridge over the moat, every bit as impressive as the road to Oz.

A roadway, paved completely with a carpet of diminutive shells.

It was exquisite. It reminded him, somehow, of King Tut's tomb: an archeological treasure for some future generation to boggle over.

But for the encroaching tide; Marty suddenly wished himself the camera-toting type, that he might somehow become a part of this fleeting moment. Give them, and himself, something to remember it by . . .

Then the five children clambered around him, enthused. He waded through them, closing in on the wonder they'd wrought. The jokes, the customary glib patter, weren't forthcoming—he was too much in awe—and when the eldest boy withdrew from the pack, he scarcely even noticed.

The tallest of the girls—very pretty, reed-slender—said,

"Take a look inside. That's the best part of all." He nodded, obliging, and peered over the wall.

The dog was there, belly-up. The back of its skull had been staved in; a layer of sand had encrusted the exposed brain and bone. Its thick head pointed skyward, dead eyes flecked with sand and confusion. Marty expended perhaps another second in terror and disbelief, staring down at the body.

And then the eldest child returned.

The first blow of the Boy Scout hatchet caught him squarely in the stomach. He could feel his guts blow open. He could hear them. See them. Smell them. He had been wheeling as it happened, so the blow caught him off-balance. He teetered at the edge of the hole, while the hatchet slid wetly away.

The next blow caught him bluntly at the bridge of the nose. It was not quite enough to kill him outright, but the force of impact was sufficient to topple him backward into the hole.

My name is Marty Swansick I'm a very funny guy were the words that crowded his brain as he landed on the stiffening hound, the sky roiling crazily above. A genuine burst of thunder erupted; when Aberdeen followed, it seemed pale by comparison.

But the kids; they loved it. They thrived on it. Suddenly, as he stared up into their happy, busy faces, he knew that *they knew*! Suddenly, he knew exactly what the sound meant to them.

It made him almost glad that he was leaving.

Almost.

Then the walls of the castle caved in under a flurry of laughter and limbs, sending sand down to drown him. And Marty fought like hell; he kicked and spat and thrashed with a newfound will to live that might have saved him, a month or a week or a minute earlier. Marty Swansick actually had some edge left, after all.

Too little, too late.

More sand tumbled down. Little stones.

Little shells.

When the tomb was sealed and the ritual concluded, the children clasped hands and smiled. The Big Voice le out another volley of approval. They were thrilled, of course, although they didn't dare let on; they had too well mastered the innocent faces that were so much a part of their current roles. The youngest stared out across the water in awe as the eldest explained once more:

Soon, very soon, they would inherit the earth. The Big Voice told them so. And there would be so very much to do in that brave new world.

Many exquisite holes to dig.

Many, many rituals to perform.

As they left the beach, more thunder erupted. It was louder—maybe even stronger—but the Big Voice was the one that spoke directly to them.

Soon, it said.

Very soon . . .

■

A little while later, the tide rumbled in.

And the rain began to pour.

12
VOLITION

He was, sad to say, not surprised in the least to find her at his door.

Oh, bloody saviour on a stick, he thought. Here's just what I fucking need.

"Colin," she said, her voice a high peep that slurred only a trifle, her balance unsteady against the doorframe. "Colin, please. I need to talk to you." The mingling reeks of gin and heartbreak preceded her with an unsavory zeal, fogging up the corridor.

"Why?" That seemed direct enough. Just the sight of her was curling the hair in his nostrils, not to mention her unbottled sachet. Evidently, the headache he already had, had been deemed insufficient by the heavenly host.

"Colin, please..." Ah, the taste of fine whine. Any moment now, he expected that she would fling herself against him. He held the door ready to slam in her face, just in case she decided to prove him prophetic. "Please, I'm scared. You gotta let me in..."

"Well, that's not exactly true, though, is it?" he said, letting the words *I'm scared* sink in subliminally. "Seems to me I don't 'gotta' do any such thing. What are you doing here? What the hell do you want?"

"I need to talk to you, Colin! Please!"

"You need to bloody well sober up, that's what you need. You're talking in fucking circles, and you're stinking up the foyer. Why don't you just stumble back to whoever's bed you're flopping in currently and sleep it off?"

"But I can't! You don't unnerstan'..." The first true slur, tripping off of her tongue. "Please!"

"Please!" He mimicked her tone. "Please bugger off!"

True to form, she flung herself forward. He pushed the door between them, and she thudded against it. The screech that ensued was a hideous thing, ratlike when compounded by the scrabbling and *thwunk*ing. He had not shut the door completely, and it required all his strength just to keep her from forcing her way inside.

"PLEASE!" she shrieked.

"Get away from my door!"

"OH GOD, COLIN, PLEASE!"

"Leave my fucking door alone!"

Pummena-pummena-pummena-SLAM! A flurry of fists and feet, culminating in a full-bodied assault that sent him sliding three inches inward. He countervolleyed, digging in with his heels, adrenaline surging through him as he regained the ground he'd lost. She yelped and shrieked some more, and he was amazed to discover that he'd begun to wildly grin. Just where the grand segue from annoyance to amusement had transpired was beyond him, but there it was.

A delightful little strategy occurred to him then: a wee, wicked snippet of transcendent slapstick. Since it seemed evident that she would not go away, the least he could do was control her method of entry. Momentarily lamenting the lack of a handy banana peel, he sighed and then stepped back, away from the door.

At that precise split-second, Katie rocketed inward, an expression of epic surprise on her face. Said face went hurtling toward the floor, the rest of her in close pursuit.

"Perhaps you'd better come inside, then," he quipped as she impacted. The door, of its own volition, slipped quietly shut behind.

Katie just lay there, sobbing rather disjointedly. Evidently, the humor of the incident eluded her. Ah, well. At her present level of intoxication, it was likely that little in the whole of creation was failing to elude her just now.

"So," he said. "You needed to speak with me."

"Urmgh," she replied, between sobs. It raised the faintest flicker of alarm within him.

"Beg pardon?"

"Uh, Gah . . . urmgh!" More emphatic. All at once, he understood.

It was a very short jaunt to the kitchen wastebasket,

replete with its scented plastic liner. He traversed the distance with lightning speed, prayed that he wasn't too late. There were a few fairly foul-smelling items already therein; perhaps she would see them as inspiration. Not that she appeared to require any.

"There," he said, placing the basket in front of her face. She struggled to a crouch before it. "For God's sake, take care how you aim."

"OhhhHHHUALP!!!" she exclaimed. A rush of rancid frothing vomit accompanied her statement. Colin winced and stepped back, watching only to ascertain that she'd respected his wishes. Once that much was clear, he retreated to the kitchen and waited for her biological backfire to run its course.

While he waited, he thought about the little she'd said. I'm scared, I can't. An atypical approach to rewinning his heart, that much was for certain.

Perhaps she was sincerely frightened. In fact, knowing Katie, her sincerity was the last thing he had reason to doubt. And it was common knowledge that—present company excluded—she exercised stupendously poor judgment in her selection of partners. Perhaps she'd found yet another tragic psychopath, God help her; and if that were the case, then surely it behooved him to hear her out. At the very least, he could give her the benefit of his counsel before booting her back out into the maelstrom.

And at most...

He shuddered to think of it. The temptation was too great. Though she was far from enticing at the moment, what with heaving her guts and all, the truth was that the last two months had found his life wanting for something poignant as well as perverse. And the past had proven, if nothing else, that a vulnerable Katie was a savory morsel indeed.

And so the wheel turns once again, he mused, warming to his options.

In the hallway, her retching had tapered to nothing. Perhaps she would achieve coherence soon. If so, perhaps they could proceed apace toward the bottom of things. In a manner of speaking.

And in those final patient moments, he wondered what sort of trouble she'd gotten into this time.

And with what sort of man...

GENTLEMEN

TO BE A MAN.

The words are carved on the sweat-smeared oak of the bar's surface. They're the only four that never seem to change. Like the troll at the taps, the regulars that surround him, the TVs and the black velvet painting of the Hooter Girl that hangs in sad-eyed judgment over all.

TO BE A MAN.

As if that were all there is.

I always hated Bud. He loves it. We drink it. One after another, we pour them down, while Ralph Kramdon bellows about trips to the moon.

And the guys all laugh. You're goddam right.

They know about being a man.

And now, at last, so do I.

I remember the night that my edification began. Every nuance. Every shade. The phone started ringing at 12:45, precisely. It was LeeAnn, of course. She'd just crashed and burned with another asshole relationship, and she needed to talk. And drink. Right now. I knew all this by the first ring. No one else ever called this late. No one.

"Damn," I muttered. "Not again."

There were a lot of good reasons for not answering. It was a shit-soaked night outside, cold rain falling in thick sheets. The steam heat had finally kicked in, and I was down to my jeans. I was halfway into a lumpy joint of some absurdly good Jamaican. *Star Trek* would be on in fifteen minutes. Seeing LeeAnn would make me miserable, and I'd just wind up sourly wanking off when I got home. Yep, a lot of good reasons. I took another toke and settled back in my chair.

The phone rang again. I choked. The smoke exploded in my lungs. I began to cough violently, great redmeat

185

wrenching hacks. The phone rang again. I roared back at
it, defiant, my eyes tearing and my throat desperately
lubing itself with bile.

The phone rang again, and I got out of the chair. What
was the point? The phone would ring forever. The night
was already completely ruined; LeeAnn's face had control
of my mind. I snubbed the joint and placed the butt in my
pocket, for later. The phone rang once more before I
caught it. I coughed a little bit more at the receiver as
I brought it to the side of my head. What did it matter? I
already knew what the first words would be. First, my
name. No *howdy, stranger*, no *long time no see*.

Just:

"David?"

Then:

"David, I need you . . ."

Like clockwork. I gave brief, fleeting audience to the
idea of just hanging up, of pitching the receiver into the
cradle without so much as a whimper. But then her voice,
so characteristically vulnerable, spoke the final two words
in the equation:

"David, *please* . . ."

I was slaughtered.

"Where are you?" I asked. Coughing had made me
roughly twenty times more stoned in a matter of seconds;
the air seemed thicker, my head felt muddier, and the
crackle over the phone line raked like needles in my ears.

She let out a laugh I recognized: the resigned and
barely-in-control one. I coughed. She laughed. I spoke.

"I still don't know where you are."

"I'm at this place called . . ." She paused; I could almost
hear her neck craning. ". . . dammit, I can't tell. It's at
48th and Eighth. The beer is cheap. The guys are all jerks.
It's my kind of place. Can you come?"

"Shouldn't the question be, 'How fast can you get
here?' "

"Jesus, I really *am* predictable."

"You're not the only one," I assured her wearily. "Give
me some time, okay? I don't have any clothes on."

"Hubba hubba."

"Don't tease me, LeeAnn. I'm not a well man."

"Aw, poor baby."

I closed my eyes, and LeeAnn was behind them: leaning against a bar with brass rails, china-doll lips pouting, green-eyed gaze languidly drifting as her T-shirt slowly hiked its way past her breasts and over her ash-blonde head. *Never happen,* my rational mind reminded me flatly. It sounded barely in control, too.

LeeAnn must have heard it. The teasing stopped. "Please hurry," she said. "I need you."

"I'm on my way. Stay there."

The phone went dead. LeeAnn never said goodbye anymore; it was too commital. I set down the receiver and caught a glimpse of myself in the bureau mirror. Gaunt, sensitive features. Aquiline nose. Deep-set eyes. Quietly receding hairline. An interesting face: not handsome, certainly not repulsive. I smiled. Loads of character. The face of a poet, even . . .

Who was I kidding? I thought. *It's the face·of a fool.* The reflection nodded in sad affirmation. I looked at the piles of dirty clothes on the floor, and grabbed up a dirty sweatshirt. Dress for success, I always say. Or *said,* rather.

Whatever.

At any rate, I was suited up and out the door before manly Captain Kirk had pronged the first of this evening's deep-space bimbos, way out where no man had gone before. The last three words from her lips echoed through me like a curse.

I need you.

Sure.

■

The cab ride was long and wet, cold rain pounding on the windows like a billion tiny fists. The whole way up, I brooded about LeeAnn. The whole way up, I hit alternately on the dwindling vial of blow in my jacket pocket and one of the two jumbo oilcans of Foster's lager that I'd scored just for the trip. The irony of getting wasted as a prelude to meeting a friend for drinks was not lost on me, but what could I say? LeeAnn made me crazy: the same kind of crazy that would inspire me to tromp out into a maelstorm on a moment's notice and woefully underdressed, from my army-surplus field jacket down to a pair of battered

Reeboks with a dime-sized hole in the right sole. She unnerved me that thoroughly. I snorted and watched the passing streets slip by: each one rain-slicked and on the verge of flooding. Each one dark and bleak and utterly depressing.

Any of them an escape route: infinitely preferable to where I was going.

If I'd been stronger, maybe, I'd have taken one. Sure. Of course, the same line of inarguable reasoning could be applied to any other quarter of my world, from my unpublished short stories to my unfinished novel to my utterly unrequited love life, with exactly the same results. The gross total of which, combined with fifty cents, would buy me a packet of Gem safety blades.

The better to slit my miserable fucking throat with.

The thought deflated as quickly as it came. Of course I would never really do that. Neither, of course, would I tell the cabbie to turn around and take me home, or just grab LeeAnn by the hair and force her to my heap big masculine will, or do *anything* but what I always, always did. Which was to go to her: whenever, wherever her next whirlwind sortie ended. In tears, in disaster. In rain, sleet, or snow. Good Ol' Dave would be there, day or night, with the right words and the right drugs and a shoulder to cry on. Good ol' Dave was never more than a phone call away. I hated myself for being such a stooge to this endlessly cyclical farce, for being so hapless in the face of my own flaccid desire.

The cab sploshed indifferently onto Tenth Avenue, heading uptown. The beer sploshed in my roiling guts, heading south. And the memories came boiling up . . .

We went back a little ways, LeeAnn and I. Long enough to count. Worked for the same messenger service: humping the bullshit of the business world by day, pounding at the walls of our dreams at night. She was in the office, I was on the streets. She was sharp and funny and smarter than anyone else in the whole fleabag organization; I was the only one in the entire company who would talk to her without staring incessantly at her tits. No easy task, let me tell you. But I did it, because I valued her trust almost as much as I hungered for her touch.

So there we were, sharing in the adventure of being

young and piss-poor in New York, trying desperately to make it in our respective careers: clone of Kerouac meets fledgling Bourke-White. Came to spend a lot of time together; scrutinizing my first drafts and her black-and-whites over a dinner of ravioli and Riuniti; wandering the streets and parks in search of inspiration and free entertainment. We grew very tight. Very close.

With one rather glaring exemption.

You see, for all that deep meaningful contact it never quite gelled for LeeAnn and I. It was ridiculous, yes. I mean, I'd heard the most heartfelt feelings she'd ever cared to offer without blushing or batting an eye; I would have taken a bullet or thrown myself gleefully into traffic to save the tiniest hair on her head.

Sure. I could do all that. But somehow I couldn't bridge the safe, comfy distance between friend and lover. I just couldn't bring myself to tell her how I felt, to grab her and give her the kind of kiss that would make her reciprocate my passion, my love.

In retrospect, I realize that I was waiting for *her* to do it. I cringe to think of it now, but it's true. Part of my heart sincerely believed that she would wake up one day with the realization that no one would ever love her like I did. No one else could be so tender, so compassionate, so understanding. No one else would bear with her through her tragedies and madnesses, be so selflessly and completely devoted to her needs.

She would wake up one day, I told myself, kicking herself for her foolishness. And she would throw herself, weeping, into my arms. And I would tell her that it was okay, it was over now. And we would be swept away into a love that not even death could destroy.

One day, I knew, she would realize just how much she was saying when she said the words *Dave, I need you.*

That was the bullshit *I* believed. I preferred it to the cold hard truth.

As for LeeAnn, well . . .

LeeAnn preferred a different kind of guy.

A guy like Rodney, for example. I grimaced as his sneering pug loomed up like the answer in a magic Eight-ball toy. Rod the bod, punk hunk *par excellence*. Took her on a three-month nightmare tour of the Lower East Side, every nook and alley and rathole club that charged four bucks a beer. Rod, the artiste. Rod, the super-intense. He was inspiring her, giving her photography a whole new edge. Sure. Asshole inspired her, alright: eventually O.D.'d on crack and went nuts in her apartment, damned near inspiring her to death before heading off to be shot by the police.

I upended the first can, draining the dregs, and popped the second in a ceremonial toast. *Rot in hell, Rodney. If they'll have you . . .*

After that it was Willis, the far side of the pendulum. I think she met him at a Soho gallery opening. Willis of the shining white mane, who was strong and stable and financially secure and about old enough to be her father. Willis wined and dined her like a princess; my god, he even proposed to her. And she actually accepted, to my unending shock and horror, though I think it was more political than emotional. He had connections. He could *help* her. That is, until she found that her Svengali absolutely forbade her to work after the wedding. Not a woman's place, you understand. LeeAnn shouldn't worry her pretty little head with thoughts of careers. LeeAnn should worry about tending to Willis's earthly needs.

Or how 'bout Roger, her latest disaster. Yeah, Roger was great. Handsome and fortyish and too hip to hurt; cut him and he'd probably bleed Ralph Lauren aftershave. Now *they* were an item, and *soooo* good for each other. He was doing a book on Central America, was going to take her along as his photographer. Maybe her big break. I remember her coming out of the office at checkout time, pulling me aside to tell me the great news . . .

The great news ended rather abruptly at the Midtown Women's Services clinic, at precisely the same microsecond that the urine test came back positive. That was six weeks ago, give or take a millenium.

Well, he *did* pay for exactly his half of the costs, which was awfully decent of him. But he wasn't there for her on the day it happened, with a smile or a hug or a hand to hold. I was. And he wasn't there in the guilt-wracked weeks after, or ever again.

I was.

Yeah, Roger was slime, and Roger went the way of the wind. But even he wasn't the worst. First, there was Martin.

There was *always* Martin . . .

The cab cut up Tenth Avenue like a shark through dark waters. Forty-second Street floated by; I blinked back fractured patterns of garish light and color that winked like beacons to hungerlust and loneliness, previews of coming attractions that would never hit town. The moron-parade marched on in my brain: an onslaught of compelling, charismatic bastards who, for all their disparate differences, had held one thing in common. Which I had not.

LeeAnn.

Lithe, lissome bane of my existence. An otherwise intelligent woman who wouldn't take two ounces of the same shit on the job that she ate buckets of in her personal life. And who, for some equally unfathomable reason, liked her men either old and sensitive or young and macho. Old, macho men were chauvinistic pig-dog bastards.

Young, sensitive men were wimps . . .

I winced, biting back the thoughts, denying any possible truth. The cab turned onto 48th and crossed Ninth Avenue as the last of the Foster's slid down my throat. I felt bilious, and I needed to take a leak. My mind was burnt crispy. My nerves were live wires.

But as the cab slid up to the corner, I resolved that this time, *this* time it would be different. Tonight would mark the end of her love affair with the scum of the earth. I felt a queasy determination that I underscored with a toot of cocaine courage, an alkaloid surge of ersatz bravado. *It's my turn, dammit!* I told myself. If it could be done, it would be done.

It wasn't until I paid the cabbie and hit the pavement that I started to get nervous.

Maybe it was the way she sat, back framed in the grimy bay window, red and green neon backwashing her features like some DC Comics damsel in distress. Maybe it was the window itself, which hung dripping like a plate-glass gullet. The way it displayed her.

Like bait . . .

I felt it, alright. As I hunkered over and puddle-dodged

toward the door, it was there: a small, wormy gut-rush, synching with the Bud and Stroh's signs that blinked wanly behind the glass, vestige of some primal warning mechanism not entirely obliterated by the drugs. Saying *No . . . No . . . No . . . No . . .*

It was enough to register. It was not enough to stop me. The place was a dump, alright, but I felt sure I'd seen worse. It was nestled in the middle of a block dominated by drug dealers, pimps, and pawnshops, with the occasional ratbag adult emporium tossed in for good measure. The sign above the awning read simply BAR, with a badly painted-over prefix that looked as though the name had changed hands so many times that they'd just given up. The grime on the big window was thick enough to carve my initials in. The street itself was mercifully void, thanks to the rain; a sole Chicano bum not too far from his teens sprawled by the doorway, oblivious to the pounding. He twitched and muttered sporadically.

I fingered the folding knife thrust deep into the right-hand pocket of my jacket, the one that I'd habitually carried since being mugged last summer. It was long and thin and very sharp; stainless-steel casing, stainless-steel blade. I had never pulled it, never even used it, and often wondered if I carried it as a kind of a talisman more than a weapon. I hoped that I wouldn't need it in either capacity tonight. The thought *oh shit, LeeAnn, what are you into now?* loomed forth. The only possible answer was directly ahead.

The smell of bridges burning lay behind.

■

The first thing that hit me was the stink, a palpable presence that grew exponentially as the door shut behind. The usual stale smoke/stale beer bouquet, yes. But something else, underneath: a vague, foul underpinning. Familiar. Like—

Sewage, I realized. *Great.* My stomach rolled. I grimaced and took in the layout in an instant. The interior was long and low and dark, the furthest reaches of it enshrouded in greasy shadow some forty feet back. A psuedo-old-time finger-sign pointed down some steps near the back, one word emblazoned in large gold script.
GENTLEMEN.

The source, no doubt. This must be my night. My bladder begged to differ. It wouldn't be long before I had to hit the hopper. It was no longer an idea I relished.

I noted that the rest of the decor was strictly Early K-Mart: imitation-walnut paneling and formica as far as the eye could see. The bar itself was unique, hugging the wall to a point halfway down the far side. It was a large and graceless structure replete with tarnished brass hand and foot rails, and somehow managed to be constructed entirely of oak without being the tiniest bit attractive. Twin ceiling-mounted Zenith nineteen-inch TVs blasted cablevision mercilessly on either end.

The Hooter Girl adorned the center.

She looked like one of those paintings of the hydrocephalic sad-eyed children, pumped full of silicon and estrogen. The kind of black velvet sofa-sized monstrosities you see cranked out by the yard and offered up on abandoned gas-station aprons across America, right next to Elvis and Jesus and the moose on the mountain. Big moon eyes and tits like basketballs. Pure class. The neon color scheme had faded over the passage of smoke-filled time, leaving her once-electric tan lines merely jaundiced.

It might have been funny, under other circumstances. At the moment it was making me ill. That and every other sordid detail, from the fly-specked ceiling tiles to the screaming vids to the sodden regulars that lined the bar like crows on a barnyard fence. What the hell was I *doing* here, in this hole, at this hour?

The answer crossed the lateral distance of the room and wrapped herself around me before I could mutter a word. We stood there for what seemed a very long time. I probably would have remained in that position forever, but for the eyes that had followed her course to me. They were hungry, angry, gimlet eyes.

The hunger was for her.

The anger was all mine.

"Would you please tell me what the fuck is going on here?" I said under my breath. It came out a little more hysterical than I'd wished. *Good start, chump.* I thought. *Don't whine.*

"Thanks for coming," she whispered into my armpit. I

waited for more. It did not seem to be forthcoming, but she added a squeeze for emphasis. The warm flesh of her back shuddered beneath my touch, but for all the wrong reasons.

"Hey, are you okay?" I asked, not entirely certain that I wanted to hear the answer.

She nodded and snuffled just the tiniest bit, but she didn't let go. It worried me. Very gently, I pried her arms from around my waist and started to say, "C'mon, Lee, what's going on h—"

I never finished. LeeAnn looked up.

She had a black eye. Slit-swollen. Nasty. A tiny crescent-shaped cut had congealed just under her left eyebrow. She smiled gamely, chagrined. Her right eye crinkled with little smile-lines; the left remained fixed and droopy, like a bad impression of the Amazing Melting Woman.

I don't know why I was so surprised. Maybe I wasn't. I'd seen it before. But I couldn't bear to see it again: not now, not ever. My gaze flitted spastically to my shoes, the tubes, the goons at the bar. Anywhere but her face. Her face was dangerous. Her face made *me* dangerous. I stared in red-eyed rage as twin Rambos dispensed endless all-beef lessons in how real men take care of business.

But the goons at the bar weren't watching that. They were watching us. They were watching me.

They were smiling.

It was too much. There was nowhere to turn with my anger but back to the source. The words that came were clipped and vicious, in a voice I barely recognized as my own. I didn't like it. I couldn't help it.

"Who. Did. It."

LeeAnn shook her head. "Beer first," she said. It was not a suggestion. "And we'd better sit down." Then she pulled away, turned, and strode over to her place at the window end of the bar, next to the very pay phone she'd probably used to call me, and gathered up her things. She gestured to the bartender, a withered old troll in a baggy white shirt who looked as if he'd spent all his younger days on some Lower West Side dock, trundling the very same kegs he now presided over. He grunted imperceptibly, ash falling from the Lucky pinched in one corner of his lips, and began refilling her emptied pitcher with deft, wordless efficiency. She was back in control that fast. However tenuous, she was in charge. Of herself. Of me.

I stood in stunned silence, the rage draining impotently out, as LeeAnn returned. She squeezed my arm lightly, imploringly, and then walked back toward the shadowed and empty booths. I was supposed to pay; it was understood. I watched her graceful trailing trek across the room. I watched her hips. I watched her ass.

I wasn't the only one watching.

Two of the clientele, a pair of drunken dimwits interchangeable as Heckle and Jeckle leered at her in brief, neck-craning abandon. The third, a hairball with thick gold chains and too many teeth, managed a sidelong snickering appraisal before resuming his ogling of the washed-out and weary-looking blonde to his left.

The blonde, meanwhile, was oblivious to it all: staring off into her drink as if it were a gateway to another world entirely. She was the Hooter Girl made flesh, and then stepped on. Not pleasant.

I stepped up to the bar, stoned and shellshocked, drugs and wasted adrenaline making the seamy details painfully apparent. I fished out a crinkly ten-spot and stared blankly at the wooden expanse of the counter. It was scarred and pitted, with initials and epigraphs and other vital pearls of wisdom. Ritual scarification. One stuck out like a message in a bottle: four words, carved deeper than all the rest.

TO BE A MAN.

To be a man. A bitter sneer engraved itself across my face. *To be a man.* I'd heard enough of that shit to last me a lifetime. My old man had said it. My peer group had said it. The first caveman to bludgeon his object of desire and drag her home by the hair had grunted its equivalent.

To be a man. You bet. If my mind had lips, it would have spat out the words. *Somebody got nice and manly with LeeAnn tonight. It's written all over her face . . .*

I looked up. The blonde was glancing at me with weak and wounded eyes. I could see every crack and sag in her features. Ten years ago or so she must have been a real looker, but that was ancient history now. That kicked-around look spilled off of her in waves: the way she hugged her vitals, as if waiting for the next blow to fall; the way she'd sort of sunken into her own caracass, as if the extra padding might help; the way her eyes kept darting to the back of the room.

I stared, waiting for the pitcher to fill. And I wondered how the hell she could have let that happen to her.

Then the men's room door squealed open like a thing in pain.

And up stomped the Mighty Asshole.

The gnarled little man with the pitcher of beer was forgotten. So were the drunks and the hairball, the blonde, the dueling idiot boxes where Rambo played out his bloodless charade. Even LeeAnn slipped from my mind for one long, cold moment, as the entire spinning universe funneled down to the behemoth pounding up the cellar stairs.

Big as life and twice as ugly, he swaggered toward the bar, fumbling absently with his fly. Arms like girders. Eyes like meatballs. Feet pounding the floorboards like an overblown Bluto in a Max Fleischer cartoon, sending shock waves up my legs from halfway across the room.

The impulse to retreat must have come on a cellular level, because I had backed into a barstool before I even knew I was moving. Connecting with teetering solid matter jostled me back to the broader reality, and I cast a nervous glance over to LeeAnn. She was watching him, too.

We were *all* watching him.

It wasn't just that he was tanked, or that he was built like one. Or even that he was bearing down on us like some angry moron-god. Rather, it was his presence: the sheer force and volume of his rage. It was as vivid as the glow around a candle's flame, and black as the dead match that first fired it up.

The Mighty Asshole thundered over to his seat next to the blonde. The terror in her eyes answered my previous question quite nicely: they were an item. Like hammer and anvil, they were made for each other. I shuddered involuntarily.

Then the troll was back, pitcher and mugs clunking down onto the bar. He grinned at me, a toothless rictus, as

I handed him the money. Looking into his eyes was like staring down an empty elevator shaft and never quite seeing the bottom. He smiled as he handed back my change, smiled as I hefted the goods, and kept right on smiling as I made my way back. The Asshole shot me a beady-eyed and territorial sneer as I hustled away.

I crossed the room like the guest of honor at a firing squad. The screaming of my nerves eased up only marginally the farther away from the bar I drew. LeeAnn was already seated, tucked into one of the half-dozen claustrophobic, dimly lit booths that ringed the desolate rear of the room. I joined her, setting down the pitcher and mugs, peeling off my wet jacket and tossing it into a heap on the bench. The beer sat untouched on the table. I sighed, grabbed the pitcher, and filled both our mugs. LeeAnn watched. I handed her one, took a swig off my own, and waited.

Nothing.

"Well?" I said. It was meant to sound level and controlled, but it came out all wrong.

LeeAnn looked away. "Finish your beer," she said. She was serious. She was miserable.

"What?"

"Your beer." She was adamant. "Finish it."

I glared at her exasperatedly, then tipped back the mug, drained it in two gulps, and banged it on the table. "There," I said, "All gone. Happy?"

"Very," she said, refilling my mug. "Have another."

"What?! C'mon, LeeAnn, this is bullshit."

"Trust me, Dave. Drink up."

I stared at her for a moment longer, weighing the situation. I didn't want any more beer. I really didn't. In fact, the whole situation was beginning to grate on my nerves. My clothes were wet, the night was old, my bladder ached, and my patience was wearing thin. The words *don't play games with me, dammit* flickered through my mind on their way to my mouth. I caught them just in time.

But the anger remained. It was not lost on LeeAnn; she knew who it was for. Her whole body flinched back for a microsecond. The gesture was mostly surprise; but there was no getting around the fear, iris-black and widening, at its center. I'd seen fear in her eyes before, but I'd never been its cause.

I felt like a total shit.

"Jesus, kiddo," I whispered. "I'm sorry." Now it was her turn to avert the eyes. I looked at the mug of beer before me. It wasn't that much to ask. I wondered what the fuck was wrong with me.

I drained the goddam mug.

"Okay," I said, deliberately, with as much aplomb as I could scrounge up. "The beer is drunk, and so am I. I'm sedated. I'm fine. I will not get angry.

"So tell me: was it someone you know?"

She nodded, still looking away. Her good eye glistened.

"One of your lovers?"

Another nod, with an accompanying tear; that one hurt. It wasn't phrased to hurt. It couldn't help itself.

"Who?"

No answer.

"*Who?*"

A small voice, barely there at all. "Martin."

For one terrible moment of silence, the world went cold and dead.

"Come again?" I said. Vacuum voice, through a throat constricted. I knew I'd heard it right, was terrified that I'd heard it right. My temples began to thud. The bile swilled in my guts.

"Martin," she said. Louder. Defiant.

"*The* Martin?" I pressed. She shrank back again; inside my skull, there was thunder. "Scum-sucking douchebag Martin? Originator-of-this-whole-downhill-slide Martin? *That* Martin? Is that what you're telling me?"

"Yes." Less a word than a squeak. She was still shrinking back, her spine flush with the booth. Retreating, now. Into herself.

"Are you serious?!"

"YES!" She screeched, the tears flowing freely.

"*JESUS!!*" I screamed, clapping my hands over my forehead. "You're sick!" She winced. "How could you *do* that?!"

But I already knew the answer. It was easy. She had help.

Martin.

The first, and the worst . . .

LeeAnn had broken up with him about two years ago, right around when we first met. I'd only seen the guy once or twice, when he came by the office to meet her after work. He seemed alright enough; tall and good-looking in a yuppified way. Real confident. Real smooth. They seemed like the perfect couple, and I was crushed.

But then I started hearing the horror stories: about how he constantly bullied and sniped at her, how the emotional abuse had begun to turn physical, and the physical act of love became brutal, supply on demand . . . until, when she finally grew sick of him and was no longer willing to offer herself, he went ahead and took her anyway . . .

Repeatedly.

No charges were ever filed. I hadn't really known her then, had only admired her from afar, and it wasn't my place to speak out. But I remembered seeing the bruises, and hearing about the asshole ex-boyfriend following her around, making threatening phone calls and an ugly nuisance of himself.

And I remember, even then, wanting to tear his stupid throat out.

She'd been with him for almost two years: a very gradual descent into hell. She never talked about it much; I had to piece most of my knowledge together from the rumor mill and an outsider's perspective. But the bitch of it was, I think she really did love him. And that's what scarred her so badly: she cared, and she trusted him. She'd truly given him a piece of her heart. His betrayal was tantamount to a traumatic amputation; even after the shock she could still feel a twinge of the missing piece. The phantom pain, where it used to be.

And tonight she'd gone back, once again.

To find it.

I really didn't want to hear the gory details; I could fill them in well enough by rote. She was scared; of him, of herself. She had good reason to be. It was a twisted sort of *ourobouros*, the snake forever consuming its own tail, forever vomiting itself right back up; victim and victimizer, locked in an endlessly spiraling deathdance.

And for the very first time I saw her, flung head-first off the pedestal and down into the slime. I saw her the way *they* must.

Flawed. Vulnerable.

Pathetic.

And for one bone-chilling moment, I thought that maybe Martin had a point . . .

No. The word was vehement, the voice very much my own. *No no no No!* The vision ran completely counter to everything that I held dear, everything that I'd ever believed about the nature of love and the dignity of the human spirit. It made me crazy to think that such a thought had even entered my head . . .

. . . but still I could see it, in psychotic Technicolor clarity: LeeAnn, cringing before my swinging fist; the moment of glorious frisson, as flesh met surrendering flesh . . .

WHAT THE FUCK IS WRONG *WITH ME?* I silently screamed. My eyes snapped shut. The vision vanished. I whirled in my seat, away from LeeAnn and toward the bar, not wanting my face to betray the merest hint of what had just gone on inside my mind.

Then the bartender turned toward me. And nodded. And smiled.

And the pain in my bladder went nova.

It was remarkably like getting kicked in the balls: the same explosion of breath-stealing, strength-sapping anguish. It doubled me up in my seat, brought my face within inches of the tabletop between LeeAnn and I. At that distance, with the dim light etching them in massive shadow, I couldn't help but see the four words crudely carved across its surface:

TO BE A MAN.

"What is it?" her voice said in quivering tones. Her tears were subsiding; she was regrouping in the rubble. I dragged my gaze up to hers with difficulty, still drowning in the pain.

"It's nothin', kiddo. Honest." I was trying to brush it

aside, to hide it. It wasn't working. My voice was even more wobbly and wasted than hers.

"Don't bullshit me, Dave. You're in pain. Is it an ulcer?"

"I don't think so. I never had one before." But I had to briefly consider the possibility, because, *Jesus,* did it hurt!

"You look horrible."

"Thanks a lot."

"No, I'm seri . . ."

"LEEANN!" I thudded my fist against the table in pain and frustration and rage. "We didn't come here to talk about *my* goddam pain! We came here to talk about yours! Now will you stop trying to change the fucking subject for a minute!"

She was stunned. In this, she was not alone. I could no more believe what I'd said than I could what I followed it up with.

"Baby, I'm not the one who got smacked around tonight! I'm not the one who went to Martin's and asked *him* to do it, either! I didn't even ask to come here! I only came because you begged me to, and I only did *that* because . . ."

I stopped, then. It was like slamming down the brakes at 120 mph. The only sound in my head was the *screeeeeee* of rubber brain on asphalt bone. I blinked at the dust and smoke behind my eyes.

"Because why?" Her voice was soft as a whisper, warm as a beating heart. Her good eye was green and deep and inscrutable. It unnerved me, that eye, even more than its battered mate or the question that accompanied it. It scrutinized me with zoom-lens attention to every blackhead and ingrown hair on my soul.

Because I love you, my mind silently told her. *Because I'm a goddam chump, that's why.*

I couldn't decide which conclusion was truer. I couldn't even sustain the internal debate. If I didn't get up and drag my ass down the stairs, I would let loose in my pants, and that was all there was to it. It was a matter of Piss or Die now, and there was no holding back.

"Excuse me a moment," I managed to mutter, rising up at half-mast and away from my seat.

But suddenly, LeeAnn didn't want to drop it. She grabbed my wrist just as I cleared the table. "David, please..." she said. It took everything I had to force the gentleness into my voice.

"I gotta pee, baby. Please. I'm gonna blow up if you don't let me go."

She actually smiled, then. In retrospect, were it not for the pain and embarrassment, that might have been the finest moment of my life. "I really do want to know," she said, soft as before. And her hand stayed right where it was.

I laid my free hand over it. The fingers meshed.

"Hold that thought," I whispered. Not entirely romantic; speech had gotten very difficult. Then I turned and beat a hasty retreat.

She watched me go. I could feel her eyes.

I knew what they were saying.

I will never forget.

■

Mark Twain once said that if God exists at all, he must surely be a malign thug. I wish it were true. It would be easier to blame God, or Fate, or the drugs, or the bar, or even LeeAnn.

But I know where the blame lays.

Right where it belongs.

I waddled away from the table with a smile on my face. The pain was still there ... it kept me half-doubled over ... but those last few moments had rendered it nearly insignificant. I was aglow with proximity to my heart's desire. I was aglow with impending triumph.

And that, of course, was when the Mighty Asshole chose to speak.

"Hey! Lookit the fuckin' *creampuff*!" he bellowed. "Guess you gotta go WEE-WEE, huh?"

There was a pause that crackled in my ears like static, dispersed by a ripple of harsh, raucous laughter. I turned to face a dozen mirthlessly grinning eyes: the Asshole and his punching bag, the troll and the hairball and Heckle and Jeckle. All of them watching. Most of them laughing.

The Mighty Asshole, most of all.

Something clicked inside me. The words *I don't need*

this took control of my brain. Under ordinary circumstances, I might have been scared. Not now.

I stared him down for a long defiant second.

Then I smiled. And curtsied. And blew him a kiss.

"Eat shit," I said.

Crude, but effective. I felt better almost instantly. The shock on his face was a joy to behold. I turned and scuttled down the stairs before he could rally; my mind raced in mad tandem with my feet.

Never mind them, I told myself. *You've got to get your butt back there, tell her that you love her, give her the kiss that you've been dreaming about. The time has come. She WANTS you, man!*

Then the stairway ended, and my thoughts screeched to a halt.

I had reached my destination.

And the source.

The door itself was ill-hewn and splintery, lusterless and finger-smeared where the finish hadn't worn away entirely. The word GENTLEMEN was spelled out in eight-inch metal caps that glimmered flatly in the glare of the overhead bulb. I yanked on the handle; it was surprisingly heavy, beyond its mass. I pulled harder, and it reluctantly gave way.

I'd forgotten about the hinges, the terrible screeching sound they made. *Like a thing in pain.* The small hairs on the nape of my neck stood up like frightened sentries as the sound sawed through my eardrums and raked along my spine.

I stepped inside. The door creaked shut.

And the presence of the room assailed me.

There was the resonant *boom* that sent echoes bouncing off the filthy tiles. There was the overpoweringly ammoniacal sewage-stench, jolting up my nostrils like smelling salts. There was the dim insectoid buzz of the overhead fluorescents, spackling the interior with blotches of pulsing, spasming shadow.

And there was the *size* . . .

Mad, twirling Christ, it was huge. I stood in stunned amazement of what lay ahead. Now, the claustrophobic crapper of any midtown Manhattan working-class watering hole is just about big enough for the average-sized man to squeeze in and out of with an absolute maximum of discomfort. By comparison, this place was a fucking castle.

Twin rows of nonfunctional, moldy sinks: ten, in all. They lined a long tiled corridor on the way to the main room, from which I could make out a solitary stall.

A solitary stall...

Its door hung lopsidedly askew, as though wrenched violently off its hinges. An enormous pool of black, fetid water extended around it in a widening berth, apparently stemming from the blockage of gray, spongy effluvium that floated in the bowl like the lost continent of Atlantis. By craning my neck I could make out a pair of urinals just around the corner, clinging for dear life to the wall beyond.

One stall. Two urinals. Ten sinks.

Under any other circumstances it would've been weird enough to ponder. At the moment, my priorities were far more basic. I groaned, surveying the terrain. There was no way around it.

Only through it.

So I started in, holding my breath, gingerly skirting one of the main tributaries. Each of the sinks had its own mirror bolted to the wall above it. Nine of them had been smashed into glittering shards, held in place by inertia and thin metal frames. The buzzing light refracted off of them, making the streamlets of the pool appear to ripple with a malignant life of their own. The last mirror, the one nearest an adult novelty dispenser proffering big-ribbed condoms in tropical colors, was intact. My reflection fought its way back through the grit and haze; it looked pasty and haggard, forlorn.

"No wonder she's crazy about you," I muttered. "You gorgeous thing."

Something burbled, distinctly, from inside the stall.

"Huh?" I sputtered, startled, and turned to see a fresh ripple of foul water expanding outward in ever-increasing concentric rings. My thoughts turned to my quality footwear and nervously gauged the odds of making it over and back unscathed. It didn't look good.

The stall belched in agreement, sending out another wave.

I peeked around the corner, into the main body of the room. It was infinitely worse: the water actually deepened, and though it could only reasonably be a few inches, it looked bottomless. Some of the floor tiles were warped enough to form a series of little dry islands.

It was my only hope. Taking a last, desperate glance at my reflection, lips curled in disdain, I began to hippy-hop from dry spot to dry spot like a little kid crossing a creek. The beer made me clumsy, the drugs hypersensitized me, and the fumes burned like lye in my eyes and nose. But I made it, awkwardly straddling the sole oasis beneath the far urinal.

The stench was incredible. I momentarily regretted leaving my jacket upstairs, where a half-pack of Merits were serving no useful purpose. The joint was there, too, as were all my matches. There was nothing I could do to abate the smell.

Those were the facts I had to face as I, at last, unzipped my fly.

And not a moment too soon; no sooner had I freed my screaming pecker than the pee blasted out and splished against the procelain like a runaway firehose. I sighed, a deep and vastly relieved "Ahhhh . . ." and leaned forward to brace myself against the wall, feeling slightly dizzy and a vague surge of pride at having made it.

I looked at the wall, while the bladder pain receded. There was a profusion of graffiti there; the same sort of jerkoff witticisms that probably graced the Pissoirs at the Dawn of Time. Crudely optimistic penises pounding into yawning pudenda. Tits like udders, hanging from faceless, howling female forms. Phone numbers advertising good times at someone else's expense. Initials. Dates. Dreams of seamy grandeur.

And the same four words.

TO BE A MAN.

In the stall, something big went *squish* and then sputtered. I could hear the tinkling of falling droplets, delicate as the tines of the tiniest music box as they sprinkled the surface of the pool.

My spine froze. My pissing and breathing cut off instinctively. I leaned back as far as I could and listened.

Nothing.

"This is stupid," I informed myself by way of the room at large. My paranoia burgeoned. "There's nobody in there."

Still nothing. Ripples, expanding quietly outward. I exhaled. My pissing resumed with great difficulty.

And the door to the men's room flew suddenly open.

I jerked, nearly spraying myself. From inside, the echoing screech of the hinges resounded like a billion bat-shrieks in a cave. The door *screeeeed* and slammed shut like thunder. The walls boomed with the sound of amplified footsteps.

Every alarm in my nervous system went off. It was like pissing on the third rail of a subway track, a thousand volts of terror sizzling through me in the space of a second. The footsteps got closer, and I found myself wanting to get out of there very badly. *Relax,* I hissed silently, as internal organs tightened to pee faster. *You're stoned. This is stupid. Nothing's going to happen. Nothing's—*

"Well, well, well," he said, sneering. "Lookit what we got here."

The footsteps came up behind me and paused. I didn't want to turn around and look.

I had to.

The Mighty Asshole stood at the edge of the swamp: arms crossed, legs spraddled, a hideous grin on his face. He said, "Looks like we got us a live one."

Something burbled and glooped in the toilet stall.

What the fuck did he mean by that? I wondered. The images it conjured were not very pretty. The smile that flicked across my face was meant to look cool and unruffled. It failed. I flashed it anyway, trying to hide my desperation. He grinned back at me, flat-eyed and mean as a mouthful of snakes.

The Mighty Asshole sploshed, indifferent, through the pool of rancid liquid. He came up beside me, unzipped his fly, and finagled himself into trajectory with the urinal to my left. I took a deep, nasty breath and exhaled it at once, not looking at him. His pissing chorused with mine.

A moment passed.

"You're a faggot, you know it?" he said casually. "You're a little fucking faggot."

I looked at him then, peering straight into his idiot face.

"Yeah you," he continued. "A little fucking *faggot*."

" 'Zat so?" I said. "Geez. This is sure news to me." My bladder was draining, like air from a flat; and with it, the pain and the fear.

"A faggot," he repeated, as loud as before, but his sense of utter mastery had dwindled a bit. Our eyes were locked, and I could see the sudden twitching of dimwitted uncertainty there.

" 'Zat a fact," I said, marking time 'til I was done. I didn't want to fight him, that much was for sure. My knife was upstairs, with the Merits and the joint. He wasn't all that much bigger than me, but he was blitzed and stupid; even if I jawed him, he probably wouldn't know it, and we'd end up rolling around here in the slime of the ages.

"Thass a fact, alright." He slurred it, and it took a long time to get out. Good sign. My pissing was almost done; by the time he formulated another thought, I'd be gone.

"I know a woman who'd be interested to hear that," I said. "Yessiree. She'd find that pretty goddam funny."

He laughed. I joined him.

He stopped. I didn't.

He hit me.

It was a short, straight-armed punch, with a lot of muscle behind it. It caught me square in the side of the head, sending hot black sparks pinging through my skull. I lurched to the side, off my little island, and straight into the sludge. Cold putrescence flooded up through a hole in my shoe.

"Shit!" I yelled. "Shit! Shit!" I splashed around to face him, waiting for my vision to clear. I could feel my ear starting to cauliflower, feel the hot trickle of blood seeping down. I thought about booting him right in the nuts, grinding his face into that same black water. I was furious. *"You stupid motherfu—"* I began.

And then stopped.

Suddenly.

Completely.

Stopped.

■

In the pool. In the slime.

It started with the sole of the right foot: a numbing sensation that I at first mistook for the cold. In the thin web of flesh between the first and second shafts of the metatarsus, seeping up through the sodden expanse of my gym sock, the horror took root and spread. Up along the flexor tendons, through their fibrous sheaths. Soaking into the flexor brevis digitorum. An impulse, shooting out at the speed of thought, socked into the motor nucleus at the fifth nerve of the brain.

I couldn't move.

The numbness spread.

In the grume. Where He waits. Forever and ever.

Up through fibula and tibia, dousing bone and soaking marrow. Up through muscle and sinew, tendrils snaking up arteries and conduits, putting frost in my ganglion, ice in my veins. Up through the femur and into the hip, the pelvis. Numbing my cock, my balls. Spreading down the other leg.

Ancient. Eternally crawling.

Blitzkrieg in my bladder. In my spleen. Worming a finger up through my intestines. Oozing through the superficial fascia of the abdominal wall and then outward. Seeping through the pores. Bleeding through my sweatshirt.

Eternally struggling toward form.

And taking it.

For His own.

My eyes riveted on the eyes of the man before me: moist and pulsing, the color of slugs. A spasm ran through us both, synchronized and uncontrollable. Then I was pivoted and slammed face-first into the filthy tiles above the urinal. I couldn't feel it.

I could feel nothing.

In the stall, the burbling became violently frantic. I managed to lift my head away from the wall. The magic-marker scrawlings hovered inches from my eyes.

Then they began to shift. To change.

And He began to speak.

YOU'RE JUST A LITTLE FUCKING FAGGOT, He said. **OH YES YOU ARE.**

My eyes were glued to the words as they synced with the voice booming inside my head.

JUST A LITTLE FUCKING CREAMPUFF FAGGOT WHO DOESN'T KNOW HOW TO TAKE CARE OF BUSINESS.

I thought about the blonde at the bar, her groveling eyes. I thought about LeeAnn. I wanted to scream.

He sensed it. It made Him happy.

LIKE HER, He said, immensely pleased. **OH, YES. EXACTLY.**

Something slithered out of the toilet bowl and landed on the floor with a thick wet splutting sound. LeeAnn appeared in grotesquely animated caricature on the wall before me, silently screaming as a monstrously bloated penis plunged in and out and in and

YOU DON'T KNOW HOW TO BE A MAN. YOU'RE *AFRAID* TO BE A MAN.

I tried to scream. I couldn't.

YOU'RE AFRAID TO GO OUT THERE AND *TAKE* WHAT YOU WANT.

Sliding up my larynx, out over my tongue. Pouring into the hollows behind my eyes. Oozing into the billion soft folds of my brain. Black static, eating inward from the periphery of my vision. Blocking out everything.

But the realization.

Forever and ever.

It was crawling toward me. I couldn't see it, couldn't turn my head, but I could hear the horror revisited in the breath of the man beside me.

And I could hear it, slithering. I could feel its hunger. I could taste its boundless greed. A tiny voice in my head shrieked *it's only the drugs:* but the voice was tiny, and hollow, and fading.

Something small and moist grabbed onto my pants leg.

NOW YOU'RE GOING TO KNOW WHAT IT IS

Crawling up.

TO BE A MAN

Coming closer.

Struggling toward form.

TO BE A MAN

Tiny fingers clawed the base of my skull. My jaws pried open. A caricature appeared on the wall, mocking me.

OH, YES.
And there was nothing I could do.
But let Him in.

■

When I came to, some ten minutes later, the Mighty Asshole was gone. I knew that I'd have no more trouble from him that night, or ever after. In fact, I could come back as much as I wished. Again. And again.

I belonged now. Completely.

He had not let us fall, cunning fuck that He was. When I came to, we were in front of the sole surviving mirror, and He was splashing freezing water in our face.

He cleaned us up: meticulously washing away the blood, smoothing back the disheveled hair. Tomorrow we'd get it cut, He informed me. Nice and short, maybe a flattop. And we'd start working out, put some meat on these bones.

A real man, He said, *always takes care of business.*

When we were nice and clean, He turned and bought us a big-ribbed condom. For later. He smiled at our face in the grimy mirror. It was a cruel smile, and infinitely calculated. His smile. The mirror grinned coldly back.

And He smashed it.

With my fist.

When he finally came up the stairs, twenty minutes had passed. LeeAnn was waiting anxiously at the table. "David!" she demanded. "What happened to you? I was really getting worried."

He lifted one finger, and told her to shush.

She obeyed.

"You're a sweetheart," He said, moving close.

Then He kissed her.

Passionately.

With my lips.

There is a book on the history of photojournalism on the endtable beside me. It was one of LeeAnn's favorite's, but that's not why He keeps it around. He likes the pretty pictures.

And He likes to torture me.

Right now, it's open to the page on the liberation of the concentration camps, at the end of World War II. One

photo in particular stands out, flickering in the dim light of
the TV's hissing screen like footage from some long-
forgotten newsreel. It's a black and white picture of the
gate to Auschwitz. Perhaps it's even one of Margaret
Bourke-White's; that would be nice, but I guess it doesn't
really matter. So what if I can't make out the credit? I can
make out the inscription clear enough: **ARBEIT MACHT
FREI**, in huge iron letters. That's what's important.

ARBEIT MACHT FREI.

Work Makes Freedom.

I've thought about that alot. One of the many thoughts
that help me in the night, long after He's passed out in His
favorite easy chair, drunken and still dressed. Tonight, He
didn't even get the damned field jacket off.

I'm so glad.

I'm sure that LeeAnn would be, too.

It took her over a year to tear away: thirteen months of
steadily escalating madness. Oh, He was great, for the
first month or so: strong and sensitive and very, very
sincere. He made all the right moves, said all the right
things. And she welcomed my newfound assertiveness,
with an ardor that both amazed and destroyed me.

He waited with the patience of the ages, until the hooks
were planted nice and deep. Until she fell for Him. Until
she trusted Him. Until He could destroy her. It was
amazing, how much groundwork I'd already lain. It made
it inifinitely easier for Him. And infinitely worse, for me.

And then, when the moment was right, He showed her
His true self. Repeatedly.

I'll never forget the look of betrayal on her face.

It took her over six months to escape; we were living
together by then. He tried to break her, and she fought
Him. Escape cost her dearly: emotionally, mentally.

Physically.

But escape she did, and I love her for it. I've thought of
her often, God knows. I've wondered how she's doing,
wondered where she is.

But I don't really want to know.

And, besides, I never will.

Because every night after that, He dragged me down-
town and back to the bar. The guys were all there, of

course. The guys were always there. We got along famously, round after round, while the Hooter Girl sadly presided.

And every night after that, we went out in search of fresh meat. There were always women out there, waiting to be punished for something. He was always eager to oblige. He wanted me to watch. He needed me to forget. His failure. Her victory.

But I didn't, dammit.

I remembered.

Within the month, he'd found a suitable distraction: Lisa. She wasn't as sharp as LeeAnn, or as strong. But her blue eyes were bright, and her curvature dazzled, and her smile could have sold you the moon. We've been married now, the three of us, going on four years. We have kids, to my unending sorrow: Patricia, little David, Jr., and another damned soul on the way. Lisa's eyes no longer sparkle, and she hardly ever smiles. Thirty pounds of purpled padding grace the skeleton of her beauty like a shroud.

But tonight, that's all behind her.

It's taken four years. Four years of practice: at night, while He slept drunkenly on. Cell by cell. Inch by inch. Four very long years. LeeAnn would be proud.

I can move my right arm, you see.

Only when He sleeps, true, and not very much. It's not very strong, either. Yes, life is a bitch.

But it was strong enough to open the book tonight. And with a little strength to spare . . .

It'll be enough to reach the knife.

And so what if it takes me all night. **ARBEIT MACHT FREI,** right? Sometimes, that's just what it takes.

To be a man.

13
THE HOUSE THAT JACK BUILT

And this is how Meryl's Halloween went:

She awoke at 8:45 A.M. to the distant sound of her bedroom alarm. A clanging hangover was there to greet her, but nothing and nobody else. She was a bit surprised to find herself on the couch, until pieces of the previous night came crawling back to remind her. From there, her biggest surprise was that Katie was no longer with her.

By 9:00, she had remembered how to walk and swallow aspirin: the morning was off to a roaring start. She stripped off the little she was wearing and hit the shower, turned the hot water up high until the steam-level of the room matched the fog inside her head, then cut it with a seering blast of cold water. The effect was stunning; her nerves had never seemed quite so acute as they did while she dressed, in regular Meryl-clothes this time, and hobbled off to class.

At 10:20, her day's dosage of higher education kicked off with a one-two punch of stultifying proportions: "Lost Gods and Legends: Myths of the Ancient Mediterranean," and "Hey Diddle Diddle: The Secret Messages of Mother Goose." It was all she could do to keep her eyelids hoisted. Had modern-day psychologists unlocked the real secrets of Pandora's Box? Was there really a wealth of evidence to support the contention that nursery rhymes originally carried cryptic encodations vital to the outcome of the War of The Roses? Did anyone honestly give a shit? She could answer only for herself.

Which brought her up to 1:45, where an hour-plus of breathing time took her out in search of fresh city air. Washington Square Park, just across the street, seemed just the place to do it. Already, the preparade production crews were setting up for the long night ahead; their excitement required no exchange of bodily fluids to prove infectious. *Tonight is gonna be quite the experience,* she told herself. *Now, if I can just survive today . . .*

It wasn't more than a minute later that the day began its downward spiral.

Halfway past the fountain at the center of the park, she was accosted by a gap-toothed punk: naked stubbled scalp, cracked leather jacket, T-shirt emblazoned with the surreal and anomalous legend SKINHEADS FOR JESUS. He graced her with a brain-damaged smile that made her think *ye gods, Nancy Reagan was right,* and then shoved a pamphlet into her hand.

"Only Jesus can save you!" exclaimed God's Uncle Fester.

Looks like he did a bang-up job with you, she thought, but kept it to herself, moseying onward and away.

Ten feet past, she finally peeked at the thing. It featured a dumb-looking Reaper and scythe and the words "Death: YOU could be the next!" She could scarcely contain her excitement.

"Even while reading this tract," she was informed, "you could be having a slight pain in your chest or head, but WITHIN A FEW HOURS, YOU WILL BE DEAD of a heart attack or brain hemorrhage . . ."

"Oh, Jesus!" Meryl grimaced, wadding the offending paper up and tossing it. She already had a major pain in her head, thank you very fucking much. It brought her hand up to rub her scalp, in the hope of easing the thrum somewhat.

In the process, she seemed to dislodge a snippet of drivel from her previous class: a synaptic tape-loop of one of the nursery rhymes, spliced into her subconscious and humming, mantra-like, over and over . . .

> " . . . this is the priest, all shaven and shorn,
> who married the man all tattered and torn,"

Meryl crossed the park, struggling to think about things that mattered, like maybe getting some lunch in her

stomach and heading up Broadway to the Strand Book
Store to score the prep material for her last class of the
day . . .

". . . who kissed the maiden all forlorn . . ."

. . . the amazing "The American Short Story," in which
she was informed that its golden age had already come
and gone: an annoying thought, when one considered
that she'd personally rather be reading the next J. P.
Rowan than be dragged through the literary pretensions
of one more insipid F. Scott Fitzgerald upper-crust
pity-party . . .

". . . who milked the cow with the crumpled horn . . ."

. . . despite the frightening downward turn the stories
seemed to be taking, or the fact that the book was almost
over, which meant two things, only one of them good . . .

". . . that tossed the dog that worried the cat . . ."

. . . no more stories, but also no more excuses: she
would have to bag her fantasies, or nail her tail to the
grindstone and track that mystery man down . . .

". . . that killed the rat that ate the malt . . ."

. . . and she knew that there really wasn't any choice at
all, even if it did mean seeking the help of dear old Dad,
to check out the realtor who rented the pad, to track down
the writer she wanted so bad . . .

". . . that lived in the house that Jack built."

"Gah," Meryl groaned. "Enough, already." Pain wanged
in her head. She rubbed her temple. The rhyme went
back to whatever gray-matter hell had disgorged it.

She looked at her watch: almost two o'clock. She was
already well past the park, on a collision course with the
corner of Broadway and Eighth Street. She knew she

should be buckling down a little here, playing the good little studious type, maybe trying to salvage her academic career before mid-terms reared their ugly heads. She checked her notes for today's class: Eudora Welty. Oboy.

And that, as much as anything, decided her.

It was a short jaunt from there to her building. She managed it much better, relieved of the burden of good little literary studentdom. Her path took her past a spate of Greenwich Village fashion-risk emporiums—Unique Clothing, The Antique Boutique, One of A Kind, and a host of others—where the slumming hordes were busily plunking down cash to score that elusive and pricey Halloween accessory: Day-Glo studded underwear, earrings that looked like aborted launch wreckage from the Star Wars defense initiative, the basic necessities of life on lower Broadway. Meryl ran a mental checklist of her own outfit, did not find it lacking, and so wished them well and went on her way.

But the whole thing made her think of Katie, so she stopped by Bayamo on her way upstairs, to see how her partner in crime was holding up. *If she's not at least half as hungover as I am, she's a dead woman.* She stepped inside.

It was then that she got the next piece of weird news.

At 2:15, Meryl discovered that Katie hadn't shown up for work today. Nor had she left any word as to why. Her boss was profoundly displeased by this development; so much so, in fact, that he was talking termination. The hostess confided in Meryl her doubts with regard to her boss's sincerity, but the ugly truth remained: it didn't sound like Katie, and it didn't sound good.

Alarmed, Meryl hightailed it up to the loft, checking for clues that she might have missed in her early-morning stupor. There were none. At least none visible. No notes, no microfilm, no lipsick messages on the mirror. That left nothing to do but fret and stew and chide herself for her mother-hen-ism and wait around, fretting and stewing some more.

By three o'clock, she had gotten the shits. There were four stories left. She settled back on the couch and dug into the first of them.

Shells.

Depressing was too mild a word.

She sat there, thinking about it, thinking about what it could possibly mean. Structurally, it was a very odd piece; beyond that, it was dark as dark could be. She could literally see the hope trickling out of him, like a slow leak in an inner tube, hissing away one micromillimeter at a time.

And it frightened her.

Because she knew what lay at the end of hope. Her mother had shown her that. The tiny scar at the thin of her wrist was a road map of that place.

But she didn't want to think about that . . .

"Nuh-uh," she muttered, and got to her feet. No time to waste on that bleak thought terrain. It made more sense to worry about Katie, the more mundane unpleasantries of everyday life. Whatever reason the girl had for blowing off work, it must have been a good one. Probably some festive jumbo surprise. Chocolate-covered vibrators, perchance.

The humor in that vastly eased her mind, for almost fifteen seconds.

Then it was back to the fret and the stew, coupled with a gradually mounting annoyance. Since when, she inquired of herself, have you taken to letting the comings and goings of other people get so far under your skin?

A darn good question, she had to admit. Too bad the answer was so fucking uncomfortable. It was ridiculous, for example, that she should be antsy: in her own apartment, in the privacy of her own selfhood. It was preposterous to whip herself into a tizzy just because someone (surprise!) gave every appearance of having gone back on their word. It was utterly absurd, after all these years, to have her sense of well-being suddenly hinge on the presence of another.

But there it was: and much as she hated it, she couldn't seem to rationalize it away. Without Katie here to warm things up, the place felt cold and strange. The fact that she was certainly manufacturing those weird vibes herself only made it worse.

Because, alone here, there was nothing to do but read the book.

And reading the book was starting to freak her out.

At four, she noted the absence of spirits in the apartment with some dismay. Her hangover malaise had not dispersed, had only changed in shape; perhaps a little hair of the dog was in order. She threw her coat on and headed back down to Broadway, hit the nearest liquor store. Got what she needed. Headed back up.

Still no sign of Katie.

Three stories left to go.

By 4:30, Meryl had cracked open the brandy, poured herself three fingers' worth, and sipped half of it down. The fact that she had neglected to eat made her cautious; she didn't want to get crocked. At least not yet. She would wait for the party to begin.

The brandy helped a little: taking the edge off, putting the nice warm glow in her belly, restoring a bit of her former enthusiasm. She hadn't really expected Katie until 5:30, anyway, so what was there to get anxious about? She gave herself a halfhearted kick in the tush and started thinking about getting ready.

Her costume was right on the bed, where she'd left it. Thank God it required next to no maintenance. She'd considered the possibility that she might have to hand-wash the blouse and stockings in the sink; but no. All was hunky-dory.

She took her time changing and arranging herself, let herself space out in the process. To assist, she slapped some Suzanne Vega into the compact disc player, let the sad sweet music take the back door in to settle over her subconscious.

And in that realm of thought unfocused, she thought about J. P.: his sweet and sad and savage sides, the pain-filled heart sliced razor-thin and draped across his every word. What would it be like to know a man whose walls were so thin, nerves so close to the edge? What would it be like to be such a person?

She thought about herself, then, with uncustomary scrutiny: thought about her own walls, their staggering density; thought about the things behind them, so well

concealed that they scarcely touched upon her surface life
at all, so utterly sealed off from light and life that they had
begun to mummify, turn dry and brittle, flesh paper-thin
over sharp-boned petrified husk...

...and it flashed her back to the Mexican expedition
immediately preceding this phase of the Meryl Daly Story.
The endless party weekend that ranged up and down the
Mexican Riviera: falling in with the batch of rowdy rich
kids who trashed the lobby bar at the Hotel El Mirador in
Acapulco, slugging back margaritas until she passed out on
the beach in Puerto Vallarta, causing a scandal on the
Baja by bare-breasting herself by the pool at the Hotel
Mision de Loreto.

And, of course, that fateful trip to Guanajuato.

It started out as a goof: chartering a private plane to
León and then cabbing the twenty miles over to the town,
all to check out the stiffs in the *Museo de Momias*. She
didn't even remember the name of the guy who showed her
the postcards, the guy she dragged with her, Todd or Tad
or whatever.

But she remembered the postcards themselves: the
bodies dried and yellow as old newspaper bales, lined up
along the narrow corridor that two hundred pesos would
gain you entrance to, dozens of them, naked and stiff and
held up with baling wire, ex-citizens of Guanajuato or
unfortunate visitors who opted to stay forever, their families unable to purchase them more permanent rest. She
looked at the postcards and knew that she wanted to see
them, those dearly departed sons and uncles and fathers
and mothers, the papyrus flesh of their sunken faces
pulled into something that looked like a laugh and looked
like a scream, a hideous shrieking belly-buster at their
own eternal predicament, cavities caving in where life
used to burst forth, withered loins attesting to the light-
years between the place they occupied and the passions
that once ruled over them, brittle-stick fingers reaching up
to curl around absolutely nothing.

She looked at the postcards and knew, deep inside, that
she had to see them, had to gaze into their dead dry eyes,
had to reach out and rap upon their hollow breasts...

Her disappointment upon arriving there was a mystery

to poor ol' Tad, as was the fit she threw when she found that curators had tidied up a bit since those postcard photos had been taken: laying the mummies out in wood-and-glass display boxes, encased and enclosed and utterly out of reach. He didn't understand why she stood shaking when she got to the last chamber, were the cesarean madonna and child stood, alone in their case, frozen in time. He didn't notice the bulb-headed infant, grinning its blind and gummy grin, still cabled to the sagging belly of the mother who stood hunch-shouldered, mouth wide, bare and bald and ready to howl until the end of time.

Poor ol' Tad didn't pick up on any of that, and he certainly didn't connect it to the fact that Meryl dragged him back to the hotel without so much as another word, blew back a bottle of tequila, and just about fucked him blind . . .

. . . and that was just about enough reminiscing for now, thank you. She had come too close to the cracks in the vault where the things she did not care to know were kept. It was time, once again, to clamp down hard. Get down to business. This business of life. Certainly, Katie would be home soon. And then the fun—tittee rump, tittee rump—could begin.

Meryl looked at the clock, was amazed to discover that more than an hour had passed. It was closing in on six o'clock, and she was still sitting around in her underwear. Hastily, she kicked herself into motion: sliding the spider-web stockings on, the lacy tap pants, the complete ensemble. By 6:15, she was ready for Katie to put on her face.

But Katie was nowhere to be found.

Fine, Meryl thought. A little late. No problem. There was still a little brandy in the glass, lots more where that came from.

And three more stories to go.

At 6:25, she turned the first page of GENTLEMEN. Twenty-five extremely uncomfortable minutes later, she laid the folder shut. If the last story had been depressing, then this one was positively numbing in its cold and hopeless horror. Even the ending, with its worst-case optimism, could not overcome the terrible chill his words had placed at her core.

And the scar on her wrist had begun to dully throb.

"That's enough out of you," she told him, by way of addressing the walls. "This shit is the last thing I need right now." The walls said nothing in response, merely soaked up her energy and fired it right back, even weirder than before.

Meryl spent the next hour drinking and pacing, drinking and pacing, while Suzanne Vega played over and over and the darkness deepened outside her window. Periodically, a thought of comparable darkness slipped into her brainscape; she slapped it back as soon as it came. She would not let her demons get the best of her. No way in hell. She would keep herself level and steady and cool.

And when Katie got home . . . oh, when Katie got home . . .

She stopped herself, lest she get carried away. There was no point in getting mad at Katie. The girl was a flake; that was all there was to it. A cute little flake with a heart of cotton candy and the better judgment of a moth that has just hit the flame.

Like this whole parade business, for example. In certain respects, blowing off the parade was the good news: the longer she waited, the less she believed that letting herself get eyeball-fucked by the freaks in Washington Square was such a terrific idea. They wanted fun? They should go as clowns. Preferably asexual ones.

But that was Katie's problem: the Powers That Be, whatever they were, had fashioned her into a blonde ticking bombshell and then said, "Okay, honey. You're on your own." And look where it had gotten her. In many ways, she was just a ditzier version of the girl in J. P.'s story, doomed to bounce from loser to loser, and never quite getting the message.

"So," she muttered, announcing her decision. "That settles that. I'll just keep this on 'til she gets here, rub her face in it a little." She laughed, swigged a bit more brandy down. "Let guilt do the rest. A little Jewish jiujitsu."

There was only one problem.

It was already eight o'clock.

So what would she do if Katie never showed up? How to spend this lovely fun-filled Halloween night? Already, she could hear the ruckus echoing down the streets: evidently, the parade was well under way. Should she just forget her date completely, put on some normal clothes, go check out the spectacle? Should she sit down and master *150 Ways to Play Solitaire*? Should she—heaven forbid—do the sensible thing: maybe get a good night's sleep?

On the stereo, Suzanne Vega sang:

> "And she says, 'I've come to set a twisted
> thing straight'
> And she says, 'I've come to lighten this
> dark heart'
> And she takes my wrist, I feel her imprint
> of fear
> And I said, 'I never thought of finding
> you here'"

She didn't know why her emotions chose that moment to bushwhack her: the brandy, the tension, the mummies within, the haunting dreamlike quality of the music itself. Whatever it was, it put a ripple in the world that stopped Meryl dead in her tracks: her eyes grown suddenly hot with warning, a liquid chill rolling down her spine, a tightness in the back of her throat that spread out into her shoulders, her fingertips, the small of her back.

And one other thing: a feeling so incongruous—so familiar and yet so out of context—that it dizzied her in its grip. Not just the feeling of being watched: that came and went. No, this was more of a physical thing, like sensing a warm body just behind you.

A feeling of proximity.

Of someone, very close...

"Jesus," she whispered, catching herself. The air felt suddenly leaden; she needed to sit down. She turned, brandy glass sloshing slightly, and moved back to the couch.

But the echo of the feeling lingered, brought strange thoughts to roost with it. She looked at the last two folders beside her. The last two stories. All that stood in the way.

It didn't matter what the feeling really meant. She would never know.

And so, was free.

To draw her own conclusions...

DEADLINES

Kane watched the old man kill himself for a good fifteen years before he finally got it right.

It took that long, he supposed, to prepare the intricate implements of his destruction: to allow the dissatisfactions, the failures and the unfulfilled dreams of a lifetime to simmer to perfection, like some old secret family recipe.

"The accumulation," his father said, clear as a bell. Kane stood by the big hospital bed and watched his father fumble with the restraints, canvas tentacles tethering his wasted limbs to the cold steel frame. His hair was an ash-white nest of snakes rimming the dome of his skull, static electricity from the sheets making the individual strands waft in the perfectly still air of the ward.

"The accumulation."

His eyes stared quizzically up through the ceiling: even half-focused in fear, they were blue and piercing as shards of ice. They were a fine family trait, like the aquiline nose, and the intelligence and the wit, and the penchant for substance abuse and self-destruction. They had been engaged, for the last few hours or so, in bewildered contemplation of the miracle undulating before him: a sooty, black snow that drifted in from the corridor and across the ceiling, piling up in zigs and zags and artful twirls and swirls, only to rain down like mist and stick to his fingers like tiny, gummy bugs.

"Don't you see them?" he asked Kane anxiously. "For heaven's sake, they're plain as day."

"I don't see 'em, Dad," Kane replied. "I'm sorry."

It was true. Kane was very sorry, and he really wished he *could* see the black snow, or the gummy bugs, or the endless corridors that stretched out past the walls, or any of the sundry other visions his father had wandered through in the last fifty hours. It might give him a clue to what lay

223

behind the shadowy, fluttering hoods that shaded those icy eyes, a key to unlock the hell the old man had built.

"It's accumulating," his father reiterated, twisting purposefully toward the edge of the bed. "This is terrible."

No shit. And the old man was damned well going to do something about it. He struggled weakly against his bonds, expending what little strength remained in pull after pull. Eventually the simple physics of the situation prevailed, and he slumped back against his pillow in defeat. The gaze he turned back to Kane was that of an ancient, frightened child, encased in a prison of uncomprehending and dying flesh. The straps had left deep, purplish-brown bruises on his wrists and ankles. His upper torso was clad in a johnny harness, it utility disguised in an ugly plaid cloth that was possibly someone's idea of a jaunty robe but more likely somebody's idea of a bad joke. The restraints did their duty: not allowing him to get up, nor turn over, nor allow any limb to touch any other. They kept him centered on the bed.

They kept him under control.

A necessary evil, the night nurse said. He had pulled out his catheter twice last night; Kane winced to even think about it. Hell, he'd even yanked his IV out four times, all in similar moments of delirium.

But that's what the DTs are all about, aren't they? Kane thought bitterly. *Delirium Tremens. Hallucinations. Disorientation. Panic. Terror. If the stroke didn't kill him outright, the DTs still might. Isn't that what the doctor said? We'll just have to wait and see.*

Kane was tired of waiting. He'd been waiting for a long time now. He wondered if he was a monster for wanting to just get on with it. Or maybe he was just impatient with the method. Because, when push came to the shove, Kane's old man had chosen to kill himself the old-fashioned way.

Inch by inch.

He had measured his death each day in his glass, with a squirt of reconstituted lime juice and a dash of club soda. But mostly with an endless, incremental measure of Bowman's Virginia Vodka, which had to rate right up there with Orwell's Victory Gin in pure viscosity and brain-rotting vileness. Kane's old man went through a bottle every other day; sometimes more, never less.

Kane could never understand it, though he was able to log the ritual in meticulous detail: every morning, sometime after hacking up great burbling clots of the previous day's tar 'n' nicotine quotient but well before lunch, he'd start to drink. A couple of years ago he was able to wait until after lunch, when it became somewhat more respectable, even rakish. But as time wore on, it became harder and harder to resist the urge to sneak just a squeak of it into his coffee. To get the ball rolling.

By early afternoon, it was downhill all the way: lime and soda time, and to hell with the hindmost. The glass would seem almost magical in its ability to maintain its inch of sauce, no matter how many sips he took. Of course, he'd have to freshen it up periodically. But he only really drained it two, maybe three times in a day; hence, if pressed he could ever claim that he had only two or three drinks a day. It was a neat trick, one that allowed him to damn near buy his own bullshit.

Until now, Kane thought. *Kinda hard to deny the fucking hallucinations, isn't it, Dad? Hard to have a mild case of the DTs. Like being kinda pregnant.*

Or slightly dead . . .

Kane could hear the *tik-tik-tik* of high heels echoing up the hall. Mother coming, he just knew it. He watched his dad settle into the pillow, watched those tired eyes roll deep into their plum-colored sockets. Out again. The doctors said it might be a reaction to the Librium and the Haldol, or any of the other drugs that formed the narcotic insulation that held his demons at bay. Then again it might be simple swelling of the brain. Kinda hard to tell, until the delirium subsided.

Tik-tik-tik. Any second now. He didn't know if he could handle it; comfort and solace seemed as utterly beyond him as the sun and the moon. He tasted the bile and the frustration welling up somewhere deep inside, and contemplated spewing it out even as he understood the essential pointlessness of the act. Why bother? At this late stage, it would be like kicking sick puppies. Anger would accomplish nothing, and solve even less. There was nothing left to do with it.

And nowhere for it to go.

But closer, ever closer.

Toward the deadline . . .

Explanations were always cheap, always plentiful, and always off the mark. The socially acceptable suicides were like that. If you were a misanthrope, at least, it was different: if you ate a bullet or stuck your head in the oven or jumped off a bridge, you usually left a note, some pathetically touching, unheeded cry for help. Tsk-tsk. Everyone knew your number.

But if on the other hand you subscribed to the approved methodology, note-leaving was unthinkable. After all, that implied choice. You couldn't suck down two packs a day for twenty or thirty years and then pin a note to your lapel, now could you? And you couldn't very well be expected to piss on such great American institutions as the happy hour.

No, the upright suicides were a different breed. They built the instruments of their destruction bit by bit, so that when those suckers finally fired up it was almost like a miracle, almost like an accident.

And they left their notes, such as they were, pinned to the people they left behind. You didn't so much see them as feel them, probing like blind fingers over braille, reading the bumps of the ritual scarification. Playing connect-the-dots with the moments of a lifetime.

This, of course, led to endless speculations, endless readings of clues. The old man had no coping mechanism. The old man just gave up trying. Booze did it. Smoking did it. Stress did it. The devil did it. The list went on and on. Kane always figured that if he had to pick, it would have to be *all of the above* and more. Much more.

Now that it was in his face, Kane saw a whole 'nother reason altogether.

> Deadline. (ded' lin') n. **1.** A time limit, as for the completion of newspaper copy or other work, payment of debts, etc. **2.** Originally, within the

limits of a prison, a boundary line that a prisoner
might not cross under penalty of death.

It seemed as though the torture would never end.

First, the stroke: number two, with a bullet. He'd been
warned; number one hit the charts five years ago, and he
got off with no paralysis, no impairment, a clean bill of
health. His doctors told him he was incredibly lucky, give
up the cigarettes and the booze and the fatty foods and
he'd live another twenty years.

He took their advice, for a couple of months. Then he
went back to the old ways.

"You can't keep this up," Kane told him. It was one of
their home-from-college-man-to-man-late-night-drink-'n'-
rap sessions: Kane downing too many beers while his
father nursed that bottomless inch-deep pool in his glass.
A great time for honest forthrightness and candor. "You'll
die if you do. Is that what you want?"

"I'll die anyway," his father replied.

"Yeah, but this way you'll die sooner."

"Listen, little buddy," Kane's father said authoritatively,
using a tone that he was sure reeked of wisdom but to
Kane simply reeked. "A man only has four pleasures in
this life . . . Food . . . Sex . . . Smoke . . . and Drink."

Kane couldn't believe his ears. It was a lunatic reasoning, like listening to Boris Karloff as Frankenstein's monster, going "MMMMM . . . Food, good . . . Drink, good . . .
Fire, BAAAADDD . . ." It was nuts.

He watched as his father sucked in a thick acrid plume
off a Winchester cigarillo. He actually inhaled it; Christ,
he thought, who inhales cigar smoke? It was the smoker's
equivalent of mainlining. He exhaled in a violent coughing
fit, as if something wanted out of his chest desperately.
Kane watched him contort, choke, and gradually bring it
under control.

"Anyway," his father grumbled, "the doctors say I can't
have the first one anymore, and I'm sure as hell not
getting any of the second."

He gestured back toward Mother's bedroom; Kane rolled
his eyes. "So you'd rather die, is that it?"

"I don't know," his father sighed, "but I'll tell you this

much. Every once in a while I think to myself: if I could go to sleep tonight and just never wake up at all, that would be just fine."

Their eyes met then, for the first time in ages: two souls exchanging glances as they passed in the night; one going up, the other down. Kane didn't often look at his father anymore. It was too uncomfortable; it was like staring at a ghost. He killed off the last of his beer and took a long deep breath before answering.

"You might not get off that easy, you know," he said, very slowly. "You might not get to pass blissfully in your sleep. You might just wind up in Riverdale ICU with a tube up your nose, blinking once for yes and twice for no."

Kane stood, surveying the wreckage. Another stray clot had been inspired to fire down that tube and lodge in some dark fissure of the brain. It had happened in his sleep; he woke up, got up, went to the bathroom, and fell over.

Boom.

Kane heard about it fifteen hours later. He drove all night, coming down from the rustic little cabin in upstate New York where he'd holed himself up to work on his new book. The whole way down, his thoughts drifted back to that long-ago conversation. The whole way down, one thought kept repeating, over and over again.

"Nice try."

Stroke number three had followed in short order, within hours of being admitted. It sent him into a medically mystifying stupor; they simply couldn't keep him awake. For two days, he drifted in and out of consciousness.

On the third day he rose, miraculously reawakened, weak but lucid. The first thing he asked Kane for were his cigarettes.

By mid-afternoon, the DTs kicked in.

And the black snow came.

It fell for four days, a bleary-eyed wash of delirium and sedatives, needles and tubes and canvas restraints. Kane slept very little, poised on the death-watch while his father took many strange journeys.

By the morning of the fifth day, the DTs had passed. By the afternoon of the fifth day his system had an adverse reaction to the sedatives, and he went to sleep again.

Two days later he awoke, coughing horribly. Seven days on his back had produced a spectacular case of hospital pneumonia. Again modern medicine came to the rescue, with bronchial dilators and ever more tubes and needles and pills.

And he just got weaker and weaker, inch by inch, closer.

To the deadline.

Kane had been forewarned about the paralysis, and the bilateral swelling of the brain, and the dozen-odd other biological disasters that had transpired. They were all dire, all terrifying.

But they all paled, next to the look in his father's eyes.

The uncertainty was the worst. In a bad movie Kane might somehow know, just by looking at him. Real sad violins and cellos in the background, swelling with passion at that moment of true contact.

Real life didn't work that way. Six inches from his father's grizzled, swollen face, holding the claw of his frozen left hand and staring into those eyes with only the hiss and burble of medical machinery for accompaniment, Kane couldn't tell if his father even knew who he was.

Worse still was to consider that Dad might indeed know, and want to react, but not be able to, betrayed and imprisoned by a conspiracy of blood and brain and bad habits.

Outside, Kane appeared calm. Inside, he felt numb. He was aware of the presence of feelings, in a kind of cold, abstract way. He watched the synapses fly from a great distance, even heard exact replicas of emotional reactions coming out of his very own mouth. But he didn't really feel attached to them.

Not that there was any shortage of emotional grist: guilt, anger. Remorse. Rage.

Pointless rage: at his father for courting misery and death, at his mother for aiding and abetting the cause, at both of them for not having the guts to work it out or the balls to call it quits; at God Almighty, author of this mad melodrama and architect of Original Obsolesence, the only One who would deign to build creatures so terrifyingly fragile that a lifetime of knowledge and experience could be wiped instantly from the face of the earth by a lump of cholesterol no bigger than a goddam booger, for chrissakes, an insignificant speck of matter hurtling through an infinitesimally small space to run amok among even more perilously delicate matter.

"Do you know who I am?" Kane stared at his father's eyes. "Can you say my name?"

Nothing. The eyes stared at him, registering awareness but no emotion. They did not track any movement; six inches to either side and his father was staring blankly at the ceiling. Kane tried to center himself, tried to meet the gaze.

Finally, he did. Those blue, frozen orbs locked on his.

And Kane gazed into the abyss.

His mother and sister were talking to the doctor; it was all a burble of incomprehensible modulating tones, coming from some distant galaxy. Kane gazed into the abyss.

The abyss, through his father's eyes, gazed back.

It held for thirty seconds, give or take a lifetime. Then the old man's gaze just drifted away, toward some distant inner space, and he was gone again.

No one noticed as Kane walked out into the corridor, and kept on walking. He found the bathroom with the quiet urgency and aplomb of someone about to be violently, desperately ill. He entered softly. Locked the door.

And cried. Until the tears wouldn't come anymore.

■

"I've been thinking about your father's last wishes."

Kane sat across from his mother in the hospital cafeteria, a congealed lump of tuna fish salad sitting untouched before him. A glass of iced tea that tasted like runoff from a Jersey chemical spill sat next to it. He wanted the food about as much as he wanted to hear his mother's next words, which was not very. But like the food, he figured he'd better take it all in. So he ate. And listened.

"He always said he wanted to be cremated and have his

ashes scattered at sea," she said. "So I've decided that, when he dies, I'm going to take a cruise and do just that."

She nodded her head, in complete agreement with herself. The absurdly mercenary logic of her survival instinct was genuinely impressive. Kane looked at her flatly, trying not to react. It wasn't too hard; he felt as if his heart had scabbed over damned near completely. *Bon voyage*, he thought. *What a great way to start fresh: no plot to keep weeded, no urn to clutter up the mantlepiece, no unpleasant reminders. Just anchors aweigh as we sail into the sunset . . .*

"Good plan, Mom," Kane mumbled. *Maybe I can bribe the mortician to save a bone hunk for me.*

"Don't feel bad about your father," she said, by way of comfort. "He chose to do things this way."

Kane nodded. *Yeah,* he thought. *That's very true. He did choose this fate.*

But he had help . . .

It was so perverse. There came a point where it was possible to see one's parents, not from a child's point of view, but more as peers: people who grew up, grew older, made decisions, made choices.

Made mistakes.

Had they ever really loved each other? He didn't know. Maybe *they* didn't even know. They must have, once upon a time, when they were young and nothing in the world was beyond the grasp of their imaginations. They had it together for a while, anyway; Kane had memories of a happy, stable childhood.

And then something clicked, like a forgotten land mine waiting years for that one misplaced step.

Kane's father had given him some scraps of information, from time to time. Others he had gleaned from his mother, or his sister. But piecing together the story of his parents' lives made Kane feel like an archeologist deciphering the cuneiforms of a lost civilization. Fragments surfaced. Most were probably lost to him forever.

It was during the heady last days of the Big War. He was a lieutenant in the Navy: handsome and cocky, fighting the good fight with the world by the balls. She was a model and a nightclub singer: a flighty, pretty girl with great gams and a gold digger's streak. She'd married him less for love than for security, thinking him to be better off than he was; at best, she very likely loved him a whole lot less than he loved her. Kane couldn't really bash her for climbing—from what he knew, she'd grown up working-class poor, abandoned by her natural parents and raised by relatives—but he always thought if she'd wanted to be *nouveau riche* she should have done more thorough research.

She accepted her fate like a trooper, and their years together ran the middle class gamut of the postwar years. They begat their fair share of the baby boom—Karen, Kevin and Kane—and juggled kids and careers in a kind of all-American ascendancy. He studied and eventually went on to become a university professor; not a lot of money but it had a certain class, and it was something he believed in passionately.

She gave up performing but eventually discovered a talent for art, and went on to become a sculptor. Their social life burgeoned as they worked their way into a lively local art scene, with lots of friends, lots of shows, and awards and parties galore.

And then somewhere along the way they lost their footing. The parties got wilder. The drinking got harder. Make no mistake; they both drank. But there was a difference, a line crossed, made clearer by the passage of time. Mother had a drinking problem. Dad was an alcoholic. Dad lost his tenure at the university, some terrible scandal the kids weren't let in on.

Kane never did find out what that was; another fragment lost in the great excavation. All he knew was that when he was fourteen they moved to a bohunk cowtown ten years behind the times. Dad had secured a position at a smaller, infinitely less prestigious college in a distant state, uprooted the family, vaporized the art shows, the parties, the social whirl.

She never forgave him.

They hobbled through the changes, growing ever more depressed and alienated from themselves and each other. He ultimately quit teaching altogether, no longer able to breathe fire into complacent, indifferent students, no longer able to see any reason why he should care. The world was going to hell in a handbasket, and he just didn't give a shit.

Kane grew away from them; searching for his own life, determined to define it on his own terms. He was their baby, the youngest. When he left, the remnants of the nest went with him.

Middle age, when it came, found each of his parents blaming the other for their own unhappiness, until their union ultimately degenerated into a bloody war of attrition, where they punished each other for the things they should have done by denying each other the things each needed most.

She had always wanted security. He had failed to provide her that. So she punished him, by denying him: her affection, his self-esteem. He punished her back, and himself in the bargain, by ceasing to care: about his life, about his health, about much of anything.

And he started the serious drinking.

Not the falling-down drunk kind; at least, not until much later. No, his was the brand that happened slowly, insidiously; a disconnecting process so gradual that you might not even see the change if you didn't know the man. In the mornings, there'd be the semblance of the father Kane remembered: soft-spoken, though tired. A gentle and intelligent man.

By afternoon, invariably, the torture had resumed. The voice raised. The temper flared. Everything became an irritant: the dog, the house, his wife, his job, his world.

Life itself.

Life irritated him from early afternoon through late evening, and on into the dead of night after night after night.

And after a while, it never stopped at all.

Still, they clung to the marriage: working at cross-purposes, antagonizing each other, racking up the years like points of some imaginary scorecard. *We might be miserable, but we'd been together three decades and that counts for something, goddammit!*

Eventually, she couldn't imagine a scenario in which

she actually felt like she loved him again. She needed him, yes, indeed. In ways that she couldn't see, which would become very apparent when he was gone. But she couldn't let that through. She was marking time, she said, waiting for him to die so that she could get on with her life, afraid that if they split up now what little insurance he had would end up in the hands of some twenty-year-old chippie. He was actually worth more dead to her than alive.

Eventually, she said it so often that she came to believe it.

Kane couldn't fathom why his father even remained in the game. Probably because he loved her still, beneath it all. And he needed—desperately, more than he could say—to *be* loved. By her.

But he had maneuvered himself into a lose-lose situation: the more he drank, the less he cared. The less he cared, the worse it got. The worse it got, the more she harped. The more she harped, the less she could ever hope to express her love for him. The less she loved, the more he drank. The more he drank . . .

And on. And on. It was a downward spiraling vortex, a doomed duet, with death at its heart.

His.

You were supposed to be understanding; yeah, sure. You were supposed to forgive, to remember that we're only human, after all, that each of us has their faults and their shortcomings. Like the saying went, *"If you love someone, you don't expect too much of them."*

"Fuckin' aye," Kane muttered, bringing the axe down with all his strength. Wood cracked like a rifle shot in the cold night air. *Don't expect too much of them.* Right. Tell it to the worms. Tell it to the fucking carpet beetles. Kane saw it differently.

The exact inverse, in fact. If you love someone, you expect an awful fucking lot. More than from anyone else on earth. If you love someone, you couldn't help but let them in, close to the soft, beating mass of your heart. It was an inescapable risk. You let them in and hoped that they didn't hurt you. You hoped that, if they couldn't find it in themselves to live for their own sake, maybe they could get it up for the sake of those they loved. You hoped that there'd be enough time for everyone to work it out.

No matter what they did, no matter how often they did it, you held out Hope.

As the death watch ticked, toward its inevitable end.

You held out Hope.

Til the end of the line.

You held out.

Until you just couldn't hold it anymore, until you were burned and burned and burned past all hope of recognition. Until something inside you one day just snapped...

Kane gathered up the load in his arms to carry into the cabin. Inside, he laid the damp wood down on the hearth, laid a fire in the fireplace, and coaxed it to light. Then he sat down at the table that held his Smith-Corona and fed in a clean sheet of paper. He had to get back to work; the chore of cannibalizing his experience for posterity beckoned.

There was a small bone-dry aquarium among the clutter of the tabletop, with a string of colorful postcards propped up against its glass wall. They were all from tropical ports-of-call in the Caribbean, all postmarked recently, all signed *having a lovely time wish you could see this love mother*. Lots of beautiful sunsets. Kane stared at their colorful cavalcade for a moment, and wrote:

> I see the deadlines in my father's face. They grow deeper every day: prominent in the harsh winter light; drawn from the hollow sockets of his eyes, sketched in papyrus skin, and sadness, and time. Too much time.
>
> Too little time.
>
> I see the walls of his prison. I see the boundary, and the debt to be paid. Though we are close enough to touch, there is no contact. It is as though he has been sealed away, locked in a hell the depths of which I cannot fathom. We look, but do not touch.
>
> For a long time I wanted only to tear down the walls, to smash those fuckers into dust. I wanted

to pull him back from the edge he seemed so determined to cross.

Now, I welcome his departure. I celebrate his passing from this veil of sorrow, that he may join the all-consuming light, embrace his karmic destiny, reflect upon his travails in the sweet repose of eternal Night. I welcome his departure, that I can better get on with the process of honoring his memory.

So that I can better deny the spark of him that lies buried within his son.

There was a small pile of wood shavings filling the aquarium's center. Nestled on the shavings was a skull. Carpet beetles crawled across its cracks and crevasses, diligently cleaning the surface. Its hair was an ash-white nest of snakes rimming the dome of the skull, the movement of many tiny bodies making the individual strands rustle in the perfectly still air of the tank. They'd been at it for a long time now.

They were almost done.

I catch a glimpse of it every now and again; in a cough or a gesture, some nuance or tone of voice. I see my reflection out of the corner of my eye and it's him, an updated version of the beaten-down man with the sad blue eyes.

And it frightens me.

Because there's a mad rhythm to his, palpable as the *tiktiktik* of shoes down a hospital corridor, as the clock that runs down a life that lasts too long and ends too soon; a mad logic that says: if we are the younger versions of our parents, are they not older versions of ourselves? Are we as much a product of their struggle as their blood? Are we also doomed to roll over, to murder our dreams one day at a time, to endlessly replicate the sad patterns of this pathetic, genetic code? And are our children, when they come, likewise doomed to repeat our mistakes, as we repeat those of our forefathers?

I think not.
I will not.
I will find the key to this prison. I will end this
game.

*It wasn't a very hard thing to do, physically speaking.
Certainly no harder than bribing the mortician. It was a
private room, at the end of the hall, and the acoustics
were such that you could hear approaching footsteps from
clear down to the nurse's station. It didn't even take very
long. The pillow was big, and very soft, and he was so
weak. His lungs were godawful bad, practically emphysemic.
Who would notice one more brief choking spell?*

I will know what lies behind those sad blue eyes.

Kane looked at the skull. The beetles went about their
task, unmindful of the audience.

Very soon.

Meryl turned the last page with trembling fingers, reached for the brandy, pulled her hand back sharply.

He had come too close, too close this time. He had dragged her down to the secret place and ground her face against its walls. The reek of self-destruction was a tangible thing in the air, a rotting stench that clung to her like night sweat. She could almost hear the flies.

"Please," she said, imploring the walls. The walls hung on her words. "Come back. Come back. Don't take me all the way down here and leave me, don't . . . just don't let it end like this, please . . ."

She reached out her hand for the final folder, hesitated an inch from its manila skin. There was no way around the dread she felt. It was as real as the paper on which it focused. She prayed for the next words to bear her some comfort, to shine with some shred of the vanishing light.

She prayed for those things.

But only the walls were listening.

THE DIFFERENCE

Part I: Terminal

Blood and dust and frozen rain: the tastes and textures of the world. Max Hart carried the first through the second and out into the third: away from the screech of the South Ferry station, to be wetly pelted and embraced by a night as black as a cancerous lung. Boot-heel clack and puddle splash, step after step, in pain and on purpose.

Then through the smoke-caked door of glass.

And back to dust again.

Inside the terminal, only one of the escalators was working. Up and up, not down and down. "This must be some kind of a joke," he said, wiping ice and water from face and hair. "You got your metaphors crossed. To go down is easy. Going up is what's hard."

Nothing new. God was lying again. He'd have thought that he'd have gotten used to it by now, but no. God's treachery was one big fat endless surprise. The world was His jack-in-the-box, and He held the crank, so you never knew when or where that sinister clownface would rear up, leering. You only knew, if you ever got wise, that it would. Sooner or later.

Max Hart stared at the broken escalator and wished that it was working. He'd have liked to walk up as it rolled down, bucked the tide one last time before drowning beneath it.

No such luck.

Blood and dust and frozen rain.

He took the escalator, as God had willed, secure in the knowledge that what goes up must come down.

The Manhattan terminal of the Staten Island Ferry was a sprawling concrete Purgatory. Max slipped his quarter in the slot and slid through the turnstile, began the final wait.

He wasn't alone. Dozens of lost souls were in atten-

239

dance, scattered throughout the vast interior. Most of them didn't seem to know exactly how lost they were. They were lining up for coffee and beer, hot dogs and cookies and grim psuedo-pizza; they were milling about the magazine stand, lapping up scandals from the alleged lives of vapid celebs and corrupt politicians, some straining their craniums all the way up to the V. C. Andrews and Judith Krantz–populated heights of contemporary literature. For every dozen that kept to themselves, a cool dozen more were shucking and jiving. The air was alive with their echoing laughter.

They didn't know—they *couldn't* know—how completely the joke was on them.

Max didn't care. He was beyond caring. Max was just waiting for the great door to open. Depending on which clock he believed, it would be anywhere from five to twenty-five minutes. He prayed for the former and banked on the latter, tried very hard to keep his mind as empty as his eyes and his heart had become.

Fat fucking chance.

There was a pane of glass in front of him, windowing in to the drunks lined up at the terminal bar. He didn't see them, didn't see them at all. His eyes were locked on the pale reflection that stared back at him, a ghost already...

The shade in the glass stood just under six feet. Its face was puffy and milk-spider pale, the cheekbones buried under scruff and swelling. The soul-black eyes were moist glinting islands, adrift in pools of purple bruise-flesh surrounding either side of the broken nose.

The shade was dressed in battered chic, high style gone to brawling seed. There was blood on the scarf around its neck, blood down the front of its open jacket. The white cloth wrapped around its hand was almost entirely red: a quaint reminder of the last mirror that had reminded it of who it was...

Max Hart stared at the shadowed glass one moment longer, then turned away. He did not want to see himself, but at least the urge to smash was gone. It had been beaten out of him some forty-five minutes earlier, along with the rest of his will to live, by a surly McSorley's waiter who'd had every right to punch his lights out. He had, after all, chosen to go nuts in a public place, destroying private property and screaming his lungs out; it had earned him a very public beating, and a boot out the door into his own private hell.

It was no big deal.

It was just the last straw.

Last straw plucked from a scarecrow's gut, leaving the empty fabric shell to cave in on itself . . .

And that, of course, threw the whole thing wide open. *Let it all hang out,* as the groovy denizens of the sixties had been wont to say, fucking baby-boomers who'd grown up thinking they were the only important generation in human history. Yeah, they'd been known to say all kinds of shit that the darker days a-comin' had proven pathetic: things like *sock it to me* and *I really grok your vibes, far out, man* and *flower power* and *you can't trust anyone over thirty.*

But of all the stupid things they'd said, the dumbest and most pernicious of the batch was *all you need is love.* Mostly because it sounded so good, it sounded so right; when the Beatles sang it, you had to believe it was true.

More lies from God. More goddam lies. All Max had to do was look around him—even easier, look inside at his *own* charmed life—to blow that misbegotten bastard sentiment right out of the water for good.

Oh, yeah, Max growled to himself in silence, tears taking form in his pummeled eyes. *All you need is love. But a rubber ain't a bad idea, either, because all you really need is herpes or AIDS or maybe just a nice simple unwanted pregnancy. In which case, all you need is an abortion, and all you need is for them to fuck it up. Yeah, that's the ticket! all you need is a botched abortion. Then all you need is to run away. All you need is a series of accidents, a healthy dose of cowardice, and a nice ledge to jump from. All you need is an empty bed to scream in as you lay awake in the dark of a night that never ends. All you need is a butchered baby whose face you'll never see, a woman who you thought you loved and whose face you'll never see again, all you need is love but all you'll get is the hate she feels and the hate you feel for yourself . . .*

Then the great door opened, and he took his tears with him as he followed the lost ones who now filed out.

Toward the death ship.
And the other shore.

Part II: Death Ship

It was one of the old ones, for which he was grateful. It was, in fact, his favorite: the one and only Death Ship. Max felt a pang of something almost like joy, more like vindication, as he set foot on its icy deck.

He hated the new boats. *Floating bus stations,* Cassie had called them, and Max could not improve on the appellation. Plastic seats of orange and yellow, as far as the eye could see. Ticky-tack snack bar. Balconies enclosed with smoke-shittied safety glass. They were horrid contraptions, bereft of charm, funkless as the smooth expanse where Barbie and Ken's genitals were meant to be.

But *this* one—the Death Ship, the John F. Kennedy—was without a doubt the cream of the Staten Island fleet. It had character out the ass. It had character like Humphrey Bogart's face had character, and was probably just about as old as the best of Bogie's films. The seats were made of solid wood; no goddam plastic here. They looked lived-in, the way your grampa's favorite rocker did. The snack bar was crummy, but at least it didn't look like a Burger King caught in a trash compactor.

Best of all was the upper deck, with the open-air balconies adorning the sides. You could stand up there, leaning out over the rails, and stare straight down at the brackish water of the upper New York Harbor. No murky, spittoon-flavored safety glass between you and the Jersey insecticide vats, the eternally waving Statue of Liberty.

That was the important thing: no safety glass.

Max stood on the lower deck, watching the last vehicles wheel aboard, nestling themselves in the three aisles of parking womb that the ferry provided. Then the crewmen cordoned off the end zone with a stout length of chain, unhooked the boat from the loading ramp, and they were ready to cast off toward the black horizon. This had always been his favorite part of the journey; no way was he going to miss it now.

Standing there, watching the boat's slow disengagement and retreat, was purest real-life cinema. The rumble of the massive engines, shuddering up through the soles of his feet. The white foamspray of the deep dark water, madly churning in the widening gap between the hull and the receding shore. The gates at the end of the vehicle ramp, fading back to the vanishing point, the great weathered and beaten wooden walls looming up and out to either side, the vista slowly widening, broadening, spreading out as rumble turned to roar and foamspray segued into cold mock-percolating swath and trail, the black-irised camera lens panning regally back and further back as the panorama quantum-leaped in magnitude, majestic sweep too huge for tiny camera-brain, sucking air from camera-lungs as the edge of the city unfolded, revealed itself, bared its infinite glittering glimmering blind glass eyes, doorways to the soul of the city, to him . . .

. . . and he felt the pull of it, the yank of his spine, the tug of lifelines playing out and playing out, searching for just an inch of slack and finding none, the reel unraveling, hot as it spun, melting the ice that his heart had become, ice water trickling down into his belly, cold as the frozen rain creeping down his back as he stood there, watching the city fade back into distance . . .

. . . and it was his life he was leaving behind, it was a stinking shitty life in a stinking shitty world but it was the only one he knew, and he couldn't stop the sadness, the sense of pain and the sense of loss, any more than he could stop the boat or the waves it rode or the earth it adorned, speck of dust in an empty universe, speck of dandruff on the lapel of the empty laughing lunatic God that manufactured it all, from the primordial slime from whence it came to the bombs that would send it right back where it came from, back to nothing, dust to dust . . .

. . . and when the line was all played out, and the high-tension hum was the roar of the engines, he turned his thoughts to Cassie and his blown last chance at love. He thought of her as she had been when their eyes first met, when their smiles first alighted. He thought of those eyes, and the promise they'd held. Promise of warmth, an inner spark, infusing his life's cold bleak terrain with light and heat and meaning...

...and it had been good, it *had* been good, he could remember nights so sweet their ghosts still ached in the pit of his stomach, days so fine and full of laughter he could almost believe in the words to the song. He could remember them all too well, because there had been so few of them, and they had been over so quickly...

...and then had come the mornings when he had awakened, not to her willing warmth, but to the sound of her heaving in the bathroom down the hall. It had taken no genius to figure out what that meant. Those harsh, wracking tonalities harkened back to the world he understood, the one he'd hoped was left behind: the world where dreams were cannon fodder, where love was an artificial carrot on a stick, a reason to live for the donkey-faced hordes...

...but, lo and behold, that world was back; indeed, from all the evidence, it had never really left, just been pushed back for a while by his own mad desire to see the little dreamy dream come true, to hold God to His fucking word for once, just for once...

...but no...

"*Stop,*" he whispered. "*Stop it. Now.*" Absurd, of course: there was no end. Only in the water.

Only beneath the waves...

Max took a moment to get his bearings, dragged a clipped breath in and out. The city was small now, a toy box in the distance. He could take the World Trade Center and crush them in his hands. Off to his left was Ellis Island; slightly behind him, the Liberty Belle. She was waving hello.

She was waving goodbye.

It was time to go inside now. It was time to go upstairs. Somewhere in the course of his quaint reminiscence, the lifelines had snipped and gone falling away. *Arrivederci, mon ami. Sayonara. Bon voyage.*

There was nothing left for him to do.

But go inside.

And go upstairs.

*   *   *

They called it the Death Ship for three main reasons. First, and most obvious, was its proper namesake: our beloved President, John F. Kennedy, he of the exploding head and endless conspiracy theories. Second was the fact that, for some strange reason, it had been involved in more accidents than any other in the ferry run's history. Stupid shit, mostly: coming into the dock too fast, pasting the very occasional tugboat. Some people had died along the way. The way of the world. The world as we know it.

The third reason was the most important, at least from Max Hart's point of view. It was the reason why he'd come: why his footfalls dragged upwards, step by step, on purpose and in pain.

It was at least part of the reason why the upper deck was closed at night.

But they hadn't bothered to lock the doors. He had known that they wouldn't. That was why he had come.

Standing amidships, he looked around. No one was watching. No cops at all. No one to stop him as he moved to the doors with the sign that read CLOSED AFTER 9 P.M.

Opened the doors.

And stepped into the darkness.

Part III: Voices

Blood and dust and frozen rain: the tastes and textures of the world. Max Hart, alone with his senses, took them in and savored them, a psychic gestalt snapshot to take with him.

On his journey to the other shore.

The upper deck, unlit, at night, resembled nothing so much as the inside of an abandoned church: the empty wooden benches so much like pews, row upon row, disappearing into the deeper dark; the wind, whistling through the sliding doors, like the spirit-residue of some long-ago parish choir. It stirred something in him that he scarcely expected: a flicker, a spark, of misguided but undeniable reverance.

Reverence for what? he demanded of himself, feeling bile-scented anger well up in response. *Reverence for life? Give me a fucking break. Life is cheap, and born to die. If life was worth the meat it's etched in, it wouldn't be dealt*

*in such shabby hands. Reverence for love? I won't even
dignify that horseflop with an answer.*

*Reverence for God? Get out of my face. That malevo-
lent turd is the last on my list. If God had any reverence
for life or love, I...*

And that was where he stopped, because the statement
begged a question that he wasn't sure he wanted to ask. It
struck him as chickenshit to raise those doubts at this late
stage of the game. He had all the answers he needed, all
the right and reason in the world to do this thing, this
thing that had brought him to this place...

...and the sliding doors were to his right, the wind and
the rain were calling to him, the water below was calling
to him and there was no more time to waste. All too soon,
the ferry and all the lost souls it transported would be
pulling into Staten Island, perpetuating the farces that
were their lives. Max had no intention of being among
them.

He moved toward the doors.

But as he moved, his mind raced on, speaking not in
words but in pictures. And the pictures refused to leave
him alone, they badgered him with every step, tugging at
him as he gripped the handles, pulling at him as he
yanked the doors open, tearing into him as the wind and
the rain tore into his face...

...and he stepped outside...

...and the pictures were of Cassie's face, her eyes so
bright, the bed so warm; the pictures were of a baby he
had never seen and never would; the pictures were of a
baby that had never been but still could be, it had
happened once, it could happen again, there was no
reason on earth why it could not happen again...

...and he heard himself screaming, *"FUCK THE BABY!
WHY WOULD I WANT TO BRING A BABY INTO THIS!"*
the sound carried off by the wind and the rain, his tears
subsumed by the wet ice pelting his battered face, his
burning eyes...

...and still the pictures, still they came...

...as he gripped the guardrail with trembling hands,
leaning out over the waves...

. . . and then he heard the voices, softly singing, from below.

Part IV: The Other Shore

Voices of water and voices of mist. Icy voices. Shadow voices. Voices that sang in mournful moaning choruses, voices that wailed behind, voices that sang of love and loss and infinite regret . . .

"No," he whispered.

The voices sang . . .

. . . of other nights and other days, looking down over the rails; of other emptinesses, each one different, all the same . . .

"No." His hands: unclenching, clenching. "It's all in my head. More lies from God . . ."

. . . the voices, singing Death Ship songs . . .

"More goddam fucking lies . . ."

. . . the voices, calling out to him . . .

. . . and he could see them now, could see them floating on the water: skeleton arms reaching out in welcome, skeletal jaws parting wide in song. He closed his eyes. He still could see them. He opened his eyes. He still could see them . . .

. . . and Max Hart shouted "No, you're wrong!" as the first one clung to the side of the boat . . .

. . . and Max Hart howled *"Shut up! You're crazy!"* as God's jack-in-the-box popped madly open, and the lost souls climbed the icy wall . . .

. . . and Max Hart screamed *"Goddam you, NO! This is fucking bullshit, this is fucking lies, I REFUSE TO ACCEPT THAT DEATH ISN'T THE END.*

And that was the end of the book.

"What?" she said, staring at the last piece of paper. She fliped it over, scanned the back. Nothing. "What?" she repeated, somewhat louder, leafing quickly through the folder, checking to see that she hadn't missed a page somehow, missed the redemption at the end of all this, the redemption that absolutely fucking had to be there...

"WHAT?" she hollered, but the answer to her question was already implicit, etched into her marrow, etched into the walls. She checked and rechecked the folder, the sofa cushions, the box itself. There was no more: not even a period, not even one little idiot dot of ink to finish the unfinished sentiment.

There was no more.

It was 9:23.

Ten seconds later, the telephone rang.

Meryl jumped as if cattle-prodded, jerked her gaze across the room. For a second the silence settled, and then the telephone rang again. Too loud, too loud, like a skewer through her ears. She got up to stop it. It rang again. She crossed the room and snatched up the handset before it could make that noise again, brought the plastic trembling to her ear.

"Hello?" she said in a voice so thick and dead she barely recognized it.

"Is this 254-2369?" A British voice. She didn't understand what it was doing there.

"Yes?"

"Is this Meryl speaking?"

"Yes." Confusion. "Yes. Who is this?"

"Ah, well. I'm a friend of Katie's. She asked that I call and inform you that she'll unable to frolic with you tonight."

Colin. The name was a hammer, cocking back in her head. It helped to clear her mind. "Wait a minute, wait a minute," she heard herself say. "Is this Colin? Is she with you?"

"Why, yes!" he exclaimed. "On both counts! Very good!"

She felt her composure, an embrittled thing, begin to come apart. It was all she could do to choke down her volume as she said, "What's going on?"

"Well, it's actually quite involved. In fact, I'd hoped you might be able to illuminate me as to some of the particulars..."

"You first."

"Ah." The voice at the other end chuckled. "Perhaps I will." He cleared his throat.

Oh no, she thought. She didn't know why, but it had the ring of truth.

"It seems that Katie has had a rather traumatic experience," Colin continued. "At any rate, it wound her up at my flat with a gillfull of liquor and a rather sordid tale to tell. A ghost story, in fact. Am I ringing any bells?"

"I don't know what you're talking about."

But the room was growing colder.

"Ah ha. Well, to hear her tell it, there's a rather unpleasant discorporate spirit in your apartment, which happens to belong to an old friend of hers. A rather intimate friend, as it turns out."

She wanted to say *that's bullshit*. The words seemed to freeze on her tongue.

"A writer, with whom she had been involved, and who evidently hung himself up by the neck and shuffled off this mortal coil..."

The chill in the room was a tangible thing now. A killing frost, seeping under her skin, numbing her nerves and the dopamines that tracked information from one part of her brain to the next. The words *oh, no* reappeared and then died, were rendered fossils, etched in ice, a monument blocking the flow of his words as they poured into her ear...

oh, no

"... terrified her to such an extent that she claims she can't go back..."

oh, no

"... dead to the world, but you might want to reach her tomorrow..."

oh, no

"... is that alright? Hello...?"

. . . as she slammed down the phone, and the sculpture shattered, leaving her empty and broken inside, dead cold blank eyes panning slow across dead cold blank apartment walls, the chill in the air making sense at last as she focused on the couch and the folders it bore, thought of the box

(DO NOT OPEN 'TIL DOOMSDAY)

and the

(*ghost*)

man she would never meet and the

(*dream*)

love she would never have and

(*oh no*)

then she was moving, slow and steady, slow and steady toward the bathroom, trying so hard to hold it together at least until she hit the toilet, threw herself to the tiles before it, and tried to hack up the poison within her. . .

. . . but it wouldn't come, it was lodged too deep inside, she was stuck with it until she could find a way some way any way to pry it loose . . .

. . . and she looked at the shower, she felt the tears, not here yet but coming, soon, and she scrabbled to her feet and clawed at the idiot fucking costume she wore, tearing away the serpent-clasp on the stupid tie on the sheer white blouse, she couldn't stand the feel of them, she couldn't stand her own white skin, she was stuck with the skin but the clothes weren't so lucky, they were history strewn across the floor as she climbed into the shower stall and threw the water full-tilt on . . .

. . . and the shower was sanctuary, the shower was safe, a safety zone where she could stand bare-assed and let the barriers break down under a deafening stream of boiling water, pounding down, just let it hit you and let it out, yes, let it out just enough to keep from losing it entirely . . .

. . . but things were breaking up too fast down there, the walls were crumbling, and when the first sob came it came hard as a jackhammer jammed into her solar plexus, firing away, it was almost like puking but it came from her eyes and her lungs instead, sound and saline, cinderblocks and rivers that merged with the hot-water thunder and roar that surrounded her, pelted her, pummeled her into the helplessness that allowed the feelings to surface and scream . . .

. . . and he was dead, that was the big payoff, the revelation waiting at the end of her journey: John Paul Rowan was dead dead dead dead all of the fantasies all of the dreams just bullshit wish-fullfillment unfullfilled and unfullfillable, ten million useless tears for every how could I be so stupid sobbing in hideous synchronous parallel motion . . .

. . . because now she would never even fucking know, there would be no hope of meeting him, no hope to calm the storm inside his soul or even be there for a second, dammit, one lousy miserable moment in the whole of eternity, because fucking J. P. had already killed himself he was dead and gone and she wasn't there to stop it and she never even got a chance . . .

. . . and she started to sag, and she caught herself, an almost miraculous act of will, her hands snaking out and clutching the knobs that controlled the flow of the water that pummeled her, steam seeping into her skull like fog, clouding her vision, a billowing gray-white oblivion that crowded in from every side . . .

. . . and her mind said no no no NO NO! twisting the knobs that she clung to for balance, the thunder vanishing in an instant, water suddenly stripped down to a trickle that dribbled straight down on one spot at the crown of her head, like the fabled Chinese Water Torture . . .

. . . and she leaned away, but the fog was still there, pouring in from the left and the right. I'm going to faint, she heard herself say with a terrible monotone matter-of-factness . . .

. . . and she closed her eyes and saw herself, head split open on the tiles on the floor, dark blood reaching out with rivulet fingers to spiral down the drain . . .

. . . and she would not let that happen, she would not be found on the floor like that, so she groped along the shower wall, slapped the curtain weakly out of the way. A great white terry cloth towel dangled from the curtain rod. She grabbed at it, nearly lost her balance, pulled the towel to her as she stumbled out of the stall, caught herself on the bathroom wall and propped herself against it . . .

...and now it was only the music she heard, echoing across the tiles, louder than the sound of her own heart pounding in her temples as she slid sideways toward the door...

> "I came out of the darkness
> Holding one thing..."

...and the room was too bright, the fog too thick, the doorknob a thousand miles away, her arm stretching out and out and out as her hand closed around it, twisted it, pulled...

> "I know I have a power
> I'm afraid I may be killed..."

...as the door swung open, and the cool air blew in, chilling the water that speckled her skin, cutting a wedge in the core of the fog through which she could see the living room...

> "But when I'm dead
> If you could tell them this..."

...but the air was thick was buzzing static, black and iridescent, the sound of it filling her ears...

> "That what was wood became alive..."

...buzzing like the sound of a thousand flies...

> "What was wood became alive..."

...and then she saw him: a shadow man, his face obscured by the black static cloud, his form hovering in the dimishing circle of light before her like the projection of a poorly lit hologram, shifting in and out of focus, reaching out with hands of smoke...

...and in the last moment before she fell, he came to her, moving like light through a tunnel across the room, across the veil, between the arms she held out to him in that moment of sudden mad flash recognition...

...and then, together, they went down.

....
....
....
.....................**NOVEMBER**

14
IN THE FLESH

and i am moving inside you
and you are moving inside me

The loft, transformed: the cold dispersed, the darkness clinging to the walls no longer. Behind the shut and shuttered windows, a sweet near-silence, its whisper strangely overwhelming the roar of the world beyond.

In the bedroom, a rustling on sheets.

The sliding of flesh over flesh, softly merging...

in the body, not of the body, the body moot
yet moving smooth soft mirrored
syncopation to the touch i
give to you you give to
me inside, where thought is
touch and you
are the tongue, the nipple, you
are the fingertip tracing the
wet silk thigh down
tangled thatch and i
am the snatch of clipped
breath, i am the
fingers that part the hungry
lips, one apiece and all
for one, i am the sigh and
you are the gentle rotation, the
liquid rising tide, the heart's
acceleration, the blood in my
veins as i come to you
now, come to you

quickly, come to me over
and over and

Later, much later, her eyes flickered open. Sleep had come, and soon after, the sun. Now the first had gone, and the other was fading.

"The dream is over," she whispered.

And he whispered back, *I know.*

Then, together, they rose and moved naked to the window. The room was bathed in long shadow and golden light. It was the first sunset they'd ever shared—a special thing, never to be repeated—and so she put on her glasses.

The better to savor the sight.

15
NIGHTLIFE

It was cozy and warm in the back of the cab, and the driver spoke next to no English at all. It was a perfect combination: what better way for her man to enjoy his first night out in months?

Oh, God, check it out! he enthused, leaning them into the window. *Just look at all this!*

"Look at all what?" Meryl wanted to know. His enthusiasm was infectious; there was a smile on her face.

Just . . . everything, he replied. *The city. The people. Times fucking Square. Life's rich pageantry . . .* He laughed, did a little bouncy-bounce inside her skin. *I just didn't know how much I'd miss it. It's all just so beautiful, and ridiculous, and wild . . .*

"Yes."

It's just so goddam wonderful to be back, I can't even say . . .

"You don't need to say a word," she affirmed. "Just enjoy it. It's your coming-home present."

You are my coming-home present, he whispered, and she felt him move inside her again.

She felt her head shift this way and that, muscles and tendons and ligaments moving as though manipulated by a pair of gently loving hands. It was a strange and pleasant sensation, like yielding control to a another's touch; letting go, safe in the trust that you will not be hurt. Her head floated as if bobbing on the purposeful currents of an otherwise tranquil sea, as she looked first down to the sidewalk, then up to the tops of the buildings, then from side to side to side. Taking in the neon wonderland of Times Square, the sweeping expanse of Broadway, the crowds and excitement and energy pulsing around them.

Taking it all in, together.

She felt something brush against the skin of her right inner arm; she looked down to see the fingers of her left hand tracing filigree patterns upon the delicate flesh. She shivered and closed her eyes.

And so doing saw, in the darkness, his hand upon hers. Guiding it. Tracing the pattern.

"I can see you!" she exclaimed, opening her eyes. The cab driver's eyes made a fleeting, puzzled pass across the rearview mirror. Meryl's attention was fixed on her arm ... but Jack's hand was nowhere to be found. Only her own, still tracing the tiny scrollwork designs back and forth, back and forth.

Meryl's eyes fluttered shut once again: the hand was there, form etched in shadow, guiding her. *What am I saying to you?*

"I don't know," Meryl whispered. Her heart was thudding in benign overdrive. "What are you saying?"

Look carefully. What does it say?

She stopped then, realizing that the scroll-like patterns were letters, an ornate cursive script, repeating themselves in sequence.

T...H...A...N...K...Y...O...U...

She felt a tear glistening in the corner of one eye; together, they brushed it away.

"You're welcome," she said.

There was the cab ride: uptown and around town and then down to Astor Place. There was the dinner at Do Jo: intimate and intense, with much talking with her mouth full. There was the long walk afterwards, meandering through the shadowed streets of the East Village.

And there were the conversations.

Lord, how they talked: Meryl was stunned by just how much they had in common, how much they shared. Their tastes in food, in fashion, in music and film and politics and philosophy were all of a kind; even the things they didn't immediately agree upon were made more palatable simply by the other's impassioned endorsement...

"You mean, you've never heard Suzanne Vega?? She's wonderful!...."

A quicksilver flash of memory, darting across her mindscape: dancing alone in her room, while the bell-like and haunting cascades of music washed over her...

> "If language were liquid
> It would be rushing in
> Instead here we are
> In a silence more eloquent
> Than any word could ever be..."

"Can you hear it?"

Ohmigod, yes! Yes! I can!

"Isn't it beautiful?"

Yes, but I don't know how much of it is her and how much is your feeling about her...

"But it doesn't matter, does it?"

No, I guess it doesn't. So many things I never knew, until you.

"Me, too."

> "I'd like to meet you
> In a timeless
> Placeless place
> Somewhere out of context
> And beyond all consequences..."

... and they were both there, alive and together in her memory, swirling in perfect time to the perfect music of Suzanne Vega's airy whisper poured from the stereo and the sun's rays lay warm on their skin...

They walked. And they talked. Her thoughts were embers glowing bright under the breath of his touch; she felt the heat of it envelop her in its embrace. And if the world at large was alarmed by the attractive and intensely peculiar young woman wandering the streets and caressing herself, lost in the whispers of a one-way conversation, it was of no consequence. The city accepted them into its fold; one more person talking to themselves would not disrupt its flow.

And they, in turn, knew only each other.

Their lives had seemingly run in an intricately overlapping counterpoint without them ever realizing it, only to be brought together by something that was nothing short of a miracle. They marveled to each other at how easily so many things just flowed out . . .

. . . and privately, how others were sidestepped completely.

Back in the sweet confines of her sleeping loft, they found that making love was better the second time around. She showed him the photograph of the Keeper and asked if it was him, and he said it was, and she was glad. His presence was stronger inside her, and the combination of his insatiable lust for life and her near-cellular awareness of what pleased her proved irresistible. Bit by bit, she opened herself to him, and he responded in kind.

Growing stronger.

They moved on the big bed, high up in her loft, facing the mirror that leaned against the wall, watching as two became one to the nth degree. And his touch was her touch: her hands guided him to her most secret places, showed him the subtle codes that unlocked the fortress around her heart. And he, in turn, brought light to the chambers long hidden, blew the dust away and rescued the treasure long buried there.

Jack opened the box . . .

And her memories flew, mercurial bursts of thought given fleeting shadow form. She saw herself as the first- and last-born survivor of a difficult pregnancy, marred by the second-trimester miscarriage that revealed that there had in fact been fraternal twins and only one had been lost; she saw herself as the little girl, perfect only child of the perfect couple: deeply prized and adorably precocious, if somewhat overprotected. She saw herself as the prepubescent, at the tearing point of innocence: just old enough to have a grip on her will, just young enough to still believe that mommy and daddy were something like gods.

Then she saw herself in her early teens, when the first real clues to her parents' fallibility grew appallingly clear. She saw herself in the early stages of quashed adolescent

rebellion, when the fact that they'd never really under
stood her at all made their authoritarian regime an object
of rage and scorn. She saw herself fighting to become who
she was; she saw herself crimped by the world they
embodied; she saw herself as the round peg being ham-
mered into the square holes in their logic, in their worldview,
in the plans they had for the life she owned.

She saw her father: distant, imposing, successful son of
successful son, always driven, always pressing her to be an
achiever, be a winner, be like the son he would never
have . . .

She saw her mother: unfulfilled in her position as do-
mestic ornament, growing older as her child grew farther
away, coming unraveled one drink and one Darvon at a
time, forever reminding her daughter of the sacrifices
made on her behalf, of the child victoriously snatched
from death's door only to disappoint them so later in
life . . .

And she saw herself: playing the game until she could
buy her escape: graduating high school with honors, at-
tending the ivy league school of their choice, making the
grades to appease and then, boldly, refusing to come home
on the weekends. She saw herself: arguing on the dorm
phone as they guilt-tripped her half to death, wishing only
the chance to be allowed to meet the world on her own
terms, to be finally and forever out of their smothering
clutches . . .

She saw herself, the day the dorm phone summoned
her, like some demented fairy godmother, to grant exactly
one-half her wish: the voice on the other end informing
her that her mother had died . . .

And the tears came then, blurring the memories of what
proceeded, of the wake and the funeral, the reading of the
will and the downward spiral that followed, ending in that
tomb in a tiny dusty town in Mexico, in a wash of emotion
that came as first a trickle, then a torrent, then a flood of
feelings too long denied: guilt and anger, remorse and
regret, and the cursed realization of things said that could
never be taken back, the sensation of feeling the cord
irrevocably cut, now and forever, amen.

She finally found the tears to cry for these things, and

cry she did: deep heart-wracking sobs that shook her body and soul. She cried, and she was not alone. Her arms were his arms and together they encircled her, rocking her gently back and forth, back and forth. In her mind's eye she saw her lover, holding her so sweetly and whispering in low, soothing tones; the Keeper, keeping her safe from her own darkest secrets. And Meryl allowed herself, at long last, to surrender to the great hot waves of joy and sorrow and love once lost, then found.

And her walls came tumbling down...

Sleep claimed them eventually, and the need for rest. The energy expenditure of being so intensely intertwined proved exhausting; Meryl found herself falling into a deep, dreamless slumber, dark and inviting as a return to the womb. She gave in to the need, and her last conscious thoughts were of drifting away into a peaceful black sea.

Leaving Jack behind.

To contemplate his new home.

16
THE PULL

skin
touching skin
feeling bone underneath feeling
muscles
contracting and
releasing
contracting
and releasing
feeling cool sheets
on warm skin feeling
soft small breasts heave
up and down
in sleep
fingertips tap
in time with her heart
beating deep
in the darkness
pumping hot black
blood through veins
fine as lace
spun beneath the surface
of the sleeping girl's
skin
touching skin
feeling the life inside feeling
alive again feeling
alive

It was a long crawl back from hell, and he really wished he could feel as good about being there as she did. But

262

laying in the bed, alone in Meryl's supine form, he couldn't escape the painful truth of the matter. He could not stay here like this forever.

And Jack had no intention of going back.

Which doesn't leave me much in the way of choices, he thought. God, I really fucked up this time. Nestled snug inside her willing flesh it should have been easy, dammit—easy!—to feel contented, relieved even, with the prospect of just staying there, sharing the rest of her life together, living and loving and maybe righting every wrong he'd left undone.

Maybe even writing again. Yeah, that would be something, wouldn't it? Writing again: stories, books, whole libraries filled with a whole new perspective, a bold new angle that blew trance-channeling clear off the metaphysical map, a direct link to life after death, could you imagine the talk show circuit? Jesus. Oprah would shit.

It was a great plan, alright.

Except.

Except for the feeling at his back. Except for the Pull. He didn't know what it was, and he was afraid to find out. All he knew was that it wanted him, that resisting it was like trying to move upstream through white-water rapids, was like being sucked through an airplane window at thirty thousand feet. All he had to do was look behind him . . .

. . . and there it was, the long black spinning vortex with the terrifying light at the end, threatening to tear him from his fragile moorings inside this sleeping girl, to suck him spinning back into . . . what?

Into itself, whatever that was.

Into nothingness, and whatever lay beyond it . . .

. . . and he cursed himself for being so stupid, for betting his miserable fucking life that death was end of the line. Because now he was stuck, with one foot in either world and a howling abyss behind him, and only this girl's devotion to hold him here and that wasn't enough, dammit, that just wasn't enough. He needed more.

He needed form. He had none of his own.

So hers would have to do.

He started with her hands. Easy enough; she'd already

relinquished enough control that dexterity was not a problem. Her hands found each other in the darkness, blind fingertips running over each other like old men reading braille. So far, so good. But he wondered just how far he could go, without her express permission.

Only one way to be sure.

It took him a few studious moments there in the darkness, tracing his way along the ganglia until he felt comfortable enough that he could try an experiment. He flattened both her palms against the surface of the bed, tensed her arms, and pushed . . .

. . . and her torso lifted up off the bed, head tilting forward and then snapping back from lack of support.

Whoa, shit! He let her body drop back to the bed with a muted *thwump*. Damn, he cursed himself. Forget all about her head.

He lay still for several excruciating moments, listening to see if she would awaken. But his luck held: the distant murmur of her dreams remained a constant thing, unfazed by the disruption. Surreptitiously, he felt his way along the interlacing nerve fabric where arms and shoulder, neck and head converged. Tracing the threads. Pulling together.

Pulling as one.

Now, he whispered.

Her body rose.

The bad news was that there were a lot of things to account for along the lines of basic motor control, things that he'd taken for granted since he was maybe three years old, that now required a major refresher course to keep from ramming her into the stereo system or pitching her through the glass-topped coffee table and hurting her, and himself in the bargain.

The good news was that he got better with practice.

A lot better.

Within the hour, he could stand. Her legs felt fawnlike, wobbly, for the first several minutes. But that, too, wore off fairly quickly, receding with the prickling itch of sleeping limbs coming awake. And soon, very soon, he felt good enough to take his first hesitant steps. Good enough to leave the room.

Meryl emerged naked into the living room, her skin glowing a soft blue-white in the cool night air. Jack felt a thrillrush of pure adrenaline at the relatively simple act of standing and walking in her tight young form. It was the ultimate arcade ride and Halloween costume, all rolled into one. It was an amazing act of manipulation.

Jack was into it.

And he had to admit that, sweet as she was, he almost preferred her asleep. It was the difference between having a chauffeur *slash* tour guide and being in the driver's seat. Ultimately, he preferred to be the one at the wheel. The one in control.

And control he did: while Meryl's soul was far away, Meryl's body was moving more and more, exuding a surprising amount of near-feline grace. Jack was pleased as could be; he sure didn't recall his old body having such a high degree of alacrity and lightness to it. He bade it move across the expanse of the room, and it responded to his overtures, revealing a tremendous reserve of pent-up energy. Shoulda been a dancer, he mused, feeling the eagerness of the musculature. But who knows? Maybe we'll take a class.

The world, he realized, was full of possibilities.

New sensations bombarded him; there was a slightly askew feeling to her internal organs, the way they sat in her bones. Different from a man's body in so many ways. It was sort of like walking around in someone else's pair of well-worn shoes; everything seemed a little off, somehow. But he figured he would adjust, in time. After all, he chuckled to himself, what choice do I have?

Uh-oh. Jack stopped to do another internal inventory. South of the navel, it would appear that somebody needed to take a pretty fearsome leak. Well, this ought to be interesting.

He started toward the bathroom, taking in the sights and sounds along the way. All of his senses seemed overamplified, as though he was sensing things just a little beyond the normal boundaries of the spectrum. The shadows seemed darker, the lights brighter. He could hear things: vast rumblings like the sound of the earth turning, the high trilling cycles of synapses connecting in her brain. Even tactile things: her breasts felt the tiniest bit heavy and tender to the touch, and her skin seemed infused with a kind of prefeverish tingle all over. PMS, maybe? What a rush. He giggled to himself; her lips responded in kind.

Have to get used to tampons, he guessed. And women's intuition. Oh well.

Comes with the territory.

He couldn't clearly say whether it was novelty or vanity that stopped him as they passed the door. He was fresh back from a victorious episode of adventures in modern hygiene, sure in his assessment that yes, they would soon be flowing heavy. He was guiding her past the doorway, when he caught a glimpse of his reflection in the mirror.

And stopped.

She was staring back at him, but that wasn't what caught his eye. It was by the sense of recognition: of the mirror itself, the beaten-up cheval with the scarves draped across it, and the funky junk jewelry, and the plants behind it and the clothes around it and the scent, god yes, the scent of the room itself: the lingering air of tea rose and patchouli, of sachets and cinnamon and Nat Sherman cigarettes, all blended together by a bond of sweet musky sweat at once distinct and disquieting. It was a sensation beyond simple *déjà vu*, for it didn't end in an elongated second or two. It hung around, taunting him.

Because Jack had the undeniable feeling of having seen this room before. Yes, Jack knew this room very very well. Jack had seen this room in another place, in another time, in a whole 'nother life.

Omigod, Jack whispered as Meryl's hand reached out toward the mirror, delicately unhooking the strap of the silk undershirt that hung from the side. It was a fine washable, and clearly between wearings. Jack watched spellbound as Meryl's hand brought it up 'til it was right beneath her nostrils.

Omigod.

And the scent that filled his memory then was the same as the word that fell from her lips.

"Katie . . ."

Jack felt a wave of vertigo, twin fists of tension curling

tight into the small of Meryl's back. "What the fuck is she doing here?"

He felt the pounding at the back of her skull that was the Pull, trying to snatch him back, send him hurtling back into the hell that he'd made. He held on, feeling the nausea rise, fighting back the memory of the fall, and the rope, and the snap...

"Why didn't you tell me?"

And the long crawl back...

"Why?" he asked the reflection in the mirror. Sweat was beading across her brow. "Why did you have to hide it?"

The stranger in the mirror gave away no secrets. Jack stared at the reflection, shaking with agitation and rage, wanting to punch it, to smash it into bits, to grind glass into smooth knuckle skin. He watched as her tiny hand curled into a tiny fist, considering the option.

And instead watched as her fingers dug nails into the bare flesh of her palm and squeezed, leaving five angry crescents to turn red in the moonlight. He felt her stir inside and cry out, caught in the throes of an all-too-real nightmare. Jack backed off, letting her slip back beneath the waves, trying to smooth the turbulence of his outburst. The pain had done its job, acting as a grounding force, a small reminder of where he was and how he got there... and what he might wish to do about it.

He calmed her, and himself in the bargain, and noticed that the force at his back slackened as her body settled into a less agitated state. It was weird, and he didn't understand it, but the implication of causality was crystal clear.

"Shh-shhhhhhh, everything's okay," he purred. Yes. Much better. Self-fulfilling prophecy, i am that i am, doo-dah, doo-dah. "Everything's fine."

He spoke to the reflection facing him, and for the first time realized that her lips had begun to move as he spoke. More causality in motion.

"Yeah, it's fine," Jack said. "You don't have to tell me anything you don't want to."

He walked her out to the living room and plopped down on the sofa. He began to massage the angry red marks, rubbing them into submission. Staring up at the ceiling he could just make out the leftover, painted-over stub of rope. Right where he'd left it.

He stared at the stub for a long time, until long after the throbbing at the back of her skull had receded, and he contemplated the nature of deceit, and control, and the long long night ahead. Yeah, sure, he thought, you don't have to tell me anything at all.

There were, after all, other ways to find out.

17
A SLIVER OF DOUBT

In the dream, they were picking her brain apart, one layer at a time. Like onion skins, peeled back to reveal the juicier layer just beneath, peeled back again.

In the dream, she could feel her mind invaded.

She couldn't scream, of course. That had been seen to. She remembered the electric shocks, the twitching galvanic responses. She knew that they could make her body do whatever they wanted.

Now they wanted it to stay, and it did; they wanted it to be silent, and it was; they wanted to rifle through its memory banks, peruse the gray matter for fingerprints, and they did.

She looked at the table before her. They had the top of her head upside-down in a bowl. It looked like a blood-spattered, hair-matted, flesh-covered section of coconut shell, face up and brimming red. Bits of herself were floating there.

Bits of herself they were throwing away.

She couldn't see their faces. It didn't matter. She'd always known. They had her right where they'd always wanted her: utterly helpless, completely exposed.

They were picking apart her brain.

And she couldn't even scream . . .

■

Meryl's alarm went off at 8:45 in the morning, as usual. The distant bleating tone bled into her dream; the dream faded out and vanished completely, the room faded in and persisted. The light in the room was too bright, for some reason; it burrowed, unwelcome, through her eyelids, bid her keep them shut as she groped with her left hand for

the alarm, didn't find it, instead found herself alarmed
by the fact that she was sitting upright on the living
room couch, her eyes already open and staring at the
ceiling.

Good morning, he said.

"What? Jesus Christ!" she replied, one hand coming up
by itself to swab at her eyes. Disorientation was the word
she was looking for; it took her a moment to find it.

Remember me?

"Oh. Hi." It all came back. She felt the beginnings of a
pleasure rush, felt it curiously subverted. It came to her
that her body ached, pretty much all over. She wondered
why. She also noticed that she didn't have to pee immediately upon waking, which was a first.

She also wondered what they were doing on the living
room couch.

She asked.

I don't know, he said. *I just woke up. What's wrong?*

"I don't know." An honest reply.

Weren't we in the bed?

Scratching her head. "That's the last thing I remember . . ."

Do you have a history of sleepwalking?

"No."

Well, this is weird, then.

"I guess . . ." She shook her head to try and clear it.
There was a man in there, and he wouldn't come out. The
cognition of it was somewhat startling, like a guy you were
dancing with last night that you don't really remember
inviting home. Only worse. "The whole thing is kinda
weird, don't you think?"

A moment's pause. Then: *Is something wrong?*

"No," she said, though her thoughts qualified it.

Her thoughts seemed to lack their accustomed privacy.

Okay, he said. *Just checking.*

Somehow, she didn't believe him. It certainly didn't feel
okay. The vibe was all wrong, and she was pretty sure it
wasn't all coming from her. "How 'bout you? Are you
okay?" she asked him.

Yeah, fine. A little disoriented, maybe. She felt him
smile inside her, felt his touch move up to work her
shoulder blades, just the way she liked it.

Except that she wasn't much liking it now. It was making her very uncomfortable. There was something forced about it: the automatic assuaging gesture, empty and overly familiar.

It started her thinking in unpleasant ways, even as her flesh cringed. After all, she hadn't just invited him up for some saki and a back rub. She hadn't even just made the primal mistake of giving him the keys to the apartment. This whole thing ran a little bit deeper than that.

This was getting just a little bit scary. . .

Did you say something? he asked; and as soon as he said it, her spine went cold. The morning's dream was gone and utterly forgotten, but one sensation lingered, haunting. Lingered in more than memory.

An itching in her brain.

And that was when the first inklings of real fear began.

It was a long-standing paranoia of hers, perhaps her oldest conscious phobia: its roots in tiny childhood, its seeds the light of stern interrogation in her father's eyes. So many times throughout her life, she'd found herself stuck in a room with a jerk whose simple presence was wiring her out, and even as she tried to be cool and polite and inscrutable, the thought *what if he's reading my mind?* would pop up on the wings of pure, inarguable superstitious dread.

Reason had nothing to do with it, ever; the real bottom line ran much deeper than that. It was pheromones, vibes: things beyond your control. It was a thing you thought or felt so strongly that how could they not know it, reason or not?

Only this time, there was a reason.

A very good reason.

To fear.

"It's nothing," she said.

It doesn't feel like nothing.

"You asked if I said anything. I didn't say anything."

But you're shaking.

"Am I?" Of course she was. How stupid of her to think she could conceal it. She could feel his agitation, and he didn't even have a body.

No body but hers. . .

I'm sorry, he said, suddenly contrite. *I guess I woke up neanderthal this morning. This whole thing is still kinda scary for me. I didn't mean to be a prick . . .*

"It's okay." She said it a second before she began to feel it.

No, it isn't. Where's the fucking gratitude in that? Where would I be without you?

"Oh, J. P., stop . . ."

Jack. Call me Jack.

"Okay. Jack. Stop." She laughed as she said it, and the thing she referred to as rational mind began to kick in for what seemed like the first time this morning. It regarded her paranoia the same way it regarded any other nascent credulity: it dumped a full shaker of salt upon it.

It made her remember the simple fact that this wasn't just some dumbfuck yuppie who'd won his way into her bed on the strength of his pecs or his portfolio. This was the fabled John Paul Rowan: the man whose innermost thoughts she'd spent months hungering, fantasizing, feeding upon. This was the man with whom she'd spent the last and best nearly forty-eight hours of her life. Here he was, in spirit if not in substance. She should be thrilled.

So what's on today's agenda? he asked, derailing her train of thought. *I know that you've got things to do. Classes? Study? Jack LaLanne?*

"Classes," she answered. "A particularly scintillating one: 'The Novel Comes of Age.' I'm sure you'll want to sit through that."

My secret dream. This time, they laughed together. *You know, I never went to college. Who knows? I might learn something.*

"Yeah, right. More boring shit. They could learn more listening to you."

I've never written a novel.

"You should."

That's true. Maybe I will.

"I'd help."

I couldn't do it without you.

"That's true." All the while, he continued to inwardly rub her shoulders. The distaste she'd been feeling had all but receded; it was starting to feel real good again.

It was a lesson that she'd flirted with time and time again, but never really internalized successfully: relationships take time. Of course there would be moments of uncertainty. Of course there would be moments of profound discomfort. Of course there would be fights: there would always be two sets of will and self-esteem at stake.

But if you'd found the right partner, the one with whom you could spend your life, then all of that shit was manageable. It was simply part and parcel of building the life that you wanted to have. From there, all you really needed was the will to stick it out.

That and mutual trust, of course.

There was nothing more important than trust.

Right?

"Well, we'd better get ready," Meryl said, standing and stretching.

What about breakfast?

"Breakfast?" she asked incredulously.

Most important meal of the day, he offered. *Remember, you're eating for two now.*

"Oh. Right."

Only kidding. Jolly Mister Sunshine.

Meryl looked at her watch: 8:55.

We'd better get ready, he said.

18
THE DRIVER'S SEAT

I'd like to ask you a little favor, he said, much later. They had just finished breakfast at a diner on Seventh Avenue that he swore was one of his favorites, though she couldn't for the life of her figure that out. The food was dreadful, the service even worse.

"What?"

I was wondering if . . . we might be able to stop by this place for a second.

"What place?"

An apartment. It's right in the neighborhood.

"Jack, wait a minute. I'm confused."

I understand, but it's real simple. It's just a couple of friends of mine. I just want to check and see that they're okay.

"But . . ."

I know it's kind of awkward, but believe me, it'll only take a second. We don't even have to go in. See, they were having some health problems when I . . . left. I've been worried about them.

"Yeah, but . . ."

I know what you're thinking. A complete stranger knocks on their door. What are they supposed to think?

"No, I was thinking more about my profound embarrassment. I mean, what am I supposed to do . . . ?"

Tell you what. How about if you let me handle it? I think I've got a strategy . . .

"Whoa, wait a minute." It was her turn to slap on the brakes. "What do you mean, 'let you handle it'? You mean . . . ?"

I mean let me do the talking, what little there is.

"Can you do that?"

I could try. He smiled. *You wanna do a little test run?*

"I'm not sure," she said, and meant it completely. The whole concept gave her the serious willies. "You've got to understand; I'm a bit of a control freak..."

I noticed.

"Yeah, well." She wasn't sure she liked the tone of that. Perhaps it was time for a little dreaded honesty. "It's one thing to share my body; and believe me, there's no one I'd rather share it with. But to give up that much control is just..."

A little unnerving.

"So to speak."

I understand. Believe me. I mean, I'm here on the flip side of the situation. I have no mouth of my own. It's a little unnerving, it's a little bit frustrating, but it's the hand that I've been dealt.

She was tempted to point out that he'd been more than a little involved in the dealing, but let it go. Too much honesty at this stage of the relationship could be counter-productive.

"I understand, too..."

Then trust me. Please. I swear to God, I wouldn't do anything to hurt us.

"I know that."

I think.

Then just relax a second, okay? Let's see...

"...if this works," he concluded, out loud, with her lips. He made them smile. "Okay!"

Jack? she said.

"What?"

Jack, this is making me nervous.

"Relax, okay? This will only take a minute."

Jack, I want my mouth back. Please.

She felt the perturbed expression play across her face. It was not the expression she would have made; hers would have been far more emphatic.

"Meryl, calm down," he said. "Really. Trust me. Come on."

Jack... she began, and then they were standing, her body was standing all by itself, a vertiginous rush that

would have been bad enough if it weren't for the fact that
she was helpless to stop it. *Jack!*

"Up, up, and away," he said, smiling as he moved
rapidly up to the door, out of the diner, out onto the
sidewalk. He seemed to know exactly where he was
going.

Please, Jack! Stop! What are you doing? she cried out,
and realized in horror that no one could hear her. She was
staring right at the people she passed on the sidewalk—
she was making fucking eye contact—and none of them
could see that anything was wrong, because Jack was
giving everyone her cutest little smile and wiggle and
wave as he scurried her around the corner.

At that point, she began to get angry: a hallucinatory,
anchor-and-rudderless anger, but genuine nonetheless. *Jack,
this is crazy! You're scaring me!*

"I thought you said you trusted me."

Goddam it, Jack! Cut it out! I'm not kidding!

"I'm not kidding, either, Meryl. Now would you just try
and fucking relax for a minute? Jesus!" He came to a short
set of front steps, proceeded to ascend.

JACK, YOU STOP RIGHT NOW! she hollered, putting
her foot down once and for all.

There was only one problem.

She no longer had one.

She no longer had one, because Jack was using it now;
and if there had been any malingering doubts about that,
he squashed them in a second, because he felt her try to
reassert eminence, and the force of his newfound control
slapped her back so hard and fast that her consciousness
reeled, unmoored from her skin.

"You don't like it?" he said, throwing open the door and
stepping inside. "Well, then how the hell do you think I
felt? Being completely powerless like that? Being completely
subjugated to somebody else's will?"

Please . . .

"It's a fucking thrill a minute, wouldn't you say? Never
knowing what's going to happen next?"

Please . . . She was starting to cry now. The tears made
no impact on her face whatsoever.

"Meryl, relax. Enjoy the ride." He pushed against the

inner security door. It gave. He seemed genuinely pleased. "This really shouldn't take more than a couple of minutes, and then we can get right back on schedule. Wouldn't want to miss out on 'The Novel Comes of Age,' now, would we?"

But it's my *body . . . !* she wailed, her last clear shot at reason. The thought seemed to amuse him. He stopped and smiled.

"Ah. Well, that's not exactly true, though, is it?"

And then they were climbing up the stairs, taking two steps at a time. She couldn't believe how strong he felt, how completely he had taken over. Even words were eluding her now; she just cowered inside herself, like a tiny animal trapped inside a puppet's wooden skull.

"No, we wouldn't want to jeopardize those monthly checks from Daddy, right?" he continued, grunting slightly from her body's exertion. "Maybe if we learn how to kiss up properly, we can even up the ante some. I'll tell ya, I can't wait to meet him. He just won't believe the change that's come over you."

Wh-what? She wanted to believe that she hadn't heard him right. She wanted to believe that this was just a very very realistic nightmare.

"I'm talking about your motivation, darling. I'm talking about your drive to succeed. You know, that thing that you've never had so much as a nodding acquaintance with in your life?"

Jack, Jesus Christ, what are you saying?

"I'm saying that Daddy's gonna be so impressed with your new career as a brilliant and successful writer, he won't know what to do! He'll probably say, 'Dear God, I never even knew she had it in her!'"

Then they reached the third floor landing, and he stopped, fell silent, appraising the doors that lined the hall. It only took a moment for him to make his selection.

And Meryl watched the door approach, watched it helplessly through her eyes, drowning under the implications of his words, drowning under the full weight of her incredible stupid gullibility, his even more incredible betrayal. She watched her hand ball into a fist, watched it rap upon the door, felt the panic overtaking her.

And for the first time, felt the Pull...

... as if some brutal force of nature suddenly had elected to grab her medulla oblongata like the head of a cane and yank, separating it from her spine, the spasming neuron cord popping out of the shell of its bone-sheath like a hunk of steamed shrimp. It was, she realized, a wholly interior experience, as she noted Jack was still using her hand upon the scarred wooden door with impunity. She took in the details of the act as if from an ever-increasing distance, as she felt her consciousness de-rezzing, unmoored and adrift within a swirling black tunnel: the world she knew receding swiftly before her...

... as the howling abyss beckoned greedily at her back. She was terrified to turn and look at it, to behold what it was that pulled at her with such blind, brutal abandon. Meryl screamed, feeling it sucking her farther and farther in, and fought it with strength she never even knew she possessed. She screamed and slid, fought grabbed and slid...

... and finally found purchase. A scrap to hold on to. A place to withstand the battering that besieged her...

Jack felt it, too; and for a moment, he almost lost control of her bowels, so extreme was his terror. Then he felt the good solid mooring of her flesh, felt himself moving securely within it, and his terror shifted gears into something more like distinctly pleasant surprise.

He was stronger, suddenly. Much, much stronger.

Almost as if he owned the place.

Very faintly, from within, he could hear her tiny screams. Of course they made him feel badly. Of course. He wasn't a heartless bastard, no matter what anyone thought. He really liked Meryl, too, when it came right down to it: was more than happy to share, if that wound up the bottom line. I mean, he thought, what do they think I am, some kind of monster?

But that was the problem. That had always been the problem. If only they could have understood where he was coming from, they'd understand: understand that he really had no choice in the matter, and never really did.

But no. It always comes down to the same thing, doesn't it? Her body—his body—swelled with the anger he'd come to know so well. Mean old Jack against the world, man. Every fucking time. Isn't that right . . . ?

He was about to answer his own question, as he so often had to do.

When the door creaked open.

And Colin appeared.

19
HERE'S TO GOOD FRIENDS

There was no denying the power of ghosts.

It was nearly 7:30 A.M., Pacific Standard Time, when Glen finally got the message. It had been a long night, to say the least: the video he was shooting for Clenched White Flesh was already threatening to overshoot the deadline, and last night had just been one of those sessions when everything and its ugly cousin subscribed to some turbocharged variation of Murphy's Law: the smoke pots would misfire just as the lead guitar player was getting ready to take his big air solo (which took him thirty-nine punch-ins in the studio to finally get right), or they'd lay down mist with the fog machine and just as the continuity was right something would jam or someone would miss their mark and they'd have to set it up and do it all over again, and then the lead singer tried to do one of his patented flying V-kicks off the scaffolding and ended up damn near herniating himself.

To top it all off, some faceless veep from the record company was hanging around all night, trying to look important and making dumb-assed suggestions and generally getting in the way. In other words, a long night. By the time Glen hauled his tired bones home, it was all he could do to toss his bag at the couch, drop his mail on the table, and hit the message playback button on his answering machine before he bolted for the bathroom. The tape squealed as its load of messages began to rewind. The number six glowed red in the darkness of the hall.

He passed the bedroom, taking note of the fact that Mia wasn't back yet. Still in New York, on location. The pain of being bicoastal. She'd probably be there for the rest of the week; he would most certainly be here.

He pushed open the bathroom door and fumbled in, foregoing the light switch and finding the toilet by braille. He'd had to pee for roughly the last thirty-five miles, and it was all he could do to refrain from starting a white-water ride down the inside of his left leg. He unzipped, aimed, and let fly.

"Ahhhhhhhhhh . . . ouch!"

Glen had a bad feeling right then. He flicked on the light, and let sight confirm what touch conveyed. All that stress had paid off.

"Oh, great," he mumbled. "Just what I need."

Hard to believe, he often thought, that something with such a cute little name could be so fucking painful. Herpes. Herpes, the Love Bug. And don't forget the wacky sequel: *Herpes Rides Again!* It was like Walt Disney's revenge on the sexual revolution: all those moist crusty little Volkswagen-shaped clusters . . .

Not for the first time, Glen swore a pox on Jamie Morgan. Most succulent receptionist in New York City history, without a doubt, and still the most miraculous one-shot lover in all of his considerable experience. But at moments like this, with the miracle of twenty-twenty hindsight and humiliating agony at his disposal, he most assuredly wished he could trade that night in for a lifetime free of genital dysfunction. He wished that he could wish it away, turn back the clock and start all over, like in that simple dumb-ass story . . .

But he didn't really want to think about that.

Glen opened the medicine cabinet and searched for his little tube of Zovirax. All things considered, maybe it really was for the best that Mia was away, after all. He hadn't had an outbreak since well before they'd started seeing one another, and he was a little scared to tell her; she was about the most understanding woman he'd ever met, but he didn't know if her understanding went quite that far. Trust is hard to come by.

By the time he'd ministered his affliction and wandered back out toward the kitchen, the messages had started their playback. The first two were from Geffen and Indieprod, respectively, relaying updates on the latest production schedules. Good news: Geffen loved his cover shots for Human Stew's new album, *Bring the Bucket*, and Indieprod had gotten the green light on "Pretense of Innocence," their film project. Glen grabbed a Löwenbräu from the fridge, popped a lysine caplet, and swished it down.

The third was from Mia, cooing sweetness from three thousand miles away. Glen's knees went rubbery; he could barely stand upright when she cooed. Hell, he could barely stand it when she so much as changed facial expressions, she was that beautiful. On the tape, her gorgeous voice informed him that she'd be back by Sunday, barring disaster. She missed him tremendously, hug, smooch, squeeze.

After a night with Clenched White Flesh, these were exactly the things he needed to hear. He afforded himself the luxury of a very tired smile and prepared to kick back. Relax. Live a little.

Then the next message came up, and dispensed with that notion entirely.

He'd only met her that once, a little over a year ago, but he remembered her voice distinctly. The agitation behind it only amped its recognition factor. It brought back memories.

It brought home the undeniable power of ghosts.

". . . Glen, hi, you may not remember me but my name is Katie, I met you a long time ago and I'm sorry to bother you like this but I got your number from directory assistance and called it and got a message saying you were out there in L.A., so I called but you're not in and I'm sorry if I'm bothering you but I need to know what happened . . ."

beeeep.

Glen flopped down on the couch, cradling his beer in one hand and his crotch in the other, staring blankly into the pale blue wash of the encroaching dawn. Goddamn; he hated being up this late. Just hated it. It had to be the saddest time he could think of, that elastic moment between night and morning when tired eyes could see the ghosts of a lifetime in the shadows to which they were forever consigned. Already, it was rushing back; and, sonofabitch, it would have to choose this time of day to hit him.

(*I need to know what happened*)

". . . Glen, this is Katie again." More reserved this time: reining in, almost on the verge of tears. "I'm sorry, but I need to talk with you, bad. Please call me . . ." Pause, fight for control, come back hushed.

". . . it's about Jack."

He listened as she recited the number, saw them drifting before him like wraiths in the wan morning light.

(*I need to know what happened*)

"I wish I knew what to tell you, Katie," he murmured. "I wish I knew myself."

He had thrown up walls to shield himself from the memories. They were jerry-rigged structures, not built to take a pounding. Her last words came at them like a wrecking ball . . .

"Glen, please . . ." Her voice was tremulous; in the battle for control, the tears were winning. "I'm scared."

And his walls came tumbling down . . .

The scene that Katie's image conjured to mind was, of course, the McSorley's Massacre. He could still itemize the steps it had taken, like the amplified *tick tick tick* of a cinema time bomb taped under the hero's table, like a musical piece he'd memorized by playing it over and over. It was three, four months before Jack died; and even then, Glen had seen it coming.

He just hadn't known what it was.

That night, as always, the place was packed, with the ubiquitous collegiate line out front. It took Glen twenty minutes to get inside, another ten to push his way to the bar for a round, another five to locate his friend in the roaring crowd.

Jack and Katie were tucked in the back, near the nominal kitchen. Somehow, they had weaseled actual seats at a table they shared with six sloppy-drunk college boys. There were thirty or more empty mugs on the table, at least that many full ones. Quite a few of each belonged to Jack. He was already lit. This was not a surprise.

But he and Katie appeared to be fighting, and that actually was surprising. To hear Jack tell it, the last several months had been nothing but seamless and heavenly bliss. Either this was a first-time-ever schism, or Jack was deep in his bullshit again.

Jack slapped on a cracked happy mask as Glen sidled up to the table. It wasn't too convincing. "Hidey-ho, bro!" he hollered expansively. In McSorley's, you hollered if you wanted to be heard. "I want you to meet the great love of my life!"

Glen took that moment to size her up, and what he saw was distressing as hell. She was every bit as lovely as Jack had said, but that was where the similarity ended. There was no ecstasy on that face, despite the smile she affected for him, and no evidence of the legendary psychic bond, the much-heralded absolute coupling of souls. There were tears in her eyes, and painful embarrassment lurking behind the cheery facade. She looked like she'd rather be sucking on rust.

"Hi!" Glen yelled, extending his sympathy with his eyes. She mouthed an identical response that never reached his ears and looked away.

"We've just been discussing our future!" Jack continued, voice tremulous. "Actually, we're discussing our family! Katie doesn't seem to think that we're ready yet, but I'm not quite so sure! What do you think: Ward and June Cleaver material, or what?"

The words punched through Katie like hollow-point bullets, and Glen felt black oil start to churn in his gut. The situation was clear. The situation was ugly. He didn't know whether to slap some sense into the boy or just go home and let it slide.

One thing was for certain: this was not the man he knew. This was a tortured and unreasonable facsimile. The Jack Rowan he knew and loved for the last seven years didn't treat people like this. The Jack Rowan he knew didn't evoke such unpleasant pity.

And, of course, Jack had picked up on that right away. Glen hadn't even needed to say a word. From there, it was a short jaunt to the men's room, where Jack broke the mirror with his fist and set the Massacre into motion. In the resulting chaos, as Jack was escorted rather violently off the premises, Glen and Katie had managed a few quick words.

He remembered the pain, and the concern, in hers.

"I'm scared," she said . . .

That was the beginning of the slide, as he knew it. Glen had been mercifully absent for the end, and the aftermath, when they first found the body. It was hard to believe it had actually happened, until he arrived back home. Once there, there was no denying it.

The stench was unbearable. It seemed to permeate the place: walls, rugs, furniture, everything. He cleaned, he scrubbed, he hired professional cleaners and scrubbers, to no avail. The stink hung, cloying, beneath buckets of pine-scented Lysol.

He ended up tossing a lot of stuff—the leather sofa's departure, in particular, was cause for mourning—all in the hope of ridding the place of it. But it was no use. The loft was ruined.

Jack had poisoned it.

Glen ultimately abandoned it altogether, settling for something on the Upper West Side that was half the size and half again the price and transferring the bulk of his major operations to L.A. All told, he figured that he was out one home, a few thousand in durable goods. And one best friend.

But that wasn't the worst of it. The worst of it was that he'd known all along: there was no way to forestall John Paul Rowan's downward slide. Not, then, not ever. Jack had flamed out before, jettisoning from the latest wreckage his life had become and crashing in Glen's guest room; after Katie he ended up there on a more or less permanently temporary basis: one week becoming two weeks becoming six weeks becoming an easy double-dozen.

But never like this.

Jack had thrown himself into his work then; not sleeping, not eating, drinking way too much, writing obsessively, and refusing to let Glen see so much as a word "until it was ready."

In retrospect, Glen wished that there was something he

could have said, or done, to make a difference, to help chill him out. But there wasn't. The fire was part of what made them tight. Jack and Glen both burned for their art, and they always had.

But with one glaring difference. Glen had learned to channel it, to focus on one thing, or set of things, until it paid off. Glen had figured out that it was only then that you could ever hope to buy the leverage to survive, and branch out, and connect with more creative people, and do more diverse things. Only then could you hope to buy the time to work it all out.

Jack, on the other hand, only knew one way to burn.

Up.

And out.

(*I'm scared*)

By the time Glen finished his beer, it was full dawn on the coast; back east, it was pushing toward noon.

(*please call me*)

He thought about it real hard, for about ten seconds.

(*I need to know*)

"So do I, Katie," he sighed.

"So do I."

And he reached for the phone.

20
A DIFFERENCE OF OPINION

By his own admission, Colin Bates had a handful of less-than-savory peccadillos to his nature. One of them, which he reserved wholeheartedly, was the right to be just as swinish and cruel as he pleased if awakened before the God-appointed hour of noon.

However, in the event of being met by a lovely apparition such as now stood before him, he also reserved the right to rein in his baser impulses a trifle. Just a trifle, mind you; a wee little buffer on behalf of the meek and unwitting. It seemed the appropriate thing to do, given her personal appearance and all.

"What the fuck do you want?" he inquired with just a touch of puckish good humor.

Alas, the poor dear girl didn't seem to grasp his subtle wit. Indeed, her dark eyes seemed rather like coals in their keen and off-putting intensity.

"I want to see Katie," she said, as if this were news somehow guaranteed to awe and humble him.

"Well, isn't that a shame," he countered. "It appears she's not at home just now."

"Where is she?" the girl insisted, annoyingly so.

"If I may be so bold: who the fuck wants to know?"

"I'm Katie's roommate, that's who the fuck . . ."

"Well, why didn't you say so?" he interrupted, feigning delight. "Meryl, my dear, I'm so pleased to meet you! Katie's done nothing but gush about you; and now, of course, her reasons for doing so are radiantly clear."

"Colin, you're so full of shit . . ."

"And a refreshingly deft command of the language, as well. I just *knew* we'd hit it off!"

He watched her little hands and teeth clench and tremble with menace. It was a delight, almost better than sleeping. He suspected, however, that it might be best to assuage her somewhat, lest she spontaneously burst into flames and alarm the neighbors. The terrible price of civility in a savage, untamed world.

"Ah, well," he continued. "Perhaps you'd like to venture in and wait. I'm quite certain she won't be gone forever. You might enjoy a cup of tea in the meantime. Or a toot? Why not?"

He stepped back, held the door open wide, motioned her inward. She glared at him suspiciously; it was difficult not to grin in response. He so enjoyed the face of animal cunning at work.

"Come along," he insisted. "Don't worry. I won't bite, I assure you. My teeth are giving me problems at present."

"I knew there had to be some explanation," she muttered as she muscled rather daintily past him. He could tell that she was mightily impressed by the snappiness of her retort.

"*Touché*, love. *Touché*," he mouthed in simulated good sportsmanship. It was not a habit that he intended to cultivate. Still, as he watched her pert little bum sashay toward the living room, he speculated that a slightly lighter touch might serve him well in the end.

"So," he continued, following her in and pointing her toward his favorite chair. "Refreshments?"

"No, thanks." Rather curt, that dismissal. Nor did she seem inclined toward the seat he proffered. She stood leaning against the dense bookcase, arms crossed beneath her tiny breasts, making a grand display of her pique. If not her peaks. "How long do you figure before she's back?"

"That depends," he said, "upon her level of concentration. It's quite possible that an attractive window display could detain her for... what? Three hours? A month?"

"Oh, great."

"Like the weather, that girl. Utterly unpredictable..."

"Has anyone ever pointed out," she cut in, with a most unpleasant curl to her lips, "what an unctuous little pisswad you are?"

"Well, no," he replied, somewhat taken aback. "Though I admit that it's a fairly well-turned phrase. Why do you ask?"

"Because you are." Her face had hardened into a marble mask, mottled flecks of rising red against the rigid pallor. "You make me sick. You always have. You're so fucking condescending."

"Oh? Have we met before?" He was genuinely confused now. Her face was not in the least familiar.

"In a manner of speaking."

"That's odd. My only recollection is of our little chat the other night, with regards to the magnificent swinging hack . . ."

"Shut up!" she hissed with surprising vehemence. Her eyes had narrowed to feral slits. "I mean it!"

"Why?" Now this was an odd development, indeed. It seemed that the subject was rather touchy. Always good to spot the pressure points. "Did you know him, as well?"

"That's none of your goddam business," she spat.

"Well, no, of course not. I'm just surprised." Yes, definitely a touchy subject. Best to poke about at it, see what turned up. "And curious. Were you another of his adoring fans? He had so many of them, you know."

"Colin, you shut your fucking mouth . . ."

"Ah! Now I understand." He narrowed his own eyes, gave a wee conspiratorial wink. "What was it that drove you mad about him? Was it his unique and deeply sensitive perspective? Or perhaps his Olympian yet enigmatically down-to-earth sense of connectedness with the whole of human suffering?"

She didn't speak, this round, opting instead to inhale loudly through her small clenched teeth. Her eyes, however, were glazing over; they did not appear entirely sane. He dragged his own gaze heavenward for a moment, as if something remotely more enlightened might be up there somewhere, and listening.

On the credenza, the telephone rang.

"Or were you one who saw through all that?" he continued, ignoring the phone, closing in on the *coup de grace*. "Were you the one out of his vast legion of insipid bovine followers who understood that he was really just an evil, self-indulgent little shit with a poetic streak..."

The phone rang again. All things considered, the timing was perfect. Nothing like the tinkling of New York Telephone to ring the curtain down.

Given the luxury of hindsight, he would have been the first to admit that he never should have turned his back on the little twitch. But he did, in a rather grand display, as if to say *you are dismissed*.

And she hit him.

With his bust.

Of Einstein.

The blow landed squarely at the base of his skull, simultaneously fracturing the atlas vertebrae and propelling his forehead into brutal contact with the cut glass panels of the credenza's upper doors. The glass fractured into long, knife-edged fragments upon impact, slicing through the thin skin of his scalp and sending freshets of blood cascading down to blind him. He wheeled, stunned and off-balance.

And she hit him again.

The second blow caught him in a full roundhouse across the face, smashing both the right side of his jaw and the bony ridge around his eye socket, shattering most of his upper bridgework in the process. Any witty repartee remaining in his mind took flight on wings of purest pain as Colin tumbled to the floor, a spraying fountain of blood and crushed enamel.

He hit the floor hard and badly, his full body weight coming down on the floating knob of bone that was his left knee. It cracked and dislocated at once, sending an agonizing overload of shrieking pain up and down the thumb-thick ganglia of his leg. Blind, primordial instinct prompted him to crawl—anywhere, nowhere, as far away as possible, to hell and back, to the slime from whence he came. This he did: without thinking, without reason. Twenty-three million, twenty thousand, five hundred and twenty-four minutes along, and Colin Bates had virtually nothing to say.

And then she hit him again.

* * *

The phone stopped ringing on the sixth or seventh try. For a long time after, the only sound in the room was the rasp of her hyperventilating breath. An ugly sound. The best he could do.

Inside her head was another story.

Because Jack's mind was alone in there, at least so far as he could tell, and it was working overtime: manufacturing excuses and explanations, why it was an accident and how he didn't mean to and it wasn't his fault, spinning mile upon mile of webbed rationalizations to keep the gibbering panic-voices at bay.

Most of all, he knew, he had to calm down. Only the cool head would prevail. He had come too far to flame out now, and he sure as hell wasn't about to spend his second chance at life in the Women's Correctional Institute at Ithaca.

"C'mon c'mon c'mon c'mon," he said, as if he were coaching a flagging athlete at the big meet. "Think! Think methodical! Think evidence! Think medical examiner! Think..." and he smiled then, "*...forensic pathology!*"

Of course. God knows he'd spent enough time poring over the textbooks back at Glen's. He knew what they looked for, what kinds of clues were applicable to a blunt force injury. It was simply a matter of eradicating the evidence. Between that and the coke whores and customers and his stash, a botched-drug deal would be the natural assumption. "Too bad he didn't have a dog, though," he murmured, fumbling with Meryl's glasses. "Under the circumstances, canine anthropophagy would be a godsend."

He bent over and breathed deeply, calming her shaking limbs. "There, there, calm down," he murmured. "Shhhh-shhhh."

While her head was down, he checked the floor. Colin was a mess. The lacerations around his eye were still bleeding like crazy; all those arteries along the bone ridge, probably hemorrhaging away, pumping his life out onto the Congoleum. Not to mention his wise fucking mouth. If he wasn't already dead from the trauma, the blood loss got him for sure. No way in hell of cleaning it up; the best they could hope for was to blur the clues.

Fortunately the floor was a little crooked; most of it was

pooling toward the living room. He checked very very carefully for stains or smears in any way tied to Meryl's body or clothing, and, satisfied, backed up and padded over to the kitchen, giving silent thanks for that good ol' feline grace.

"Colin was a prick," he noted with amazement, "but he certainly was a fastidious prick. Just look at this!" The underside of the sink was filled with cleaning agents and solvents of all kinds. He found a pair of Playtex living gloves and slipped them on, and started rooting around.

It was during this rooting process that Jack found the Clobber.

It was a very strong brand of drain cleaner, so much so that it made Drano seem like Kool-Aid by comparison. There was a full liter bottle of it, way in the back, behind the Lemon Pledge and the Formby's Tung Oil. Jack pulled the bottle out and held it up, reading the ingredients off the label. Undiluted hydrochloric acid, for those really tough jobs.

If there was a tougher job than this, Jack couldn't think of it. He changed his mind about cleaning up.

He had a better idea.

"Yes, yes." He smiled. "This'll do it. We're gonna be okay, you'll see."

He stoppered the sink and placed the bust of Einstein on its side in the basin. Then he uncapped the bottle.

"Careful, now," he admonished. "This stuff will burn a hole right through us." Jack held the bottle at Meryl's arm's-length and tipped a third of the contents over the bust, then backed quickly away. Plumes of acrid smoke instantly sputtered up from the rim.

"So much for Albert," he said, hefting the remaining contents. He turned back toward the mess on the floor.

And had yet another idea.

"Don't look," he warned her, as he held the bottle over what was left of Colin's head.

She didn't.

Five minutes later they were out the door and down the street, leaving Colin to stew in his juices. They discarded the gloves three blocks away, in a dumpster that looked to be ready for pickup.

"Are you okay?" He asked, feeling for her presence. Meryl hadn't made a sound since . . . since quite a while ago. He hoped she was okay. He told her so.

She didn't answer, but he could feel her terror dimly in the back of her . . . no, his . . . correction, *their* . . . mind. "I guess we should head for home," he said by way of comfort. "I'm exhausted. How about you?"

No answer.

"You'll feel better, soon's we get some rest." They turned down Greenwich Avenue. Cafe Degli Artisti beckoned from across the way, right next to the Jerusalem falafel place and the Tex-Mex chili bar. Either one of the latter seemed infinitely preferable. He hated fucking snotty literati. Besides, he decided, too much caffeine might be overly stimulating just now. "We should get home," he offered. "Katie'll be back real soon. I feel sure of it.

"And everything will be just like it was before," he added. "Only better. I promise.

"Trust me."

21
THE HEART OF THE MATTER

It was just about a quarter past one when Katie found the stories.

She had come back ostensibly to get her things... at least enough of them to subsist on until she could clear her head. Finding the apartment empty was a mixed blessing: on the one hand, it had spared her the embarrassment of facing Meryl, stammering a mouthful of excuses that sounded a whole lot lamer than they felt. On the other hand, it meant facing the apartment, alone.

She was just starting to consider the unpleasantness of that option when she found the stories.

"What the hell," she started to ask, but the words just dried up in her throat. One look at the box and she knew exactly what it was.

"Oh, say it ain't so," she croaked. Now, more than ever, she wished that Meryl were here. She'd evidently known about this for some time, which pissed Katie off. She'd also left in some kind of big-time hurry, judging from the fact that the book and a lot of other stuff was just laying around. Not like Meryl at all. She wondered what that meant.

The folders sat there, all neat and tidy. Something else was there beside them.

Meryl's notebook.

Now that's really strange, Katie thought, feeling a worm of anxiety uncoiling in her guts. Meryl would never leave the house without her book. She was always scribbling in it, and she carried the damned thing around like it was welded to the end of her wrist or something. Katie avoided looking at it, as if even seeing it away from its keeper was like some sort of intrusion. "Huh-uh, no way," she muttered. "I ain't peeking."

She looked back at the folders instead, their titles rendered in the tight cursive script that was so anomalously familiar, so exemplary of control in a life so otherwise out of it. They brought back lots and lots of memories. Most of them painful.

Only the last two stories in the batch were new to her.

They didn't take long to read.

By the time she turned the last page of "The Difference," her hands were shaking. She felt cold, but not in the poetic sense; it had nothing to do with his icy metaphors, climbing up from their fogbound allegorical sea. She felt like he had jammed his hand up the hind end of reality and worked its jaws, twisting everything and making it say all the wrong things.

It wasn't the first time she'd felt utterly violated by one of his stories.

But this one sure as shit took the cake.

"Jack, goddam you," she said to herself, the room at large. "How could you do this to me?"

She already knew the answer to that one: easy. That's what loving Jack Rowan was all about. Heartbreak and torture, with just enough good in there to keep her hanging on, hoping that one day they'd work it out.

Except they never ever did. And now...

She looked at Meryl's journal, and the stories she'd sworn she never wanted to see again. Side by side. Daring her to put one and one together.

She didn't want to do it.

She had to.

The early journal entries dated back over a year. They were none of her business. Cut to the chase, she told herself.

The chase began in the entry dated October third.

And ended right in her lap.

"Goddam you!" Katie shut the journal and collapsed back onto the couch. No sooner than you think that you've finally gotten on with your life then the door creaks open and the skeletons come crashing out to remind you that there's no hope and no help and no answers, not then, not now, not ever. "It's not fair, dammit, it's just not fair . . ."

She kicked at the pile of manuscripts, sent a cascade of ivory bond spilling out across the floor. There was no comfort in it. She wanted to scream, she wanted to cry until it felt better to stop. But she didn't.

She wouldn't.

"I'm not gonna cry for you anymore, Jack Rowan," she said out loud, to herself and the world. "I cried myself out on your behalf a long, long time ago. And it's over now. You hear me?"

She was still waiting for an answer when the door creaked open.

And Meryl walked in . . .

. . . and it was her, he couldn't believe it but there she was, in all her glory: his Katie-girl, his one true love, big as life and twice as sweet, so fine it fucking made him crazy, ignited a bonfire around his heart . . .

. . . and she was rising up to greet him, rising up with a face so full of warmth and concern and relief at his return that his knees felt weak as he moved toward her . . .

. . . and then he was locked in her embrace, engulfing her tightly with his own as she whispered oh god, I'm so glad you're here and he brought his lips hungrily up to hers . . .

. . . and Katie was stunned, but the kiss was hot: a silken-soft steamroller press of lips and teeth and sweet wild darting tongue that filled her mouth, cutting off all words as it lured her in, wearing down all thought of resistance for one elongated fire-breathing moment . . .

. . . but something was wrong here. To say the least.

She tried to pull away. Meryl didn't seem so inclined. She kissed Katie again.

Katie resisted this time. "Mmmpgh . . . Mermpgh . . . Jesus!" She pulled away. "Damn, girl, what's gotten into you?"

"Nothing that hasn't been there for a long time."

She kissed Katie again. Katie pulled away. "Meryl . . . listen," she gasped. "There's something we gotta . . . Meryl . . . whoa, listen . . . Meryl, dammit, we gotta talk!"

"Yeah, we sure do," Meryl agreed wholeheartedly, her brown eyes aglow with what struck Katie as molten desire. She was still holding Katie by the waist, and one hand was actually sliding down to caress her butt, which wasn't a bad feeling by any stretch if you overlooked the fact that the whole damned universe had just been stood on its head and it was about as un-Meryl-like a thing as could possibly be and Katie thought she might just pass out from the shock.

"We've got a lot to talk about," Meryl said. "But nothing that can't wait."

She tried to kiss her again.

"Meryl, would you back off!" Katie broke free and was backing away from her now, reeling from the table-turning absurdity of the situation. Meryl meanwhile walked into the living room, sliding out of her coat and dropping her daypack to the floor, then continued walking, arcing in a broad circle around the couch and the sprawling spill of manuscript paper, never taking her eyes off of Katie, watching her in a way that somehow reminded Katie of *Wild Kingdom* outtakes of some predatory cat stalking its intended prey.

"You found the book," Meryl said.

"Yes, I found the book, how could I miss the book," Katie replied. "I found your journal, too."

"You read my journal?" Her voice sounded carefully neutral. She contined the arc. Katie kept backing up.

"I'm sorry, Meryl," Katie said, feeling scared and sick and weirded out. "I had to."

"Mmmmmm . . ." Still circling. "Well, we all do what we have to do."

"Meryl, why didn't you tell me?"

"Tell you what?"

"About the book!" she cried. "About Jack, about the dreams, about all of this shit!"

Meryl smiled slyly; she was getting closer. Katie suddenly realized that she couldn't back up anymore, that she had backed clear across the room until she had butted up against the wall next to her bedroom door. She also came to a crazy realization about why Meryl's movement was reminding her so much of *Wild Kingdom* reruns: it was a classic technique, highly regarded by predators of every species.

Herding.

Meryl drew closer. Katie pulled back. The bedroom door beckoned.

"Meryl, please," Katie asked. "What the hell is going on here?"

Meryl smiled, moving closer.

"It's a secret," she said.

And started to unbutton her shirt.

"GYAHH!!" Katie rolled around the door and into her bedroom. Meryl followed her. It was a much smaller space; not as much room to maneuver, not as much opportunity to maintain a comfortable distance. Katie started speaking as fast as she could.

"Meryl we have to talk but we can't if you keep pushing at me like this so would you please fucking back off so I can TALK TO YOU!!"

Meryl stopped, put two soft-palmed hands up, made a grand display of her restraint. It struck Katie as strangely familiar.

"So talk."

"Thank you." She paused to catch her breath. "Meryl, I just wanted to talk with you about why I left . . ."

"It doesn't matter."

"Yes, it does. It's very important. What you wrote in your journal, I've been through it before . . ."

"Through what before?"

". . . being sucked in by his stories, and falling in love."

Meryl smiled. "And?"

"I just wish you would've talked with me about it before. I . . ." Her thoughts were racing now. "I would have tried to warn you off."

"Why? So you could keep him all for yourself?"

Katie would have laughed, under any other circumstances. "Honey, I think it's a little late for that . . ."

"I know."

That stopped her cold. "You do?"

"Yes. But that doesn't change a thing."

"It doesn't?"

"Why should it?"

"Meryl, stop it!" Katie was pissed now. "I'm not playing games here. I'm *scared*. Jack killed himself in this apartment not six months ago and I think he's still here!"

Meryl smiled and drummed her fingers patiently on her biceps.

"You think that's funny? I'll tell you, girl, it's no laughing matter. I left here because he was coming to me in my dreams, and it brought back memories that I have to live with, but I don't like having 'em ground in my face because, bottom line, the man was dangerous! When I was in love with him, I was scared of him; if you're in love with him you ought to be damn scared, too."

The drumming stopped. He didn't say anything.

"I met Jack a little over a year ago," Katie said quietly, filling in the blank, "maybe six or seven months before I moved in here. I saw him at a party..." she smiled a little. "I think he struck me as just about the sweetest man I ever saw. We hit it off right away.

"Anyway, he wanted to be a writer, and god, was he determined. I never saw anybody burn for something like that. Half the stories in that box out there he wrote in the four months we were together, plus about a dozen others that he just ended up throwing away. Just throwing away! Said they weren't good enough."

He smiled.

"That was just the way he was: intense about everything. You know he never sold any of those stories? You wanna know why? There was only one way those were gonna come out, and that was in a book that was handled exactly the way he wanted it. He wouldn't let anybody touch a comma, he didn't want to hear what they had to say. He figured nobody knew how to handle his work as good as he did. I mean, he was this close, a coupla times..." She pinched an inch of thin air with her fingers.

He watched.

"...but every time, he shot it down! I never saw anybody build such beautiful sand castles, then kick 'em over every time. He used to say it made him crazy that nobody could appreciate how fucking good he really was, and why wouldn't they just leave his work in peace.

"The only problem was, he was right."

"What do you mean?" he said. He could feel the anger starting to build. The anger he knew so well.

She shrugged. "It made him crazy. It literally drove him right over the bend. It got to the point where he was just so goddamned bitter, you could barely stand to be around him. I mean, he would just fly off into a rage over the tiniest things; I mean, stupid things! A waiter would bring him his toast too dark, and he'd scream right in his face. I couldn't deal with it, after a while."

That wasn't how it was. His fingers clenched, unclenched again. That wasn't how it was at all.

"But that wasn't the worst of it. The worst of it happened when we were home alone. He would talk to me, he would tell me things, and this whole black side of him started coming out.

"He would talk to me about hope. He liked to tell the story of Pandora's Box: how when she opened it up, all the evils flew out and populated the world. And he'd say, 'everybody knows about your basic evils: your hatred, and greed, and dishonesty, and jealousy. Everybody just seems to take those for granted.

"'But everybody seems to forget about the last one, the worst one, down at the bottom of the box. You know what that one was?'"

"Hope," he said.

"That's right!" she said. "He said that hope was the worst evil there was. Because when you looked around at the state of the world, with all the suffering and agony and rage, and you looked at the direction that the missiles were pointing, and you looked in the stupid piggy eyes of the average person on the street, you knew that you had to be fucking kidding if you thought that there was ever gonna be any such thing as a hope in hell for any of us."

Katie shook her head. "This was pretty hard to live with. I was starting to get just as crazy as he was. And I couldn't let that happen.

"But then, wouldn't you know it, I had to go get pregnant. I couldn't believe it, but it was true. I'd been just about ready to tell him I was leaving, and all of a sudden...bang! Knocked up. Suddenly I'm waking up every morning and the first thing I do is run to the bathroom and toss my cookies.

"Jack figured it out pretty quick.

"And then all hell broke loose."

Go on, he thought. Tell me all about it. He wasn't going to say a word. He was letting it build.

He was letting it burn.

"I told him I didn't want to keep it. I told him I wanted an abortion. You know what he did? He went fucking berserk. He told me I had to keep the baby. He told me I had no right to do it.

"And that was where it ended for me. That was where my heart drew the line. He had no right to tell me what I could or could not do with my own body. I told him so.

"So you know what he did? You know what that sweet, sensitive, understanding man did? He beat the living shit out of me."

Oh god, Meryl thought.

"That's a lie," he said.

"Does this look like a lie to you?" Katie asked, pointing to the semicircular scar near her eye. "*He* did this to me."

Oh god. Meryl could see it clearly.

"No . . ."

"Yes. He hit me, Meryl: he hit me with a goddamned broomhandle . . ."

. . . and she was there, in his memory: two minds wielding one piece of wood, swinging a short vicious jab at Katie's face, feeling the smack of impact as hard wood hit soft skin and tore through on its way to the bone, blood and terror and self-righteous rage spinning round and round and . . .

"Shut up."

"No, I won't. You need to hear this, Meryl. You need to know the truth. Because Jack got his wish: I didn't have an abortion, after all. I would have, and felt just fine about it.

"But I never even got the chance, because John Paul Rowan beat the shit out of me and I had a miscarriage instead!"

"SHUT UP!!"

"Which just goes to show that you can't judge a goddam book by its cover, girl! The simple fact of the matter is that Jack Rowan had a gift, and in a lot of ways his stories were the absolute best part of him, but then he twisted out, and his stories twisted right out with him! He went over the edge, and everything he wrote past that point was a lie! 'Shells' is a lie! 'Gentlemen' is a lie! 'Deadlines' is a lie! And 'The Difference'... hell, honey, 'The Difference' was such a lie he couldn't even finish it! He couldn't even tell that one without killin' himself in the process!"

Jack was losing control. Meryl could feel it in her bones. She could feel it in the way they clenched as her right hand reached out, feeling for the nearest blunt object...

... and she could feel the Pull, alive at her back, alive and growing stronger by the second...

"You hear what I'm saying to you? His stories were lies! His father is *fine*! He was sick, yeah, but he got better! He got better 'cause he had the one thing that Jack came to hate more than anything on this earth! He had hope! And Jack hated hope, 'cause as long as you had it you had to keep trying, and all he wanted was an easy way out...!"

And then he was upon her.

"BITCH!" he roared. "YOU LYING BITCH!" He backhanded her across the face. "YOU NEVER FUCKING UNDERSTOOD! YOU NEVER UNDERSTOOD ANYTHING!"

Another blow, on the backswing. Katie was too stunned and shocked to stop it. The force of impact slammed her into the bureau; her head cracked hard against the wall. Potted plants and perfume bottles fell crashing to the floor. Jack's stolen breath blew hot in her face.

"I LOVED YOU!" he bellowed. No slap, this time. A punch. A glistening fissure opened up above Katie's right eye; Meryl felt the fine bones of her right hand snap under the brute force plowing them forward. She screamed; he screamed; they all screamed together. He gave up on the useless fist and used Meryl's forearm to shatter Katie's nose.

"I LOVED YOU SO GODDAM MUCH," he shrieked. "AND YOU LEFT ME TO FUCKING DIE!" His tear coursed down her cheeks, his voice her voice homicidal careening straight over the edge and straight into Katie's face, his hands her hands coming up to Katie's throat, the right balking as the pain went white, the left hand more than compensating.

"WHY COULDN'T YOU LISTEN TO ME!" he howled, pressing down, mashing into Katie's esophagus. "WHY COULDN'T YOU JUST FUCKING LISTEN TO ME!"

Katie's eyes were fogging over, pain and terror and oncoming death taking over. Her gaze groped for purchase, for recognition. Found it. Latched desperate hold.

For one moment, the three of them met, eye to eye . . .

. . . and Meryl stared into the blackness of those death-dilating irises, saw the void opening up beyond, felt the Pull at the back of them as surely as she felt it gnawing at her own back, tearing at her, eager for her, ready to snatch her away from this life already stolen, stolen by the bastard she harbored within . . .

. . . and she had been weak, yes, she had been hiding, she had spent her whole life hiding from life, building walls to protect her from life, great stone walls to convince her that she was strong and sane and invulnerable even as she ran, ran from everything, ran from who she was and what it meant and what it stood a chance of meaning if she could only stop running long enough to face herself . . .

. . . and Katie was dying now, really dying, eyes and thick tongue bulging out, and it was her hand that was bringing it about, it was her hand that she had abdicated control of, handed over without a fight to a sick pathetic man who had thrown away his own life and only now had figured it out, figured out that life is precious, that life is all there is, just as she was only now deducing the brute simplicity of the equation . . .

. . . and she did not want to die . . .

. . . and she did not want Katie to die . . .

. . . and in that moment, she attacked him.

I HATE YOU! Meryl tore at Jack from the back of his soul, screaming *IHATEYOUIHATEYOUIHATEYOU* as she threw herself at him, tearing and thrashing and howling. It pulled at the tendons he had claimed as his own, yanked at the root of his claim to her being. He let go of Katie, let her slump to the floor, and reached up to clutch his temples, screaming "BITCH! SHUT UP! SHUT UP!"

IHATEYOUHATEYOU GET OUT OF MY BODY!

Her hands dug into her hair.

GET OUT OF MY BODY!

She tore a small handful out by the roots. He bellowed in pain.

"GET OUT OF MY BODY!" she screamed, and the words were out before she grasped the meaning, grasped at the hope it implied. She could feel her body, could feel herself a part of it, the battle now raging in every cell . . .

. . . while the Pull yawned wider, behind them both . . .

. . . and she saw herself in the cheval—a crazy woman, locked in the lunatic throes of epileptic seizure—and she knew that she couldn't live like that, couldn't spend her life in a body at war, it was her fucking body and she would decide, not him, no way, she would rather die than bend another second to his will . . .

The moment was crystal clarity.

She went into the mirror.

The mirror disintegrated in an explosion of glass and kaleidoscope light and slicing pain. The wooden frame and backing splintered and collapsed beneath her; she collapsed upon the floor. The pieces of glass were everywhere. She picked one up.

She brought it down.

There was a tiny scar at the small of her wrist where she'd tried this once before. Hesitation cuts were all she'd managed; the attempt had not been entirely sincere.

The tiny scar now disappeared into a deep red flowing gash. Another slash, and the wound redoubled. She heard him shriek, and slashed again.

"YOU WANTED TO BE DEAD? YOU'RE DEAD!" she bellowed. The red glass rose and fell. "GET OUT OF HERE! GET OUT OF MY BODY!"

She opened up her arm.

"YOU HEAR ME, JACK? *YOU CAN'T HAVE ME! YOU CAN'T HAVE ME!*"

The blood was hot . . .

. . . and it seemed the blood was everywhere, an amazing amount of it, coating the floor, coating her limbs as she slumped among the wreckage, her strength decreasing . . .

. . . and she could still feel the Pull, but it wasn't pulling on her anymore. There was something else moving over her now: a gentle thing. A rolling fog. It started to surround her, cool and gray and comforting. She tried to smile. It didn't work.

But at least her face was still her own.

She was dimly aware of a couple of things as the fog billowed in to take her away. She saw Jack's face. It was going away now, too, like a coin down a deep dark well.

And she also heard a distant voice. A beautiful voice.

I'm going to get help, it said.

Get help? But why?

Everything was fine . .

....
....
....
....
....
....................**DECEMBER**

Dear Katie,

How do you like the photo? Hee hee. Unbelievable, huh? Never before has such an expensive and extensive collection of tacky floral displays been assembled in one place. As you can see, the deeply sympathetic citizens of Beacon Hill and Back Bay are nothing if not generous, at least in their public displays of condolence, not to mention their prurient response to scandal. (Can you spot me in the picture? Hint: I'm the only thing not being pollinated.) By the time I get back, at least, I should be the Sachet Queen of Lower Manhattan.

By the way, thank Lee for the roses. They meant more to me than the rest put together. Except for yours, that is.

But you already knew that.

Things are not nearly so bad up here as I might have expected, although they'll be tons better when you come up for Christmas; the physical therapy is going well, and even though my right hand is little more than a claw on the end of a stick, they tell me I'll get back maybe eighty percent dexterity. Ah, well. No regrets. I may never play the violin again, but I'm hell at one-handed typing, and I'll be back in time for spring registration.

As for my return, what can I say? The Beast, in particular, did not respond as I would have thought. No I-told-you-so's, no pontificating or putting down of the great Daly foot. In fact, just the opposite: he's been very attentive, and—dare I say it?—tender,

even. I think this whole thing, particularly the publicity— COED FIGHTS OFF SLASHER, SAVES FRIEND —made him see me through new eyes. (Of course, I also think it scared the shit out of him, but he'll never 'fess up to that.) I'm not sure, but I think he respects me more, in the face of all this. And you know what? I think it's kind of mutual.

Maybe he's not such a bad guy, after all, as Beasts go. Maybe we've both changed in the face of this, maybe we can learn to respect each other's differences, and grow closer as we grow older. Yes, and maybe one day we'll build a world where men and women can live in love, and dignity, and mutual trust . . .

Nahhhh. Forget I mentioned it.

Onward. I trust the new apartment is just fine and dandy. From my end, I have been assured of that. Let me know if there are any problems.

Which leaves us with the one who shall remain nameless.

So what is there, really, left to say?

I'm glad you got rid of the stories. If somebody picks them up off the street, then fine. I hope they have a good time. Burning them really would have felt wrong, I know; on the other hand, I sure as hell don't feel any enormous responsibility for their imminent welfare. If they never get seen again, is this our problem? I don't think so.

As for where he went: who knows? Who cares? If we owe him any thanks for anything, I think he got them well in advance. All I've got to say is: Sayonara, sucker! Better luck next life! Don't let the doorway of perception hit you in the ass on the way out!

See you on the flip-side, girl.

Love,
Meryl

Meet John Skipp and Craig Spector, writers at the crest of a new wave of horror.

"SKIPP AND SPECTOR GIVE YOU THE WORST KIND OF NIGHTMARES."

—George Romero
Director of
THE NIGHT OF THE LIVING DEAD

"THESE GUYS ARE AMONGST THE FORE-RUNNERS OF MODERN HORROR. SKIPP AND SPECTOR TAKE YOU TO THE LIMITS . . . THEN ONE STEP MORE."

—Clive Barker
Author of *INHUMAN CONDITION*

"SLAM-BANG NO HOLDS BARRED HORROR FOR THOSE WITH STOUT HEARTS AND STRONG STOMACHS."

—T.E.D. Klein
Author of *THE CEREMONIES*

☐ THE LIGHT AT THE END
25451-0 $3.95/$4.50 in Canada

It's a funky guitar riff fingered by Satan.
It's bizarre graffiti splashed in blood.
Something evil is lurking in the tunnels beneath Manhattan.
Something horrible is hungry for souls.

☐ THE SCREAM
26798-1 $3.95/$4.95 in Canada

Welcome to the heart of the Nightmare!

Look for them at your bookstore or use this page to order.
